The Ghost Keeper

Devon Wells

For my mother, Vivian, whose love knows no bounds.

ACKNOWLEDGMENTS

Many people informed the characters and events in this book's pages, and as such, I owe my gratitude to these gracious souls. My thanks to the following investigators and intuitives of the now (sadly) defunct Arizona Paranormal Investigations for allowing me to pick their brains: Sandy and Kyle McNatt, James Kelly, Susan and Judy Graehling, Joe and Mikki Shelton, and Joey and Deborah Lane. I thank Lloyd Lee, Laura Tohe, and Jaynie Parrish for taking the time to share of themselves and impart to me the resilience and richness of the Diné culture. Thanks also to Suzanne Vaughan for instilling in me the importance of the research process. To my niece, Colleen; nephew, Dan; and "adopted" little sister, Pam: I cherish our time searching for ghosts and history in Jerome, Arizona, the wonderfully colorful town upon which Prosperity is loosely based. My appreciation goes to Dot DiRienzi for her invaluable editorial insight and Linda, Melissa, Mena, Scott, and Trish for being loyal and caring cheerleaders. I also owe much to John "Cuz" MacIsaac, whose love of reborn copper towns proved both infectious and inspirational.

Finally, my heartfelt thanks to my family—Mom, Dad, Jeff, Marian, Jeannette, and Nancy—for supporting me in my writing endeavors over the years. Without their constant love and encouragement, I would have surrendered long ago.

PROLOGUE

Every town has its ghosts. But few are haunted, despite what legends would have you believe. Haunted places are those with memories too dear or dreadful to surrender, cluttered so thickly that the living can scarcely breathe. In Prosperity, Arizona, both place and population are haunted by pasts that have nearly destroyed them.

Each building bears the indelible stain of sins on mortared walls and scabbed flooring. And an eerie aura clings like mist to the hillside site overrun with careless weeds and tourists. It is a locale founded on dreams and greed, a boomtown that hit a glorious heyday in 1927, before dwindling into ruin.

In its prime, Prosperity pumped out more copper ore than any mining center in the nation, and its inhabitants lived more wickedly or desperately than most can imagine. The community set high atop Salome Hill in the Sandspur Mountains repeatedly earned its reputation as a debauched setting where miners, power players, ladies of the night, and gamblers mingled in luxurious bordellos and a gritty reality that limited the average resident's lifespan to just shy of 40 years.

Like most towns that quickly find fame and fortune, Prosperity—in its original form—did not endure. In 1939, after several years as the nation's top copper producer, and many more spent in mediocrity, Prosperity's Copper Prince Mine closed, signifying the end not only of a place but also an era.

Resurrection began in the 1960s, as bohemian artists and hippie rebels discovered Prosperity's brick bones and the romantic decadence that radiated from them. The newcomers studied the town's canon of legends, both history and myth, and committed to memory every sordid detail, every wretched twist, every woefully unfortunate ending, and came to know, if only in their minds, the spirits of Salome Hill. Banding together with the

1

few die-hard natives who lived in ramshackle abodes on the fringes of the former town's chalk outline, they pulled Prosperity out of its ashes and painted, scraped, braced, and refurbished it into a new but unsettling incarnation.

The reborn Prosperity is alive with spirits and dedicated to the macabre. It is a ghost hunter's paradise, a Goth's haven, a New Age mecca, a day-tripper's guilty pleasure. Every business—from Headless Wei's Barbershop to Spooktacles Eyewear—exists, even flourishes, because the residents embrace the supernatural and revel in their town's unique, if bloody, yesteryears.

Only two balk at Prosperity's ghastly reputation: Afton Burnside, who finds the paranormal claims ridiculous, and Lloyd Chang, who knows only too well that they are real. For very different reasons, these two do not want to remember what has been. They do not want to be reminded of the past, to see its ghosts or hear its echoes. But soon they will have to.

Someone is coming to dig up the past and lay its bones bare.

It is one of the blessings of this world that
few people see visions and dream dreams.

— Zora Neale Hurston, *Dust Tracks on the Road*

PART I: THE SHADOW OF A MAN

Journal of Yee Chang
May 10, 1953

I am 67 years old today. Xu said it is a day to celebrate, but I disagree. Despite me, she brought out a bottle of wine and cooked two pots of pork dumplings. They looked like litters of pale, bald puppies lying on their sides, huddled together for warmth. Xu could not make smooth dumplings if her life depended on it. There is little she does well. However, she is an expert at spending my money, and she is teaching our son to be the same. They went down the hill yesterday to shop for worthless gifts. Xu gave me this journal and a tin of sugared pecans. From Lloyd I got a pair of fake leather bedroom slippers. They pinch my toes like hell. Lloyd must think I wear the same size shoe as his mother.

Xu, if you are reading this, put it down! I will box your ears if I find out!

When I unwrapped the journal, I thought it was a foolish gift. I asked Xu why she did not buy something good, like a new pipe and tobacco. Now I think maybe the journal was a good idea. What do old men do? Sit and remember. Think of things they cannot do anymore. Think of people who are gone. And talk about the past. Talk to anyone who listens. Talk sometimes when no one listens.

Maybe Xu bought the journal because she tires of listening to me. But I have not told her many things. The most important things she does not know. Maybe I will write them here. This is like talking but with a pen. I say what I want. No one tires of listening. Especially my wife, who talks more than I do and has nothing to offer but worries and blab. She is too young for me, too childlike. Her concerns are nothing. What to make for dinner? What color to paint the bathroom? I would give 10 years of my life for such simple worries!

She calls me a miserable old man. I am that. But my misery comes from regrets she does not know and cannot understand. When Prosperity was bustling, many villains lived here. Everyone thought Mad Molly was the worst. That was because they were ignorant of what I did and who I truly am.

Now Prosperity is quiet. Only five families remain on the hill. No business is open. The buildings where I delivered food to hungry miners and rich men and their families were burned down or are boarded up. Yesterday I found a coyote in the Canary Cage Bordello. I remember when that big house was a palace and its naughty girls like queens. That was so many years past. This has become a hill of ruins. The streetcars have disappeared, and anthills grow from their tracks. The trills of speakeasy pianos are gone. No music. No life. No one comes here. I do not recognize this town.

All the people from my youth, good and bad, are dead. It does not seem just that I still live and the good ones do not.

67. I never expected to last this long.

I miss my brothers more than I could have imagined. I miss my brother's wife and my niece. They were my joys. No bad thing in them. I miss our friend, Sadie, and my teacher, Mr. Garibaldi. These were the good ones. Not me. But still I live.

The only good I know now is my youngest boy, not weak George who went to Korea to make me proud and ended as blood and flesh shards on a battlefield. What a foolish waste. Lloyd is the smart one. His grades are the highest in his class. If his mother does not turn him soft, Lloyd will be a man of consequence. Not like me.

My opinion is this: when a man commits a great sin, he takes one of two paths. He either spends the rest of his life atoning, or he decides that further sins do not matter because his soul is already damned. I am so far down the second path that I have lost count of my offenses. As Xu suspects, I cheated on her during that trip to Tahoe. Again when she was pregnant with Lloyd and we visited her parents in San Francisco. These are only my recent sins. They are very little compared to what sent me down this road. I have betrayed. I have killed. No atonement for me. My soul is lost. Why did I start writing in this foolish journal?

CHAPTER 1

North Central Arizona
May 7, 2010

Peter Jacoby left for vacation with the worst headache of his life and a feeling of dread. He considered canceling because of the pain but told himself time off was exactly what he needed. As usual, he'd worked late again, and since it was a Friday, he'd been the only one in the business services section of Grand Canyon Hospital for the last three hours. When he powered off his computer and locked his office, he emerged into a darkened corridor and left for a week of sightseeing without any farewells or fanfare.

An hour and 28 minutes after he set his wheels on I-17 south from Flagstaff, Peter arrived in Prosperity, still clenching his jaws and squinting his eyes. He rolled down his window for an unobstructed view. The old mining town was bright with the lights of weekend revelry; yet, an unsettling darkness lingered on its edges, as if something sinister was waiting to creep in. This wasn't the quaint little tourist-trap spook town Peter had expected.

"Don't tell me I have to listen to that all night," he mumbled as he approached a crowded bar, where inebriated individuals spilled out the door, bouncing to amplified live music. Upon closer inspection, he realized the people weren't dancing but instead bobbing with bloodlust as they watched a red-headed giant fling a biker across the parking lot. Peter noted the irony of the rowdy scene occurring directly behind the "Welcome to Prosperity" sign.

He hoped his choice of accommodations wasn't nearby, though he suspected that all of Salome Hill was subject to the bombastic noise. The musical clamor was only one of his concerns. From every yard and porch and storefront, evidence of the absurd assaulted him. Between his headache and the unusual scenery, Peter could hardly maintain the needed concentration to drive safely. He gripped the steering wheel and tried not to fixate on an artist's gallery that displayed on its patio—under the glow of a bare porch light bulb—two life-size skeletons seated at a Bridge table with cards in their bony fingers, one wearing a curly, auburn wig, the other in a panama hat, a cigar clenched in its perpetually smiling mouth. Things only got weirder from there. With every turn of his car's wheels, Peter regretted his vacation plans. In fact, he wondered why he'd made them.

"Prosperity is THE coolest place in Arizona! It's got an awesome haunted-hippie-artist vibe," a coworker had told him.

"It's like walking into a ghost story," another had said. "You'll love it!"

But Peter wasn't close to his coworkers and wasn't susceptible to peer pressure. Above all, he didn't believe—and wasn't interested—in the supernatural. He just needed a break from reality, which meant a thankless job as a hospital accountant and no family or friends to cajole him away from reading or watching television in his off hours.

Peter's first impression of Prosperity made it seem like, perhaps, too much of a break from reality, but as he went along, he began to warm to its peculiar character. Despite his brain pain, Peter's humor was piqued by the playfully horrific names of the businesses that flanked Prosperity's main thoroughfare, Spirit Street, a title chosen in the 1800s for the eight saloons located along the road; after the town's ghost-town rebirth, the name fit for a different reason.

"Poltergeist Pizza Pub? Bloody Finger Tattoos? Where do they get this stuff?" Peter asked, groaning. After reading a few more ghoulish shingles and spying a yellow caution sign that bore "Ghost X-ing" above the silhouette of a Casper-type ghost in a crosswalk, he let a laugh trickle from his mouth.

Stepping hard on the accelerator, Peter adjusted his car to the steep incline of the mountain road and pushed on. The white Buick sedan was prudish compared to the vehicles in parking lots and along curbs—Vespas, a tie-dyed VW van, hybrids with personalized environmental plates, tricked-out trucks, and custom motorcycles—and Peter, himself, was prudish compared to those vehicles' owners. A man of money and means and no sense of himself, he was a handsome, hollow person, gutted of his most meaningful parts by a damaged youth and neglectful parents who'd made him believe he was an unworthy son of privilege. Instead of exploding in rebellion, Peter had let himself fade away into a straitlaced professional who dressed in pale blues and neutrals and spoke in polite, even tones. But, in a town as colorful as Prosperity, Peter's tameness made him the standout.

Swerving right onto Hangman's Lane, he left behind the business district and ascended Salome Hill at a snail's pace. Vividly painted Victorian homes, lovely yet eerie in the stark white light of celestial objects, reminded him that people actually lived in Prosperity. He imagined those people were a far different breed than any he'd ever known and, in some small way, envied them their free-spiritedness.

Peter gave a relieved sigh when he noticed the "Canary Cage Inn" sign swinging from a copper lamppost before an elegant, yellow, triple-story Queen Anne swathed in greenery and finished with red and white trim. This was his place of lodging, and a very pretty place it was, without even a speck of kitsch. No gargoyles, pentagrams, or skeletons in sight, not so much as a garden gnome. He grabbed a peanut butter cup from the bag on the passenger seat, unwrapped it, and scraped the soft chocolate candy from its fluted paper-cup liner with his teeth. He felt the rush of sugar numb his headache ever so slightly.

Stepping from the car and taking his luggage from the trunk, he perceived the reverberations of the bar music far down the hill, but atop them were the peaceful clicks of crickets and the gurgling of a water fountain somewhere nearby. Peter looped his duffle bag strap around his shoulder and stared up at the top window of the inn, then further up the hill, to the next house over: a sprawling blue Victorian surrounded by rosebushes and birdhouses on painted posts.

A woman wearing a shawl, hair bound into a fat bun at the nape of her neck, watched Peter from the porch. Although she kept her back to the porch light, Peter could vaguely see her features. She appeared to be Native American and very old, evidenced by the hunched shoulders of her silhouette.

Man and woman watched one another for a time, and Peter filled with an odd sensation of recognition, not that he recognized the old woman but that she recognized him. Peter's fingers twitched. He felt impelled to raise a hand and wave, but before he could lift his arm, the woman nodded, tightly wrapped the shawl around her shoulders, and shuffled indoors, flicking off the light.

Peter's chocolaty breath caught in his throat. If he hadn't known better, he would have sworn the woman had been awaiting his arrival.

A few paces off the sole, winding road into town, behind the "Welcome to Prosperity" sign—a copper plaque shaped like a ghost wearing a headlamp and carrying a miner's pick—stood the double-decker bar and eatery known as the Ghostly Grill, a rough-paneled Victorian edifice that once served as Prosperity's mercantile. During the day, art and antique hunters cozied up to the black Formica tables and consumed greasy small-town fare while perusing the framed photographs of early-1900s Prosperity that hung on the walls. But when the sun went down on weekends, twisting columns of bikers and hard-as-nails ruralites in trucks clogged the road from the base of Salome Hill to the Ghostly Grill's parking lot. A live band—alternating between Western and Classic Rock—played on the second-floor balcony, shaking the floorboards, while revelers danced beneath, throwing back shots of hard liquor at a rate Prosperity's original bad boys would have envied.

Some went too far and lost their souls along with their good sense, sometimes their innards, too. Afton Burnside knew this all too well. Silently cursing the weekend help—ZuZu Lorenz—for calling in sick, she attacked a puddle of chunky, pink-tinged vomit with paper towels and a mop. After several hearty swabs and a dousing with bleach, the small area of floor near the bar was fit to be walked on again, but Afton was riled.

"I still smell it. The puke scent is stuck in my nose," she griped.

Had she been a dog, foam would have been dripping from her jowls, her teeth bared for a fight. Of course, that description applied to Afton more often than not. She was a woman who lived in a near-constant state of displeasure, earning the moniker "Our Lady of Perpetual Discontent" from her affable and colossal brother, Seamus. Her fuse had been lit long ago by an unfaithful husband, the death of her parents in a house fire, and, well, life in general. Every little thing compounded her unhappiness; a vomitous pond was as likely a source of ire as any.

Carrying the bucket and mop out back while shrieking curses like a banshee with Tourette's, Afton stalked toward a granite precipice, leaving a trail of splashed mop water behind her.

"Bite me, Prosperity!" she howled, chucking both the mop and bucket—with what was left of its putrid contents—down the cliff. She wiped her hands on her apron, embroidered with a black widow spider in its web, and twisted her long, frizzy red curls into a loose knot that resembled a noose dangling at the back of her head.

In the spidery apron and a black Oxford and chinos, she was meant to look scary but instead—at five feet even, with a freckled pug nose and slight overbite—seemed a nocturnal sprite. Heading back toward the grill, leaning forward, fighting the wind, she appeared ready to go airborne at any minute. A blinding gust tore a few strands of hair from her unconventional ponytail and slapped them against her unadorned face, in her mouth, up her nose, across her watering blue eyes.

"That does it! I'm getting a buzz cut," Afton fumed. "And…and, maybe I'll quit the grill! Start over!"

Afton scowled at her rash comment. As co-owner of the Ghostly Grill, she couldn't simply throw up her hands and walk away. And deep down, she didn't want to. She was self-aware enough to recognize that the problem was her own character, not long hair or nauseated customers.

Staggering inside, she caught her breath and watched her brother pour a whiskey in front of the night's puke donor: a shaggy-haired young man in a Metallica T-shirt and jeans ripped at the knees. Her eyes bulged at the sight. With pure disgust coloring her cheeks, Afton made her way across the bar and grabbed the shot glass, sending a wave of amber liquid over the brim, onto her brother's hand.

"You," she said, angrily jutting her jaw in Seamus' direction, "why are you serving someone who's clearly wasted?"

Twisting her neck toward the offender, she pleaded, "And you, go home and sober up, kid, okay?"

"Hey, lady," he protested.

That was the extent of his defense. He tried to say more, but all that came out was a long, watery slur. Spittle gathered at one side of his mouth, and his glassy eyes gyrated in their sockets. Afton knew that look. He was about to go out, cold.

She held a hand over the boy's head and called out, "Who came with this guy?"

There was no response. Only a bat could have discerned Afton's words over the din of inebriated conversation and grinding guitar riffs. Retrieving a bright red air horn from behind the bar, Seamus gave the contraption three quick squeezes, emitting a series of rapid but deafening blasts.

Everyone quieted, even the band upstairs. The people within the downstairs area set their dazed gazes on Seamus, then Afton, as she demanded, "Who's with this guy?"

There wasn't a jot of recognition on the faces around her.

"Who gives a shit?" came a voice at the back of the room.

"Who said that?"

The crowd parted and a few unsteady fingers pointed at a tattooed cue ball of a man: bald, black-goateed, glaring at the world from kohl-lined eyes, wearing a leather vest and motorcycle chaps seamed with silver spikes. He swelled his chest, exposing a yarn-thick chain that ran between large silver hoops in his nipples.

Afton strutted over to the biker—her irritation equaled by her confidence—and stared up into his heavily accentuated eyes.

"Get out," she snapped.

"Yeah? Why should I?"

"Because I own this place. I say who comes and goes, and it's time for you to go, big boy."

"Is that right, bitch?" the man growled, folding his arms across his chest and making a move toward Afton, who fearlessly stood her ground.

"That's right, asshole," Seamus confirmed, leaping over the bar and taking quick strides across the hardwood floor, fists set, prepared to administer punishment for his sister's slander. Everyone in the grill knew the biker was about to pay dearly for one poorly chosen word.

Even in a cheesy white Oxford crawling with black-thread spiders, Seamus was an awesome figure. His wooly, red hair fit him like a lion's mane, edging onto his jaws and chin in a neat beard that added maturity to his 26 years. Drawing himself up assuredly, he showed the crowd what 6'7" looks like in the form of a brawny human frame. Almost a full foot taller than his opponent and nearly twice as wide, Seamus stood between him and Afton, letting a proud smile lighten his face.

"Can you find the door, or do you need my *little* brother to help you?" Afton innocently asked.

The biker wavered on his feet. His eyes briefly registered fear and then flickered insolently. Pride pushed him beyond the limits of discretion. "Let's do this," he challenged.

Seamus glimpsed the chain, strung between delicate pink nubs of flesh. "Nah, too easy," he said. Without further ado, he shoved the man's shoulder, spinning him like a top. He put one hand on his belt and the other on the scruff of his leather vest. The troublemaker silently rose, then seemingly levitated across the room and out the door, arms flailing, carried by the bartender and followed by a few thrill-seeking busybodies. Just like that, he was gone, and after a few eventful minutes outside, Seamus returned, none the worse for wear, to resume bar duty.

Afton slapped her brother a high five and the two giggled like kids with a secret. Seamus gave the all clear signal—one honk of the air horn—and the band picked up its cover of "Smoke on the Water." Bodies writhed in strange dances, raucous laughter and talk began, drinks were lifted to lips; it was as if nothing of consequence had occurred.

Glancing at the now empty line of bar stools, Seamus made a relieved shrug. He quickly scanned the scene and found no sign of the young man in the Metallica shirt.

"At least someone got Barf Boy out of here," he said. "I didn't see him in the parking lot, either."

Afton leaned on the counter, which was almost as tall as she was. "Let's hope he didn't get out of here on his own. He wasn't in any shape to drive. I can't believe you kept serving him. I mean, between this kind of stuff and you going AWOL with your ghost geek friends, I don't know what to think, Bro. You're not acting yourself lately."

"What do the Paranormal Investigators of Prosperity have to do with that kid?"

"Listen to that name…it almost makes your little group seem respectable," Afton jeered. "PIP is, like, all you care about anymore. What's up with that?"

Seamus pulled one of a hundred tiny, red plastic pirate swords from a cup at the back of the bar. He returned to his sister and used the miniature blade like a toothpick as he explained. "Boyd keeps lining up back-to-back investigations. I don't know why. Since he split with Amy, it's all he thinks about. Actually, it was all he thought about before he split with Amy, which is why they split."

He pulled the sword from his mouth and pointed it accusingly at Afton. "What's this really about? You think I'm not pulling my weight here? You know I'm always on time opening up, and I'm here every shift. Okay, I had to back out of one last Monday to do an investigation, but I got ZuZu to cover for me, so what's the problem?"

"Yeah, yeah. Don't get defensive. I just worry about you, Bro. Investigating dead people doesn't seem like the right pastime for someone like you."

Seamus raised a thick red eyebrow and tossed the sword toothpick into a trashcan tucked under the bar. "Someone like me? Go ahead and say what you really mean, Affie. You don't think it's the right hobby for a crazy guy, huh?"

"Knock it off. You're not crazy," Afton admonished. "But you are vulnerable."

"Let's see…a whack job who tried to off himself at 17, wound up in a psych ward, and now lives on megadoses of antidepressants. Yeah, I guess that's one definition of 'vulnerable.'" Seamus took a few steps away and put some muscle into rubbing down the end of the bar.

"Don't be so hard on yourself. It makes sense…the depression and the hobby. For crying out loud, you still lived at home when the fire happened. You're still hurting, and maybe you're hoping to contact Mom or Pop during one of your ghost hunts. That's why you do it, isn't it?"

Seamus looked around, embarrassed, his massive stature shrinking as he slouched against the bar. "This isn't the place. Do we really need to go into this in front of the patrons?"

"Please! You think anybody is listening to us?" Afton half-shouted over the screeching guitars and loud hum of blended, boisterous voices. "Listen to me, there's no such thing as ghosts. Mom and Pop are gone. You can't find them through this pastime of yours. I'm worried you're getting in over your head. You may be built like an ox, but you're a little boy inside."

Seamus' face reddened in anger. "I'm not an idiot."

"Of course not. But you're not always rational. I mean, how rational is it to chase after ghosts? How rational is it to keep serving a sick guy drinks? I'm sorry, but sometimes I have to question your judgment."

"One drink, Afton. That was it," Seamus solemnly swore. "Now, what the kid had before he came here, I can't say. And by the way, that whiskey—the one you slapped out of my hand—that wasn't for him. He was drinking rum and cola, just the one. I thought he was okay until he looked kinda funny and asked for a glass of water. That's what he was drinking when he heaved."

"Sorry," Afton quietly offered, letting the whole scene sink in. She hopped onto the bar stool where the young man had sat and thought of his blue eyes, dimmed by alcohol and threaded with red vessels. Something was tragic about them. "Did you card him?" she asked.

"Duh," her brother mocked. "Jerry O'Neil, age 23. That's what his license said, but who knows if it's right. He could be 16-year-old Joe Shmo, who printed and laminated that card. These days, it's hard to spot the fake ones, but I check cards, even on nights when I'm the only one working the bar."

"Yeah, I know you do, Bro. Sorry again." Afton's thoughts drifted back to the guy slumped on the bar stool, a pond of foamy vomit at his feet and a crumpled, stained napkin in his white-knuckled hand. In hindsight, her opinion of the boy softened. "Poor kid must be messed up," she lamented. "I saw some dissolving pills in his upchuck. That's sad…and stupid."

Seamus clicked his teeth as he worked his way down the counter, wiping away fingerprints and drops of liquor. "Drugs and alcohol—what a majorly stupid combo, but then, human stupidity never ceases to amaze me." His words gave way to a smirk that Afton took as self-deprecating. A bottleful of duloxetine and a 24-ounce can of beer was the method Seamus had used to try to end it all years earlier.

"Slide me a Zombie and a Dos Equis, stud!" yelled a scantily clad young woman, who flung herself against the bar as seductively as possible.

Afton looked away as her brother handled the order. Her eyes narrowed, voice cracking with concern as she whispered, "That poor kid…"

CHAPTER 2

It was time for another SpecTours by Night ghost tour to begin. The group gathered outside the front gate of the gloriously gaudy Canary Cage Inn, once Prosperity's high-end brothel. The bright yellow mansion was a deft blend of coziness and sophistication. Not a smudged wall or wilted leaf to be found; the place beckoned with a welcoming charm. Like the girls it once housed, the Canary Cage was both beautiful and accessible—for a price.

The picturesque B & B was the ideal starting point for SpecTours by Night expeditions. Its polished prettiness eased the less paranormal-minded tourists into the past and a night of wild stories told on a long trek to several of the near-vertical town's most notorious locations. The tour company owner and host was Clive LeBarre, an unhealthily pale beanpole dressed entirely in black save for white Adidas sneakers. Looking like a nerdy vampire, he grimly eyed each candle-wielding client in his 10:00 p.m. group: a middle-aged couple in "We hiked the Grand Canyon!" T-shirts, a lone Irishman, a New England seniors group, and three blond Northern Arizona University coeds.

"Please, good people, search your souls. If you feel any doubt about your ability to withstand this night's terror, you must tell me now. Does anyone wish to stay behind?" he gravely asked, leveling his candle before each set of eyes and gathering a negative answer before moving on.

Though born and raised in Prescott, Arizona, 28-year-old Clive spoke with an English accent, the result of an obsession with British horror films and a stint with the Arizona Renaissance Reenactors Troupe while in his teens. The Old World effect pleased his clientele, so he kept the gimmick going 24-7 to further engrain the tendency.

"You aren't from here, are you?" squealed a young woman who looked remarkably like Malibu Barbie come to life. "You have a German accent or something, huh?"

"It's English," Clive sniffed. Gesticulating theatrically, he swirled about the crowd. "England—that hallowed isle green with life and gray with the sorrows of millennia. Such a land! Her moors and hills and emerald glades are peopled with the ghosts of the unjustly condemned…the depraved…the unforgiven…the unrepentant. Armies of the disquieted roam her soil! Ah, but the only other place on earth as close to the Other World is the ground you stand upon. Take heed! Prosperity is cursed!" he warned, relishing the intrigued reactions of his audience. "Here—in the Wickedest Town in the Southwest—evil reigned for a short but powerful time…and its shadow remains in the spirits of its agents and victims. Perhaps you've heard of some of Prosperity's ghostly inhabitants: the beautiful Sadie Rue, who hanged herself just up there," Clive emoted, sweeping a hand toward the top of the yellow turret, "in the attic of the Canary Cage Bordello; or Wei Chang, loving father and husband…strung up like snared quarry, strangled and decapitated in the yard of the Graham Boarding House, which ran red with his blood that dreadful May night in 1922…"

"Ewww," one of the coeds yelped, her face puckering in disgust.

Clive turned up the drama. "Or the ruthless Amalia 'Mad Molly' Petrova, Prosperity's queen of crime, so reviled that after she was killed and her home torched, her charred remains and those of her henchman were dumped into a mine shaft rather than interred in consecrated ground. Their spirits are but a few that have lingered on after death and whose lives we'll revisit tonight. For whatever reasons, dear ones—hatred, vengeance, sorrow, love—they are still among us. They are…"

Clive twitched from scalp to toe and braced himself against the wrought-iron railing of the Canary Cage's fence, looking like someone had just lobbed a punch to his gut. He ran a hand over his slicked-back hair, a naturally ash-brown mop dyed black. A stripe of gummy pomade came off on his palm, but he was too anguished to notice or care.

"You okay?" asked one of the nubile coeds.

"I'm dizzy," Clive rasped, identifying but one symptom.

He paused in contemplation, his eyelids drooping with concern, his skinny fingers bending in uncontrollable spasms. Clive's body chilled; every nerve prickled.

"Blimey, it felt like an Arctic wind blasted clean through me," he muttered. "I'm numb. I…I feel disconnected."

As the chill subsided, Clive's being was flooded with odd stimuli—more prickles and a nearly electric vibratory sensation—and most astonishingly, his brain received the distinct knowledge that another restless spirit had been added to Prosperity's paranormal pantheon and hadn't made that transition peacefully. Never, in all his years of SpecTours by Night expeditions and ghost hunts with the Paranormal Investigators of Prosperity had he felt such a thing. Both mysterious and specific, the information pointed to a fresh soul but not its identity or even its gender, only that it was new to the scene and victimized on its path to the great beyond. Clive glanced up at the Canary Cage, driven to search the windows for a sign of that ghost. Somehow, it was tied to the old brothel or someone inside it.

A 70-ish woman in a sequined pink baseball cap reading "Sexy Granny" put a hand on Clive's shoulder, startling him. "Do you need help, young man?"

Clive remained bowed over, unspeaking, the tilted candle in his right hand dripping its wax onto the inn's brick walkway.

"Call 9-1-1, Harve," the woman ordered her husband, who fumbled through his pants pocket until he produced a cell phone in his shaking paw.

"No need," Clive assured, waving in the man's direction. He gulped and ran a set of fingers through his hair again, taking off more pomade and coating his fingers in what looked like drying mucus. "I sense a new spirit among us tonight, and it passed through me," he somberly voiced.

The sexy granny unhanded Clive. "Oh, I see. Put the phone away, Harve. It's all part of his shtick."

The blond teenagers giggled excitedly and huddled together, pushing the flames of their candles together into one enormous flare.

Incensed by the reactions, Clive glowered at the group and scolded, "I do not jest with you! This is no laughing matter! I felt a spirit walk through me and go there." Clive's unsteady forefinger pointed to the Canary Cage.

"Oooooh," howled the tannest of the coeds, sliding a fingernail up one of her friends' spines.

The girl shivered and shrieked and jumped to the side, dissolving into laughter.

"Please behave!" Clive yipped. "Tonight a human being has made the passage from one plane to another! I beseech you to conduct yourselves respectfully!"

Malibu Barbie apologized with an airy, "Sorry." But the girls continued to fight smiles and anxious laughter, believing Clive's admission to have been just another part of the act. Sadly, not being taken seriously was something to which Clive had become accustomed.

He pushed himself away from the railing and tried to compose himself so that he could resume the tour. "Give me a moment please."

Clive's chest burned with the after-ache of an unknown yet powerful emotion, which had stampeded through his body moments earlier. He felt strung out and clammy, more drained than the one time in his chaste life when he'd awakened with a hangover—the morning after his high school graduation party, when members of the Prescott High School football team had slipped past the faculty chaperones and dumped three bottles of vodka into the punchbowl.

Clive stood there, trembling, catching his breath until he noticed his audience growing antsy. The show had to go on.

"Let us begin!" he heralded.

"This is so exciting," one of the teens chirped, snuggling close to her friends.

Clive pushed open the wrought-iron gate and waved his group onward, holding his candle so that its flame illuminated only half his face.

"Let us move onto the porch, and I will tell you the sad story of Sadie Rue, the Gem of the Canary Cage." He went into storyteller mode before they'd reached the steps, even before some of them were through the gate, his voice lacking its usual enthusiasm.

Clive recited the tale just as he had during hundreds of tours before, but this time, he didn't listen to his words. He didn't pay attention to the rapt faces around him. He was busy looking over his shoulder at the inn, wondering at the identity of the spirit that had, that night, entered the grand old bordello.

"He's here, awee'," Mae said when her daughter came in to kiss her goodnight.

"He is?" Ooljee glanced around the room, half-expecting to see an unknown figure. But there was nothing out of the ordinary, just a tidy white-walled bedroom and an open window, through which the moonlight and a sprinkling of stars glowed.

Ooljee loosely tucked a quilt around her mother's tiny form and bent over the old woman to read her expression in the dimness of the unlit bedroom. The wizened face on the pillow looked peaceful, relieved even.

"The man I told you about—the grown-up boy from Tennessee—he came to the Canary Cage tonight."

Ooljee smiled. "Fantastic."

She wasn't being patronizing. She knew how important this moment was to her mother. Mae Benally had spoken of little else the last three weeks, ever since the dreams began.

It started on a Saturday night. When she made her regular 1:00 a.m. trek to the bathroom, Ooljee caught Mae prowling through the darkened house, drinking a can of Ensure. "Can't sleep," the old woman explained. Ooljee turned on the kitchen light, and they sat at the table as Mae described her dream. Two skeletons, laid out on their backs, arms crossed on chests, became illuminated, as if daylight suddenly shone on them, and they both sat up, arms still crossed over their breastbones. The dream scene pulled in tight, focused on the ribs of one skeleton, the perspective traveling around one rib bone, across the sternum and onto another rib bone, up and around to the next rib, around and up, faster and faster in circle eights, until a curved bone transformed into the bleached pavement of one of Salome Hill's hairpin turns, and a vertebra became a white sedan traveling that road. As the vision crystallized, Mae saw the man driving the car. He wore a blue shirt and looked straight ahead with dolorous eyes. His face struck Mae as poignantly familiar. She'd been hopeful of that vision, and the dreams that had come since convinced her that her initial reaction was spot on.

Prophetic dreams were nothing new to the women. Though unrelated by blood, no mother and daughter could have been more meaningfully connected. For all their differences—and there were several striking ones—the two were alike in ways that mattered. Most binding of all was the burdensome psychic gift granted to them both from the beginning of their lives—it was what had brought them together 48 years earlier. Clairvoyant, telepathic, psychically empathic: the women had been branded with many labels, all of which fit, with no one term neatly tying up all of their talents. Those who had witnessed their power knew they functioned at a level far beyond human understanding. That these two glorious aberrations had found each other and strengthened in each other's presence was a miracle.

One particular perk for the women was their ability to exchange thoughts and feelings so that most conversations were unspoken. But as time wore on, Mae relied more on verbalization. Age was changing her in ways that frightened her daughter. Not only did she speak more often, but at greater lengths and about things from long ago, things Mae had spent most of her life trying to forget, or at other times, things that seemed to have no relevance to anything at all. And then there were moments when the woman appeared to forget everything, including who and where she was. It was heartbreaking to Ooljee that the strong as steel Mae, who'd lived with dignity through events that would have destroyed a weaker soul, now occasionally became confused and lost in her own home.

"You want to show me this Tennessean of yours?" Ooljee asked, gently latching her fingers onto the woman's gray temples.

She closed her wide black eyes, listening, feeling, waiting for the transmission of a mental image, a vision, but there was no sign of the troubled boy who'd clung to her mother's psyche for nearly a month.

The old woman was thinking of the next morning's breakfast. The only thing Ooljee picked up on was a steaming pot of cinnamon-flecked oatmeal. That seemingly benign image bothered Ooljee to no end. It was yet another disconnection between her and her mother.

Frequently, they shared their visions by physically touching and focusing—one on transmitting, the other on receiving—until their minds met. It didn't always work, but so great was their shared talent that it usually did. This time, however, Mae didn't even have the wherewithal to try. Already, her mind had skipped from something it held dear to a random and insignificant thought.

Ooljee breathed out and released her mother's head from her gentle grasp. Her fingers dropped down to the woman's shoulders and gave a few soft, relaxing rubs.

"That's okay, Mama. I'll see him in person soon."

Mae turned her face to the window and smiled up at the moon—ooljee. Born to the Water Flows Together Clan for the Towering House Clan, Mae was Diné, yet she hadn't returned to her homeland since arriving in Prosperity decades earlier. She was renowned as the daughter of Rosemae Bennally, the Navajo teen practically beatified for killing Mad Molly in 1923, thereby liberating Sin Alley's sex slaves and freeing the town from the villainess' yoke. Mae couldn't escape the community that needed her as a lifeline to its celebrated past or shed the legacy she carried like a millstone. As consolation, she'd been given Ooljee, a reflection of herself and a link to her people.

Ooljee Davis was an eminent victims' rights advocate, who, for 15 years, hosted the enormously popular Silent Witness-sponsored *American Fugitives* television show, flying to Los Angeles every week to film and returning to Prosperity on the weekends to be with her mother. Having come to fame as a psychic who worked with law enforcement agencies to solve cold and stalled cases, she continued in that role, helping out as she could; her high profile and success rate earned her countless speaking engagements and a lucrative publishing contract for a series of true crime books with an action-advocacy slant.

Ooljee navigated between worlds from the beginning: past and present, life and death, here and there. Even her heritage reflected this duality. Her father was Jacob Davis, an African American who taught science on the reservation; her mother was Betsy Gorman, a gifted Navajo hand-trembler and a nurse at the same school where Jacob taught. When Ooljee was five, a sleepy trucker on State Route 264 rammed her parents' car and ended their lives, sending her to live with her mother's family in a hogan near Chinle. Two years later, as her psychic gift bloomed, frightening her cousins and challenging her aunt, a group of elders at a roundhouse meeting decided that Mae Benally—known from her childhood as an intuitive of the highest order—was the best hope for the girl's future. Ooljee was sent from the reservation to the blue Victorian high on Salome Hill and into the welcoming arms of a woman who fully understood everything she was experiencing.

Now, almost five decades on, Mae was very aged and verging on the infirm, but she was well loved and cared for by a daughter who made her proud and placed her above all others. She knew well, in her lucid moments, that no one could have had a better child.

Ooljee looked down at the tear-shaped pendant resting on her mother's clavicle, a drop of glass encasing the powdered petals of a dried yellow rose, the one item Mae was never without, not even during baths. She brushed a single strand of gray hair from her mother's forehead, planting a kiss where the hair had rested.

Mae's eyelids fluttered. She turned her focus on Ooljee, as if awakening from a deep sleep and slowly attuning to her surroundings. "Don't you worry about me, awee'. Everything's happening as it should."

Ooljee wondered if that meant the way her mother's life course was coming to a close or the arrival of the man at the Canary Cage. She thought, perhaps, it referred to both. Gone were the days when she instinctively, assuredly understood what her mother said and felt.

"Do you want to go next door and see your grown-up Tennessee boy? I'll call over there and fill Clare in."

Mae snuggled into her pillow and shut her eyes. "No, no. Go on to bed, awee'. She'll send for us soon enough. As soon as that boy starts a firestorm."

Ooljee hesitated to say what she thought needed to be said. A year or two ago, she wouldn't have bothered; Mae was almost always right about her premonitions and solid enough to roll with the punches on the rare occasions when something didn't happen as expected. But this vision—or series of visions—was intensely personal and meaningful to her mother, who was becoming more fragile every day. If Mae's sight didn't prove true in this case, she just might crumble, and that was something Ooljee couldn't bear.

"Mama, what if he doesn't know where the bones are? I know that's why you're so excited. You think he can help find them. But what if he can't? I don't want you to be disappointed."

Ooljee grew silent and drew back as a soft, purr-like snore issued from Mae's slightly parted lips. Her eyes watered as she watched her mother sleep, a loose smile bending her mouth. Batting away the tears, Ooljee looked up, quietly entreating, "Lord, please, I'm begging you; let her be right about this."

Boyd Chang lay awake, stroking the small, bleached stripe in his otherwise black hair, wondering how he was going to tell his grandfather that he'd quit college. It wasn't that he didn't want to finish; he just had to prioritize, and there was no room for homework and programs of study between his part-time job with the Prosperity Public Works Department and his mounting work as co-founder of the Paranormal Investigators of Prosperity.

"He's gonna kill me," Boyd whispered, softly pounding his head into the pillow, imagining the flabbergasted look on his grandfather's face when he finally learned the news. *Then he's gonna kill Seamus and Clive*, he thought, recalling all the barbs, gripes, and outright vitriol the old man reserved for Boyd's fellow ghost hunters.

Lloyd Chang had received his master of architecture degree from Cornell, taught for a few semesters, and went on to helm the most successful commercial and residential design firm in north-central Arizona for many years. A man with that kind of background was doomed to misunderstand his grandson's unorthodox decision and the motives behind it.

Boyd pulled the pillow from underneath him and held it against his face as he cursed into its fluff. Requests for investigations were coming in right and left, and Boyd was having a hard time saying "no." Documenting evidence of otherworldly contact and making people feel safe in their own homes was his calling, not fixing cracks in Prosperity's sidewalks or listening to a lecture on finite math. Something had to give, and for the time being, that was college.

As Boyd lowered the pillow to his chest, he heard something that jolted him from his insomniac quandary. The back door opened and shut, followed by the sound of heavy footsteps running across the wooden downstairs floor. The teen's heart fluttered with excitement, as if an old friend had just arrived. But Boyd knew no one was there. No one ever was. It was always the same: the noise of the door bursting open and slamming, then several heavy lunges on the oak planks. It always happened at 2:41 a.m., like a recording played as a sign-off for the night. He'd been hearing that routine clamor a couple of times a year since he was a boy, and even that first time, though he barely remembered it, he wasn't frightened. Only puzzled. He still was. Who was it who'd once run into the house, full of such heavy emotion that a trail of energy was seared into time itself? The options were mind-boggling. The building had been one bookend of Sin Alley, the worst section of old Prosperity, and one of two buildings spared in the fire that razed that ratty block in 1923. It had seen its share of violence, misfortune, death, and drama as Chang Brothers Restaurant—on the ground floor—where world-weary miners devoured meals next to gamblers and outlaws, and as the Chang family home on the floor above, and later, when the restaurant closed, on both floors. Of all the generations of Prosperity's Changs, only Boyd and Lloyd remained. All others were long dead, including Boyd's parents, three grandparents, and of course, the original Chang Brothers—Wei, Wu, and Yee—as well as Wei's wife, Ting, and daughter, Yin.

Old town records and newspaper clippings pointed to several violent, some fatal, confrontations in or near the restaurant. Boyd considered those events strong possibilities for the cause of the repeating disturbance, but so too, were his deceased kin, none of whom had died peacefully. Boyd had tried to discover the answer, but there was nothing left to be found, no substantiation beyond the din itself. He'd recorded the noise several times, and that was the extent of evidence. Though he'd staked out the kitchen on many occasions, there was nothing to see, no change in temperature or atmosphere or magnetic field. The kitchen door did not move. The floorboards did not vibrate. There was only the sound of something that had happened long before echoing all around him.

Switching on his bedside lamp, Boyd twisted back and scratched his thumbnail into the side of the headboard, leaving a hash mark behind. That made 31. Thirty one times he'd witnessed the unexplained phenomenon. He ran a finger over the six sets of five and the single line, yearning to know the meaning behind the early morning disturbances in his home and questioning if he ever would.

CHAPTER 3

Pouring herself a mug of decaf, Clare Bowers gracefully stepped onto the porch of the Canary Cage Inn, a thin black braid bouncing against her purple kimono, and took a seat in one of the rocking chairs.

"Hello, Sahara, Tropicana, my darlings," she cooed, reaching down to pat the gray tabbies that slid between her ankles.

Clare breathed in, then out, exercising her lungs, filling them with dry mountain air and the conflicting baked scents of spicy jalapeño quiche and ginger scones, the showpieces of the breakfast she'd serve to her 10 guests.

Refashioned around the bones of the old brothel—which had flourished throughout the Victorian, Edwardian, and Roaring 20s eras before being shuttered as the Copper Prince Mine tapped out and its workers, then the surrounding town's people, moved on to other places and other lives—the Canary Cage Inn was one of Prosperity's greatest treasures. Clare played up the building's raunchily romantic past to draw a steady stream of historians, lonely bachelors, run-of-the-mill tourists, and ghost seekers. It didn't hurt promotional efforts that several visitors to the red-wallpapered oasis claimed to have seen Sadie Rue, a buxom specter that usually appeared nude and sometimes nuzzled against men in the dark of night. The transparent form was said to be the ghost of a prostitute who hanged herself in her attic room after a failed elopement. Of course, the story, like Prosperity itself, was a blend of fact and fantasy. It had been so long since Sadie's life and death that it was difficult to know which details held true. Nonetheless, Clare continued to tell a liberal version of the tale to anyone who'd listen.

The ghostly hubbub kept the inn's once-widowed, once-divorced geriatric ex-showgirl proprietress in the spotlight. So did Clare's role as the reigning queen of the Resurrectors, the hodgepodge of entrepreneurs, craftspeople, artists, and hippies that reclaimed Prosperity in the late 60s.

Like all Resurrectors, she held a reverent love for her chosen hometown and the people who'd lived there before.

"Ah," Clare hummed, prolonging the sound. She widened her mouth and loosened her throat, sending the "ah" up and down the scale. "Mi, mi, mi, mi." Her voice wasn't quite what it used to be, but it was still impressive.

Though she would beg to differ, age had been kind to her. Any unflattering trait was her own doing, such as her harsh cat-eye makeup and hair dyed so unnaturally black that it had a bluish sheen, like Wonder Woman's; that hair was habitually worn in a tight braid or bun that gave Clare an instant facelift.

She warbled on, until she turned about and observed one of her guests hunched at the curve of the porch, trying very hard not to be noticed.

"Heavens! I didn't know anyone was out here," Clare explained, approaching the man, who jumped from his chair, rubbed out the creases in his pants, and nervously slid his hands into his pockets.

"Are you a professional singer?" he asked in a deep, Southern-nuanced voice.

"Why, you are a flatterer, sir!"

With a demure smile, Clare greeted Peter Jacoby—temporary resident of the Séance Suite—who had arrived late the night before with a young male companion. He was older than she'd thought. The soft gaslight of the foyer had cast a complimentary spell upon him. Now, in the glare of dawn, she noted the webs of shallow lines around his eyes and the furrows that ran from the corners of his mouth to the side of each nostril. *Thirty-five, if a day,* Clare thought, beginning a thorough assessment. *Sandy hair, powerful brown irises, square jaw, full features. Impeccably pressed dress shirt tucked into leather-belted khakis—a far cry from the usual T-shirt and shorts tourist uniform. Such a refined and handsome man!*

Clare's lips fluttered and pursed throughout her internal conversation. Peter thought to ask if something was wrong, but he was a perceptive creature. He quietly watched the twitching of her crimson-painted mouth—which appeared fuzzy due to small quantities of lipstick radiating into the flesh fissures around her lips—and waited for her to finish making her appraisal.

"You're an early riser, Mr. Jacoby. Did you sleep well?"

"Yes ma'am," Peter fibbed. He'd experienced a brutal headache and a devil of a nightmare the night before, but there was no point in burdening his hostess with that information. Rocking on his heels, he let his eyes absorb the magnificent scene before him and then turned them to the scrolled details of the porch railings. "This is one of the best examples of Queen Anne architecture I've seen."

"Thank you kindly. The Canary Cage is my pride and joy. Best views in all of Prosperity. Best rooms, too."

Feather beds, tasseled pillows, Persian rugs, and antique lace coverlets weren't exactly his style, but Peter couldn't deny the attention to detail his hostess had lavished on her establishment.

"I don't doubt it. All my coworkers recommended the Canary Cage…or the Skullery Inn."

"Oh, that place," Clare dismissed with a tone of distaste. "That isn't an inn. It's a sandbox. It caters to bikers and roustabouts. There's no proof of a haunting, merely reports of an occasional unholy odor…which is probably the clientele. But the owners claim it's a spirit and call him Pooter the Flatulent Ghost. They even printed merchandise with him on it—a floating sheet with cutout eyes and mouth, and smoky puffs trailing behind him at waist level! Unbelievable!" Clare leaned in secretively and said, "I'll have you know, they serve a cold breakfast of cereal and pastries. Isn't that dreadful? They get you all sugared up so you carb-crash halfway through the day. I'd never do that! Heavens, no! I have high-quality protein available at every breakfast, and everything is homemade with the freshest of ingredients. Organic, if possible."

Peter worked to digest each sentence the chattering woman had made. "Do you run the Canary Cage on your own?"

"Yes, sir, for going on…" she blushed and genteelly swiped a hand at Peter. "Let's just say longer than you've been alive! I think of the Canary Cage as my baby. She was a hovel when I bought her. A year and a half of loving restoration efforts made her come alive. I've been pampering her ever since." She inquired, "So, does Prosperity agree with you, Mr. Jacoby?"

"I don't know yet, ma'am. What I saw of the town was…" Peter picked through applicable adjectives until he came to a positive one, "interesting."

"Oh, yes, it is that! At its peak, Prosperity had over 15,000 people, many of them wilder than the dickens. Now we're a quaint hamlet of 439 colorful but decent souls—no, my mistake, we're down to 438 after last month; I forgot dear old Ada Barbary passed away. Sometimes we seem much bigger because well over a million tourists come here annually. But don't let that fool you. Prosperity is an excellent place to live. We have a true sense of community, a fine police department and all-volunteer fire department, and…well," Clare gestured widely. "Just look at the view from up here!"

"Yes, ma'am," Peter granted, gazing beyond the inn's flowery grounds to the grandeur of the Verde Valley below, hemmed in by ancient mesas and craggy buttes painted with striations of buff, plum, mauve, and blue.

"If you want to learn about the town's history from an authentic source, you should speak with Mae Bennally next door. Her mother…good heavens, now there's a story straight out of a Hollywood movie! Anyhow, her mother, Rosemae, was kidnapped from the reservation when she was just 13—taken while watching her grandmother's flock of sheep—and sold to Mad Molly. Rosemae was one of the poor unwilling girls kept in leg irons in the basement rooms along Sin Alley. Eventually, she escaped her chains, freed the other girls, and stabbed Molly in the heart with a letter opener. Got one of her bodyguards, too. She became known as the Savior of Prosperity. With Molly gone, crime leveled out, and many innocent souls were saved. Rosemae died long ago, but Mae and her daughter, Ooljee, are considered royalty in this town—the nicest people you'll ever meet, and…" Clare whistled in a breath, "eerily psychic. Ooljee's our own celebrity, but no diva. She's totally devoted her life to her mother and her work with crime victims. Remember her? She hosted *American Fugitives* on TV?"

Peter looked blank.

"Or, you could talk to Lloyd Chang. His family's been here since the turn of the twentieth century. Lloyd's father and uncles ran Chang Brothers Restaurant on Sin Alley, and his uncle, Wei Chang—rest his soul—was hanged by a lynch mob for bootlegging and carrying on with Sadie Rue."

Changing directions, Clare dared to ask, "By the way, Mr. Jacoby, did you have the great good fortune to meet Sadie last night?"

Peter's face tensed in confusion. "Sadie?"

"Sadie Rue, our resident ghost." Clare seemed wounded by the lack of recognition, but she quickly regained her enthusiasm as she began to gush about her supernatural houseguest. "Sadie Rue was Prosperity's favorite lady of the night, a golden-haired beauty, who in 1922, took her own life up in the top turret room—the Séance Suite—why, the very room you're in." Clare rested her free hand on her chest, as if calming an aching heart. After a dramatic pause and a slurp of her decaf, she looked at the white porch planks beneath her feet and then peered suspiciously around her. "But Sadie isn't gone. No, sir." Clare lowered her voice to a whisper. "She's still with us."

Peter grinned. "I'm not one for ghost stories, ma'am."

"Ah, a nonbeliever. Well, perhaps it's best that Sadie didn't call on you. After all, that boy of yours is still at an impressionable age, and Sadie is known for her…how shall I put it?…lusty ways." Clare gave Peter a wink, not noticing his confounded expression. "I take it your son isn't the early riser you are."

"I don't have a son, ma'am."

Clare was chagrined. The teen who'd trailed Peter into the foyer and up the staircase could have been anyone—a nephew, godson, friend, quick hookup, among others.

"I'm so sorry, Mr. Jacoby. I just assumed the young man was your son. I beg your pardon."

Peter stared at Clare while her words tumbled through his brain. "I'm not traveling with anyone."

"No?" Now Clare was more than embarrassed. She began to question what she'd seen, what was true, if she was being scammed or whether she'd reached that age when, for some, being addled is the norm. "There was a young man with you last night. He stood behind you when you signed in, and then he followed you up the stairs."

Only a mockingbird's lullaby and the loud purring of Clare's contented cats filled the air as the discomfited twosome considered one another, measuring personal acuity against the knowledge that had been shared.

Peter wondered if his hostess was suffering from dementia or trying desperately to turn him on to the ghost angle she'd tried to ply earlier. Either way, he felt pity and a terrible awkwardness.

"Maybe he was with another guest," he politely offered.

"Yes, of course," Clare mindlessly agreed, backing away. "You'll excuse me, won't you? I should check those muffins."

"Up and at 'em!" Afton shouted, using the same phrase their mother had roused them with every school day when they were kids.

The horizon was glowing, readying to spew out the sun. There wasn't time to laze about. Saturday breakfast was the Ghostly Grill's busiest meal. Afton and Seamus always arrived by 5:30 to get things going. Un-stacking chairs from tables and stools from the bar, setting out paper placemats and napkin-wrapped utensils, putting biscuits on to bake, and so on. At 6:00, Ordway and Monette—an old hippie couple who'd lived on Salome Hill since the '70s—would arrive in their spidery uniforms, ready for a busy day's work slinging hash and waiting tables.

It had been only three hours since the Burnsides left the grill after shooing away the hangers on, stacking up the seats, mopping the floors, and putting a load of glasses and snack plates into the dishwasher. The scant few hours of weekend sleep never seemed to affect Afton, but her brother usually had difficulty coming fully awake Saturday and Sunday mornings.

"I'm getting too old for this," he moaned, plodding down the stairs from his loft apartment. He was completely dressed and groomed, but he looked like a walking corpse, green eyes shrunken to slits above puffy dark flesh bags, mouth slack, head listing forward.

Afton cooed, like a mother watching her toddling baby waver on its feet. "Aw, come on, Bro. I've got coffee ready: French roast. That'll get you going." She met him at the base of the stairs with a hot mug. "Just a few sips. We're running behind."

"How can you be so...alive...at this hour? I need a nap."

Afton laughed. She wasn't the type who took naps. Every hour of the day was spent on the go, or more like on the run, from her thoughts and feelings and the reality of what life had become. She was a constant whirlwind of activity that amazed the hardest of workers. But she wasn't more energetic than those people. Without her recognizing it, she was simply trying to stay one step ahead of any quiet time that would invite self-reflection and profound musings. She was trying to outpace her own existence.

In one long, drawling slurp, Seamus drained the coffee and handed the empty mug back to his stunned sister.

"That was steaming, Bro!"

"Yush!" Seamus spat, clutching at his throat. He flung himself forward and coughed. When he straightened up, Afton was standing on her toes, shoving a glass of tap water in his face. He downed it, coughed a few more times, and red-faced, whispered, "I'm good," while the interior of his mouth went numb.

Afton used her sleeve to dab beads of water from his beard. "See? Sometimes you're like a little kid."

Seamus frowned as he carried the glass to the kitchen. Stepping through the old Craftsman-style house, glancing at family photos and Afton's haphazard decorating, which amounted to some scented candles, throw pillows, braided rugs, and plants, he wondered how his sister would feel if he ever managed to transform into the responsible adult she constantly reminded him he wasn't. Would it really make her happy? Would she even recognize or admit that he'd become a capable grown man? If so, Afton would lose half of her identity. Being Seamus' protective pit-bull of a sister was what defined her. Since the fire that claimed their parents, she'd been sibling, mother, and father to Seamus, but she didn't know when to let up. Every day, Seamus felt himself diminish under her influence, losing a bit of confidence, a bit of freedom, a bit of self-respect, a bit of who he was.

He set the empty glass on the cracked yellow tiles of the kitchen counter and listened to Afton lay out their plans for their day off without his input.

"I thought we could drive to Sedona on Tuesday and check out that new Farmer's Market, maybe do lunch and catch a movie. That'd be fun, yeah? I know there's a PIP investigation that night, but I think you should table that stuff for now. We only get one day off a week, and we should unwind. PIP is not relaxing for you, Bro. It's stressing you out."

After a while, Afton's words sounded like the drone of a bee swarm to Seamus. It didn't matter what she said. It didn't matter what he thought. He was Seamus Burnside, the gentle giant, Afton Burnside's henpecked baby brother, the man who could knock a guy out cold with one pop to the nose yet couldn't stand up to his sister. He just couldn't. That would be changing both their identities.

CHAPTER 4

"Sam, you there? Come in, Sam," the silver-haired man in coveralls asked, holding his cell phone away from his mouth like a walkie-talkie. Lloyd Chang had been using the phone and a shiny white Super Duty F-250 XLT for over a year—ever since the town council replaced his trusty old radio-dispatched Prosperity Public Works truck with the newest tools of the trade—but he still didn't feel comfortable with either contraption.

"Morning, Lloyd. How are you and Boyd today?" answered Sam Alvarez, mayor of Prosperity and owner of the Skeleton's Closet, a thriving antiques store housed in the old schoolhouse. Sam was known throughout the greater Verde Valley area for two things: being a moral politician and resembling a mustachioed turkey wearing Teddy Roosevelt glasses. He and Lloyd had been good friends since 1976, when Sam went through a painful, public divorce—the only kind known to occur in small towns.

"We're fine, Sam, but I can't say the same for the park. Looks like Mad Molly had one of her tantrums last night. Over."

"What's the damage?" Sam hesitantly inquired.

"Plants uprooted, benches standing on end. There's a bloody handprint and 'help' written on the back wall of the visitors' center. Tree trunks are burned and..."

Lloyd was distracted by his grandson. The teen with a skunk stripe on his spiked bangs was crouched behind the Prosperity Visitors' Center, twisting shut the water main with a T-wrench. The collar and front of his wrinkled surfer shirt waved from the unzipped torso of his coveralls. It was too hot to comfortably wear anything beneath the khaki maintenance uniform, but Boyd would've rather died than be seen swaddled toe to neck in the high-waisted twill bodysuit.

Lloyd positioned the cell phone at arm's length as he kept his eyes on the teen. "The fountain has blood in it again. We're going to have to replace this one, too. A real pain in the patootie, Sam. Over."

"Damn it! We've spent more money on that park over the years than all our community programs put together. We can't afford a total overhaul. And the Prosperity Days Festival is right around the corner! What do you suppose set off Mad Molly? It's not the anniversary of her death or Wei Chang's lynching, not any of the usual dates. She's done random acts of crud before, but this sounds like a whole heaping pile for no reason."

Lloyd surveyed the scene, scowling at the destruction. "There's a reason," he answered, "I just don't know what it is."

"Who would think a pretty little park could be so haunted?" Sam mused. "I thought we were out of the woods when we demolished the buildings on that land."

"Suppose Boyd and I need to start making our rounds even earlier. The tourists shouldn't see this. They want mysterious figures in white—romantic fluff—not violent spirits. Over."

"True enough. And they shouldn't be around the park when there's activity…safety issues and all that. But I don't know what more can be done. You and Boyd get out there before dawn as it is. What's next, you camping there? Molly would probably set fire to your sleeping bags."

Lloyd suspected Sam wasn't far off the mark.

The Visitors' Center Park had always been Prosperity's evil heart, an area locals first dubbed "the Crib District" for the rinky-dink rooms that housed prostitutes along Sycamore Alley, which eventually earned the nickname "Sin Alley." With the seven deadly vices regularly enacted throughout the town, the fact that this stretch of road became known as particularly sinful was an indication of how irredeemably foul the area had been.

Since her arrival from Chicago in 1898, Mad Molly, nee Amalia Petrova, had controlled the entire Crib District of old Prosperity. The block of shabby buildings—a wedding gift from her railroad magnate husband—at one time or another included gambling parlors, an opium den, saloons, a restaurant, a three-story apartment slum, and of course the infamous assortment of rooms used to accommodate her throngs of prostitutes. Many worked for Molly of their own accord—ladies of the evening too unappealing, infirm, or just plain unlucky to find employment at the luxurious Canary Cage further up Salome Hill or the smaller Cajun Queen on the town's periphery. But sadly, some were virtual slaves in her employ—immigrants sold into bondage or the wives or relations of unconscionable men who turned them over to settle gambling debts or insurmountable drug and bar bills.

No one was more reviled or feared in old Prosperity than Mad Molly, who regularly lived up to her name on either interpretation: irate or insane. A tall, cool blonde with the chiseled cheekbones of a Nordic queen, Molly didn't look like a nasty piece of work, but that's what she was—and then some. Her sins ranged from business-related murders to keeping her unwilling prostitutes in leg irons, and most notoriously, personally disposing of her husband shortly after moving to Prosperity. Yet she freely walked the winding streets of Salome Hill for 25 years, until being stabbed in the heart with a letter opener and torched.

Some said that after her death, Molly became an earth-bound entity because she was too possessive of the district she'd created and ruled over to ever leave. Others held that she was so nefarious that the devil himself wouldn't have her in Hell for fear of the competition. Whatever the cause, a chilling presence permeated Sin Alley, and sightings of what were perceived to be the spirits of the villainess and her victims were commonplace: streaks of light; shadowy figures; faint faces emerging from the trunks of trees or the back walls of Chang Brothers Restaurant and the Prosperity Visitors' Center—the only two buildings on the block to survive the fire sparked by Molly's assassination. Locals believed a war was being waged on that unholy ground, a never-ending battle between Molly and an army of wronged women who couldn't forgive her and move on.

The land was developed a few times, but each building was abandoned almost as quickly as it was erected. Eventually, the town council took over the plot and created a charming park that gave tourists an uneasy feeling and spurred them along toward Prosperity's shops and restaurants, which worked out great for business owners. The only problems stemmed from occasional paranormal vandalism during the night.

This morning, the Changs would resort to using yellow "Caution" tape to cordon off the area until repairs could be made. There was too much to tackle before the tourists were out and about.

Sam gave a defeated sigh. "Just do what you can...but deal with the fountain first. Remember the smell last time?"

Lloyd couldn't forget. One hundred gallons of blood and the blazing Arizona sun isn't a good mix. "Will do, Sam. Over and out."

The man leaned into the pickup bed and rifled through metal compartments until he found two sets of rubber gloves and six feet of flexible tubing. He slung the coiled tubing over his shoulder as if a purse and lifted a stacked set of 10-gallon buckets from the bed. It was going to be a hellish cleanup.

Victoriously shutting off the water main, Boyd trotted over, his eyes alight with enthusiasm. "Dude, can you imagine the evidence Seamus and Clive and I could have caught if we'd been here last night with our gear? Maybe we can get something tonight—EVPs, infrared images, photos, who knows. But it's a challenge...usually, the activity is so strong here it drains the batteries on our equipment, and we can't use it."

Lloyd made a disgusted hiss. "Leave that junk alone, boy," he spat, whisking callused hands in all directions. "Look around you. This isn't Casper the Friendly Ghost here. It's bad stuff!"

"But maybe we can help figure out why it's happening and…"

"I said to leave it alone!" Lloyd cut in, leaving no room for debate. "No wonder Amy broke up with you. You're obsessed with this ghost junk."

Boyd tossed the T-wrench into the pickup bed and grumped, "The breakup was mutual. We outgrew each other."

"Sure, she grew up, and you didn't."

The man grabbed the buckets and stomped over to the white cement, three-tiered Spanish fountain that was now non-functioning thanks to his grandson's actions. The three large basins were filled with maroon blood as thick as setting gelatin. Clotted drips hung over the edges, darkening to reddish-black as they dried. The stench was overwhelming, a nostril-singeing, eye-watering scent of death. Lloyd believed this was the blood of ages past, literally the life source of Mad Molly's victims, supernaturally conjured to prove that Molly continued to rule Sin Alley from beyond the grave.

"This is going to be a real mess, boy. First, we drain it, then we dismantle it and move it somewhere it can't be seen or smelled. I guarantee we'll need some Ben-Gay tonight."

Lloyd wheezed and sighed. He already felt exhausted, and the day and his work were just beginning.

Boyd slapped on the rubber gloves and started to snake some of the tubing into the biggest basin. "Dude, it stinks like a butcher shop!" he shouted, letting his breath out quickly and then holding it again.

Lloyd grinned. "That's why you're in college. So you don't have to work at a job like this forever."

"Uh-huh, right, Grandpa. Remind me again how many degrees you have."

"Do what I say, not what I do, boy."

Boyd submerged the tubing before realizing the blood was too thick to siphon. "It smells like death," he said.

"Death," the older man mouthed. His smile disappeared as he recalled a morning 16 years earlier, when Sam Alvarez—at that time a town councilman—appeared at his McBrideville office, grim faced, to inform him that the commuter plane carrying his son and daughter-in-law had gone down in the woods of northern Arizona. It wasn't the first time Lloyd had to raise a child alone. His dear Viola had suffered a stroke giving birth to their son. But Lloyd had been a robust young man back then, and was perfectly willing to pay childcare workers to tend to his son's needs. Fast-forward 28 years, to when he was less energetic, less patient, more set in his ways—technically, a senior citizen—and yet chose to walk away from his successful architectural firm to become the sole caretaker of three-year-old

Boyd. The transition had not been difficult. In an instant, Lloyd realized his grandson was all that mattered. Even when the boy reached school age and was out of his sight most of the day, Lloyd couldn't imagine going back to the four walls of an office and placating a roster of demanding clients. He took the public works job and never looked back. In the outdoors and historic buildings he'd found solace. Working with his hands had given him a new sense of fulfillment, and years later, his grandson as a partner, though he knew Boyd only assisted him out of pity.

Things were changing. Mad Molly and aging joints were testing his resolve, as well as his contentment with being Prosperity's senior public works technician. Soon, Boyd would be graduating from Yavapai Community College and transferring to Arizona State. It would be just Lloyd in the narrow two-story house with steep stairs that cranked up his knee pain with every ascent.

Lloyd gazed into the bloody pools, bracing himself for one of the most horrific maintenance tasks he'd ever undertaken. His chest throbbed. His fingers felt like rusty hinges. He wondered how many more good years, good days he had left. Lloyd questioned how much longer he could hold out for his grandson and for Prosperity, and how much more he had to sacrifice to keep the past at bay.

"You're one mean old broad, Molly, and I'm tired of cleaning up after you," he whispered.

Peter was too preoccupied to enjoy breakfast. His first night in Prosperity had produced a doozy of a nightmare, an oddity, since Peter rarely remembered his dreams and, in fact, doubted that he had them on a regular basis. Chalking it up to a change in elevation and setting and the anticipation of a long-overdue vacation, Peter tried unsuccessfully to brush off the nightmare.

When he'd first awakened—before dawn, heart pounding so hard his left breast trembled in matching cadence—he'd opened the curtains of his room and sat in the turret window seat, looking down three stories at the shadowy flowerbeds of red geraniums and white alyssum, hoping to fill his mind with peaceful impressions. Instead, he'd turned woozy. He'd showered, dressed, and quietly walked through the inn, admiring artwork and antiques, making his way down to the main floor and onto the porch, where he'd met Clare in the fresh first rays of the day.

The meeting had helped take the edge off. Yet now, as he sat eating breakfast with the inn's other guests—all struggling to maintain perfect posture at the long, lace-covered table in the dining room—he found his mind uncontrollably replaying the nightmare in vivid detail. He tore at a muffin and stuffed it into his mouth without tasting it.

Peter's eyes were wide and unblinking as the episode unspooled in his mind. He'd seen a wounded boy with lips and eyelids swollen from weeping, red handprints burned into the flesh of his neck. He was shirtless, his back and chest bearing long bloody lash marks or claw marks; Peter couldn't tell which. Wearing only unbuttoned brown knee pants—the kind Peter had seen in old photos of golfers and baseball players like Babe Ruth—the boy huddled in the corner of a room, crying and kneading the cloth of his pants. He was perhaps 10 years old, with wavy blond hair and dark eyes.

The room was small and dingy. Peeling green and beige wallpaper blighted two of the walls. A slim, high window shed a shaft of light onto a blood-spattered bare mattress, the only furnishing. Peter comprehended every gradation of the boy's agony; even in a dream, the sense of suffering was overpowering.

Abrupt pounding rattled the door to the small room. Peter had felt the boy's body tighten and panic balloon within him as his eyes swung to the brass knob, watching it slowly turn while a key worked its way through the lock. Every feeling gave way to fear as the boy stared at the unopened door, shaking, waiting…waiting. Then, the scene faded.

Peter had awakened from the dream in a traumatized state. After examining the images again—this time, in the Canary Cage Inn's filled dining room—he felt cold and nervous. He snapped to and peered around the table at the other guests, who were feeding on Clare's lavish breakfast banquet while engaged in conversation. Peter wondered how long the chatter had gone on and whether anyone had tried to draw him in only to be met with silence and glassy eyes. Thankfully, the attention was on a round-shouldered young Irishman at the end of the table, who was explaining the culture shock of navigating a four-lane Phoenix freeway amid honks and rude hand gestures after leaving his rural hometown, where most traffic jams were due to flocks of sheep or slow-moving tractors.

"More juice, Mr. Jacoby?"

"What? Uh, yes, thank you, Miss Bowers."

Peter chuckled with the others, though he'd caught only the last portion of the Irishman's tale. He took a deep breath and studied the scene of levity, slowly gaining security amidst the happy strangers. He drank his orange juice and finished a second helping of jalapeño quiche.

It was just a dream, he told himself until he believed it.

CHAPTER 5

The lunch crowd was gone, except Clive, who lingered over a cup of cold coffee and a plate flecked with strands of Coleslaw-ter and the last bite of a Chicken Cordon Boo Sand-Witch. He was reading *Putting on a Brave Face: Living with Phobias*, a far cry from his usual literary fare.

"Mind if I join you for a minute?" Afton asked, pouring him a refill.

Clive glanced up from his book, looking as if he minded the interruption more than anything in the world. However, he kicked out the chair on the other side of the table and said, "Be my guest, lass."

Afton sat down, unhanding the coffeepot as she noticed the book's title. "I don't think I've ever seen you reading anything not work-related—you know, paranormal."

"This is related. I'm endeavoring to make myself a better investigator by conquering my jitterishness. Is that a word?" Clive sipped his coffee and admitted, "I know I sometimes disappoint your brother and Boyd on investigations."

Though she played innocent, Afton was pretty sure Clive was alluding to his legendary cowardice, which was the source of many jokes around town. His career lowlight came during an investigation of a private residence noted for poltergeist activity. While setting up a video camera in the attic, Clive claimed something blew on his neck, sending him into escape mode. Grappling with the room's sticky doorknob, he thought an evil entity had trapped him and began shrieking with the fervor and pitch of a terrified five-year-old girl. Seamus quickly sprang him, but in his haste to vacate the premises, Clive knocked over the homeowner, as well as his large-screen TV and the urn containing his deceased wife's ashes. After that, Seamus and Boyd had a deep conversation about the liability Clive posed but decided against booting him from PIP. They did, however, secure a vow from him to avoid caffeine and sugar eight hours prior to any investigation…and Clive bought a new large-screen TV and antique urn for the aggrieved client.

Afton couldn't figure out why someone as gutless as Clive was obsessed with ghosts. It was illogical for him to mold his career and hobby around something that scared him.

"Listen, Clive, ghost-o-phobia—or whatever the clinical term is—is an irrational fear. There's no proof ghosts exist…or Bigfoot or werewolves, so try to relax and be reasonable, okay?"

"Ah, ye of little faith! Spirits are all around us. You may not see them, but they're here. Some people and places attract them more than others. Some people are more perceptive than others." Clive looked Afton up and down disapprovingly. "By the by, have you heard of any of our fellow Prosperityites dying recently?"

"Ada Barbary was the last I know of, and that was, what, about a month ago?"

"Yes, poor Ada. God rest her soul. No one else, though? You're sure?"

Afton bobbed her head with certainty as Clive turned brooding. She wanted to leave him alone with his thoughts but couldn't abandon so pitiful a character. He looked like a deflated balloon, his skinny frame bent in a defeated "C" shape, his thin black brows upturned in worry.

"What's wrong?"

Clive's eyes lifted to Afton's. "Last night was abysmal! The first part, you wouldn't believe. Suffice to say I had a supremely unsettling paranormal experience. Then, as I was recovering from that shock, another came. As is my custom, I led the tour group to the hanging oak in Ooljee and Mae's yard, where I recounted Wei Chang's lynching." Skating off on a tangent, Clive lamented, "When I tell that story, there isn't a dry eye to be found!" He dabbed his teary eyes with a crooked pinkie. "I hate to lose that venue!"

"Why would you lose it?" Afton asked.

"Well…we had an incident. Ooljee told me to get the blankety blank off the property and stop trying to turn a historic site into a blanking circus act."

Clive might have been a supernatural freak, but he was every ounce the gentleman. Under no circumstance could he imagine using profanities in front of a woman, and by this point Afton knew that "blankety blank" and "blanking" were Clive's substitutes for words he found offensive.

"Wow, what set her off?"

"I positioned every person under the hanging oak so they had a good view of the monstrous tree. Then I began telling the story." Clive closed his eyes and was transported back to that fatal day, as his often-used script played from mind to mouth.

"May 19, 1922, in the hours before dawn. A drunken mob happened upon Wei Chang and Sadie Rue transporting a load of illegal liquor out of town in Deputy Warrington's supply wagon. There was a violent confrontation. Wei was summarily charged with bootlegging, kidnapping, and theft of the wagon and mules…a list of crimes the inebriated thugs believed warranted execution. And like that," Clive snapped his fingers, "Wei Chang was condemned." He laughed scornfully. "What hypocrites! I wager that mob likely broke every law in the book at least once a week."

Lifting a finger pleadingly into the air, Clive made a dramatic documentarian. "Wei was dragged back to town, to the massive tree at Pearline Graham's boarding house—the oak that still stands, now half dead and bent with shame.

"It took five men with sticks and clubs to beat Wei into submission and slide the noose around his neck, and not one of those men who knew Wei as a kind and gentle human being—a man who'd served them meals in his Chang Brothers Restaurant, whose wife died acting as nurse to the victims of the Spanish influenza epidemic that decimated Prosperity, whose daughter and brother died in the same outbreak—gave ear to his cries of innocence and pleas for mercy. Once the noose was fitted, they tied the slack end of the rope to the wagon's mule team and drove the beasts across the lawn and onto the street, slowly lifting Wei up, up, high into the air, choking the breath out of him. The team bolted, jerking Wei up, then down, and the thin rope sliced into flesh and sinew, severing his head from his body. Witnesses say that when the body struck the ground, so much blood spilled from the neck cavity that it colored the earth red for years."

"Enough! I've heard it all before, and it makes me so mad I could punch something!" Afton slammed her fist onto the table three times, like a judge rapping her gavel.

Clive's dark eyes narrowed to microscopic, wild dots as he shuddered with rage. "It should infuriate you! An inebriated mob hanged a man for a load of moonshine! Grotesquely ironic, yes?"

Afton fell sullen thinking of the horrendous event. Her eyes roved across a line of sepia photos on the wall, stopping at the framed likenesses of a Chinese family: a young teen in a tam and bow tie; an older teen and a young man wearing bowlers; and a slender woman in a long, dark dress with enormously puffed sleeves, the whole group displaying hopeful stares. "My heart breaks every time I see that picture of Wei and his brothers and his wife, Ting, lined up in front of their restaurant, so…unaware of what was to come." Afton frowned, clearing her mind. "Tell me why Ooljee went off on you."

Clive bowed his head in disgrace. "I suppose I told the tale too well. I ended with a moment of silence, and while we were paying our respects, a car came down the hill, and its headlights lit up a round glass birdfeeder hanging from a tree. One of the senior chaps screamed, 'Look, it's Wei

Chang's head!' And all Hades broke loose. It was dreadful! The three blond tarts in the group began shrieking, and one of them jolly well almost trampled an old woman as she fled. I tried to calm the mindless horde, but Ooljee came out of the house at the height of the mayhem and gave me a right good tongue lashing."

Afton wasn't close to Ooljee—in fact, the two shared a tense acquaintanceship—but she'd heard the gossip and seen Ooljee work at being courteous to Clive during unplanned encounters in town. Word was that Ooljee referred to Clive as "that ghoulish clown" and his tour business as the "Hysteria Express." Nonetheless, the local celebrity had always been gracious about people's interest in her historic dwelling and its hauntings. It wasn't like her to lose her temper at harmless folks, not even Clive.

"Something else must be going on with Ooljee. I wouldn't take it personally. She didn't tell you not to come back, did she?"

"Not in so many words. I suppose on any other night her outburst wouldn't have affected me so. It was the earlier experience that staggered me. I shan't rest until I determine whose spirit I encountered outside the Canary Cage..." Realizing he'd broadcast his ghostly encounter to one of the few nonbelievers in Prosperity, he apologized with a quick, "Pardon me."

"Actually, that reminds me of something I wanted to discuss with you."

"Truly?" Clive was astonished.

"I'd like you and Boyd to not include Seamus in your next few PIP outings. He's really...impressionable, you know? The last one—in the Copper Veins Mineral Museum—didn't go well. He swears something slapped him on the back and whispered in his ear. He had the heebie-jeebies all night."

"Yes, he reported the phenomena, and we included it in the personal experiences portion of our documentation. That activity is similar to what others have encountered there. It's an unpleasant location with a strong negative vibe. How can it be anything but? It was formerly the restaurant where Mad Molly poisoned her husband. Witnesses said he writhed about and foamed at the mouth for nigh on an hour while Molly and the wait staff watched, and when he stopped, Molly ordered a bottle of champagne. The current owners have done little to help its aura. They've painted the inside walls black and hung sharp silver stalactite-type ornaments from the ceiling. Have you seen it? A feng shui practitioner would condemn that place."

Afton didn't know why she'd tried to approach the situation from her logical point of view. She and Clive had fundamentally different philosophies. Her factual, practical universe didn't match his.

"Let me put it this way. I don't want Seamus going someplace he considers dangerous. He's been doing some strange things lately and getting really wrapped up in this ghost business. It's stressing him out. There are just too many investigations. Promise me you won't ask him on any for a while."

"How do you propose I handle that? Seamus is my superior in PIP. I'm only an investigator."

"Please talk to Boyd. See if PIP can take a break for a few months. You can give more tours during the hiatus. Sounds win-win, right? So, will you promise me?"

Clive glanced over Afton's shoulder at Seamus whistling as he scraped lunch debris into the sink, his giant hands almost as large as the white ceramic plates he cleaned. He was so strong looking and so solid on investigations that Clive had a hard time believing Afton. He'd never seen any sign of Seamus' vulnerabilities. Quite the opposite; Seamus usually did the best job of allaying clients' fears. And he was always the one to calm Clive when he began his slapstick Barney Fife routine in the midst of a daunting ghost hunt.

"I like your brother, Afton, ol' girl. He's an honorable bloke and an exceptional paranormal investigator. I'd never do anything to harm him. That includes treating him like a child and taking away his right to make his own decisions."

Afton's thin lips twisted contemptuously. She pushed herself away from the table with a puff of hot breath and stood, peering down her Peter Pan nose at Clive.

"You don't have any idea what he's been through or how fragile he really is. If he breaks, Clive, you bet your pasty butt I'm coming after you and Boyd." With that, Afton snatched up the coffee pot, shot him a withering look, and angrily stalked away.

It was two weeks until the annual Prosperity Days Festival, a weekend that included such diverse entertainment as an art fair and a go-kart derby down Spirit Street. Clare always reveled in planning her portion of the event, the Canary Cage stop on the historic homes tour. She would—according to Prosperity Historical Society requirements—wear period attire while welcoming visitors into her establishment and plying them with appetizers and non-alcoholic drinks.

The costuming was no problem for Clare. Her closet was stuffed full of elaborate gowns, every one of them well used from hosting various tours, murder mystery weekends, Halloween parties, and fund-raising balls at the Prosperity Community Center.

"Hmm...maybe the gold-spangled flapper dress. Or, the red Victorian?" she asked herself, putting pen to lipstick-encrusted bottom lip and rifling through sequins and feathers. Clare hadn't lost her showgirl flair for the theatrical.

The woman was so caught up in her costume fantasies that she didn't hear the rapping on her bedroom door until it grew into a fierce banging.

"Ma'am!" a man's voice urgently called.

"Be right there," Clare answered, quickly smoothing down the few black hairs that strayed from her braid and adjusting the collar of her tropical print shirtdress. She straightened herself, assuming a regal posture, and opened her door.

"Mr. Jacoby, what is it?" she asked, noting the concern on his face.

"The Irishman fell down the stairs. He's complaining about his ankle. I didn't feel any bone damage. It's likely just sprained. But he's in shock…saying preposterous things." Peter made a brief nervous smile.

"Good heavens!"

Clare threw up her arms and flew from her bedroom in a rustle of florid rayon, her exotic jasmine perfume trailing her so thickly that Peter hacked a few coughs as he hurried along in her wake.

"I'd just come down to the parlor when I heard him up on the landing. He yelled—or screamed—and then I heard a crash and turned around, and he was somersaulting down the stairs. Luckily, I think he's fine except for the ankle and the shock."

"The dear, dear man," Clare whispered over and over, imagining the worst.

When they reached the parlor, Clare almost went into hysterics at the sight of wounded Jamie Clancy, the freckled young man who'd flown all the way from Carrowkeel, Ireland, to visit the haunted town and reside two weeks in the second-floor Mystical Dreams Suite, a luxurious, rose-petal motif extravaganza designed as a honeymoon hideaway. He was outstretched on the red-velvet settee with Sahara curled up on his stomach, her paws tucked under her, a loud purr emanating from her throat. Jamie looked straight up, his eyes two unfocused pools of brown, his black "SpecTours by Night: Get Spooked in Prosperity" T-shirt making him appear even paler than he was.

"You dear man!" Clare was all over him, feeling his pulse, his forehead, holding his hand. "I'll call the doctor!" On her way to the telephone in the foyer, Clare scooped up the cat and handed her to Peter. "Would you please keep Sahara from bothering Mr. Clancy? Oh, I do hope Dr. DiConcini is there."

Clare's fingers moved quickly over the rotary dial of her antique wall phone. A few seconds later, she began her conversation with "Thank heavens you're home, doctor! We have an emergency."

Peter suppressed a grin. Since when was a sprained ankle on an otherwise healthy young man an emergency? Nonetheless, Clare's maternal concern was touching. It seemed that Jamie was in need of mothering at the moment, and Clare was a willing stand-in.

39

For the briefest of moments, Peter drifted away, wishing he could remember more about his own mother, his childhood, the past. Only fleeting glimpses, like shadows of his life, occupied his memory. Most of his recollections involved his Nanny Lotta, a prune of a person with a black bob and the face of a fruit bat. She was his primary caretaker and playmate, a fiercely ungracious competitor at chess, a woman who rarely smiled or inspired smiles in others. Consequently, his feelings toward her were lukewarm at best. There were other people in his mind—his popular, big-haired mother, who was never home; his intimidating business magnate father; Lotta's husband Deke, the family's groundskeeper; Mr. Jameson, a finicky old fart who breathed halitosis over Peter's shoulder during weekly piano lessons. But they were mainly just images, two-dimensional characters. Their context regarding his life seemed guarded in a padlocked chamber of his brain. Yet despite the frustration, there was something comforting in not knowing, and that was, perhaps, most disturbing of all. Only one figure was spotlighted in happiness in his memory: Granny Weston. When Peter thought of her, he smelled roses and sugar cookies and felt sunny inside, like a child again. How he wished he had more memories of her, but she'd been an embarrassment to his moneyed parents, with her poor grammar and ham-leg limbs stuffed into polyester prints, and so she'd been kept at arm's length, rarely allowed into the hallowed rooms of their palatial Brentwood house. Even less often were the times Peter had visited his grandmother in her ramshackle home. As a young boy, he remembered sitting on her front porch, in a rocker, nestled on Granny Weston's lap, listening to a slow rain beat off the tin roof and the tune she softly hummed as she held him. Peter smiled at that one, firm memory that was rooted like a sheltering oak in his psyche.

Soon, the receiver was back on its rest, and Clare turned with a somewhat relieved expression. "Dr. DiConcini will be here shortly, Mr. Clancy. Not to worry. He'll fix you good as new."

Reclaiming the cat from Peter's arms, she thanked him for his assistance and moved to the injured Irishman, setting Sahara on the floor.

"Is there anything I can get you in the meantime? A pillow? A drink? Cookies?"

Jamie shook his head. "No, mum. Tank you."

"Are you sure you're not hurt elsewhere?"

"Don't tink so, mum."

Clare knelt so that she could easily caress the young man's face and soothe him with a few strokes of her hand. The knobby knuckles, laden with gaudy cocktail rings, scraped over his forehead. "You poor, poor thing. Did you fall all the way down the stairs?"

"Yes, mum, doon da whole flight."

"Oh, my goodness sake's alive! Did you trip?"

"Tripped over me own feet, mum. I tot I saw someting oop dar." His eyes drifted over to the staircase landing, its mahogany banister shining beneath a gaslight chandelier. "I…I tink I saw a ghoost."

Clare clasped her hands in delight. "Oh, I'm so happy for you, Mr. Clancy. You saw Sadie!"

"Tell me agin what she's suppoosed to look like, mum."

"I've never seen her myself, but reports hold that she's a voluptuous golden blond."

The outer corners of Jamey's mouth bent down. "Well, den, mum, I doon't tink dis was Sadie. It was lean and tool and wearing denim pants. I tink it were a boy. It didna look like a ghoost, not pale or sceery—not until it turned aroond and walked true da wall. Den, I saw it didna have a face. No face at ool, just blackness, like it were hollow. Dat's when I tried to roon, and I fell doon da stars."

The Irishman looked particularly perplexed by a certain aspect of the experience. "I doon't know how dis can be—it didna have eyes—but I tink it were watching him." He nodded toward Peter as he spoke those last few words.

Peter reared back, a wilted smile hanging on his lips. Briefly, he thought the freckled young man and Clare were in cahoots in the ghost-story business, determined to make a believer out of him. But that thought fled, chased out by chilling confusion, as he watched the innkeeper's eyes widen with genuine fright.

Clare's mind grappled with the idea of another spectral housemate. It had to be the same teenager she'd seen traipsing behind Peter the night of his arrival. But why had this young spirit joined her at the Canary Cage? Clare's mind jumped to disturbing possibilities. Perhaps the inn's dynamics had changed, and Sadie had been forced out by another Prosperity ghost. Or was the old brothel beginning to collect departed souls, like a supernatural honey pot? Whatever was happening, Clare wasn't pleased.

Jamie covered his face with his long, alabaster fingers and groaned. "I doon't feel so good, mum. I doon't believe I want to see Sadie Rue, after ool."

CHAPTER 6

"Hooo," Lloyd exhaled, dropping himself into the F-250 and closing the door. He was too fatigued to drive away immediately. Leaning back on the headrest, he closed his eyes and let his cramping hands fall limp on his lap. An hour of climbing up and down a ladder to install new third-floor vent filters had left him breathless and numb from the chest up. The solo after-hours projects at the center were becoming too difficult. But, Lloyd didn't have a choice. It was either do all the work in the most haunted areas by himself or throw his grandson into the direct path of supernatural forces, something he was determined not to do, no matter how much Boyd wanted that.

The Prosperity Community Center was a ghost hunter's dream after sundown. Originally the Copper Prince Miners' Hospital, it now held all town offices, as well as an auditorium and several large rooms used regularly for social events and youth and senior activities. The four-story behemoth constructed on a 30-degree incline was an incredible architectural feat, a rambling Spanish Mission-type fortress built by the mining company to serve all of Prosperity and the Verde Valley, whose smelter was linked to Salome Hill by a narrow gauge railway. During the influenza outbreak of 1918, Wu Chang perished in the hospital's southeast wing, despite being feverishly tended by medical staff and a few selfless volunteers that included his sister-in-law, Ting. Weeks later, Ting and her seven-year-old daughter, Yin, succumbed to the same disease in that very hospital wing. The building later served as a tuberculosis sanatorium and then briefly as a mental hospital before being vacated.

It sat not so quietly in its abandoned state. From its roost atop Salome Hill, the structure seemed to keep watch over the dormant town below. Screams, moans, scraping and banging sounds, and disembodied voices echoed down its corridors; lights were seen flickering on and off in the windows, though electricity had been shut off in the fall of 1948. Sometimes teens would drive up to the building and prove their courage by walking through its darkened halls and rooms, calling to the dead. Some of the less ethical youngsters broke beer bottles on the floors and spray-painted words and symbols on the walls. The shenanigans continued until 1975, when the Prosperity Community Center was unveiled and the town hired an overnight security guard, a half-cocked redneck named Roy Pervis, who prowled the grounds with a Colt .45 and his German shepherd, Lula; a string of big, progressively meaner canines followed as Roy aged and grew battier. No unauthorized person dared set foot near the Prosperity Community Center after dark.

Though Boyd and Lloyd shared an office in the community center and spent several hours there each week—sometimes doing paperwork in the office, sometimes doing repairs in the building—Lloyd didn't want his grandson spending any more time at the center than necessary, and he didn't want him spending any time inside those walls after dark or alone.

Whenever Boyd found a reason to stay late or return to the center after hours, Lloyd managed to throw a wrench in his plans. And each of the three times PIP requested access for an investigation, Lloyd saw to it that the petition was denied. Everyone who worked in the center, from Mayor Alvarez to the post office clerks to the senior center volunteers, had been instructed by Lloyd to keep Boyd out of the building after dark, and they did just that.

Though some activity occurred during daylight hours, the most intense paranormal experiences were at night. Lloyd had quickly become accustomed to lights, faucets, and machinery mysteriously turning on and off and hearing voices—sometimes entire conversations—always just beyond where he was and disintegrating into nothing when he approached. Whatever had settled in the Prosperity Community Center was haunting in the truest of senses. It made Lloyd uneasy because the lingering sorrow was part of his own, personal heritage and stirred thoughts of the last days of his aunt and uncle, and especially little Yin, who'd died before knowing much of life. The energy and full knowledge of the Changs' tragic past were what Lloyd wished to spare his grandson.

A loud bang rattled the driver's-side window of the F-250, and Lloyd snapped his head forward and his eyes open, orienting himself after the fleeting nap.

Roy Pervis knocked on the glass with the butt of his trusty pistol. "You plum tuckered out?" he shouted, giving a semi-toothless grin. After startling Lloyd awake, Roy backed away, laughing, his task accomplished. A black dog resembling a bear slobbered at his heels.

Lloyd wiped some spittle from his chin and gave a thumbs-up to the security guard before starting the pickup and driving from the parking lot, descending Salome Hill. His sleepy eyes grew sandier by the second until they fell on something that brought Lloyd fully to attention: his grandson and Clive patrolling the Visitors' Center Park in full ghost-hunting mode. Gravely alert, they prowled around taking photos and video footage, measuring the ambient temperature and electromagnetic fields in different sections of the park.

"Damn foolish kids," Lloyd mumbled. "I should've known Boyd would pull something like that."

He turned off his headlights and took a sharp turn, trying to avoid detection. He then tracked over to Sin Alley from the opposite direction and parked in the public lot next to his house. When Boyd got home, Lloyd was sitting in his recliner in his bathrobe doing a crossword puzzle, seemingly having lounged there for hours.

"How'd it go studying with your friend in McBrideville?"

Boyd stepped in from the kitchen with a freshly opened orange soda, looking like a teen surfer model in flip-flops, a tribal-print Crazy Shirt, and board shorts, his black and white hair stylishly disheveled.

"Okay, but I'm wiped out."

Boyd started to move on, toward the stairs, but Lloyd wouldn't be deterred.

"Ready for your first day of final exams?"

Boyd stopped and faced his grandfather. "Yeah, I think so," he nonchalantly answered, taking a swig.

"Is ghost hunting one of the subjects?" Lloyd asked, his eyes unmoved from the puzzle grid.

Boyd almost choked on the soda. He slowly lowered the bottle.

"The way I understand it, the only subjects you studied for tonight were ghosts and goblins."

When Boyd made no answer, Lloyd prodded further. "Were you at the park with Clive?"

"Who told you that?"

"Were you?" Lloyd repeated impatiently.

Boyd cleared his throat. "With all the activity last night, we had to do an investigation. I thought something might happen again, and we could capture some evidence."

"You make it sound so scientific by using the word 'investigation.' That doesn't change what it is: a damn foolish waste of time! You're in college now. You should prepare for your future."

Boyd stiffened his spine. "I'm sorry you don't approve, but I'm 19 now. I'm an adult."

"So, act like one." Lloyd dropped the puzzle on his lap and critically eyed his grandson. His chest heaved with emotional exhaustion. "Let the dead be, Boyd."

"I'm not playing with a Ouija board or conducting a séance or calling up the dead. I'm just investigating what's already here. You know there are all kinds of spirits in this town, Grandpa! I'm just trying to figure out why."

"We've been through this a hundred times! I don't want you doing that spook work. You're living in my home, so you play by my rules," Lloyd demanded.

Boyd took a wounded breath. "I thought this was our home, the Chang family's home, just like it's always been." When his parents were alive, the bottom story was their home, and the top floor was his grandfather's apartment; each section had a separate entrance. But Lloyd had worried about Boyd's safety when he became a rambunctious kindergartner. He removed the exterior stairs, sealed off the upstairs door, and made the building one big house, two sleeping quarters above and living area and kitchen below. There was no privacy for the men, and while that didn't bother Lloyd, Boyd felt imprisoned by the physical and intangible restraints of living with a person who ruled their home without consult or consideration.

"It's bad enough I don't have any say in how things work around here. Why do you have to try to run my outside life, too?"

Lloyd pointed an angry finger at Boyd. "I'm the elder here! I raised you, not the other way around!"

"Look, Grandpa, I love you, but why can't I do my own thing? I'm not doing anything wrong!"

"Abnormal is more like it! At your age, you should be dating. You should play sports or backpack across Europe. Not make your whole life about this ghost junk."

Boyd paused, putting the pieces together. "Dating, huh? It's Amy isn't it? I think our breaking up was harder on you than it was on me."

"She's a fine girl, Boyd. That's what you need in your life. Someone positive who makes you feel happy. There's enough negativity in the world without seeking it out, and that's exactly what you're doing by devoting your life to dead people." Lloyd shook his head. Anger and sorrow mixed in his gaze. "Boy, there's a separation between worlds for a reason. Don't go messing where you don't belong."

"Don't you wonder? I mean, why does the park get torn apart every few weeks? Why does Sadie Rue hang around the Canary Cage? What about the activity at the community center? And us? Right here! Why do we sometimes hear our front door opening at 2:41 in the morning and footsteps race across our kitchen? I've heard it 31 times since I was a kid. 31 times! What is that?! Don't you want to know what's going on?"

"No, I don't. I want to let the spirits rest in peace."

"That's the point. Prosperity's dead aren't at peace, Grandpa. Don't you see that?"

Lloyd took a hard look at his grandson. He stared so long at Boyd's face that the teen became disquieted and fidgety.

"You've changed so much," Lloyd said at last. "These last couple years—after Seamus moved here and you two started PIP—you've been different. You were always interested in ghosts, but you used to smile and laugh a lot. Since you were kids, you and Amy were always on the go, doing things, full of life. Now, it's all about spirits and despair and grief and mystery. No, Boyd, it's not about Amy. It's about you. I've seen you go from a happy kid to an intense young fellow…and that worries me."

Boyd bowed his head. He knew his grandfather couldn't understand the change in his life. "I can't explain it, but it's like meeting Seamus and getting into paranormal science awakened something in me. When Clive came onboard, it got even stronger. I almost feel like I'm on a mission, like I have to do this. It's part of who I am and why I'm here…"

The room grew cold and still and filled with a musty odor. A heaviness descended upon it and upon the men inside as the overhead lamp sputtered and dimmed to half its brilliancy.

"Do you feel that?" Boyd asked, watching goose-bumps form on his forearms and the thin, black hairs atop the bumps rise straight up, like antennae. He placed his soda on the coffee table and began to slowly turn, gauging the change in the air around him with every sense.

Lloyd stood up from his recliner, letting his puzzle and pen slide to the floor.

"Who are you? What do you want?" Boyd asked.

"Stop that!" Lloyd barked.

Boyd held out his hands in the static-charged room that had fallen 10 degrees in temperature and was now in half-light.

"Mom? Dad? Grandma? Great-Grandpa Yee?" Boyd methodically called each name and paused, awaiting a response. "Wei? Ting? Wu?"

"I said to stop!" Lloyd reiterated, his face heating to a bright red.

"Can you make a noise? Move something? I know you're here. I want to help you."

The lights turned up to full potency and the feeling lifted, the temperature returning to normal. The men were alone again in the living room.

"Wow!" Boyd shouted. "If I'd had a recorder going I bet I could've gotten a hell of an EVP! That was a sign, Grandpa. You know it was. Someone's trying to communicate with us."

Trembling, Lloyd gave his grandson the fiercest look he could muster. "Don't you dare use any of those ghost gadgets in this house! No tape recordings, no pictures, nothing, hear me?" he ordered, stomping upstairs to his room, shaking the whole building with each crash of his foot onto a wooden stair and then the landing. He slammed the door behind him and turned the lock.

Seated on the edge of his bed, he remained deep in thought for close to 10 minutes. Then, he slid out the drawer of his bedside table. Beneath a zippered case with fingernail clippers, the bylaws of the Prosperity Historical Society, and a small stack of keepsakes—a handmade valentine from Boyd, the memorial handout from his son's and daughter-in-law's funeral, an anniversary card signed from his wife with a lipstick kiss, one of his old business cards—he found the item he wanted. It was a small journal, old and worn, bound in deep red leather. He pulled it out, reverently, and held it for a while on his lap. Slowly, he opened it to an age-stained section and read the familiar words his father had penned decades earlier. Lloyd began to cry.

CHAPTER 7

Mae's shaking fingers found the numbers on the phone after a few tries. When she was certain she'd pressed the right sequence, she lifted the cordless receiver to her ear and listened to the ringing, and then a man's voice.

"Hello, Lloyd. I haven't caught you in the middle of anything, have I?"

"Not at all, Mae. How's life? I've been meaning to stop by with my Scrabble game one of these evenings. I won't let your winning streak go unchallenged."

After a few minutes of polite small talk, Mae opened up about the purpose of the call. She rolled her rose-petal pendant between a thumb and forefinger.

"Have you had a chance to visit the Canary Cage lately?"

"No, I haven't been by in a spell. I replaced a ball cock in one of the toilets and had some pie with Clare around…oh, must have been the third week in April. Does she need help with something?"

"Nothing like that, Lloyd." Mae hung on the phone, silent, for so long that Lloyd had to prompt her to continue.

"Mae? You still there?"

"I was thinking of the best way to say this."

"Say what? You're worrying me. What's wrong?"

"Nothing's wrong, but…I'll just say it. There's a man at the Canary Cage who's the spitting image of Charles Avendon."

Now it was Lloyd's turn to be silent. Following several seconds of uneasy quiet, he said, "But Charles died long ago, when he was a kid."

"I know that well enough, Lloyd. I knew Charles better than anyone. That's why I recognize him in this man."

"You aren't saying he IS Charles, are you? Reborn or something?"

"No, no. He's his own man. I sense they have kin in common, which

48

must account for the similarities. This man doesn't just look like Charles, he's been...treated...hurt...as he was. Has second sight, like Charles, too, only much stronger."

Lloyd pensively chewed on his words. "Hmm, that's a hell of a coincidence."

"No such thing, Lloyd. You know that."

"So, why's he here? What does he want?"

"He doesn't know yet. He doesn't understand that he's been summoned."

"By whom? Did you call him?"

"No, I didn't call him." Mae let out an exhausted sigh. "Lloyd, you take everything much too literally."

"Well, then, spit it out. Tell me what's going on without all the dramatic hooha!"

Lloyd and Mae were like siblings, usually supportive and loving but not above the occasional perturbed outburst.

"Alright, then, Lloyd. Here it is. This man—Peter Jacoby is his name— has a powerful mind that he can't yet control. He's going to see visions of things we thought were long gone and forgotten. He's going to see your father and Wei and Sadie Rue, and all that energy from the past is going to take him to the edge of madness."

"That doesn't sound good for him or us. Can we stop him? Get him to go back home?"

"Course not. But we can help him make sense of what he's experiencing, and Ooljee and I can teach him to harness his gift."

Lloyd's voice shook uneasily. "You know I'm not a hocus-pocus kind of fellow, Mae. I don't know what good I can be to this Peter Jacoby, and I don't know exactly what you're asking of me. I hope it isn't what I'm thinking..."

Mae clutched her pendant like a talisman. "Let him read your father's journal. Or tell him what happened back then."

"How can you even suggest that? You know I made a promise to my father."

"Yee was disturbed and sick when he made you promise that. Look what the dishonesty did to him. The shame he carried all those years is what made him miserable and finally put him in his grave. I felt that pain then, and I feel it now. It's still here, Lloyd. For pity's sake, I live where his brother was lynched. You know how many times I've stepped into my side yard and had it replay in my mind's eye? I've watched Wei being beaten and strung up over and over, watched his head pop clean off his body...the things I've seen and felt in this town...one of the worst feelings is from your father. I've felt it in your home, in my home, every place he walked. When he was alive, his guilt and grief was so thick that I could sense it like a stink coming off him! Sometimes I can still smell it!"

Lloyd let an inaudible complaint dribble from his lips. A sharp pain flashed inside his chest, leaving a heavy ache behind. Mae had riled him worse than Boyd ever did. "You aren't telling me anything I don't know! But I don't see what his misery has to do with one of the Canary Cage's guests."

"Go take a pill, Lloyd. I can tell your angina is acting up," Mae calmly instructed.

"Damn it, Mae! I'm a grown man, and I'll take a pill when I think I need it."

"Stubborn. Always have been. When are you going back to that cardiologist of yours? You need to see him. You hear me?"

"Stop playing mother hen. You want to talk about my ticker or this fellow at Clare's? I only have the patience to listen to you nag about one subject."

"Now, look here, Lloyd, this man at the Canary Cage needs us. He's so lost and alone. The poor soul doesn't remember what he's been through. And aside from everything else, I believe he can help me find the bones."

Lloyd relaxed a bit. "Good grief, is that what this is really all about? These last three or four years, that's all you think about. You're obsessed! How many times have I told you that it doesn't matter where the bones are? There's no restless spirit attached to them. You said yourself that Charles moved on. You're the only one who cares where they're at."

"It isn't right that he was discarded like trash. After everything he suffered in life, he doesn't deserve to spend eternity in the same grave as the woman who made his life hell on earth. Yes, Lloyd, I want to find Charles' bones, but even more than that I want to help Peter, and I'm going to do that. I am, and he's going to see the past and all the things you don't want him to. I can only tell him so much. I only know so much. I can't see it all, Lloyd. You know that. You have the journal and the stories your daddy told you. You could make this much easier for all of us if you'd just share what you know. Might as well. One way or another, Peter Jacoby is going to find out what happened here."

Mae took a few ragged breaths. She hadn't talked so much in ages, and the very act of it had worn her out. "You think about it, Lloyd. Think about what you need to do to really honor the Chang family. It seems to me you've been given another chance. Think of this man as Charles Avendon. Are you going to help him? What do you think Yee and Wei would want you to do?"

"I don't intend to dishonor my family—or you, Mae—by revisiting events that hurt us all. I feel genuinely sorry for this fellow at the Canary Cage. I do. But I can't break my promise. I'm not going to talk about that whole mess, and I'm begging you not to either. What happened to Charles and everyone back then doesn't matter now. It's over and done with."

"Does what happened to me matter now?" Mae gently asked.

Lloyd choked on his answer. "I...I'm sorry. Just...please, don't."

"Then, the only thing I'll ask of you, Lloyd, is to go read that journal again. Read what your daddy wrote, and think about it."

Mae pulled the phone away from her ear as a loud "clack" informed her that her old friend had hung up. Finally, she released her pendant, letting it drop against the top button of her long-sleeved blouse.

She shuffled over to the front room's big picture window and took a seat on the window sill bench. When Ooljee arrived three hours later, after doing a book signing in Scottsdale, Mae was still sitting there, looking out at the Canary Cage and the rooftops of Spirit Street's businesses further down Salome Hill. It was a bustling Sunday afternoon. Now and again, Mae could hear the speakeasy music that occasionally played from inconspicuous speakers mounted on lampposts along Spirit Street, creating a fun ambience for most tourists and heartache for the very few who remembered the days when that music was new.

Ooljee walked up behind her mother and cupped her hands over her bony shoulders as she planted a kiss on the top of her head. Mae's fingers rose, overlapping Ooljee's, and a smile colored her cheeks.

From the back, petite Mae appeared to be the child to Ooljee's tall and robust mother figure. In a brilliant yellow suit, with a silver concho belt at her waist and her curly black hair drawn up in a loose up-do, Ooljee was a flash of vitality, like the sun rising in the window of the old Victorian. Mae, stoic and earthy in a brown camp skirt and rust-red blouse, lavender shawl, was Ooljee's grounding force.

"You sure you don't want to go over to Clare's?" Ooljee asked.

Mae shook her head with certainty. "Not yet."

"Do you want to go looking for the bones?"

"No, awee'. How many years have I...we...looked for them? We've explored every mine shaft in these mountains at least twice, and nothing. I think maybe I'm not meant to find them. I know Charles has gone on. He doesn't care where his bones are. It's me who cares. I can't stand the thought of them resting for eternity with that wicked woman's..." Mae took a steadying breath and squeezed Ooljee's fingers hard. "Maybe that's the lesson for me to learn. Stop trying to do something that matters only to me."

"It matters to me, too," Ooljee said. She paused before saying anything else, hesitant to fuel her mother's possibly hollow hopes, but as she weighed the strained force surging from the old woman, she realized that hollow hopes were better than no hopes at all. "Don't give up on your grown-up Tennessee boy, Mama. He's going to help us find Charles. I just know it."

She patted her mother's shoulders and gently let go, sliding her hands from under the old woman's fingers and walking toward the kitchen. "Come on, Mama, we've got food in here. I picked up Casa Roja for supper!"

Mae took her time getting to the dining room. A slightly thinner and twisted lower left leg and ankle—from an ancient wound—had produced a faint limp that had been with her most of her life. But regardless of her gait, Mae was the kind of person who took things easy and carried a grace with her everywhere she went. By the time she arrived in the dining room, Ooljee had set bright blue placemats and utensils on the table and filled two tumblers with lemonade. A circular aluminum container holding a bean burro, Spanish rice, and a fistful of shredded lettuce garnish sat on each placemat. The table's centerpiece was an opened Styrofoam box heaped high with puffy golden-brown sopaipillas and individual packets of Arizona mesquite honey.

Mae looked at the food disinterestedly.

"I know you have a lot on your mind, Mama, but you have to eat." Ooljee was concerned about the already small woman's recent loss of weight.

Mae took up her fork, then put it back down. She had no appetite.

Ooljee tried to stay upbeat. "I ran into Lloyd on my way out of town this morning. He's planning a graduation party for Boyd next week. It's hard to believe that boy's already finishing community college. I still see him as that little kid wearing a red cowboy hat and boots, riding his horse tricycle up to our place for cookies." Ooljee laughed and cut into her bean burro. "Remember when he was a baby how he had so much black hair it looked like an Elvis wig?"

Mae twitched a brief smile. "The years go fast, awee'. Seems like my young years are miles off, and these last 20 or 30 happened just yesterday," she answered, drifting away. "I feel cold." She tugged on her lavender shawl, pulling it up to her neck, jingling her glass pendant against its gold chain, and immediately grabbing it, steadying it with a hand, as if she'd upset a fine crystal goblet. "I've been thinking of things I haven't thought about in so long."

"Things about Charles?" Ooljee asked.

"Yes." Mae cocked her gray head to one side, her eyes fixed on the mound of sopaipillas. Ooljee knew the woman's mind was traveling to another time. What she didn't know was that Mae was shifting between her own past and Peter Jacoby's, connecting the two through memories of a boy named Charles Avendon.

Two thin lines of tears began to slide down Mae's face. The sight startled Ooljee. Only twice before had she seen her mother cry, and those had been on monumentally sad occasions.

"Mama, come back! Those memories are hurting you. Don't let your mind go there!" Ooljee's sturdy arms shook the table, rattling Mae from her trance. "I don't think you should relive some of those things," she quietly censured.

"I have to, awee'. Sometimes we keep the past locked up so it won't hurt us, but there comes a time when we have to open it up and go back there." She looked up at Ooljee with a delicate smile. "It's time…for both me and Peter Jacoby."

"We brought something for Captain," Seamus said, handing a rawhide chew bone to Roy Pervis.

The potbellied redneck in a white T-shirt and leather vest took the item and waved it in front of his mastiff's nose. The big black dog sniffed it and yawned, settling onto his haunches, letting the leash go slack.

"He's used to the real McCoy: beef cooked up with potatoes. Dogs is meant to eat meat, not dried leather." The man returned the rawhide to Seamus without a hint of gratitude. Accusingly, he turned to Boyd. "And don't think I don't know you boys is trying to buy me off. I give your grandpappy my word you ain't getting inside the community center after dark."

The man spat out a stream of brown tobacco juice, letting a thread-thin line dribble onto his grizzled chin. "Go on, git!"

Boyd took a step back, trying to appear innocent. "I don't know what you mean. We're here to repair some water damage in the basement."

Roy laughed so hard that it alarmed his dog. As he bent forward to slap his knee, Captain let out a low, bubbling growl. "Whoo! You one a the worst liars I ever heard! Lloyd told me you boys'd come up here and try to spook hunt. It ain't gonna work. This place is off limits, hear?"

Boyd was thoroughly embarrassed and by now realized that his grandfather would be hearing about his latest attempt to investigate the Prosperity Community Center.

Seamus peered behind the man and dog—both of whom eyed him with distrust—at the enormous Spanish Mission building that dimly glowed under the haze of tall, amber streetlamps, a few of its dozens of windows softly lit by indoor security lights. As Seamus scanned the hulking structure, he was drawn to the panes of glass—vacant and shadowed like sleepy eyes. He glanced down one line of windows and up to the next floor, expecting a spectral face to appear in one of the transparent squares.

He yearned to go inside and put his equipment to work but suspected that would never happen. The Prosperity Community Center was the only place in town PIP was barred from, and that taboo—as well as its stories—made it the one place the young researchers hungered to explore. Seamus felt a twinge of anger toward Lloyd Chang, whose dislike for PIP, and his son's involvement in it, was no secret.

"Look, we just want to go in and take some readings on our instruments. Would you be okay with that?" Seamus pulled his backpack from his shoulder, willing to display or demonstrate his ghost-hunting gear.

"No, I wouldn't be okay with that, boy. It took a long time to keep loco kids like you from comin' 'round here and causing problems. I'll be damned if I'm gonna let you two inside. You two dawdle off, hear?"

"This is ridiculous," Boyd said, exasperated, as he produced a heavily filled key ring from one of his cargo shorts pockets. "I have the keys to every room in there. I work in there. Why can't I go in after hours?"

"Cause those is my orders. I ain't gonna tell you again. Git!"

As Roy's voice deepened and his agitation became clear, Captain began to snarl. Seamus and Boyd decided it was best to just walk away.

"Have a good night, sir," Seamus said. As they turned to go, he hesitated and asked, "Just one thing, would you tell us if you've ever experienced anything strange here? Lights, noises, apparitions, anything?"

"Hell, yeah I done experienced me strange things!" Roy roared back, laughing maniacally, his toothless, wrinkled face reminding Seamus of an animatronic pirate from a Disney ride. "They don't bother me none, though. Like my grandmammy told me, 'it ain't the people in the next world you gotta fear; it's the ones in this world.'"

Proving his point, Roy slipped a Colt .45 from a shoulder holster under his vest. Brandishing the gun, his laughter simmering down to a smile, he aimed the barrel at the trespassers.

"Your grandmammy was right on," Boyd agreed as he and Seamus bolted.

Their steps across the graveled parking lot were hard and quick. Both knew that even if he didn't shoot, nutty old Roy was liable to let Captain off his leash and onto their tails just to amuse himself. When they heard the mastiff baying behind them, they threw all pride to the wind and broke into an all-out run for their lives and kept it up—their legs spinning beneath them as gravity pulled them clumsily downhill—until the dog's barking and Roy's laughter were far at their backs. When they came to a stop, they were at the junction of Mine Cart Way and the skinny dirt road that split from it, leading to the community center.

"Man, I haven't run...that fast...in years," Seamus panted. "I think...I'm gonna die!" He took a deep breath and clamped his hands on his knees, bent like a man about to retch.

Even Boyd, who was fit as a fiddle compared to Seamus, pressed his fingers deep into his abdomen, massaging away a sharp side stitch. "You run fast for a big dude! After working all day and night..." he quickly looked at his watch, "at 3:42 in the morning, you still had it in you to do that wind sprint…wow."

"Yeah, well, I had the motivation. I don't want to go out of this world as a pile of dog shit."

Boyd tried to laugh but grimaced. "I don't think my heart's beat this fast since the *Battlestar Galactica* finale!" He paused incredulously. "I can't believe my grandpa asked Roy Pervis to interfere. That's desperate."

Seamus gradually pulled himself upright and, still breathing hard, took a pack of Big Red from his hip pocket. He handed a piece to Boyd and kept one for himself.

Boyd folded the stick into his mouth and chomped hard on the gum, his anger showing with every fierce gnash of his teeth. "He doesn't trust me at all and doesn't want me doing anything he doesn't approve of."

"Why should he trust you? You lie to him all the time."

"Don't get all righteous on me, Shay. If I didn't, I'd never get to do anything," Boyd protested. "He's like a prison warden."

"Yeah, well, you better tell him you quit college," Seamus advised. "The longer you wait, the worse it's gonna be. He called me last week about giving you a surprise party. Man, do you know how much talking I had to do to convince him that you really, really would not want that? He's disappointed you're not attending the graduation ceremony, and he was upset about you not wanting a party. You know he's gonna do something for your quote, unquote, graduation, and you better hope it doesn't involve the whole town. Seriously, man, you have to tell him, or this could get embarrassing."

Boyd looked down into the valley, at the myriad white lights of McBrideville—and the big red and yellow specks, which were the Bashas' grocery and Denny's signs, respectively. Far to the north, 12,637-foot Humphreys Peak, the tallest mountain in Arizona, poked above a long, purple ridge of land. Captain had stopped barking, and the night was quiet except for the rustling leaves of the Chinese sumacs that lined nearly every road in Prosperity. Boyd's heart slowed, and remorse replaced resentment.

"I know it's wrong to lie, especially to my grandpa. But I feel trapped. He won't let me live my own life. I'm a good investigator, and I love PIP, but he wants me to quit. He thinks I spend too much time with you and Clive and that it isn't natural for us to not have girlfriends. Can you believe that? Like its 1950 or something! I told him you have girls all over you, but you're just too freakin' shy, and Clive…what can I say about Clive? He can't help what a dork he is."

"What about Amy? You were with her since high school."

"Even before that; we've been friends our whole lives. I've never not known Amy. I guess I'm not over her…and neither is he. He's always thought of her like his own grandkid. Did you know he babysat her for years so I'd have a playmate?"

Boyd grew sullen and then recalled his indignation with an agitated outburst. "He's been pissing and moaning since we broke up. You should've heard him berating me about her…and PIP. It's just hard to take, you know." He spit out his gum in a high-arcing trajectory and whined, "Do you have any idea how hard it is to have someone constantly making decisions for you, thinking they know what's best for you?"

Seamus locked down Boyd with a disbelieving stare.

"Oh yeah, sorry, Shay. You do know how it feels."

CHAPTER 8

The green Chevy Blazer looked like an enormous squashed aluminum can someone had thrown into the steep ravine. How long the SUV had lain, unseen, in the thigh-high wild grass and brittlebush of Dead Horse Canyon was anybody's guess. Ruined beyond salvage, its occupant had been totaled along with it. If not for Peter deciding to go sightseeing in the mountains and passing that spot of road at just the right time—when the sun beat down on the wreckage at such an angle that reflected light half-blinded him—the accident would have remained unreported and the victim's fate unknown.

For the time being, the victim, himself, remained unknown. Aside from being smashed beyond recognition, his face had been chewed away by vermin, and the rest of his flesh was beginning to decompose in the Arizona heat. Dental records would be required for a positive identification. Judging by the victim's attire—men's size-12 sneakers, a pair of ratty jeans, and a T-shirt too bloodstained to identify the original color—the officers were inclined to put his age below 40. That didn't narrow things down much, but it did help them compile details for a bulletin. The license plate and VIN were hidden inside folds of metal, but the color and make of the SUV were apparent. The officers were sure that a tentative match would come soon, whenever their details aligned with those in a missing person report.

Peter, however, was too shaken to feel any certainty. His visit to Prosperity had been nothing but bizarre from the start, when he discovered that his place of lodging was a former house of ill repute run by a dotty old showgirl with a penchant for suicidal prostitutes. Now, in this town centered on the resurrected dead, Peter had come face-to-face with a corpse: a crusty, half-consumed cadaver petrified in a quasi-fetal position. Peter sat on the roadside massaging his tense jaw as a team of EMTs and welders cut away the vehicle and exhumed its occupant, finally, mercifully, covering him with a white sheet. Peter watched the wordless pallbearers struggle to carry the loaded stretcher up the canyon bank and load it into the back of an ambulance.

"I'm sorry to put you through this again, Mr. Jacoby, but would you tell me where you were when you saw the light in the canyon?"

Peter looked up to see a figure in a gray and black uniform wielding a pen and notepad with uptight doggedness. He'd already talked to this officer, and two others, since he called in the discovery on his cell phone. Pure happenstance, really. He hadn't witnessed or committed a crime. He wasn't a suspect in any way, and what was done, was done. Why did it matter where he'd been when he'd seen the sunlight gleaming off the wrecked Blazer? Yet, there was no point in being obstinate and bringing disrespect to the scene with a flippant comment. The officer was trying his best to do a good job of reporting.

"I was right about there, going north," Peter said, pointing to where he thought was a reasonable estimation of the sighting. "Anything else?" he calmly asked.

The officer's eyes ran down the notepad as he mentally checked off each item he'd written. "No, don't think so. Thank you for getting involved, sir."

Peter nodded and stood, dusting off the seat of his khakis. He took one last look down the canyon and then lifted his eyes to the open back doors of the ambulance and the shrouded bundle inside. It was hard to recognize man or machine now. Peter couldn't help but envision how the victim must look beneath the sheet. He wondered who the man had been. Whose brother, son, or husband? What was his story? And why had that story wrapped itself around his own?

On the way back to his car, Peter finally noticed the long, undulating guard rail to the north and another, arced section to the south, with a 30-foot unsecured stretch that had allowed the SUV through. "What an unlucky break," he whispered.

Instead of going back to the Canary Cage Inn or continuing his sightseeing, Peter drove on through the rust-ocher crags of the Sandspurs, to the end of the pavement, and parked at the wide spot where a primitive path led to a tumbledown homestead ringed by barbed wire and red-wooded manzanita. He sat in his car with the engine off, looking at everything and nothing, thinking. He'd wanted to get away for a week to see one of the most talked-about towns in the state he now claimed as his own. It had begun with promise, with him visiting a few museums and doing a walking tour. Plenty remained on his itinerary. He was supposed to travel to some Sinagua ruins, take a train ride through the Verde Valley, and visit a recreated Wild West town for a dinner show with mock gunfights.

But none of it mattered anymore. It all seemed soiled, as if even considering such frivolity was sacrilege. He rested in his car, windows down, a small breeze moving through, until the day was lost. At one point, he reached for the sack of peanut butter cups on the passenger's seat, but the candies had melted into mush. It was then Peter realized he wasn't hungry, just in need of comfort. Watching the sky change from palest blue to indigo to lavender, then into the more passionate shades of the spectrum, he was reminded of life's multihued stages and its inevitable closing. Bullbats darted past his windshield, chasing insects. Outside, the land buzzed with crickets and came alive with evening creatures.

Peter mouthed a quick prayer for the body in the canyon—more accurately, for the soul that had been housed in that body. Opening his eyes, he looked into the sunset, feeling the burn on his straining pupils. He shut his lids tightly, pushing tears out onto his cheeks and onto his collar. "Whoever you were, I hope you're at peace, and I hope those you loved have the strength to go on."

He started the car and drifted back down the mountain to Prosperity. When Peter entered the Canary Cage, Clare's evening social hour was wrapping up. It had been a long day, more holistically exhausting than could be guessed by any of the inn's other guests, who talked about their whirlwind itineraries and the fatigue and sore muscles they produced.

"Do join us, Mr. Jacoby!" Clare invited. "Jamie is about to regale us with stories of dear old Ireland. He's even promised to tell us about his recent brush with the otherworld!"

The Irishman sat in a wingback chair, his bandaged ankle resting on a padded footstool. Grinning at Peter, his fears obviously long-since allayed, he raised his glass of port to his lips and basked in the attention of the inn's occupants.

Peter couldn't so much as pretend to be cordial for the few minutes it would take to tour the room, greet his fellow boarders, and have a nip of jewel-toned liquor. That was beyond him at the moment. He shook his head and gave Clare a despondent wave, then trudged up the stairs to the carefully crafted comfort of the Séance Suite.

Boyd held his cell phone to his ear and listened to Seamus' voicemail prompt click on. He hit the "end" button and flung his arm back and down, pretending to throw the phone.

"You're kidding me! That woman is..." Boyd fumed, his words trailing off to a hiss. "Wanna bet Afton confiscated Shay's phone again?!"

Clive watched Boyd without the faintest expression on his face. One spidery leg dangled off the edge of the tall stool at the Changs' breakfast bar; the other was crooked under him, his rubber sneaker sole gripping the top rung. He looked to be demonstrating a bizarre yoga pose, but Clive was simply so gangly that he had a hard time keeping track of his limbs.

"You won't reach him if the old girl doesn't want you to," he calmly stated. Diligently, he ran the point of a pen down a column of check-boxed items on a sheet of paper and stopped when he found an unmarked box. "Do you have the Sony Nightshot? Everything else is accounted for."

The Changs' kitchen was littered with ghost-hunting paraphernalia caught in an electrical wire web of recharging equipment batteries. Unzipped backpacks vomited various tools of the trade: K-II and EMF meters, compasses, digital and analog recorders, an infrared camera, temperature guns, flashlights, digital cameras, notepads and pens, and a first aid kit, which was used most often by Clive after his graceless flights of terror from investigation sites. The collection represented thousands of dollars and was another reason Clive was allowed to remain with PIP despite his occasional lapse in professionalism: he'd purchased the better pieces of equipment.

"Shay has it."

"It's imperative for our emergency investigation." Clive shrilly reminded, "That camera represents all proceeds from the sale of a vintage Lon Cheney poster and a rare Hammer Brides of Dracula autograph card."

"We're grateful, Clive."

Once more, Boyd tried calling his PIP cofounder, but one ring gave way to another. After leaving a curt message, he slid the phone shut and derided, "Shay should re-record his message: 'Hi, this is Seamus Burnside. I can't come to the phone right now because I'm being verbally castrated by my sister. Please leave your name and number, and I'll get back to you as soon as I grow a pair.'"

Clive winced. "I say, chap, that's rank. The old boy can't help that his sister's a bloody harpie."

"It pisses me off that he lets her treat him like a freakin' doormat! If he'd stand up to her once in a while, maybe she'd respect him more. It's pathetic, dude."

"Yes, well," Clive harrumphed, sliding from the stool and stooping low to detach the recharged batteries. "Shall we go to the grill? We need that camera."

Boyd knew that was the worst possible plan of action. "I'm pissed, but I don't want to totally humiliate Shay. Afton would tear him a new one in front of the customers."

"Ah, right-o. Not to mention the tongue-lashing she'd give us," Clive added, recognizing that the scene wouldn't be agreeable for any of them.

Boyd drooped onto Clive's vacated stool, elbows bent, cell phone clutched in both hands, like a man praying. "We don't have a choice. We'll have to do this major investigation without the Nightshot...and our wussy cofounder." He glanced at his watch and pushed himself up. "Let's roll, dude. Clare's waiting for us."

Clare frantically rapped on the door of the Séance Suite. "Mr. Jacoby?"

"Maybe he's not in there," Boyd suggested.

"I'm sure he came up earlier this evening." More raps. "Mr. Jacoby?"

Boyd looked uncomfortably at Clive, who voiced what they were thinking, "Perhaps he doesn't wish to be bothered."

"I must let him know."

Clare's fist was raised, poised for another knock, when the door cracked open. Darkness appeared between door and jamb, and in the shadows an even darker figure, features obscured.

"Mr. Jacoby, forgive the disturbance. I simply wanted to let you know that a paranormal investigation will be conducted here tonight. You're welcome to act as witness or participant. We'll gather in the parlor at 10:30 for a debriefing." Clare flushed red splotches behind her thick pancake makeup. "Where are my manners?! This is Boyd Chang and Clive LeBarre, founding members of the Paranormal Investigators of Prosperity."

The young men nodded as their names were mentioned, but Clive quickly corrected Clare. "Beg your pardon, Boyd and Seamus are the cofounders of PIP. I'm but a humble investigator…" Clive bent over with a swoop of his arm, taking a gallant bow, "at your service, my lady Clare, Queen of the Resurrectors."

Clare giggled and curtsied, waving her fingers before her face as if fluttering a fan. "You're too kind, noble sir." At least there was one person who appreciated Clive's eccentricities.

Peter pushed his face closer to the light. "What's this about?" He'd been awakened from a hard slumber and had picked up only about every other word from the odd trio in the hall.

To his unfocused eyes, none was recognizable—but judging by the voice and the ruby blur of painted lips, he assumed Clare was one of his callers. As his eyes adjusted, Peter made out the forms of the others: a long, skinny, pale fellow with a widow's peak and an average-size young man with striped black and white hair, both wearing gray T-shirts with "PIP" emblazoned on a tombstone and hefting equipment that looked like a cross between photojournalist gear and an electrician's tools. The blanched man held a device that resembled a stud sensor.

Boyd spoke up. "Sorry to bother you. Just FYI, we'll be studying the inn's paranormal activity tonight. You can assist if you like—we'll show you how to use the equipment, talk you through it. If not, that's cool. We're not intrusive. We're going to stay in the common areas. Just be aware if you leave your room you might run into us, so don't freak out or anything."

"Isn't it exciting?" Clare gushed. "I called in PIP posthaste because of the specter Jamie Clancy encountered and the boy I saw following you up the stairs. Something new is going on here, and I want them to get to the bottom of it. They're very good. PIP's done many investigations throughout the town—and Prescott and McBrideville, if I'm not mistaken."

Clare looked to Boyd for confirmation. He quickly added, "Thank you, yes, also Sedona and Vulture Mine."

"I…I see," Peter said.

Clive tilted his head to the side, picking up on a change in the environment. "It's getting chilly. Are you feeling this? What does the Mag-Temp reader say?" he asked Boyd.

A line of multicolored lights—green to red—began flashing on the gauge in Clive's hand. "Cripes, look at that!" he squawked. "The K-II meter is going mad!"

"Are you pressing down with your finger?" Boyd asked, unready to jump to a paranormal conclusion.

"No, I have the toggle switch engaged! Barring cell phone activity and electronic interference, this is a genuine event! Mag-Temp, Boyd! Mag-Temp!"

Quickly, Boyd pulled a similar-sized contraption from his satchel and held it out, noting the drop in temperature. "We're down to 67° Fahrenheit…65°…63°…"

"Over here," Clive directed, thrusting the meter toward Peter and watching the lights dance.

Boyd stepped around Clare, who was riveted to the spot, her smile sagging.

"Holy crap! The EMF's 3.2, and it's going up!" Boyd enthused, watching the digital numbers on his device's illuminated screen climb and then hold steady at 8.1.

The investigators moved about, holding the gauges in different directions and at different heights. Whenever the equipment was pointed away from Peter, the lights went dark and the readings returned to unimpressive ranges. As they neared Peter, they lit up and the numbers climbed higher and higher.

"It's you, my good man, or something near you!" Clive declared. In a rush of fearful excitement, he nudged open the door and pushed past Peter, seemingly tracking something through the suite. "Great ruddy Nora! Look, it's moving!" he yelled, as the lights on the K-II flashed furiously between long pauses of constant display.

Clare's mouth opened and shut like a dying fish's. She felt the blood drain from her scalp. The experience was taking a turn for the worse in her mind. Every time a guest had shared an encounter with Sadie Rue, Clare had quietly envied the event. Now, above all things, she realized she didn't want to experience anything eerie in the dim upper recesses of the Canary

Cage, not even with two seasoned paranormal investigators present. She'd already seen a phantom teenager trailing Peter up the stairs; he'd looked solid and normal, but the knowledge of what he was frightened her. Clare didn't think her heart could take anything scarier.

"You boys do your thing. I'll see to the guests," she squeaked before hastily retreating downstairs, her black braid beating against her back like a whip.

Boyd and Clive didn't notice Clare leave. They were intently tracking the K-II meter's lights through the darkness, Clive as he held the meter, and Boyd as he watched, astonished, from the hall, depositing the Mag-Temp reader in his satchel and pulling out a digital camera and clicking away, taking dozens of photos in a matter of seconds.

The K-II lights stilled. As quickly as the unseen entity had made itself known, it disappeared.

"Nothing now. It's gone." Clive covered the whole room, bumping into things in the darkness, losing the trail of energy.

Boyd looked at Peter, who was barely visible in the unlit suite. The scant tinge of gaslight from the hall was enough to show Boyd the expression of a deeply distressed man who'd stood there, eyes locked in distant thought, as Clive and some invisible force paraded around him.

The moment lost its thrill for Boyd. "Come on, Clive. Let's start the investigation downstairs."

"Start the investigation? Blimey, we just did! That was brilliant!" Clive emerged from the darkened room ecstatic as a kid on Christmas morning. "Perhaps we can ask this Jacoby chap if we can do some EVP work in here tonight or set up a camera. The activity is unquestionably centered on him."

"Let's leave him alone."

Clive saw the concern on Boyd's face and peeked back at Peter, who was still looking intently at nothing.

"Do you think he's alright?" Clive whispered.

Boyd lifted his shoulders. "Don't know, but we're not helping."

"I wonder if he knows he's a spirit magnet."

"I think he's finding out." Boyd leaned toward Peter and grabbed the doorknob, raising his voice as he addressed the catatonic man. "We're sorry to have bothered you. Have a good night, okay, and let one of us know if we can help with anything."

Peter didn't look up as Boyd pulled the door closed.

The evil that men do lives after them;
the good is often interred with their bones.

— William Shakespeare, *Julius Caesar*

PART II: SINS OF THE FATHER

Journal of Yee Chang
May 12, 1953

For the second time I take my journal into my room and lock the door. I write more thoughts. More memories. Xu is sleeping on the couch. She is angry with me because she smelled liquor on Lloyd's breath this afternoon and felt the back of my hand when she asked about it. I am glad she is avoiding me tonight. I can write at will. Filling these pages is liberating.

My father said that regrets are an old man's poison. I better understand that as I age. My younger days were not golden. I could not bear to relive them unless I could change them. Every year, my regrets weigh heavier on me. All my memories are attached to them.

Today, I shared my story with Lloyd and made him swear not to tell a soul. I poured us bourbon. His eyes watered when he chugged it. I was younger than he when I had my first liquor, taken with my uncle in his shop on Dupont Street. I remember how the whiskey flamed in my throat. I drank a glass of milk after to soothe myself. But not my Lloyd. He did not make a fuss. He belched and cried emotionless tears.

I told him every horrible thing, even the things so horrible I do not think he understood what they mean. He will keep his promise. But I knew by the way he looked at me that he is now more ashamed of his father than he has ever been.

It felt good to share with him, even though I sensed some of the burden shifting from my shoulders to his as I spoke. And, yes, I am cruel enough to wish that I could transfer all of that burden to someone else. Even my son.

Who else can I tell? Xu is too weak to bear it. She would be worthless to me if that sickly heart of hers worsens. She taxes it enough working in the cafeteria and bait shop; I do not want to tend an invalid. There is no one else I trust except Rosemae, and she lived much of it. It is no revelation to her. Besides, she is gone now, not dead, but dead to me. She has been keeping apart from me since George shipped out. These last 14 months she has declined every invitation to our house, though I know Xu and Lloyd have been to her home several times on the sly. Rosemae told me once that she has forgiven me, but how could she? Because of me, she stayed locked in chains and was sold to man after man. Because of me, the love of her life died. Because of me, Sadie Rue was murdered. Because of me, her would-be savior, my own brother, was hanged. I know she counts George's death against me, too. I think when she told me she forgave me she meant to say that she was through with me. She must have found her own way of dealing with the past, and that includes wiping me from her thoughts.

I miss Rosemae. I wish Xu were as intelligent and pretty as she is. No, not as intelligent. That would be difficult for me. But as pretty would be good. Most women are prettier than Xu. When I am irritated with her, I remind her that I should have married her middle sister, the flirtatious one with perfect skin and a mouth as plump as two plum slices. Xu already looks like an old woman though she is 20 years my junior. Her complexion is like used tissue, and her lips are thin and lilac-gray. I know that is because she is sickly and because I have not made life easy for her. But Rosemae has been through far worse, and she is still comely. I recognize that, as a man recognizes beauty in his daughter, but I cannot see her as a man sees a woman. To me, she will always be the little girl in the dirty red dress, locked in a cell.

CHAPTER 9

The morning newspaper was spread out before Afton. An uneaten bowl of milk-bloated cereal rested on the weather forecast. Afton's arms pressed down each side of the printed sheets, a position she'd held for 17 minutes, since she'd read the front page of the *Verde Valley Trumpet*.

Seamus walked down the stairs, loose shoelaces slapping the wood, and stopped to tie on his apron, wondering why his sister was wearing her sleep shirt and white bootie slippers, her hair an untended fuzz ball. "You're not dressed? We're gonna be late, Affie. Ordway and Monette'll be there soon."

Afton didn't move.

Seamus bent over and laced up his size-15 black Converse hi-tops. "You sick?"

Afton remained as quiet and motionless as a mannequin.

Seamus made his way over to the kitchen table. As he approached, he noticed that his sister's nose was red and dripping onto the table, the snot pooling in a thick puddle on the oak veneer; her eyes were nearly swollen shut, the lids mottled pink.

"What's going on?"

Afton seemed focused on a particular section of the paper, and Seamus leaned over her shoulder, craning his neck to see the same thing she did. It took him a few seconds to locate it, but once his eyes were there, like Afton's, they wouldn't budge.

"Shit, no…"

There, in a black-and-white high school yearbook photo, was the same boy who'd made an appearance at the Ghostly Grill the Friday before. Above his face, in big bold print, blared the headline "SANTA RITA TEEN KILLED IN CANYON ACCIDENT." Below his picture was his name: Martin Schrader; and his age: 17.

"He wasn't Jerry O'Neil, and he wasn't 23," Afton whispered.

Seamus skimmed the story. Certain words and phrases stood out, striking him with accusatory force. *Assumed to have been drinking. Underage. Lost control of the vehicle. Plunged to his death.* He forced himself to reread one particular line: "Martin was reported missing by his mother Friday afternoon when he failed to return home from school."

The room spun around him. Before he knew he was falling, Seamus was seated on the scuffed pine floor planks, his back resting against the under-sink cabinets. "How was I to know?"

Afton's stricken expression didn't change. There was enough guilt to share. She pushed herself away from the table, away from the story that sickened her heart. Slack-shouldered, she padded toward her room like a condemned prisoner on her last walk. "Don't open the grill," she muttered before shutting the door behind her.

Peter's whole body jerked. His hands reactively grabbed the coverlet. He'd had another dream, the worst yet. The setting had been his room, though it was decorated differently—ecru lace everywhere and a large oval mirror draped with hair ribbons and beaded necklaces. At the center of the room, a naked woman hung by a sheet from a still ceiling fan, her body slowly turning clockwise, then counterclockwise. She was a beautiful but ghastly figure—purple-lipped and ashen, with long golden tresses spilling from her head in a morose halo. A pearl bracelet was the only article she wore, save for the twisted sheet around her neck. It was Sadie Rue.

A ruddy barrel-chested man stepped down from the chair beneath Sadie's limply swinging body and looked up at his work, listening to the ominous creak of the overtaxed fan. He casually rolled down his sleeves and steadied his breath, as if completing a laborious but meaningless task.

Intuitively, Peter knew the immediate background to the scene. The man had strangled Sadie with his bare hands. That had been the easy part. The difficulty had come from slinging her over one shoulder, crawling onto the chair, and holding her dead weight in place while he tied the end of the sheet-rope to the fan. There was no life left in Sadie, no thoughts or feelings for Peter to detect. But he knew what passed through the man's mind: slight sadness at forever removing the possibility of another intimate moment with the woman; he wished he'd had sex with Sadie once more before killing her, but it would have taken more time and weakened him—too risky. Overall, he was satisfied. With a grunt, the man entered the shallow closet and ran his hands across the paneling, opening a small, secret door and crawling inside, shutting it behind him. As the man secretly exited the room, Peter woke.

He silently counted the nightmares he'd had since arriving in Prosperity: one about the ill-fated prostitute and two about a boy in peril.

"How impressionable am I?" he whispered.

The first had been heart-wrenching and completely perplexing: a bloodied, cowering boy awaiting some unseen horror on the other side of a door. Then, the night before, punctuating Peter's coma-like sleep, came another vision of the boy, older, dashing through what appeared to be the stubbly, moonlit Sandspur Mountains as if running for his life. Fear was etched on the child's face, and desperation pounded out of his being with every bounding step.

Peter assumed the dream would have gone on had Clare not knocked on his door to tell him about some supernatural treasure hunt. Though he tried to dismiss the vision as the random conjecture of an anguished mind, he wondered what he might have seen with a few more minutes of slumber.

"I'm going nuts," he whispered, rubbing the sprouting follicles on his chin and then warily sinking back into the soft bedding.

Seamus paced the floor of his apartment, checking voicemail messages on his cell phone. There were calls from two of the grill's helpers—ZuZu and Monette—wondering about the Burnsides' welfare, an automated message from his phone service provider reminding him that his bill was overdue, and a new message from Boyd.

"Hey, Shay, what's up? Dude, I've called you, like, five times today and went by the grill, but it's closed. Everything okay? I want to tell you about last night's emergency investigation at the Canary Cage. It was awesome! The Force was definitely with us. Clive and I went over some of the data today and found two amazing EVPs! Clare is asking Ooljee and Mae to help. Call me back, Shay. Later."

Normally, that news would have sent Seamus over the moon. But on this day, it barely registered. He cleared out his voicemail inbox and turned off the phone, tossing it onto his bedside stand. He kept pacing and considered whether the constant, "thump, thump, thump" of his feet on the floorboards was annoying Afton on the ground floor of their home. Usually, when he paced, she threw something at her ceiling—his floor— and yelled a colorful phrase, but he hadn't heard a peep from her since he'd retreated to his apartment earlier in the day.

An acoustic guitar sat on a stand in the corner. Seamus picked it up and began plucking the strings, producing "Leezie Lindsay." He played beautifully, but the one song was all he could manage. Every tune in his head had a melancholy edge to it. He didn't want to chance deepening his depression.

Seamus returned the guitar to its stand, turned on his television and, setting it on low volume, flipped through the stations until he landed on an *I Love Lucy* rerun. He flopped down on his bed and watched, thankful the episode was one of his favorites. It had always made him laugh in the past, and he knew that's what he needed now, but this time, when Lucy set her fake nose on fire in front of an astonished William Holden, Seamus didn't feel a thing—at least, nothing good. He continued to feel what he'd felt all day: nauseated by guilt and sorrow. Though he hadn't intentionally done anything wrong, he knew Martin Schrader was dead because of him. He couldn't rid his thoughts of the sweating, intoxicated boy who'd sat hopelessly at his bar until Afton forced him out. Maybe if he hadn't served him the rum and cola. Maybe if he'd moved quicker and cleaned up Martin's vomit, so Afton wouldn't have noticed. Maybe.

Turning off the TV with a flick of his thumb, Seamus rolled onto his side, curling up like a scared child. As much as he wanted distraction, nothing could hold his attention except memories of that hectic Friday night at the grill…and another catastrophic time years earlier, when his world collapsed.

Seamus' eyes roved over a family photo hung on the wall between a window and a tattered Old Blind Dogs concert poster. The photo showed Seamus at the age of 12, untamed hair in a red afro, a gleam of braces for a smile, and Afton wearing her horror of a sweet 16 dress, each standing on either side of a matronly brunette in glasses and before a distinguished-looking graying man whose spread arms encompassed them all.

Seamus closed his eyes, blocking the faces of his parents only momentarily. Their images quickly reappeared in his mind, stirring thoughts of the morning they died, trapped in their basement, asphyxiated by the smoke of a house fire. That March day had seemed like any other when Seamus woke and dressed for school. There was nothing portentous about his routine except that he'd overslept—not uncommon. A quick shower and dressing, a toasted bagel and cream cheese for breakfast, a belly rub for Banjo, a kiss to his mother's forehead, a wave to his dad, and Seamus hurried out the door, barely catching the bus. He was glad to find a seat near the back so he could try studying for a chemistry exam.

When Seamus left the house, his father was reading the paper; his mother was feeding their scruffy terrier a can of Alpo. The usual morning routine. After breakfast, man, woman, and dog would hole up in the basement office, where the Burnsides ran a Celtic music mail-order business. Seamus loved to visit the office—where music, whether a lively reel or a wistful ancient air, was always in play—and peruse the stacks of old vinyl albums and cassettes and new CDs and DVDs; if allowed, he would have spent every day listening to the Old World offerings of acts like the Corries and the Clancy Brothers. On the bus that morning, he couldn't keep his mind on chemistry for all the music in his head. He decided the rowdy chorus of "Pills of White Mercury"—which ate through his brain—was a good enough review of the subject.

Less than three hours later, the Burnsides and Banjo were dead. Theirs was an old house with bad wiring. The fire department investigator traced the source to the kitchen—specifically, the toaster. It seemed a cruel joke to Seamus and Afton that their family had been destroyed by a small appliance. For Seamus, the tragedy was especially bitter because he'd been the one to use the toaster that morning and had forgotten to unplug it. He'd never told a soul, not even Afton.

Seamus had carried that guilty secret with him into young adulthood, through a suicide attempt, an involuntary stay in a psych ward, and years of counseling. Though he knew better, he couldn't help but wonder if, in some cosmic way, his parents blamed him. Even if not, he surely blamed himself. And now he had another burden of guilt to shoulder. In his mind, Martin Schrader was his latest victim.

CHAPTER 10

"Mr. Jacoby? I beg your pardon."

Clare's words startled Peter awake. He didn't recognize his dim surroundings. Then, as the setting became clear, his momentary shock faded into the despondency he'd felt all day.

With the heavy drapes pulled to block the sunlight, Peter had succumbed to a foggy sleep punctuated by yet another horrendous dream sequence—a replay of finding the body in the canyon intercut by flashing images of an Asian man being lynched by a jeering mob.

"I heard your name mentioned on the TV news."

Peter uncontrollably walked toward the door. It drifted open, though he couldn't feel his hand on the knob. He didn't recall making a move to turn on the overhead lamp, yet light flickered into being, illuminating Clare, who stood meekly in the doorway, her harshly lined eyes round with feeling.

"Would you mind telling me what the report said, ma'am?" Peter reluctantly asked.

Clare peeked at the floor, avoiding the misery in her guest's expression. "It said the body of a boy was found in Dead Horse Canyon yesterday. He was a 17 year old from Santa Rita. Martin was his name. The last name was something German. Schroeder, no Schrader. The police suspect the boy was driving while intoxicated and crashed in the canyon, where he remained for upwards of 48 hours before one Peter Jacoby, a tourist," here Clare chanced to look at Peter for the swiftest of moments, "found the wreckage and notified authorities. The boy was driving a stolen 2005 Chevy Blazer." Clare lowered her neck in a pose of regret. "I'm so sorry, Mr. Jacoby."

"Only 17," Peter murmured. "I couldn't tell how old he was. He was just a blood-encrusted body with no face."

Clare covered her eyes with her hands. "Oh, that must have been horrible to see."

"Forgive me, ma'm. I was thinking out loud. I didn't mean to say such an ugly thing." Peter patted Clare's shoulder, as if she was the one in need of comfort.

Clare wiped her eyes with the backs of her hands. "Look at me! Here you are going through a tragedy, and I'm acting like a baby. Shame on me! Please let me get you something. Could you stomach a snack? Maybe something to help you rest?"

"I can't think of anything that would help, and I don't want to go back to sleep. I'm having one nightmare after another."

"You're traumatized. Time will help. I learned that when I lost my first husband. But talking about your feelings and thoughts can help, too. Do you have anyone close you can speak to? Is there someone you'd like me to contact?"

Peter couldn't think of a soul. The nurturers in his life—at least, the ones who should have been his nurturers: his parents and his Nanny Lotta, the woman charged with his upbringing—were long gone, and the only person who'd genuinely cared, his devoted Granny Weston, had preceded them all in death. There was no spouse, no significant other, and never had been; Peter was a true celibate. The closest thing to friends he had were the few coworkers who occasionally stopped by for a minute or two of meaningless chat or forwarded him funny e-mails or infrequently joined him for lunch in the hospital cafeteria.

"No one," Peter answered.

Clare could relate to his loneliness. "What about me, Mr. Jacoby? I'm a good listener, and I care."

Peter watched the woman's eyes flit back and forth like gray moths at a porch light, welling with tears for a boy she'd never known and a man who was drowning in despair in her presence. He couldn't stand to see anyone cry. Purely out of kindness, he held the door open wider, and Clare scurried inside.

"I'm listening," she said, folding her thin frame into an antique armchair, crossing her legs and primly adjusting the constricting waistband of her purple silk pantsuit.

Peter situated himself on the edge of the high bed, nervously kicking his legs off the side. "I don't know what to say."

"Let's start with how you feel, Mr. Jacoby."

"I don't know. I've run the gamut of emotions since yesterday. But now? I'm mostly empty...numb."

Clare nodded encouragingly. "That's it. Tell me whatever comes to mind."

Silence persisted. Peter laced his fingers together and stared at the small white flecks in his thumbnails. "You can see that I'm not exactly the world's best communicator."

"You're doing fine. Tell me, have you ever experienced anything like this before?"

"Death? Sure. I lost the people I loved when I was young. My grandma passed when I was 12, my mom when I was 14. My dad passed when I was...what, let's see...19."

"I'm so very sorry," Clare offered. "But this is a different kind of grief, isn't it?"

"Yes, and I don't know why it's affecting me so strongly. I feel like I've been sucker punched in the soul." Peter couldn't prevent his mind from returning to the scene of the wreck. The thoughts effortlessly became words. "I went on a drive through the mountains. I parked in a wide spot and took a hike—not very far—and then returned to the car. I was on my way back to Prosperity. I remember Johnny Rivers' 'Poor Side of Town' was playing on the radio when a bright light from down below briefly blinded me. I was near the 'Dead Horse Canyon' sign."

For a moment, perhaps as a defense mechanism, Peter lost his train of thought and contemplated how and when a horse had died in the canyon.

"And then what, Mr. Jacoby?"

"I'm sorry, where was I? The light... So I pulled over, got out, and looked down into the canyon. I had to walk a ways to see where the light had come from. There it was—a smashed vehicle, the sunlight ricocheting off the rearview mirror. That mirror was about the only thing intact." Peter sullenly rolled his head away from Clare. "When I first saw the wreckage, I thought it was old and had been left there because it was too difficult to remove from the canyon. What if I'd kept that thought and walked away without telling anyone? That boy's parents would still be wondering what happened." Peter paused contemplatively. "Maybe that would be better for them."

"I don't think so, Mr. Jacoby. A parent's imagination must be quite active when a missing child is concerned."

"It's a good thing they didn't see what I did."

"What was that?" Clare was the squeamish sort. She steeled herself for his answer.

Peter's breathing became shallow. He set his sweating palms on his knees and dragged in two long sustaining streams of air.

"I decided to climb down to the wreckage, just to be sure. When I was about 20 yards away, I saw a body inside. That moment, when I realized someone was trapped in there, my mind split. Part of me wanted to run away and hide and part knew I had to help. The better half won out, and I ran forward—or more like fell forward. I ran because I thought whoever was inside might still be alive." A sardonic laugh erupted from Peter's lips. "Imagine my surprise when I reached the wreckage and saw a zombie sitting at the wheel."

Slowly, Peter dissolved into distraught sobs, his fingers combing through his hair and tugging at the short, blond strands. "The poor kid was smashed, just like the SUV! I saw where creatures had eaten him. He didn't have a face!"

Clare scrambled from her chair and crawled onto the bed beside Peter, squatting on her knees so that she hovered over him. Pulling him sideways against her body, she rocked him like a baby in a cradle, smothering him in her arms and her scent: jasmine perfume and talcum powder.

"Let it all out. Martin deserves your tears."

She rubbed his neck and shoulders, trying to massage away the pain, but it was too deep, beyond muscle and tissue, beyond bone. And then she held him.

Peter couldn't remember the last time he'd been touched by another human—truly touched, not shoved in a supermarket or had his hand shaken by a colleague, but touched with genuine meaning. A sense of comfort overwhelmed him as he snuggled against Clare. There was no shame, no need to lie or hide or act as manly as he thought the world demanded of him. He just let the woman hold him in her flaccid arms until he stopped shaking and was able to breathe steadily again.

"You know what bothers me the most? That bashed body with no face reminds me of something I've seen…somewhere." Peter gently pushed away. "I shouldn't have come here."

"Now, now, Mr. Jacoby, you were meant to come to Prosperity."

Peter grimaced, pressing a hand to his forehead.

"Headache?"

He nodded.

Clare started to get up. "I'll get some aspirin."

"Thank you, ma'am, but no medicine helps. It'll go away soon."

Clare settled back onto the bed beside Peter, the tassel end of her braid brushing against one of his arms. She had more to say, but she didn't know if the time was appropriate or if he would be receptive to her words. Peter wasn't a typical free-thinking Prosperity tourist.

"Mr. Jacoby," she hesitantly began, "what I'm about to say is going to sound crazy to you, but I simply must say it."

"Go ahead," Peter allowed, concentrating more on ridding himself of his headache than Clare's words.

"I saw a teenage boy with you when you checked in."

"Mm. I remember you saying that."

"Brown hair, blue eyes, serious. He was wearing a pair of jeans and a gray concert T-shirt. Mr. Jacoby, I know he was there, with you. I watched him follow you up the staircase. Forgive me for saying this, but…" Clare hesitated, suspecting that her next words would bring either scorn or ridicule.

Peter twisted his head to look her in the face. He noted the apprehension in her eyes and could tell she was afraid to continue. "Yes?" he urged.

The two searched one another's eyes, each waiting for the other to speak or make a move. Before their mutual discomfort caused an emotional implosion, Clare gave in.

"The news showed a photo of Martin Schrader. It was the boy I saw with you. I know it was him, but according to the reports, he was dead by then." Clare uncomfortably looked away, hoping to avoid any negative reaction. "Think what you will of me, but I saw the ghost of Martin Schrader walking behind you when you entered the Canary Cage Inn."

Afton left her room and moved in a trance down Salome Hill, passing a SpecTours by Night group at the Prosperity Visitors' Center and four bikers vacating the Bloody Bucket Saloon. The young woman in a baggy sleep T-shirt slung off one shoulder was fortunate to have gone unnoticed by Clive's group and received nothing but whistles and whoops from the retiring motorcyclists.

The soles of Afton's bare feet were gray when she came to the front door of the grill; a wad of pale pink gum was wedged between two toes. Unlocking the deadbolt and turning on the lights, she walked across the main dining area and breached the bar. Moving methodically, she emptied the taps into metal buckets and poured the contents down the kitchen's utility sink. Her next chore was substantially more involved. Making five trips in all, she gathered the bottles of liquor from behind the bar and toted them out back in her arms. There, she poured out their contents, dousing the parched earth with malted brews that smelled of ancient recipes and musk, and flinging the containers from the rocky precipice near the storage shack, raining shattered glass in every direction. She stood on the overhang, looking down at the gemlike glitter that was McBrideville, and further off—resembling fairy dust sprinkled across the desert—the late-night glow of Santa Rita. Afton reached out to touch the radiant haze, her fingers curling in, snatching nothing but air. "Hey, lady…" she whispered.

Nobody noticed her on the walk back except Roy Pervis, who was doing a perimeter check at the Prosperity Community Center.

"Who goes there?" he bellowed as he shone his megawatt flashlight down the hill, onto Afton's distant figure; the fringes of the beam lit her slightly, but she was too far away for Roy to make out who she was. It shouldn't have mattered, anyway, since she was far from his territory. The crabby coot transferred the flashlight into the same hand as Captain's leash loop and pulled his pistol from his shoulder holster, brandishing it above his head. He shouted proudly, chest swollen, "that's it, keep on walkin'!"

and the black dog bayed, backing him up.

Afton returned to her home, to her room, to her bed. In the morning, she wouldn't remember her nighttime activities, but she would question the stains and gum on the soles of her sore feet and the smell of liquor on her shirt.

Peter tossed on the bed, trying to avoid hard slumber and the nightmares that were sure to come. The fight was valiant, but ultimately unwinnable. His body and mind finally surrendered, and two hours later—though it seemed like mere seconds had passed—Peter's eyelids popped open.

His mind became quickly alert as he sensed another presence in the room and heard a deep intake of breath that wasn't his own. Slowly, something lowered onto the mattress, like someone crawling into bed beside him. His insides squeezed, and his eyes widened, looking into the darkness. He wished he hadn't drawn the lined velvet curtains on the turret window; it was blacker than tar in the room. Though his heart bounced against his ribcage, Peter didn't move. He felt heat against his back as a leg gently wound around him. A bony arm slid down his own, a set of thin fingers searching for his hand.

His instincts told him who it was. Peter felt the withered flesh and protruding joints and wondered how anyone could confuse Clare with the supposedly buxom Sadie Rue. Fear became resentment.

"Clare, I don't need this," he whispered.

The body went rigid against his. After a brief pause, limbs continued to entwine his arms and legs.

"Please get off me!" Peter yelped, nudging the form away.

He jumped up, thrashing through the dark until locating the lamp and lighting the room.

Just as he suspected, Clare sat amid the rumpled bedding, her legs pulled up to her chin, her mascara-smeared eyes peering guiltily over her bony kneecaps.

"Here." Peter yanked the inn's complimentary white-terry bathrobe from a coatrack and tossed it to Clare. He kept his eyes to the side, head turned, hoping to spare both of them further insult.

Assuming a modest stance, hands crossed over the front of his boxers, Peter accused, "So, you're Sadie Rue."

"Oh, no! She's real! Many guests have encountered her," Clare assured, tucking the robe around her. "I'm just trying to help. This isn't common...I only do it when someone needs Sadie."

"You must have desperately wanted to prove that ghost legend to me," Peter fumed.

"That's not it. I know how upset you've been, and I thought a night with Sadie might help. I may not be a spring chicken, Mr. Jacoby, but I know what I'm doing in the bedroom. Remember, I used to be a showgirl. I perfected my moves when I dated the biggest names on the Strip. For years, there was a joke in Vegas that I'm the one who made Sammy Davis Jr.'s eyes go askew."

Peter tried not to envision what sexual feat could possibly have caused that.

"This is so inappropriate I don't know what to say." To Peter there was nothing flattering or even humorous in the awkward seduction attempt. Though most men who saw fit to rebuff such a ploy would have laughed it off that very night and trotted out the tale at every get-together with the guys, Peter deemed it a betrayal. "I don't need Sadie—or anyone right now," he said, choosing the kindest words he could to rid himself of Clare.

"That's not true. We all need someone." Clare stared imploringly at Peter, who was having a difficult time looking her in the eyes.

"What I need is some rest...and privacy." Peter forced a smile. "Please retire the Sadie Rue act before you give someone a heart attack."

Clare cocked her head. "I never thought of that," she uttered, inching off the bed.

Peter moved toward the door, starting to unlatch it to escort her out, but as he reached for the locked deadbolt, he wondered how she'd entered.

Clare walked to the slightly ajar closet door, opened it, and stepped inside, pushing past the few clothes folded over hangers. At the back of the small room was a thin, concealed door, its seams hidden by the slats in the paneling—the same exit used by the killer in Peter's dream.

"All the rooms have them," Clare explained, opening the low door. "The bordello was built with a labyrinth of tunnels to discreetly convey clients from one room to the next, indoors to outdoors. You'd be amazed at how easily I can maneuver through the inn. Would you like to see?"

"No, thank you, ma'am." Peter was dumbfounded by the escapade but perhaps most intrigued by Clare's lack of understanding concerning her impropriety. He contemplated whether the guests who were seduced by Clare-Sadie really believed they were romping with a prostitute's ghost or just so lonely or libidinous that they unquestioningly took advantage of a naked body in their beds.

"I'm sorry to have upset you, Mr. Jacoby. I promise to respect your privacy from now on," Clare swore, slipping into the dark secret tunnel and closing the door behind her.

CHAPTER 11

It was 4:30 a.m., the normal waking time for the Burnside siblings. Seamus was wearing his Halloween-inspired uniform and eating a raspberry Toaster Strudel while gazing into their 29-gallon aquarium, watching rummy-nosed tetras swim through the surging greenery of plastic plants and waiting for his sister to appear.

Afton was a light sleeper who rarely relied on an alarm clock or woke after her brother. Seamus expected to see her at any moment, bushy hair on end, stumbling from her room. But at 5:00, there was still no sign of her.

"Affie! It's getting late! Hurry up or we won't open on time!" Seamus punctuated his words with a couple of raps on her bedroom door.

Eventually, Afton emerged. There was little similarity between her and the woman Seamus was used to seeing. Her face was shaped and colored like a radish, the lips swollen to enormity, the eyes horizontal commas. The crimped red hair rose in a static charge above her slight form, which was swallowed by the same oversized T-shirt she'd been wearing for two nights and going on two days.

"Ah, sis, you look even worse than yesterday."

Dragging her bruised, sullied feet over to the couch, Afton stiffly bent in two and sat, ramrod straight, on the tweedy cushions. She sniffed her chest and arms. "Why do I smell like whiskey?"

"I think it's B.O. You haven't changed clothes in a while." Seamus positioned himself opposite her in an overstuffed recliner with coffee stains on the arms. His eyes zipped around the room, looking everywhere but at Afton. The sight of her was too painful to withstand. She looked as broken as he felt, but he couldn't tell her that; it would have only added to her agony. "You stay here. I'll take care of the grill today. There shouldn't be much traffic since it's a weekday."

Afton's bloated lips curved down. There was no way to read the expression on her face, but Seamus knew her well enough to sense the disgust housed in that slight facial movement. "How can you even think of the grill after what happened?!"

"Monette and Ordway will be waiting for us to unlock the back door," he reminded, deliberately keeping the edge off his words. "The grill's our responsibility."

"Responsibility? Ha! We don't know the first thing about that," Afton scornfully clucked.

"Hey, come on now, don't get all riled up."

"I mean it, Seamus. What was our responsibility? Profits? A stupid restaurant? Serving people drinks? What? Our responsibility should have been to that kid! To a human being, not a bar, not our pocketbooks!"

"I can't talk about this right now."

"When are we gonna talk about it? Huh? When? We killed a kid!"

"We didn't kill anybody," Seamus said, squeezing his eyes shut as if that could keep reality out.

Afton rested her neck against the couch's tall back and began to think aloud, purging herself of some of the poisoned blame that had been festering inside. "I don't know what else you'd call it. A kid gets wasted in our bar, gets chased off by us, gets into a vehicle, and goes flying off into a canyon. Hmm, let's see, where does the fault lie there? The underage drinker or the grown idiots who make their living by fueling peoples' alcoholic tendencies?"

"Stop it." Seamus wilted in the recliner, forehead tensely wrinkling, hands slipping up, over his ears.

"If we'd shot Martin Schrader with a gun it wouldn't have been any worse...though it might have been less painful for Martin."

"This isn't helping anyone."

"I wonder how many others we've killed. How many families and marriages have we helped destroy? How many car wrecks did we cause? How many drunken bastards have we sent home to beat the living daylights out of their spouses and kids? Huh?"

"Shut up, Afton!" Seamus roared, exploding from the recliner, his hulking form eclipsing all objects in the room. His arms swung out around him like falling timbers, his huge fingers bent in frustration. "It isn't our fault if people act irresponsibly! Not all of them are alcoholics, Afton! Not all of them do wrong! I can't control what they do when they leave the grill! You know I don't serve them when they're shit-faced or close to it! I check IDs! I throw out the troublemakers! You know all that!"

Afton provided a patronizing smirk. "I know."

"I didn't do anything wrong! Do you hear me?! I was just doing my job!"

"That's the problem, isn't it? If we hadn't gotten a liquor license and started serving alcohol, Martin Schrader would still…"

"Be dead!" Seamus finished. "He'd have gone somewhere else and gotten his alcohol. Whether we gave it to him or someone else did, he'd still be a drunk kid in an accident. We didn't do that to him, Afton! He did it to himself."

"Well, somebody else, someplace else, isn't the way it worked out. He walked into our bar. You poured him the drink. I chased him out. You and I provided him with the means to the end." Two fresh tears slipped sideways from Afton's eyes, running back into the spongy web of her tangled hair. "Wouldn't Mom and Pop be proud of us, little brother?"

Seamus' face was pure deprecation. The green eyes were disturbed yet defeated, the mouth a tight line above the rich auburn hairs of his beard.

"And don't act like you're not as jacked up as I am by all this. Look at you, ready to go to work…it's Tuesday, Bro. The Ghostly Grill is always closed on Tuesdays."

Glancing down at his uniform, Seamus felt disjoined from reality, foolish, like every weakling notion Afton held about him had just been proven. *I thought I was getting better, but I'm still insane,* he told himself, and that admission triggered a rage in him he'd never before experienced. "That's it! I've had enough! I don't need you and your high and mighty micromanaging shit! You're not my boss or my mother…or whatever the hell you think you are! I'm outta here!" He stormed from the room, sending the framed photographs on the walls into clattering convulsions as he slammed the front door behind him.

The house shuddered anew as Seamus' Yamaha Royal Star Venture engine roared to life, traumatizing the early morning placidity. The motorcycle seemed to be speaking for Seamus as it grumbled obscenities, then a final good riddance, its mechanical voice a tirade that soon shushed to a distant hum.

Peter came awake gasping, with tears in his eyes. Unable to stay alert all night, he'd fallen asleep and again journeyed back to Prosperity's painful past, as he knew he would. In this gut-wrenching episode, he'd watched an Asian man running down a darkened alley, sheer terror on his face. The man pushed through the backdoor of a two-story building, under a small shingle painted with "Chang Brothers Restaurant" in red. He darted through a kitchen and locked himself in a storage room among sacks of dried beans and rice, balling up in a corner, wrapping both arms over his head as if trying to hide. He rocked on his knees and wept for what seemed an eternity. Then, a commotion came from outdoors, as if the town was awakening with anger. The man mouthed words Peter couldn't decipher, standing, wavering, trying to move but shrinking back into the corner. He pulled his hands into fists and raised them to the ceiling before pounding them into his chest, bowing over at the impact. There he lay, a soft, grievous cry leaking from his mouth. His fear was great, but it was overpowered by shame. Peter felt both emotions strongly, and they stayed with him, sickening him, as he opened his eyes, feeling his wet lashes beat against his cheeks.

That did it. Peter didn't think he'd survive another Prosperity nightmare. He hoped that leaving the inn would put an end to them. He couldn't stay another night at the Canary Cage anyway. He couldn't face Clare. Their last encounter was a humiliation he was destined to relive every time he locked eyes with the unconventional innkeeper.

"I have to leave this madhouse," he muttered.

Shouldering his bulging brown duffel bag, Peter slunk down the winding turret stairs, hastened down the second-floor hall, and made a break for the final tier of steps while breakfast was being served. Lulled into a false sense of security by the happy talk and fragrance of huevos rancheros coming from the dining room, Peter skidded across the balcony and descended, unaware that Clare had left her guests to enjoy breakfast on their own.

Peter came to an abrupt halt. Looking down into the parlor, he saw four intent faces staring up at him. Clare and Boyd shared a red-velveteen settee. Two women sat nearby in carved parson chairs. Peter didn't think he knew either, yet something was familiar about the older one, a sweet-faced Navajo woman who rose to her feet. Wrapping a loosely crocheted lavender shawl around her shoulders, she shuffled to the bottom of the stairs and took in the sight of him with what seemed like elation.

"Hello, Peter," she said.

"Do I know you, ma'am?" Peter asked.

"We've met...in a way," she answered. "I'm Mae. Come." The woman held out two small, sun-spotted hands, beckoning to him.

Peter timidly continued down the stairs, toward the group that lay in wait. As he took the last step, he swung his duffel bag behind him and slid his hands into Mae's outstretched ones, thinking it would be rude to not reciprocate.

Mae's fingers tightened around Peter's with a strength that surprised him. Her black eyes never left his, and her smile never faded. "I've been told that strange things have been happening here—to you and others— since your arrival."

"I...I can't say what's been happening to others. What happened to me is I found a dead body."

"That's all?" Mae asked.

"Isn't that enough?" Peter laughed uncontrollably before settling down, watching the eyes around him grow softer with concern. "Well, I've been depressed since finding...what was his name?" he asked, looking toward

Clare, feeling a pang of embarrassment as their eyes met.

"Martin Schrader," she answered before quickly gazing down at the lacy handkerchief she was nervously kneading into a wad.

"Yes, Martin Schrader. Poor kid. Like I said, I've not been myself since finding him…which I think is understandable, don't you? But these ghost stories people have been telling…well, I haven't seen any ghosts."

The woman reached up to cup Peter's chin. She nudged his head to one side, then the other, giving her a full view of his face.

"You look as he would have if he'd reached your age. Don't you think, awee'?" she asked Ooljee over her shoulder.

The seated woman gave a smile. "Suppose he does."

"Who? Martin?" Peter said.

"Not Martin," Mae assured. "Someone I knew long ago. Another boy from Tennessee. Another only child. Charles was his name."

"How did you know I was an only child and born in Tennessee?" He looked accusingly at Clare before turning back to Mae.

"No one told me anything, Peter. I have second sight. So does my daughter…and so do you."

Peter chuckled. "If I had second sight, I'd know it, wouldn't I?"

"I didn't mean to scare you."

"I'm not scared," he harrumphed.

The woman's hand dropped from his chin to his chest. "So, why is your heart pounding like this?"

"What's going on here?" Peter asked, withdrawing from Mae and stepping over to Clare and Boyd.

The hostess and ghost hunter glanced at each other, questioning their next move. It seemed best for Boyd to explain.

"I've reviewed the data from the investigation, and some very interesting things have come to light. I believe…we believe…that you're at the center of a haunting. I have two EVPs—electronic voice phenomena—recorded outside your room that I'd like to play for you. A disembodied voice, a spirit voice, I believe, answers two of my questions."

Peter numbly plunged his hands into the loose pockets of his tan Dockers and looked at Boyd with a knitted brow. If a witch had flown by on a broomstick, he couldn't have felt more disassociated from the here and now. It seemed that the drive to Prosperity had taken him about 100 miles and 600 years from home, right into the Dark Ages.

He pivoted on his heels to face Mae and Ooljee. "I assume one of you is a medium or some such thing, and you want to do voodoo to conjure up the spirits around me or send them into the light or whatever it is you think needs to be done. Well, I've already told Clare I don't believe in that stuff."

Ooljee was inclined to feel warmly toward Peter, based on her mother's feelings and what she'd shared with her, but he'd gone too far. Pushing herself up, her orange camp skirt floating out around her like poppy petals, she put a fist on her hip, jangling her turquoise bangles, shooting a fiery scowl at Peter.

"Too bad. Because you're involved, and now we are, too. You can believe what you want to believe, but we're here to help. The sooner you accept that, the better for us all. I suggest you have some respect and listen to my mother, who came over here, worried about you, at the request of another woman who's worried about you." Ooljee sat back down and huffed a last response, "And, I assure you that no one here practices voodoo."

Peter squinted at Clare, and then Mae, who'd never lost her smile. He was ashamed of his outburst. He couldn't hold their superstitious leanings against them, not any of them. The boy with the skunk-striped hair, the older women, the feisty lady in orange. They all seemed to care about him, and that wasn't something to disparage or disregard. Besides, considering his nightmares, perhaps there was something worth looking into.

"I'm sorry. As I said, I've not been myself lately. I'm on edge, but that's no excuse." Peter peripherally noted the empty seating in the room, stepped toward the closest option—a cane rocker—and unloaded the duffel bag as he sat. "This kind of thinking is all new to me. I know you mean well." He took a deep breath and forced out the next words. "Will you please play the EV…EP…EPB…whatever that was you recorded?"

Boyd produced a small, hand-held digital recorder and gave a brief introduction to what they would hear.

"I conducted three EVP sessions using my Olympus digital recorder and an external microphone. One session was outside your room, Peter, one in the parlor, and one on the second-floor landing. There were no unusual sounds on the last two recordings, but this one hit the jackpot. You have to understand that when we conduct EVP sessions, we don't hear the answers to the questions we ask. It isn't until we go back and listen to the recording that answers are apparent. There are a few theories as to why that is, but we won't go into that. For now, let's just deal with the recorded evidence. In a moment, you'll hear me ask a question. Listen very closely after that. There will be a few seconds' pause, and then the answer. This was my fifth question. All the previous ones went unanswered."

Boyd held out the recorder and thumbed the play button.

"Why are you following Peter Jacoby?"

Silence, and then a tinny voice whispered, "Help."

Peter scoffed. "Maybe that's one of the inn's cats…or a glitch with the recorder. A million things could have caused that sound."

"Then listen to this," Boyd said, fast-forwarding a ways. He clicked play, and his voice asked, "How old are you?"

There was nothing.

But the next question brought a quick, definite response. About 10 seconds later, Boyd inquired, "What's your name?" Almost immediately, the same tinny voice, clearly young and male, replied, "Marty."

Peter's feet and hands tingled. He wagged his head from side to side like an agitated baby. "I don't know what's going on here, but this isn't funny."

"No, it isn't," Ooljee answered. "You've got a dead boy chasing you, trying to get your attention."

Boyd played the final response again. Then, again.

Peter shot up, frantic as a hunted deer, horrified by the unearthly voice. "I can't listen to this. It isn't real. It isn't right. That isn't a dead boy!"

"Please don't be afraid, Mr. Jacoby," Clare implored. She stood, reaching out for him. "Mae and Ooljee can help you with this. They're about the only people who can."

But before she could touch him, Peter bolted, forgetting his manners and his duffel bag of belongings.

As he dashed by, Ooljee sprang from her chair and grabbed his wrist, pulling him close to her. As tall and solidly built as Peter, she had no problem restraining him. She wanted to speak to him, calm him down, help him understand. But as she touched him, her mind flashed to a long-buried memory Peter had hidden for so many years that it was no longer in his consciousness. Ooljee was transfixed, her grip tight on his forearm, her eyes looking into his wild, blooming pupils. Peter couldn't move. Something held him firm—something other than Ooljee's muscled arms—and he knew that the woman was somewhere far inside him, acquainting herself with a part of him that even he didn't know.

With the exception of the whimsical tink tink of Ooljee's dangling turquoise earrings, the room was quiet as she and Peter stood face-to-face, eyes fixed. At last, Ooljee released Peter's arm and, slack jawed, drifted down into her chair, watching him with eyes full of pity.

Peter darted to the foyer, out the door, to his car. He had to distance himself from the intrusive quartet and their backwards, magical thinking. He had to leave before he heard another ridiculous theory or was again physically restrained by an Amazonian psychic...before he had to listen to Martin Schrader's pleading voice one more time.

CHAPTER 12

The retaining wall behind the Old Graham Boarding House had sprung a dirt leak. It was nothing serious but enough to give Lloyd an excuse to see his old friend and patch up what he perceived to be a strain in their relationship.

"Can you stay for some coffee?" Mae asked, walking onto the porch to greet him before he reached the door. She already had two mugs in hand.

"You know I can. Why do you even ask?" he remarked, taking his serving of the black brew and joining her on the swing. Lloyd crossed his legs and looked forward uncomfortably.

"Don't get cantankerous. You never were good at apologizing."

"Apologize? I stand by what I said."

"Mmhmm, but you hung up on me. That's rude."

Lloyd held his head low over the warm mug. "I'm sorry. You know I'm overly sensitive about my father."

Mae patted his knee. "I know. Apology accepted." Between sips she asked, "How's that grandson of yours?"

"Good."

"You sure?"

Lloyd guardedly approached the subject. "You know something I don't?"

"I dreamed Boyd was standing on the edge of an open pit, looking down into darkness."

"Well, what does that mean?"

Mae lifted her shoulders and rubbed a fist in one eye, appearing exhausted.

Lloyd did a frustrated double take. "That's no help. Should I be worried?"

"I suggest you keep your eyes and ears open."

"Maybe I should give him a call before I get to that retaining wall." Lloyd looked at his watch: 10:36. If he remembered correctly, Boyd's next final exam was at 10:45. He took out his cell phone and dialed his grandson, who answered before the first ring ended.

"Yeah, Grandpa?"

"Aha! So, how are finals? Over."

"Okay."

"What's the next subject?"

"Uh…anthropology."

"Anthropology, huh? Sounds difficult. I don't want to disturb your last-minute studying. Just wanted to say 'good luck.'"

"Thanks, Grandpa. See ya."

"Over and out."

Lloyd gave a pleased little chuckle as he shut his cell phone and slipped it into his pocket.

"He's fine," he told Mae.

Lloyd had no idea that his grandson was only a few streets away, conferring with Clive about some recently acquired paranormal evidence.

Peter's first instinct was to go home: a sleek condo in a guard-gated community on the outskirts of Flagstaff, where no one and nothing of consequence waited for him. Instead, he pushed up the volume on the car radio and, at the junction, turned toward McBrideville. It was bigger than Prosperity, a slightly wider dot on the map. Its kelly-green fields of alfalfa and key-lime pastures spread like a patchwork blanket before him, an agrarian oasis in the midst of a chalky desert.

A Denny's was just off the road. Peter parked his Buick between an old Chevy pickup and a green tractor and pushed through the restaurant's double glass doors. Inside, it became even more apparent that he'd left Bohemia for a thoroughly rustic retreat. Older gentlemen lined the coffee counter, chatting over steaming cups with their cowboy hats balanced on their knees; Peter had thought such rugged John Wayne types were extinct.

"Hi, how many?" asked a freckled young waitress with a pregnancy belly the size of a washtub.

"Just one."

"Follow me, sir." The woman waddled away, trying not to look beleaguered. She seated Peter at a booth and handed him a menu. "My name's Martha; I'll be your server. Can I get you something to drink?"

"Black coffee, please, and biscuits and gravy," Peter quickly improvised, returning the menu without looking at it.

"Right away, sir."

Peter drank the coffee and tried to get comfortable. Over the clatter of rattling silverware, plates, and cups, he caught an occasional word from the oldsters at the counter.

The setting and the sight of aged yet vital men bonded by a common thread were foreign to Peter. How he wished he could claim a place and a people with which to find that sense of belonging. But he'd been molded into a solitary man by wealthy parents who died relatively early in his life, leaving him with plenty of money and very little else, least of all acquainted blood relations. As Peter aged, he realized just what a disservice his parents had done him. Friendless, orphaned, he was the last of his kind, whatever that was.

When he snapped out of his trance, Peter noticed a plate of biscuit islands afloat on a sea of thick white gravy. How long the food had sat in front of him, he didn't know.

Martha slipped his bill under his reheated coffee cup, directing, "I'll ring you up at the register when you're ready."

She then moved through the dining room, refilling coffee cups and inquiring after customers' dining experiences, as well as their health and personal business, using first names during almost every interaction. The familiarity only heightened Peter's sense of disconnectedness. He ate the biscuits, sopping up every ounce of gravy, finished his coffee, and refusing to loiter, left the booth for the register.

"How was everything?" Martha asked.

"Excellent food and service," Peter kindly extolled. He slid his wallet from his hind pocket and rifled through a collection of cash and cards before handing over his American Express.

Martha ran the card through the authorizing machine and tore loose the receipt, handing it, along with a pen, to Peter. As he signed, she flipped over his card and compared the signature on the back to the one he made. Her mouth slackened, her eyes slowly rising to Peter's face.

"Peter Jacoby," she muttered. "Aren't you the guy who found Marty Schrader in Dead Horse Canyon?"

"Yes, ma'am," he admitted.

Martha held his American Express card in her outstretched hand, unable to let go. She searched Peter's eyes, face, torso, as if some significant message was written thereon. "I'm from Santa Rita, same as Marty was. My little sister went out with him a couple times." Her eyelids batted back quickly summoned tears. "He was a sweet kid."

"I'm sorry about what happened."

"Me too. Stealing Coach Jensen's Blazer and all that. I don't get it—that wasn't like Marty."

Peter slipped his card from Martha's bent fingers without her notice. Her gaze was directed down, through the glass counter, at a display of candy bars and Wrigley's chewing gum. Peter knew she was far away from him, far away from Grand Slam breakfasts and credit card machines, pulling up melancholy reflections of a boy who'd lost his way.

"I'm sorry," Peter repeated. A gnawing need to make things better in whatever way possible led him to scratch out the original tip and total lines on his receipt and add a few more dollars to what was already a generous amount. He left the white slip of paper on the counter. "Good luck with the baby."

Martha was in the same pensive position as Peter got into his car and exited the parking lot, but she soon revitalized and, ignoring the exorbitant tip scribbled on the receipt, found her way to each occupied booth and counter stool in the restaurant, then into the kitchen, to spread the news that Peter Jacoby—THE Peter Jacoby—had dined at Denny's that very morning.

"The one who found the Schrader kid?" came the same reply.

Yes, the one who found Martin Schrader. That was the way Peter was beginning to define himself, too.

Outside, Clive's house looked like many of the old homes in Prosperity. The 1,000-square-foot miner's cabin was a nondescript white box with its front half wedged on Cliffside Street and the backend precariously propped up by wooden stilts that bore into pylons 18 feet below, set in the bed of a weedy hillside wash. Inside, the house was anything but typical. Classic Hammer horror movie posters hung on the walls—slick-papered images of monsters and screaming women with long, flowing hair. Other decorations included a garlic wreath and a framed *Arizona Highways* article on SpecTours by Night. Mounted on the ceiling of every room was a small, inconspicuous camera. Clive left the security system running every night while he slept and sometimes checked the footage for anomalies. He'd never found any and hoped he never would. That's why he checked the footage only sometimes.

Clive's kitchen was PIP's evidence room, a space devoted to research and the storage and processing of data collected during investigations. This day, though his grandfather believed he was facing another round of finals at Yavapai Community College, Boyd was at Clive's kitchen table, hunkered down over his laptop, trawling the web for anything on a hospital accountant named Peter Jacoby, a wealthy Tennessean and only child who'd lost his parents while in his teens. That was all the background Boyd had; it came courtesy of Clare. After an hour of online searching, punctuated by the occasional air-drum solo performed with two mechanical pencils, he'd found only two positive hits: Peter's White Pages and Grand Canyon Hospital staff directory listings. There were many other mentions of a "Peter Jacoby," but Boyd couldn't tell which referred to the man in question.

One item, however, held promise. "Dude, I may be on to something here. Listen up."

Clive left his own laptop investigation—into Martin Schrader's life and times—as Boyd began reading aloud an archived newspaper article.

October 12, 1989
Nashville Herald
Brentwood, Tenn. – Redbud Chemical CEO Franklin Deeds Jacoby, 63, was arrested last night for the murders of his wife, former Nashville television news anchor Samantha Weston, 48, and their groundskeeper, Deke Goeckler, 51. The partially nude body of Goeckler was found yesterday at the Brentwood estate shared by Jacoby, his wife and their son. Goeckler had been shot once with a .22 rifle and was pronounced dead at the scene. Weston's severely beaten body was later discovered in a shallow grave on the property.

Goeckler is survived by two grown daughters and his wife, Lotta, who is employed at the Weston-Jacoby estate. Jacoby is being held without bond at the Johnson County Jail. He and Weston have one child, Peter, 14, who is in the temporary care of Tennessee Children's Services. Since their marriage in 1972, Weston and Jacoby have been high-profile fixtures on the Nashville social circuit.

Boyd paused reflectively. Pushing his top lip into deformed shapes with the erasers of his mechanical pencils, he mused, "So, if he was 14 in 1989, he'd be...like, what, 35? That sounds about right, don't you think?"

Clive nodded, engrossed, rereading the article over Boyd's shoulder. He heard his cell phone ringing in the other room but let it go. The theme from *the Exorcist* played out while he leaned on the back of Boyd's chair, making enthralled clicks and whistles.

"Let me try something," Boyd suggested, typing "Peter," "Franklin," "Jacoby," and "Redbud" into the search box of his browser.

A slew of articles popped up, all related to the news feature he'd just read. Scanning through them, his eyes caught on an obituary from *the Tennessean*. It was a staff-written piece—the type reserved for luminaries—from September 2, 1994, memorializing Franklin Deeds Jacoby.

Boyd rattled off the highpoints. "Redbud Chemical CEO...cleared in wife's death...guilty of manslaughter for death of groundskeeper...hanged himself...and...oh, wow, Clive, this is it! This has to be it! His body was found by his son, 19-year-old Peter Jacoby, a sophomore at Vanderbilt University."

Boyd spun around on the kitchen chair and fist-bumped Clive. "Lost both parents when he was a teenager, an only child, from Tennessee, a poor little rich boy. This is him! Shit, no wonder the guy is so messed up! I bet Martin Schrader isn't the first ghost to visit him. He has a lot to choose from: mom, dad, that Goeckler guy. Damn, dude, what's the story with that family?"

"Good job, ol' chap!" Clive gave Boyd a congratulatory pat. "I'm going to see who called. It may have been Seamus."

"Yeah, go ahead," Boyd said, moving on to another article about the sensationalistic Weston-Goeckler murders. After reading two more online pieces, he had a pretty good picture of the events as reported. The bottom line: Goeckler had attacked and beaten to death Samantha Weston when Franklin Jacoby—summoned by his wife's cries for help—grabbed his hunting rifle and went to her aid. He found Goeckler over the body and blasted away, killing him. Jacoby had admitted that much in court and confessed to burying his wife's nearly unidentifiable body on their property. His excuse: in his grief and shock, he wasn't thinking straight; he didn't want anyone to see his beautiful wife as a mangled, bloody cadaver, and couldn't bear the idea of strangers taking her away from him and their beloved home forever. Boyd considered if Franklin had truly been a grief-addled romantic or just a well-connected corporate mogul sprung by his team of ace lawyers. From the sound of things, public sentiment had run strongly in Mr. Jacoby's favor and even more so after his suicide. "He just couldn't go on without her," a family friend was quoted in one piece.

Boyd was digging into another item from *the Tennessean* when Clive came sweeping into the room in a frenzy. "You must hear this!" He pressed the replay code on his cell phone and held the device to his friend's ear.

A hysterical wail issued from the earpiece, and Boyd motioned for Clive to take it away. He continued to hear Afton's high-pitched ranting as the phone was removed from his ear. "Did she say she was going to tie your wiener into a knot?" he asked through laughter. "Dude, she's majorly pissed!"

"What you didn't hear—she regains her composure at the end, and you can understand her again—is that Seamus has gone missing. Afton said he served liquor to that young bloke who crashed in the canyon. She thinks Seamus blames himself and is off somewhere plotting suicide!"

All levity was gone. After three years as Seamus' friend and colleague, Boyd knew the depth of the man's empathy and sense of responsibility for things far beyond his control. He'd seen him grow troubled over the hurt of others as if he were the injured party. One particular incident came to mind. Almost a year earlier, local widower Art Krupps asked PIP to investigate his house after his wife's passing, not because he'd experienced any activity but because he desperately hoped some remnant of his spouse of 58 years still lingered in their home. Boyd remembered that Seamus had gone wet eyed when he explained to Art that they'd found nothing unusual after investigating for three consecutive nights and reviewing the gathered data. The following morning, as the PIP trio unwound over breakfast at the Ghostly Grill, he recalled Seamus acting withdrawn and speaking of how he'd failed Art; his gray mood had lasted more than a week. If Seamus had been that torn up by a fruitless investigation, Boyd could only imagine how he was feeling now.

Snatching Clive's phone from his hand, Boyd dialed the Burnsides' home number.

"Hey, Afton, it's Boyd."

The woman started to rail at him, but Boyd raised his voice above hers. "Stop yelling and listen to me! It's about Seamus!"

The keening on the other end ceased.

"We're worried about him, too. Clive and I are going looking for him at his hangouts, but you need to do something. And I mean it; you really need to do this, no matter how hard it is for you or how stupid you think it is. You understand?"

"What is it?" she asked.

"Go to Ooljee and Mae."

"Are you kidding?"

"If you think something's wrong, you better get over there right now and tell them what's happened."

Afton screeched her disapproval, but Boyd cut her off mid-rant. "If you care about your brother, you'll swallow your pride and do it—now!" He turned off the phone and handed it back to Clive.

"Perhaps you and I should pay Mae and Ooljee a visit," Clive suggested. "What if Afton doesn't?"

"She'll go." Boyd was sure of that.

CHAPTER 13

People had settled in the Verde Valley for centuries, putting down roots and building up structures as diverse as mud cliff dwellings and military forts. Some of the oldest impressions remained the most magnificent. Tuzigoot National Monument was first-rate substantiation of early human activity in the region, and Peter had long wanted to see it. Postcards on a rack near the Denny's entrance reignited his interest.

Since he had the time and opportunity, he paid $5 and toured the small museum, reviewing glass display cases of potsherds, metates, jewelry, and other artifacts recovered from the area. Afterward, he trekked up the ruins trail, exploring the eroded 110-room, multi-story Sinagua pueblo, feeling as empty as each crumbling chamber he viewed.

Peter thought he was alone at the site until he heard a squall of high, babbling voices rushing toward him and braced himself, backing against a wall. A park ranger crouched through the doorway, leading a very young school group into the room.

"Excuse us," the sinewy man told Peter, tipping his Outback-style hat to him. He returned to his tour script, "Many cultures have made their homes in Arizona. Did you know that the oldest continuously occupied settlement in the U.S. is just a three-hour drive from here?"

The children squirmed and looked around without answering. Peter showed the most interest, and he wasn't even part of the group.

"It's called Orayvi, and it's on the Hopi Reservation. Have any of you been there?"

The children continued to fidget, especially one tyke who multitasked by aggressively picking his nose while grabbing the seat of his shorts like a colony of red ants was marching up his crack. Every time the child's finger slipped up past the first knuckle, his eyes would cross and his tongue would curl over his top lip. If Peter hadn't been polite—and psychologically overwrought—he would have laughed.

But he wasn't up to dealing with the tot or the high-energy crowd. "Good luck," he told the guide, wading through the short-statured horde and exiting the irregular stone walls of the old village.

Stopping at his car for a bottle of water and the novel he'd stowed in the glove compartment, he then set out on an impromptu hike. The further he walked, the faster he went, his legs pumping harder, his tan loafers deftly finding footing among plants of staggered heights and stones smooth and sharp. Scenery meant nothing. Sky and earth blurred around, above, and below him. On he went, thinking of nothing in particular, and yet consumed by the need to go, move on, move ahead. A couple of hours later that urge wound down, leaving Peter panicked by the lost time spent in unconscious travel. Winded and with an aching head, he stopped, looked around, and wondered where he was.

Peter stood on the rim of a high pink mesa marbled by stubbly green and gold growth. Far below, a stream cut through stands of cottonwood and salt cedar and shrubs that resembled pom-poms. Railroad tracks paralleled the water, and a blue engine painted with an eagle's head traveled them, pulling a chain of cars through a riparian canyon. Peter watched the chugging wheels until feeling the beginning of vertigo swirling up from the pit of his stomach into his already hurting head. He never was good with heights.

Crows cawed overhead, and the wind sailed past mercilessly, whistling an angry tune. With the train gone, the overhang evoked desolation. It was beautiful but lonely, seemingly far removed from the rest of the world.

Instinctively, Peter turned to his left and moved along the sheer rock face, keeping far enough away to avoid danger. With his mind fully in the present, he began to sense the toll the hike had taken on him. His feet ached from heel to toe inside soggy loafers; the lower few inches of his pants were damp—Peter didn't remember splashing along the bank of the Verde River and wading through its shallow offshoots. His prickly skin flashed hot then cold and back again; he'd forgotten to slather on sunscreen, and his face, neck, and forearms were already paying for it.

"What's wrong with me?"

He walked back, or what he assumed was back, mumbling to himself. Peter was lost, no two ways about it, but that didn't frighten him. The inexplicable loss of time, memory, and consciousness did.

Peter started to uncap his water bottle but found that it was empty, though he couldn't remember taking a single drink. *Did I have a stroke?* he wondered.

He patted the side of his khakis, feeling for the paperback he'd dropped into the baggy pocket; it was there, and the touch of it reassured him that some things were as he remembered. The sun was straight up, no indicator at all of where he was in relation to direction. Clutching the drained water bottle, he hurried along the cliff.

A few minutes of brisk walking brought Peter to an unexpected sight. Standing perilously close to the mesa's rim was the biggest man he'd ever seen in person. His thumbs were threaded through the belt loops of his black pants, bearded chin down, facial features obscured by a blast of wiry red hair. Peter felt weak-kneed just looking at the man, whose shoe tips extended over the cliff's edge.

"Hope you aren't thinking of jumping."

The man on the overlook stepped back and wheeled about, clearly surprised by the presence of another human. The strained look in his eyes informed Peter that his jest hadn't been far off. Something besides a love of nature and the need for fresh air had sent the hulking man to the top of the rose-hued precipice. Desperation etched worried creases onto what was an otherwise young face. Peter's mind spun to find the appropriate reaction to someone so observably in need of a lifeline. He opted for an unconventional approach: acting ignorant of the man's intentions and painting himself as victim.

"I seem to be lost."

It appeared the large man hadn't heard him. He stood there, looking down at Peter with the startled and irritated gaze of one whose inner sanctum has been breached. Peter moved forward and put out his hand for a friendly shake, praying he didn't trigger the wrong response in the man. "Peter Jacoby. I guess it's pretty obvious I'm a tourist."

"Seamus Burnside," the man grudgingly responded, clamping Peter's hand.

There was something familiar about Seamus. Peter could have sworn he'd seen him somewhere before, but he'd learned not to trust his mind of late. He thought he must be confusing the man with someone else, though to match Seamus, it would have to be a wrestling superstar or a character from a superhero movie.

"Are you from around here?" Peter took a look at the embroidered spiders that swarmed Seamus' shirt and speculated that he might be from the haunted hillside town he'd just fled.

"Prosperity."

"What a coincidence. I've been staying at the Canary Cage Inn. Do you know it?"

"Yes."

Peter balked at the ridiculousness of his question. What Prosperity resident wouldn't know the Canary Cage? It was like asking a hermit crab if it was aware of the shell on its back.

"Listen, I have no idea where I am." Peter ran a knuckle over his sweaty brow. He conveniently left out the part about not knowing how he'd arrived there. "If you'd help me get back to Tuzigoot, I'd be much obliged." Peter strained to sound casual.

"Keep going that way." Seamus pointed in the direction Peter had been walking. "When you get to the highway, go to your right and follow the asphalt."

Seamus turned back to the ledge, thinking the exchange had ended. But Peter stepped up his intervention strategy, intuiting the urgency. "This is awkward." He coughed, the exhalation evolving into an uneasy laugh. "I'm not used to this heat. I think I may have suffered sunstroke." That wasn't a lie. He had no reason to think he was doing anything wrong, especially with a man's wellbeing on the line. But Peter was such a straight arrow that he felt a pang of guilt for the modicum of dishonesty in his next words. "I'm not sure I can make it back. Would you help?"

Seamus hesitated, looking into the canyon, wondering how it felt to fly and if any of that feat's exhilaration was possible when one knew the flight would be short-lived and followed by a bone-crushing, soul-draining impact. He twisted his neck, studying Peter over his shoulder—a damaged man lost in unknown territory.

"Yeah, sure," he agreed. This time, when Seamus faced him, his eyes seemed more focused. He walked away from the bluff and gave Peter a good looking over. "Do you need me to carry you or something?"

Peter felt every bit the martyr as his dignity faded. "I can walk, thanks."

"Okay. Go straight ahead, and I'll follow."

A few times, Seamus verbally guided Peter along the proper course. "Go toward that big mesquite." "Turn a little to the right." "You're zigzagging; stop and rest."

Near the bottom of the steep incline, the brush grew denser and higher, and it was harder for Seamus to keep track of his hiking cohort, who seemed remarkably mobile for a man with a serious health condition. Seamus' vision blurred as sweat slid into the corners of his eyes.

"Hey, what..." He wrinkled his nose, shaking off the stinging salt drops and an image that couldn't be. There, peripherally, he saw someone standing with Peter, walking off to his side. The ripped jeans and T-shirt, the brown hair, the hunched shoulders, they were familiar to him as belonging to a boy he'd seen only once but whose every characteristic he couldn't forget. It was Martin Schrader.

Two blinks later, and the boy was gone.

"Wait!" Seamus cried out.

Peter stopped dead in his tracks. "Rattlesnake?"

"No, I thought I saw...forget it, man. This heat is playing tricks on me."

Peter was ashamed of his wild imaginings and even more afraid that they were right. But he had to ask. He had to know. "You saw a boy didn't you? A teenager."

Seamus' ruddy, sun-blushed face drained of all color. "Yeah. I saw someone I knew…kind of. His name was Martin…"

"Yes, I know," Peter finished. "Martin Schrader."

Even a psychic can be surprised. Ooljee never expected to find Afton knocking on her front door. The two hadn't swapped more than a few polite words in passing since Afton chastised Ooljee for setting up a feeding station for feral cats on the Ghostly Grill's back stoop and forced her to move it to where it wasn't likely to merit a citation from the health inspector. That was shortly after the Burnsides' arrival in Prosperity, before they knew anything about the local celebrity or her role as an advocate for all vulnerable populations, including animals.

"Ya'at'eeh. What can I do for you?" Ooljee asked from behind her screen door.

Afton held out a $50 dollar bill. "I need you to do a reading."

"Come again?"

"A reading. Isn't that what you call it? You know, when you read a palm or something, to see what's going on in someone's life." She looked away, discomfited by being so desperate as to consult someone she considered a charlatan.

Ooljee opened the screen door and watched Afton walk by, avoiding eye contact. She waited until the elfin fireball was completely indoors before telling her, "I don't do readings, but tell me what you want to know. Maybe I can help."

"Is this enough?" Afton asked in advance, displaying the money again.

Ooljee waved away the money, insulted. "I don't charge to help people. Go on in and have a seat."

Inside, the house was far less flashy than Afton had envisioned. Buttery walls held a giant landscape of Monument Valley and a few framed photos of Ooljee and Mae in various stages of life. On the ground, stretched out between a red couch and two white- and red-striped armchairs, was a Wide Ruins Navajo rug.

Afton took her place on the couch and tried to look comfortable. She gave a tight-lipped smile as Mae walked in, carrying a glass of iced tea with a mint sprig sprouting from the top.

"Here, child." Mae handed the glass to Afton, who hesitated to take it, wondering if the old woman was giving up her own drink or if the stories about her and her daughter's psychic abilities were actually true.

Mae puttered away, through an archway, disappearing into the next room and reemerging with two more glasses of tea. She handed one to Ooljee and kept one for herself.

"Mind if I join you?" she asked, settling into the armchair beside Ooljee, who questioned her with a silent *You knew she was coming?*

Dazed, Afton proceeded. "I'm worried about my brother. We had a big fight this morning, and I haven't seen him since."

Ooljee bristled. "So that's what happened. I heard Seamus' motorcycle at the crack of dawn. Ch'ish, what a racket!"

"It's not like him to be gone this long without being in contact. I checked around; no one's seen or heard from him." Afton's whole face quivered with worry.

"It's only been a few hours."

"Eight-and-a-half hours."

"Maybe he just needs to be alone for a while." Ooljee—and everyone else in town—knew that Afton kept closer tabs on her brother than most parents keep on their preschoolers.

"You don't understand." Afton looked exasperated and anxious. "He's not like most people. He's so…sensitive…fragile. He's on antidepressants."

"So is half the country," Ooljee replied.

"Well, half the country didn't try to kill themselves and spend time strapped down in a psych ward!" Afton said, her words exploding out of her before she had a chance to think about them. "Sorry. I'm at my wit's end. I know Seamus is upset enough to try something. The look he gave me this morning…I've seen it before…it's not good."

Ooljee peered sideways at her mother, disturbed by the revelation that finally made sense of the woman's overprotective attitude toward her hulking brother, a man who on the surface didn't seem to need any looking after whatsoever.

"Do you have anything of his on you? A keychain, jewelry, anything?"

Afton shook her head. She still wasn't sure if Ooljee would be of any use, and she felt foolish asking, but she had to try. She'd do anything to find Seamus as soon as possible.

"That's okay. Sometimes that makes it easier, but it isn't required. Let me have a go and see what comes to mind."

Ooljee loosened her neck and shoulders and shut her eyes. Five minutes passed, and Afton thought the woman had fallen asleep. But she looked to Mae, who reassured her with her sparkling black eyes.

Sleepily opening her lids, Ooljee revealed, "I didn't get any specifics about his location, but he's fine. He's out of the woods now."

Afton blinked hard. "That's it? He's fine? You want me to be satisfied with that?" Her expression showed Ooljee how duped she felt. "I'm sorry to have taken your time." Starting to stand, she told Mae, "Thank you for the tea."

"Child, what do you want to know?" Mae asked. "I'll tell you."

"Where's my brother?" The words came out as more of a demand than a question.

"He's going to an ice cream parlor in McBrideville with a friend."

"I've talked to his friends. They haven't seen him."

"This is a new friend. His name is Peter Jacoby. He saved your brother's life today. You were right to worry, child. Your brother was thinking about jumping off a cliff, but Peter found him in time."

Afton went goggle-eyed and limp in the couch. She began to shudder, and instinctively, Ooljee rose and pulled a knitted afghan from the back of the sofa, covering Afton's shoulders. Many times, she'd been with people as they went into emotional shock and their bodies followed. Almost always, they felt a rush of cold and lightheadedness.

"There, there, now," she soothed, wrapping Afton. "You sit still for a spell and let it all sink in. Your brother's fine."

Speaking in a comforting tone, Ooljee added what she could. "I'm going to tell you what I picked up on. This may sound strange, but I kept seeing Seamus' hands. First pouring a drink, and then plugging in a toaster and putting two halves of a bagel in the slots. The two scenes are linked. He has a huge amount of guilt about those actions, can't forgive himself for them. I don't understand why toasting a bagel is such a big deal, but there you go."

Paralyzed by shock, Afton sat still and let tears fill up her lids and cascade down her cheeks as she fit the pieces together in her mind. When she could move, she touched a hand to her mouth and spoke through spread fingers. "He must have been the one who left the toaster plugged in."

"You know what it means?" Ooljee asked.

"Our parents were killed in a house fire. They traced it to faulty wiring and an old toaster. No wonder he can't get over their deaths…" Afton began to chide herself aloud. "I've been so mean to him, giving him grief for his ghost hunting and trying to make him face up to the fact that our parents are gone forever."

Mae struggled from her chair and went to Afton, placing a hand on each shoulder and rubbing gently, as her arthritis allowed.

"Your parents are gone from this existence, but that isn't the end of them. They've disappeared from your sight because they've gone far ahead of you."

Afton was afraid to ask what she wanted to know, what the town of Prosperity and its specter-loving residents had put in her brain. "Are they stuck here on Earth, you know…" She smacked her dry lips, forcing out the words. "Are they ghosts?"

"No, baby. They went where they should have gone." Mae made a radiant, close-eyed smile. "It's very, very good where they are."

Craning her neck to look up at Mae, Afton sputtered, "I want to believe that so much."

"Then believe it," Mae said matter of factly. "Stop blaming God for taking them away from you. Drop your defenses and open up your mind and your heart."

"It's not that easy," Afton sobbingly protested.

"Child, you look deep down into your heart and ask yourself: do you really believe those two complicated, gifted people who raised you came into being by coincidence, for no purpose? And, in the end, everything they were, everything they experienced and thought and felt, every loving thing they did, will ultimately amount to nothing?"

Afton was still for a moment. Then, her head lolled from side to side, conceding defeat. "What do I do?" she asked, looking back and forth between Ooljee and Mae.

The old woman smiled and patted Afton's shoulders, beginning a retreat to her chair and the glass of iced tea that had wept a ring on the coffee table. "Go home. Wait for Seamus. He'll be there soon. When he comes in, tell him you know what happened today—everything Ooljee and I said. Tell him that no one blames him, especially your parents, so he must stop blaming himself. Listen here—this is most important—apologize for treating him like a child, and promise him that things are going to change. Then keep your word, Ms. Burnside."

.

CHAPTER 14

The subject of Martin Schrader was left to smolder in the minds of the two men, who wondered how much to share and how much to ask of the other. After walking in silence half an hour, a time that allowed them to reach Seamus' motorcycle—parked under a juniper tree on an off-road trail—Peter tackled the topic. "How did you know Martin Schrader?"

"I'd seen him around. How about you? You aren't from around here. How'd you know him?"

"I didn't. I'm the one who found his body."

"Oh, wow…that's sad, man. I'm sorry." Seamus hid his guilt-ridden face by pretending to look for something in his cycle's stash box. "I guess me seeing Martin and you feeling him around you is one of those psychological things, huh? He's on our minds—we kinda hallucinated. Makes sense in a weird way."

"Sure," Peter easily agreed, hoping to put it behind him.

"So, how are you feeling now? Do I need to drive you back to your car or to the hospital or what?"

"My car would be fine. Listen, I appreciate your walking down with me. I wish you'd let me buy you a beer."

"No, but thanks."

Peter was having a hard time reading Seamus. The walk appeared to have improved the beefy man's state, but he couldn't gauge by what degree. Though he was intrusive, he felt justified in not yet allowing Seamus to slip away unsupervised. "How about lunch, then?" Peter looked skyward, deciphering the sun's position. "It must be well after noon."

Seamus rounded his shoulders and leaned on his handlebars like a defeated boxer hanging on the ropes. Even at a time when he felt his worst, when he wanted to be alone or simply not be, he was too decent to bundle his emotions into a selfish package. He observed Peter and considered the reasons the man could have for wanting, so desperately, to hang out with him. Superficially, Peter seemed too good-looking and well-bred to be emotionally afloat, but Seamus was wise enough to realize that even the beautiful and wealthy can be lonely. "Tell you what, there's a place in McBrideville that makes the best root beer floats ever."

Peter hadn't consumed one of those confections since high school. It was an unorthodox but appealing suggestion. "Sounds good."

"Get on." Seamus shoved his metallic blue helmet over Peter's blond hair and swung a leg up and over the bike. He patted the seat behind him, then revved up the Yamaha.

As Seamus tore down the road, Peter hung on for dear life and contemplated if all people with motorcycles had death wishes. When they stopped at Tuzigoot for Peter to transfer to his car, he was worn out by fear. He was still panting as he followed Seamus into town and under an arched pink sign that read "Sugar Hut" in sparkly white letters.

Peter parked next to a dented Volkswagen van with a tie-dyed paint job. As he got out, he heard Seamus say, "ZuZu's here."

"What's a ZuZu?" Peter asked.

For the first time in days, Seamus laughed. "ZuZu Lorenz is a friend and one of my employees—part-time server and bartender." He nodded toward the van. "That's her ride."

"I see. So, you own a restaurant?"

"Co-own. My sister, Afton, and I run the Ghostly Grill. I like to cook; she likes to boss."

Mistakenly, Peter assumed that financial problems with the grill were the root of Seamus' depression. "I've heard it's difficult to make a go of a restaurant."

Seamus smirked. "Not when a bar's attached, but I'll tell you, being a bartender and bouncer is no bueno. That's what I do every weekend night instead of cook or serve. You oughtta see some of the nut jobs who come through there."

"I can imagine," Peter said, picturing a cowboy bar or a pool-hall dive teeming with bikers, like the ones he'd seen in movies. He assumed such places existed, though he had no hard evidence. His own drinking experience amounted to cocktails at work-related functions and an occasional glass of wine.

Suddenly, Seamus' familiarity fell into context. Peter remembered his introduction to Salome Hill and the wild scene he'd viewed as he'd passed the "Welcome to Prosperity" sign. Seamus had been the red-headed giant who'd propelled a biker across the parking lot, much to the delight of several bystanders. Yes, the black-and-white uniform, the enormous stature, that fiery hair—it had to be the same man. Peter realized he'd witnessed a bouncer evicting a troublemaker, not a bar brawl. He also realized it would be best to not bring up his first impression of Seamus.

"Come on, I can't wait to get into the air conditioning." Seamus stacked his helmet on the back of his bike and swaggered toward the eatery that looked like Hansel and Gretel's candy house. Peter was amused by the picture of mammoth-sized Seamus entering a building roofed with foam frosting and studded with big plastic peppermint candies and light-up gumdrops. He was even more entertained by what followed—he and Seamus sitting on pink vinyl stools at a pink marble counter, sipping the froth off cherry-topped floats. They were the only male twosome in the crowded sweet shop.

"Yeah, this place is corny, but it's comforting. Reminds me of being a kid. I guess you can't go back, though. Things'll never be that simple again." Seamus drank his float until he was sucking air. "Geez, wouldn't it be great to be eight again? Playing in the mud. Family barbecues. No worries. Well, nothing your parents and a root beer float couldn't handle."

Peter agreed, without honestly relating. Whole chunks of his childhood were missing from his memory, but what he did have down pat wasn't pleasant. For him, childhood had meant interminable studying to earn the straight As his parents expected of him, stiff-collared galas, piano lessons, and spending more time in museums than in parks or stadiums or on playgrounds. The only playtime he could recall was sanitary and stationary, mainly drawn-out games of chess with his dour Nanny Lotta, who seemed ever-present in what childhood memories he did have. Peter struggled to recall a friend. He couldn't remember any except Granny Weston, the person he loved most and saw the least.

Seamus mindlessly traced with his straw the mosaic pattern of drying carbonation bubbles at the bottom of his glass. "I'll level with you, Jacoby. Everyone sees me as this big, strong guy, but I see myself as a kid. Honestly. It's funny to me when I go to evict some asswipe from the bar, and I see fear on his face, or when I actually throw one down the steps. It's been a long time coming, you know. I was 6'3 by the time I was 12. That's when childhood stopped being fun. I just shot up and out," he said, adding emphasis with a quick movement of his hands, and went back to poking his empty glass with his straw. "Every jerk in school wanted to fight me to prove how tough he was. Grown men tried to pick fights with me. I'd just be walking down the street and some turd would come up and try to start something. It was like being a target for guys who felt they had to prove something. And every single one of those times I didn't stand up for myself. I backed down. But then, I came to Prosperity with my sister and took over the Ghostly Grill, and things were different. I hate being a bouncer, but I'm good at it. I'm strong, and I've got the moves in me— don't ask me how, but I do. Now, I face down the bullies. I fight because I'm standing up for my sister and our business, which means the world to her. But I still can't stand up for myself."

A tattooed hand planted itself on Seamus' shoulder. "Lookee here, I caught the boss man getting a sugar fix!"

Peter turned to view the epitome of "the odd couple": a skinny old hippie in a Fu Manchu and a buff 30-ish woman with bi-colored eyes, a platinum crew cut, and so many tattoos and piercings that Peter was in pain just looking at her.

"Hey, ZuZu. I saw your van out front. Hey, Ivan." Seamus politely launched into an introduction. "Peter, this is ZuZu Lorenz and Ivan Raleigh. You guys, meet Peter Jacoby; he's staying at the Canary Cage."

Ivan blinked acknowledgement and the woman greeted Peter with a slap to his back before he spun around and stood for a proper greeting.

"Howdy," ZuZu said. "Yipes! You two never hear of sunscreen, or what?!"

Self-consciously, Seamus and Peter touched their faces, feeling the redness in the heat of their skin. "Oh that, yeah, we met on a hike today. Ran into each other out by Mesquite Trail," Seamus said.

"That's cool." ZuZu leaned over, peered into the men's drained glasses, and sniffed. "What'd you have? Floats? We polished off banana splits."

Ivan remained quiet while the others made small talk. His eyes never left Peter but watched him with unnerving intensity. When he finally opened his mouth, he interrupted with the force of a foghorn, "You're the spirit magnet Clive LeBarre spoke of!"

Spoons dropped, and heads swiveled in the group's direction. Peter fished for words until ZuZu—ignoring her companion's outburst—graciously put the derailed conversation back on track.

Ivan remained wordlessly fixated on Peter and, when it was time to trade farewells, did not turn from him but stepped away, walking slowly backwards, his pupils boring steadily into his new acquaintance until he slipped through the door ZuZu held open.

"That was demoralizing," Peter remarked.

"Don't mind Ivan. He's harmless. He's ZuZu's painting mentor. Actually, he's a pretty big-name artist. Owns the Night Gallery on Spirit Street. The guy does a lot of freaky-looking stuff, but he's good."

Peter's hands shook. The encounter had raised the specter of Martin Schrader once again, and Seamus could sense that. It had done the same for him.

"Listen, don't let him get to you. He's a wackadoo." Seamus laughed and elbowed Peter's side. "He swears his studio's haunted by the ghost of a miner who keeps using his bathroom and leaving the toilet seat up. He tried to find a shaman who'd come out and do a ceremony to un-possess the toilet, but nobody would. See what I mean? Wackadoo."

Peter whistled in disbelief.

The men chortled and stuck their faces into their float glasses, licking up sugary residue and inhaling sweet fumes, being as barbaric as possible for grown men in an ice cream parlor.

Seamus started to pull out his wallet, but Peter insisted, "I got this…and I don't want any argument."

He settled their tab, and the men left the faux candy cottage. Seamus narrowed his eyes as they stepped into the brilliant sunlight. Strangely, the heat felt good on his red skin after an afternoon inside the chilly walls of the Sugar Hut.

"You feeling better now, Jacoby?"

"I am, thanks."

Seamus lifted his helmet from the motorcycle and peered soulfully into the visor. "Yeah, me, too."

CHAPTER 15

Mae was napping on the couch, snoring soft, percolating puffs. Ooljee was curled in a fetal position on a chair, her fingers locked around her shins, eyes closed. She wasn't sleeping. She was thinking. What she'd seen when she'd touched Peter and gazed deeply into his eyes had made her queasy, and the aftereffects were still eating at her.

In the last few weeks, her mother had spoken often of the pitiable boy from Tennessee. She'd mentioned how this now-grown man reminded her of someone dear from her past and alluded sketchily to his painful childhood. Now, Ooljee understood why her mother wouldn't share the details of her visions. Mae wasn't senile or secretive. She was protecting her daughter. And Ooljee knew why. Something she'd seen inside Peter reminded her of a case that haunted her.

All the police investigations she'd assisted with troubled her, but one in particular was of such a sickening magnitude that it had settled in Ooljee's soul, transplanted there to fester forever. That was in 1983, when a detective with the Tempe Police Department—lusting for justice in a dead-end murder investigation and tipped off to the psychic women by a friend on the rez—came to the house on Hangman's Lane with a plea for help and a torn shirt belonging to the deceased. Ooljee answered the door, listened to the request, and immediately agreed to help. She retreated into her bedroom with the long-sleeved Henley and sat on the floor, clutching the ripped jersey article, waiting for her inner sight to come into focus. Four minutes into her trance, she began reliving the crime in a vivid, first-hand account, seeing it as the victim—Raymond Aguilar, 35, married, father of two—had.

Early evening: Two men approached from across a dark parking lot. Raymond was in his car, counting money he'd just extracted from an ATM for his eldest daughter's flute lessons. The men outside were merely peripheral blips until one was situated beside him in the passenger's seat and the other had his arm inside the rolled-down window, pressing a gun against Raymond's chest. "Here, take the money. Take the car. I swear I won't go to the police," Ooljee heard herself say, her unfamiliar voice a deep baritone, uneven with fear. It was quiet as the man with the gun opened the car door and climbed into the back seat, moving the .32 Magnum to the base of Raymond's skull. Then, Ooljee heard, "Drive."

There was a long ride into the desert with no words exchanged except Raymond's frantic defense: "Why are you doing this?" "Do you need money?" "I can help"; and the assailants' alternating commands to "shut up!" and "turn here" or "go straight." They parked at the end of a dirt road, against scrubby foothills Raymond didn't recognize. In the wide-sky wilderness, the captors got freer, their voices loosened, and their sadistic intent became evident. They marched Raymond into the darkness, among low-growing mesquite, and began toying with him. They'd already decided to take his car, his money, and his life. But they wanted more. This wasn't about poor desperate men stealing to get by. This was about two vicious tormentors, for the sheer pleasure of it, decimating a fellow human—a man who would have stopped to help them change a flat tire or held the door open for them at Circle K and asked, "How's it going?" Somehow, taking everything away from a decent man made these creatures feel bigger, more powerful, like more than the filth they were.

"Take off your clothes." "Come over here." "Bend down." "Beg."

Their orders became viler as the two tried to outdo one another with creative humiliations of their prey; they found amusement in their captive's quick obedience. Raymond did everything they asked because, as he kept telling them, "I have kids. I have a wife. Please, I want to see them again."

But men who give themselves over to evil have no qualms about extinguishing the very spark of humanity they are charged by their Creator with tending.

The last thing Raymond heard was contemptuous laughter and a faraway owl's dirge. The last thing he saw was a black, starry sky, for he refused to look at the two men kneeling over him or the metallic barrel of the handgun aimed between his eyes. The last thing he felt—after the battering and shoving; after the violations of flesh and soul; after scraping his knees and shins on jagged rocks and sticks and cactus thorns as he crawled from one place to the next, hoping to gain freedom by following the thugs' demands; after feeling his heart beat so fiercely with fear that he thought he might die from a burst artery, as his father had—was a quick flash of intense pain, and then nothing. He was gone before a second bullet entered his brain.

When Ooljee emerged from her trance, she was lying on her back, gasping. It took three attempts to stand, and when she finally left her bedroom, she was weak in the knees, trembling, sweat rolling off her ashen forehead and blanched top lip. She told the stupefied detective everything she'd seen, retracing in detail the route from the strip-mall ATM to the low-desert murder site. She described the murderers to a tee, and even knew their names, which they had freely used in the outdoors. After the detective left, Ooljee vomited into the kitchen sink and passed out on the floor, where Mae found her. She cleaned up her daughter and put her to bed, singing softly until Ooljee fell into a heavy sleep. But Ooljee was up and about wearing a brave face the next day, trying to move on from the ordeal. The darkness would not claim her.

She was a calming presence when she met Raymond's children and consoled them with hugs and squeezable, plush angel dolls, and when she sat beside his widow in the courtroom every day of the trial, holding the woman's hand, whispering for her to be strong for her children's sake. She viewed the defendants on the stand with mute stoicism—depriving them of any sense of power over her—and remained a pillar of strength when the guilty verdict was read and Raymond's family wept around her, holding her like one of their own blood.

But sometimes, when she was alone, she still cried for Raymond Aguilar, not for what had become of him—for Ooljee knew he was beyond all travails—but for what he had been through, for what his family continued to suffer, and for the hateful depravity of humanity's malcontents.

Though the Aguilar case solidified Ooljee's relationship with law enforcement officials and led to the offer to host *American Fugitives*, it took a high toll on her psyche. The nightmares came regularly for years and still afflicted her about once a month, waking her to damp sheets and a heart pounding as furiously as those last beats of Raymond's. She knew the nightmares would never stop altogether. And over the years, other nightmares had been added, other images from other cases. Now, she had Peter's memories, too. They were every bit as ugly and brutal, the type of scenes most people—thankfully—only read about in newspapers and witness in darkened theaters. It was understandable that Peter had needed to repress that horror in order to function. Ooljee suspected anyone else in those circumstances, anyone without the ability to self-induce amnesia, would be locked away in a psychiatric facility or prison.

"Lord, what do I do?" Ooljee asked.

How could she keep silent? How could she let Peter go on searching, wallowing in his personally created disability, when the knowledge she held might restore him? But there was no certainty. The knowledge was equally likely to push him beyond his emotional capacities. Peter had lost too much, been hurt too deeply as it was. Ooljee wouldn't risk doing more damage to an already tender soul.

She watched her mother sleeping hard now, the snores loud and deep, eyes rolling under closed lids, her rose-petal necklace riding the rise and fall of her chest like a surfer on the tide. Ooljee saw serenity in her mother's face and marveled at—and envied—it. She rolled her lips together and bit down.

"Keep your mouth shut, Ooljee girl," she whispered. "You cannot remind Peter of his part in his mama's death. You cannot bring up all that other stuff." She groaned and thumped her head against the chair's back. "No, ma'am, you cannot."

Clare lounged on her satin-and-lace-bedecked bed, stroking Tropicana and Sahara, trying to soothe herself as much as the felines. The home—indeed, the life—she'd worked hard to create was jeopardized. She'd done the unthinkable: with one stupid but well-intentioned act she'd driven away a guest, and not just any guest—one truly in need of her kindness and hospitality. Clare couldn't forgive herself for the distress she'd caused Peter. And she couldn't understand the new dynamics he'd brought to her inn.

A gilt-framed photo on the dresser caught Clare's attention. Smiling out from the past was a young woman she barely remembered: a youthful version of herself in a green-sequined bikini costume with a faux emerald in her navel and a peacock-feather crown atop her smooth black bun.

"We were once so young and beautiful, weren't we?" Clare asked herself and also the unseen presence that had shared her life more years than any corporeal entity. There were no known photos of Sadie Rue, or Clare would have kept a copy there on the dresser, where a sister's or mother's photo belonged. All Clare knew of Sadie's physicality were the descriptions fed to her by highly excitable guests claiming to have encountered the temptress' spirit: long yellow tresses around a cherubic yet knowing face and a curvaceous milk-white body. Sometimes she was nude, sometimes clad in white bloomers and a bustier. That didn't seem sensationalistic to Clare. She reasoned Sadie's ghost would appear in the garb—or lack thereof—she'd worn in the bordello.

Sadie was the centerpiece of the Canary Cage, and rightfully so. She fit. Her image, her story, her legacy were all tightly wrapped around the old brothel. Clare felt comfortable with the notion of the lusty ghost who left her alone to pursue the men beneath her roof. Sadie was something of a kindred soul, a wanton icon few could understand. But Clare understood. All too well. Fifteen years spent on the Vegas strip, in both high-end forums and gritty dives, had seen to that. As a high-school dropout on the streets of Boulder City, she'd had no options. That's what a visitor with gold neck chains had told her as he ogled her 38-inch bustline and Helen of Troy face.

"You'll make money for both of us," he'd vowed before bundling her off to the burgeoning playground of gambling, games, gangsters, and quick nuptials.

As promised, he provided her with money but also many unwanted extras. A few years into the life, and Clare felt too sullied to ever amount to, or deserve, more. But then she'd caught the eye of a major casino owner, and her luck changed. She moved up as Las Vegas expanded, producing a wealth of shows that demanded gifted lovelies. Her exotic beauty and a real talent for dance and song elevated her to the choruses of big-name programs. She even found love—twice—but both marriages ended badly. Her first husband was Freddy Fluegel, a cook who scraped together enough to finally buy a decent little steakhouse in Vegas and was killed shortly thereafter in an after-hours robbery. Next came a financier, who afforded her a sumptuous lifestyle and enjoyable companionship until she caught him in their bed with his secretary, a bar hostess, and a vat of hot wax. She ditched him on the spot. After a decade and a half of chin-high kicks, she'd made a sufficient stash of money—including a whopping settlement from husband #2—but Clare was emotionally emaciated and physically worn. She'd had enough of 20-pound headdresses, glue-on pasties that left her nipples raw, and parading around in G-strings and high-heels while she was having menstrual cramps. And she'd had enough of trying to find a sense of belonging in a town too fast and flashy to offer anything that felt like "home."

A 2" black-and-white ad in the *Southwest Realty Guide* changed her life and set her on the road for Prosperity and the Canary Cage. When the realtor toured her through the broken-down cathouse and told her the tragic story of Sadie Rue, Clare knew she was home. Many a time, she'd shepherded young showgirls through the dangers of Vegas life, telling them who and where to avoid, letting them sleep at her place, nursing them through the lows, and celebrating their successes. In a way, Clare saw herself as a madam, not as a purveyor of sex, but as a housemother to the desperate and ill-used. *How perfect!* she thought when she signed the papers turning over the old brothel and its legacy to her care.

Sadie Rue was Clare's welcome charge, or maybe vice versa, but this new spirit was another matter. Clare didn't know Martin's story, and there was great discomfort in that ignorance. PIP had extensively documented activity at the inn and reported that only Sadie resided in the temporal plane spanning the Canary Cage and the great beyond. However, Clive had warned that Sadie's potent energy, and that of her curious human suitors, could draw other energy to the site. "Be careful not to court negative forces," he'd said. "Avoid the occult—no séances, no Ouija Boards, no magic. Sadie isn't a malevolent spirit, but they exist and slip in where guards are let down."

Clare felt a shudder run through her body as she ruminated on Clive's words.

"Why's this boy here? Why not my Freddy?" she asked the air.

Her first husband had died a violent death, something that seemed to guarantee ghost-hood, but Clare had never felt his presence. Long ago, when spectral accounts first began trickling in from guests, she'd hoped someone would report a short man with dark fringe around a pattern-bald pate. No one ever did, and Clare accepted that her first husband hadn't tagged along on her move to Prosperity.

As Clare remembered Freddy—big-mouthed and big-hearted, eager to test his best recipes on her—her fearful uncertainty morphed into fearful loneliness. Queen of the Resurrectors or not, she felt forgotten and inconsequential and, worst of all, unloved by any living being except her cats.

Clare jumped at the unexpected ringing of her private phone. Tropicana and Sahara perked up their ears and made a chattering response to the rarely-used white 1970s Trimline.

Smoothing down her hair, as if her caller was able to see her, Clare sat up and gracefully took the receiver. "Clare Bowers speaking," she answered, her face sparking a smile as she recognized the voice on the other end. "My goodness, Clive, it's been ages since anyone addressed me as 'fair maiden.' I'm doing well, thank you. And yourself?"

Leaning into the pink satin pillows piled against her headboard, she playfully curled a finger through the coils of the phone cord and giggled with delight at Clive's flattering words. The ungainly young man's recent attentions were welcomed. Clare recognized the dreamy look in his eyes when he saw her and the way his words came quicker and more excitedly when they spoke. It had been years since she'd witnessed those symptoms, but the signs of attraction were apparent. And not only for Clive. Just the sound of his voice made Clare feel happy. Knowing he was connected to her through that telephone line gave her courage.

"I'm so glad you called," she murmured.

Love is strong as death; jealousy is cruel as the grave.

— "The Song of Solomon"

PART III: A CLEARING VISION

Journal of Yee Chang
May 24, 1953

This is my first sober night in a week, and I feel like hell. Writing has not eased my conscience, as I thought it might. I find myself becoming angrier with who I am. Last night, I beat Xu for refusing me the last of the gin. I struck her twice. The second time knocked her down. One of her front teeth popped out onto the floor, and she grabbed it and tucked it into her brassiere like a valuable she wanted to keep safe near her heart. It looked so foolish I laughed at my bleeding wife recovering the tooth I pounded from her head. I was ashamed but did not apologize. I bruised my knuckles, so I went for ice. When I opened the freezer, Lloyd jumped on my back and tried to fight me. That scrawny flea called his own father a "lousy bastard" and told me if I ever hurt his mother again he would kill me. I always knew my son had pluck. He is nothing like me.

Xu and Lloyd are with Rosemae. Xu probably expects me to come for her. I will not. Rosemae would not let me near them anyway. Xu will have to argue with her and escape that house.

Rosemae's is a dead place. When I look up the hill at it, I think of saucy old Pearline Graham who fought for my brother and died two years after he did. She never was right after the beating his lynch mob gave her. Damn every one of them.

That oak. It used to be a pretty sight, so elegant and tall, shading the side of the hill. It is still high and green, but now it is ugly. It is a gallows and Wei's marker, not that engraved stone slab in the Prosperity Cemetery. I have not seen that tombstone up close in decades. I have not been to the cemetery since Sadie was interred. The gates are locked anyway, the place neglected. There is not room for a single corpse more within the rocky necropolis. So, the remains of my brothers, Ting, and Yin will rest away from my body. They are together, apart from me forever, and that is apt.

I sometimes wonder where I will go when I die. My body will end up in McBrideville Memorial Gardens, where every dead Prosperityite since 1930 has been planted, but what will become of my spirit? I know there is a Heaven, but is there a Hell?

Will anyone mourn me? Maybe Xu if she outlives me, but not Rosemae, not Lloyd. My son has changed since I told him my secret. I saw whatever warm bond we had slip loose when I confessed. Now he looks at me like a stranger. I know that I have lost him forever. As surely as I pushed George from me, I have also driven away Lloyd. George joined the army and died in Korea trying to get close to me. My acceptance is what he wanted. Lloyd only wants to put distance between us.

I am a miserable father and husband. But Xu will forgive me. She always does. In a few days, she will crawl back here and apologize for being a bad wife. She will swear to make a stronger effort to please me. And I will look bothered by the request and, after pretending to consider the matter carefully, take her back.

Lloyd may live under my roof again, but he will never come back to me. When he sees my face, he will remember his mother kneeling on the floor with a bloody mouth and a hole in her gums, searching for her tooth; he will hear the smacking sound of my fist against her face and her wounded yip like a kicked dog. And he will remember what I told him about the old days and what I did to so many, those things which were much worse than anything I have done to Xu.

CHAPTER 16

Seamus' homecoming had unfolded as Mae requested, and while Afton's connection to her brother was strengthened, her relationship with herself needed work. She had a gut feeling about how to begin the improvement process. It involved a trip to Santa Rita, a shady piece of heaven, laced by roads lined with dark-barked pecan trees and peach orchards. Afton had been through the town a few times, but she wasn't well acquainted with it, preferring, as all Prosperityites did, to frequent the larger and closer McBrideville for groceries and supplies.

Slowing at the approach of every far-spaced road sign, she peered from under the sun visor and read aloud the white words on brown metal backgrounds: Buckskin, Bay, Chestnut.

"Palomino!" she rejoiced.

She turned off the main thoroughfare and idled her Honda by a pasture on which two paint horses grazed. Referring to the printed White Pages listing folded in her cup holder, she reread the address for "Schrader, MZ": 1301 Palomino Dr.

"1301, 1301," she repeated, driving away.

Small adobe houses sat on acreage containing livestock pens and corrals, lush flora, and toy-speckled play areas. The neglected street—riddled with potholes and worn to a blindingly silver patina—stretched into a copse of lofty cottonwoods. A metal mailbox, flag up, marked 1301. Afton drove a few yards into the driveway and parked, mindful of pushing too far into uncharted territory. She sat in the car, clinging to the steering wheel.

"Don't be a wimp. Go on," she nagged herself.

She opened the car door. A wave of nausea hit, but she steadied herself against it, riding out the sickening feeling and stepping from the blue Civic.

A white leghorn rooster and his hen harem strutted in from the yard's hinterlands, clucking curiously at Afton while keeping a respectable distance, and an old heeler bitch lounged in the shade, indifferently raising her head, then lowering it without a growl. Afton noticed the simple particulars of the place as she walked toward the door: a basketball hoop hanging over the carport; a two-tone Chevy pickup almost as old as she was; a teeter-totter; and a sandbox holding a plastic pail and scoop and a half-buried Barbie doll with crudely chopped hair. It didn't appear to be a home destroyed by sorrow. Life continued on here, at least to the eyes of an outsider.

Standing on the front step—a tight cement semicircle—Afton held her hand up, ready to knock.

"Can I help you?"

Startled, Afton swung around, toppling herself from the step onto the lawn, where she faced a middle-aged woman too old to be her contemporary and too young to be motherly to her. The woman had short, honeyed hair and the kind of rosy, mottled tan that comes from working outdoors. Large, dimpled limbs protruded from the sleeveless armholes of a red-checked blouse, the biceps jiggling freely as the woman reached out to steady Afton.

"Didn't mean to sneak up on you. I was in the barn, and I heard your car motor." The woman didn't smile, but there was something friendly in her manner.

"Please don't apologize. I'm the trespasser."

The woman didn't correct Afton, intimating that she was a trespasser, but one who would be tolerated.

"I'm trying to find Martin Schrader's mother."

The rural woman lost her good nature. "I'm not talking to any more reporters. Why can't you leave us alone?" she disgustedly spouted as she walked back to the barn.

"Wait!" Afton yelled. "I met your son the night he died."

Mrs. Schrader came to a quick stop, her shaky hands locked together against her abdomen, holding her stomach like a seasick sailor fighting to keep down his breakfast. After a while, she pivoted back, and her hands slid apart, reaching out in a subtle, plaintive plea. "Are you telling me the truth?"

Afton could see the emotional weariness in the woman's features. Though Afton had never viewed her before, she guessed that the haggard droops of flesh beneath her eyes, at the corners of her mouth, at the curves of her jaw, were accentuated by a recent hurt too great to be contained. It had seeped through, a watermark, a warning to others that the soul inside the physical matrix couldn't withstand much more.

"My name's Afton Burnside."

"Afton Burnside." The woman repeated the name, checking it for familiarity. It had none. She guardedly returned to her unsolicited guest.

"I'm Emma Schrader. If you knew Marty, then you're welcome in my home." She passed Afton, opening the door for her.

The women stiffly settled into separate ends of a plaid sofa—the only living room seating not covered by magazines or toys.

"Would you like some water or pop?"

"No, thanks." Afton's eyes twitched around the room, setting down first on a school portrait of Martin by a vase of yellow gladiola spikes and next on a photo of him in an orange baseball uniform, number 10. Other framed pictures—the room looked like a shrine—took him from infancy to high school. Martin was everywhere, grinning without front teeth, striking a "tough man" pose, riding a bike, wearing a tuxedo and holding a girl in a pink gown and orchid wrist corsage.

"He was a fine-looking boy," Afton said, grappling to find the right beginning for her confession.

"Thank you. Marty was my oldest." She flicked a finger, edged with a stubby nail, at a large family portrait that hung over the television set. "That's the whole family. My husband, Martin Sr.; myself; Sara—she's eight; Marty; and Tricia, 11. I have three…" Emma looked away from the portrait, mortified by her mistake. "I'm sorry. I mean, I had three children. It's just Sara and Tricia now. They're at school. Martin's at work. He's the manager at El Rancho Mexican Restaurant. Course, he has a full-time job here with our farm, too." The woman jabbered uneasily. After a sobering moment of reflection, she asked, "You said you met Marty the night he died?" Emma blinked hard, her voice going dim. "I don't know much about what happened in his final hours. No one seems to know…or they won't tell me."

Afton thought through the possible responses and decided it was least cruel to be upfront. Swallowing her fears, she clenched her fists, pushing them hard into the sofa's cushions. Her eyes shut tight, holding in tears and holding back the sight of her victim's mourning mother.

"Mrs. Schrader—Emma—my brother and I own the Ghostly Grill in Prosperity. Your son came in for a drink last Friday. My brother served him a rum and cola…really, only half and then a glass of water. I remember Martin well because he threw up on the floor. I told him to go home and tried to find someone to drive him, but he left when I wasn't looking. I swear, my brother checked his ID. It said he was Jerry O'Neil, 23. We both suspected that wasn't true, but we didn't hassle him about it. I'm so sorry. I just wanted you to know how sorry we both are."

Afton's lips pressed together, stemming the sobs and screams she wanted so desperately to release. She felt herself closing down, her emotions caving in. As if blood and life were draining away, she felt smaller and smaller, less worthy of existence with every erratic drink of air. Then, she was stilled by the touch of a hand caressing her own, lifting it up from the deep depression she'd punched into a couch cushion. She opened her eyes.

"You must hate me."

Emma patted her hand. "Course I don't hate you. Young lady, you and your brother didn't kill my son."

Afton kept talking, holding up her end of the debate. "I haven't been to the grill since…I don't ever want to go back."

"It's alright. Shh. It's alright." Emma pulled Afton against her and rubbed her calloused hands over her cheeks, spreading the tears back with her thumbs. "I don't blame anyone but myself."

Afton calmed as amazement shrouded her senses. Neither fury nor sorrow was expressed in Mrs. Schrader's manner. Afton's declaration of guilt had apparently made no impression. This wasn't the reaction she'd anticipated. "If he hadn't come into my bar, he'd still be alive," she countered.

Emma stood and ambled over to a whitewashed bookcase, making a quick search, and taking down two photographs. "Here," she said, displaying a wallet-sized portrait of Martin smiling, proudly holding a baseball trophy. "This was my son two years ago." The other photo was dangled before Afton. "This was my son last month." The 3" x 5" image from a disposable camera showed a scowling teen with unkempt shoulder-length hair and baggy clothing slouched against a tree, trying to hide between his sisters.

"He looks different." Afton stated the obvious after comparing the clean-cut baseball player to the grungy kid she remembered.

"Marty *was* different. I don't know what happened to him. He used to be a fun-loving boy. He was never the most popular kid in school, but he had friends. He dated. Got good grades. People liked him. He won the Team Spirit Award his sophomore year. Marty would do anything for his buddies. He liked to make them laugh." A smile snuck onto Emma's mouth. "He told the corniest jokes, but you had to laugh because you were happy just to watch Marty's face light up."

"Sounds like a great kid," Afton said, her body occasionally seizing in a vestigial weeping-induced hiccup.

"He was," Emma agreed, replacing the photos on the bookcase and returning to the couch. "But something went wrong. Last fall, I took him to the doctor. Mono was going around at the time. I thought he had it. But the doctor couldn't find anything. Marty wouldn't eat much, didn't have any energy, either slept all night and day or didn't sleep for days in a row. He'd lock himself in his room and play this dreadful, loud music, or sit by the pond for hours, and if you tried to join him, he'd get up and walk away. He stopped talking to me and his dad." Emma touched the rim of one eye with a thumb pad. "That hurt the most. We were always close."

"I'm so sorry," Afton said.

"I took him back to the doctor in December, and he sent us to a psychiatrist in McBrideville. He diagnosed Marty with severe depression. Gave him counseling twice a week. Then put him on—oh, I don't know how many drugs, but they never much helped. Up until the end, Dr. Williams kept readjusting his meds, trying to find the right combo and doses. Nothing worked. The talk therapy didn't help either, but Marty kept going…for me and my husband's sake." Emma sniffed back a heavy stream of mucus. "Dr. Williams said he had to honor his patients' confidentiality but came right out and told Martin Sr. and me that Marty wouldn't talk to him about what mattered, just small things about school and our farm. The doctor wasn't getting nowhere, but he kept trying."

Afton eagerly followed every word, though she didn't comprehend why Emma shared the sensitive information so freely. Instead of feeling honored, Afton felt guiltier, more unforgiving of herself, unworthy of knowing the personal history—and emotional idiosyncrasies—of a young man in whose death she was complicit.

Emma leveled her eyes at Afton, her voice tumbling forth authoritatively. "What I'm telling you is that, with all the medication in his system, Marty knew he wasn't supposed to drink and never had anything stronger than colas—never, that I know of—until last Friday. I don't know what happened to him that day. He was supposed to go on a team trip to Flagstaff. I don't know why he stole the coach's SUV; Coach Jensen always did right by Marty, even to the end. Did you know he didn't report his Blazer stolen because he didn't want Marty to have a record? I was waiting for my boy here. Had his suitcase packed and was ready to drive him and his buddy, Tyler, up north. Swear I don't know where I went wrong." Emma stared questioningly into space.

"It wasn't you," Afton reassured. "Sounds like Martin got sick, and no one could help him."

"You're right. He did get sick, real bad. I don't think he could fight it anymore. I think that's why he went to your place." Her eyes penetrated Afton's with a lamentable wisdom. "Marty knew what he was doing when he took that drink. I don't think he ever intended to come home. My son may have died last Friday night, but I lost him almost a year ago."

"You must be Coach Jensen."

The man stooped over a desk in the basement office looked up and gave an immediate smile. "That's right." He was bronzed and toned and oozing masculinity, the broad-shouldered athletic sort custom-made for teaching strapping youths the nuances of team sports.

"I'm Afton Burnside. I just came from the Schraders' residence. I gave my sympathies to Martin's mom, and I wanted to do the same here."

The glow from the coach's computer screen reflected perplexity in his pale blue eyes. "Are you a parent?" he asked, though he was certain he knew the families of all Santa Rita High School students.

"No, but I know that Martin took your Blazer and wrecked it. I feel partially responsible for that."

The muscular man motioned toward a flimsy vinyl chair that was crammed between the end of his desk and a filing cabinet peeling metallic gray paint. Afton took the seat and went straight into an apology, applying almost exactly the same tack she'd used with Emma Schrader. The litany wasn't meaningless, just easier to come by because it had been recited before and was fresh in her memory.

After relaying her encounter with Martin—from cleaning up his vomit to him leaving while she searched for someone to drive him home—Afton insecurely wriggled in the chair and croaked, "You know what happened next."

The coach drew a distressed breath. "Yeah, I know."

He raised a raw-knuckled hand and strafed his dark hair, rubbed his neck, then his eyes, fatigued by memories his company stirred. "Marty was one of those outstanding kids: respectful, honest, hard-working, smart. A real team player. He had something extra-special about him. I was privileged to have coached him." He sank back in his chair, and Afton sensed a qualifying statement coming on. "This last year, health problems kept Marty from basketball and wrestling, but his parents pushed him to keep up with baseball. That was Marty's first love. I have to give him credit; he was struggling, but he never let the team down."

"You and Martin must have been good friends."

"I thought so."

"It seems to me that Marty was a good kid, just troubled. I want you to understand that I accept responsibility for contributing to his death. I'm giving up my liquor license so nothing like that happens again." Afton tried to segue into a related act of contrition. "I'm also sorry for what happened to your Blazer. I'd like to help pay to replace it."

"My Blazer? Who cares about that? It was just some metal and a motor," Coach Jensen reflected. "I only wish I knew why Marty stole it. He'd driven it before. After he got his license and was working as my student assistant, I let him use it to run errands for me. That day, I gave him $20 and asked him to go to the mini-mart and pick up some Gatorade and chips for my drive to Flagstaff, and I told him to get something for himself and his mom and Tyler Cawes, too. Mrs. Schrader was giving Marty and Tyler a ride to the camp, like she did last year."

The man took a glass baseball-shaped paperweight from one corner of his desk and twirled the object in his hands, gazing at it intently. "Every year, my assistant coach and I rent a few cabins by a lake, and we hang out with the team for the weekend. Joking around a bonfire, swimming in the lake…it's a good way to blow off steam at the end of the year and a chance for me to show my players how much I appreciate them. The boys seem to like it, and it makes them tighter as a team. I thought Marty was looking forward to going back to Flagstaff, but he took my $20 and my Blazer and blew town. Left his mom and Tyler high and dry, too. I can't understand why. Guess he just got confused. His last season wasn't his best in any way, if you take my meaning. But I'm trying not to remember him like that. I want to remember the boy who loved to get out on the field and play the game and then share a few laughs with his teammates. Unfortunately, that kid was missing a long time before last Friday."

The air conditioning unit kicked on, rattling the bare ducts and metal framework overhead and creating a deafening hum. There was no point in prolonging the encounter.

"I should go." Afton wincingly raised her voice to what she felt was a disrespectful level. "Thanks for your time. Again, I'm very sorry."

Coach Jensen nodded and crouched over his desk, mindlessly caressing the paperweight in his hands. Gone was the genial man who'd greeted her. Afton thought Emma Schrader had taken her visit far better. At least she'd seemed touched, fortified perhaps. But not the coach. For him, Afton's visit had touched off a bout of deep mourning. Apparently, Mark Jensen had lost one hell of a team player. Maybe more.

CHAPTER 17

The bedroom blinds were tilted up in the sterile condo, splaying stripes of morning light across the ceiling. Peter opened his eyes and, for a brief moment, thought the past week was a dream. Then his mind adjusted to reality, and his stomach tangled into a queasy knot.

The previous night had produced several "mini" dreams framed around death, the last being the most terrifying. At 4:10 a.m., Peter had awakened with a start. He'd dreamed of a cadaver floating over his bed—a woman in a blood-spattered white gown, a knife-type object protruding from her chest, a plumed headband wrapped around her cottony hair. The skin of her grinning face blackened as if burning, the muscle and fat beneath bubbling and melting onto his bare chest, searing right through him. Her blood-shot eyes studied Peter until they shriveled into raisin-like beads. The dead were watching him.

"Pull yourself together," was his mantra as he forced himself into his morning routine: shower, cereal, dress, drive.

Peter slunk through Grand Canyon Hospital's doors without notice. He unlocked his office and stood in the entrance, thumbing through mail that was stacked in his inbox like the Leaning Tower of Pisa. Shutting the door behind him, he worked—rather, remained at work—for eight-and-a-half hours, dredging through e-mails that had accumulated in his absence and rifling the papers on his desk, while thinking of prostitute ghosts and dead boys. He yanked at his gray silk tie and rolled up his sleeves, unable to get comfortable in the windowless interior office and, more importantly, unable to find comfort in himself.

The next day at work was the same, an exercise in meaninglessness. That night, the dreams were more numerous and frightening than ever. In the early morning hours, Peter's neighbor called the police when she heard him scream.

He awoke to the buzz of his telephone.

Fumbling for the bedside device, he grabbed the receiver and set it against his sweaty ear. "Hello?"

"Peter, this is Mae Bennally."

Peter was quiet as the woman continued talking. His mind sliced through sleepy fog and the terror of his nighttime episodes, trying to fit a persona to that familiar name.

"Did you have bad dreams?"

Peter gave no answer. The shock of his nightmares was matched by the uncanny inquiry.

"I know you did. I've had them, too."

Mae didn't have much time to get her message across, so she went on, as Peter held his astonished silence.

"Come back to Prosperity, Peter. Come to me. You need to know what's happening to you."

There was a knock at the door—not a light, polite rapping, but serious pounding.

"I...I have to go, Miss Bennally," Peter said, letting the phone slide from his hand as he left his bed and, stupefied, stepped into the hall, through the living room, toward the front door.

Another series of hard poundings began just before Peter opened the door, disrupting it. Clad in only a pair of plaid boxers, Peter stood—unaware of his semi-nude state—before a large, uniformed police officer.

At the end of a stripe of green lawn, parked along the curb, was a cruiser with its front windows open, another officer propped nonchalantly against the hood, speaking with the neighbor who'd dialed 9-1-1 to report the scream. The car's blinding lights and the loud dispatch noises coming from the front console were stirring curious residents, who peeked out windows or leaned out doors trying to learn what was happening in their corner of the world.

Embarrassed, Peter introduced himself and invited the officer into his home and then, realizing his state of undress, excused himself long enough to slip into a gray T-shirt and a pair of loafers.

"That's better." Chagrined, Peter re-entered the living room and sat across from Officer Cobbs, a leathery man whose age and demeanor implied that he'd spent more than a few years on the force.

"Everything okay here? Your neighbor heard a man screaming. Was that you?"

Peter recalled the brutal details of one of his nightmares: he was burning alive, rolling on the floor next to a flaming corpse. In the dream, he'd tried to call out, but each time he opened his mouth, he sucked in smoke and fire. He guessed that the screams he'd tried to make in his vision had emerged successfully in the waking world.

"I'm sorry about that. I had a bad dream."

"Uh-huh," the policeman grunted.

The front door opened without a knock, and in came the second officer, a 30ish Latina, who summoned Cobbs with a subtle lift of her chin.

"Excuse me a minute," he said as he joined his partner near the door for a short, whispered conversation. When their consultation was done, the officer returned to Peter; the other cop exited the front door.

"You live alone here?"

"Yes, sir," Peter answered, wounded by having to justify his reaction to a night terror. He imagined both cops and his neighbors would have shrieked themselves hoarse, too, if they'd experienced his vision.

Officer Cobbs promptly rattled off intrusive questions about Peter's private life, mental health, use of drugs and alcohol, and the stressors at his work and home. After the grilling, he asked if he could walk through the apartment. With Peter's permission, the man strode through each room, casting a critical eye on every sterile corner and into every neatly organized closet. Begrudgingly, after a thorough canvassing, he retreated to the front door.

"Take this, sir. They have people on the phones 24 hours a day," he said, handing Peter a card for the mental health division of the city's social services department. "There are people who care," Officer Cobbs added, his distrustful face suggesting that he wasn't one of them. With a tip of his head, he was gone.

The entire night had been hellish, with the police inspection a wholly unexpected indignity. To make matters worse, Peter felt the need to go outside and apologize for the disturbance to a ring of gossiping neighbors in bathrobes.

Returning indoors, he dragged himself to the kitchen for a drink of water and stood at the sink, hands braced on the counter. Caught between total depletion and the fear of sleep, he decided to sit on the couch a while. He turned off the lights and shambled across the cool slate-gray tiles. As he passed his bedroom door, his head swung right, his eyes flying up. He jumped back, swallowing the beginning of a yell. Only for a second, Peter thought he saw someone suspended from his ceiling fan, silhouetted against the moonlight that leaked in through the blinds. He couldn't see the features, only a shadowed body and a head flopping from a crooked neck. He ducked in and slapped at the light switch. When the bulb on the fan lit up, there was nothing beneath it.

"Wha...?" Peter panted, raising the heel of one hand to his forehead, trying to hold back a swelling headache.

A quavering thumb flipped the light switch down, and Peter guardedly returned to the couch, where he remained, eyelids thick but open, until morning.

Friday was the worst day yet. Peter locked himself in his office, avoiding all human contact. He didn't answer his phone the two times it rang. He didn't answer any e-mails. He didn't do any work. He spent hour upon hour surfing the web, learning anything he could about Prosperity's storied past. He also pulled up Martin Schrader's online obituary in the *Verde Valley Trumpet*. That led to a morbid romp through every news piece he could find on the boy's sad little crime spree and death.

At 5:55 p.m., Peter typed a succinct resignation letter, printed it, slipped it into an envelope, turned off his computer, and locked his office without looking back—there were no personal artifacts to collect and few good memories. He took the letter to the Human Resources office and, without explanation, handed it, along with his keys, to the lone employee at the counter.

Night was just beginning, with the first few stars appearing in a cloudless indigo sky over the Prosperity Community Center. Boyd whooped like a howler monkey while Seamus threw his hands into the air— two heavy duffel bags of ghost-hunting gear slung over each shoulder—and yowled, "Finally!"

Walking 10 paces behind and hunched under the weight of a battery-laden backpack, Clive made a reluctant Igor. "Wait until Mr. Chang hears of this," he warned.

"Come on, man, don't ruin this for us," Seamus groaned. "We're doing our duty. The front receptionist requested this investigation because last night was so active Roy Pervis quit. Roy Pervis, man! You know it had to be wild for him to leave!"

The left side of Clive's mouth twitched nervously. "What do you suppose happened?"

Seamus and Boyd craned their necks, looking up at four floors of limestone brick and darkened windows beneath a red tile roof. The magnitude of the assignment struck them.

"And we thought the Canary Cage was big," Boyd observed with a whistle, as he led Seamus up the steps. "We can't cover this all in one night, but we'll give it everything we've got."

Clive, who remained entrenched in the parking lot gravel, hadn't gotten past the news about Roy Pervis. "You don't suppose Roy was physically assaulted by an entity, do you?" he squeaked. "With all the suffering this building has held, I'd wager a bob there's at least one demon inside."

"Would you man the hell up?" Boyd snarled. A ring of master keys dangled from an elasticized cord on his wrist. He selected a big bronze number with a square head; as he slid it into the right-side door, he felt the thrill associated with doing something long anticipated and forbidden. "No going back now," he said, twisting the key until he heard a "click."

The door popped open, creaking slowly back, exposing the foyer's worn marble tiles.

"Cripes, so we're really doing this?" Clive bleated, standing on tiptoe and peering into the gloomy lobby. This was a conundrum for a man who desperately wanted to plumb the depths of the center's mysteries yet was rendered nearly impotent by the investigation's fear factor.

The trio entered, Boyd at the lead, Clive bringing up the rear by several yards. A single security light provided dim illumination throughout the lobby, down the main hall, and into the post office. Darkness would have been less eerie than the faint silver-blue light that cast exaggerated shadows on the walls and chiseled the investigators' faces into macabre masks.

"It looks weird in here without employees and overhead lights," Boyd noted, perusing the lobby, gaining his bearings. "Let's get some baseline readings and then set up the cameras."

Seamus sloughed the duffel bags off his shoulders, unzipped one, and pulled out some papers. "Here, Clive. Since we aren't as familiar with this place as Boyd, I printed out copies of the floor plan for each level. The Xs are where Boyd thinks the cameras should go. The areas marked 'EVP' are where...Clive?"

"Huh?" Clive swiveled around and looked questioningly at the papers in Seamus' outstretched hand.

"Did you hear anything I said?"

"What? Wait, did you hear that?" Clive's eyes bulged. A trembling hand aimed toward the hall. "Back there somewhere."

"I didn't hear anything," Seamus said.

"I did. Sounded like voices," Boyd admitted, holding a finger to his lips. He grabbed a flashlight from his gear sack, flicked it on, and fearlessly headed down the hall.

Seamus paused to prepare for data collection. Squatting by the bags, he began rapidly removing equipment. "Clive, take some of this," he ordered, producing a digital camera, an EMF meter, an ambient thermometer, and a Sony video camera with Night Shot. "We need to document whatever we encounter. Start taking readings, photos, whatever, as soon as you can."

Clive grabbed the digital camera and the EMF meter and kept close enough to Seamus to be his shadow. They caught up with Boyd, who was poised outside the closed door to the auditorium, selecting the appropriate key from his stash.

"It's coming from there," Boyd whispered. "I heard something like a child's laugh but muffled. Then—I'm not making this up—I heard a woman say either, 'in here' or 'we're here.'"

Clive pled, "Please be joking."

"The temp is holding at 78," Seamus stated. When he saw that Clive was disregarding the equipment in his hand, he leaned over and read off, "The EMF is .5. Things seem normal, but of course I don't really know what normal is here."

"When we open the door, things may change. I don't know what we'll experience in there—maybe nothing—but be prepared just in case." Boyd turned off his flashlight and tucked it into his hip pocket, not wanting the singular beam of light to interfere with photographing or filming. He wrapped his fingers around the levered handle and turned the key. "Ready?" he asked.

Seamus set the video camera on record. "Ready."

Shivering, Clive raised the digital camera.

One deep breath, and Boyd pressed down on the lever and pushed in the door.

The men stared into the cavernous, pitch black auditorium. It didn't have the typical stagnant mood of a vacant room. In the darkness, shapes moved about, like shadows against a midnight sky.

"What the..." Seamus mumbled, pressing inside, keeping the video camera aimed straight ahead.

As he walked in, the lights flicked on and 79 people sprang to their feet, shouting, "Surprise!"

Clive screamed, holding a soprano's note, and spasmed from head to toe, triggering the camera, its bright flash blinding the crowd. As they roiled in discomfort, rubbing their eyes, Clive stumbled backwards out of the room, did an about face, dashed down the hall, and exited the building in a flying leap. He skittered along, skinny legs pinwheeling, even after the reality of the situation sank in.

Boyd pored over the familiar faces: his grandfather, Clare, Ooljee, Sam Alvarez, ZuZu Lorenz, Ivan Raleigh—good grief, a clean-shaven Roy Pervis in a Budweiser tie!—and other residents of Prosperity, young, old, and in between. There were even two former classmates in attendance: Harry Dukapoo and Jim Stanley, who'd met regularly at the Chang residence a semester earlier to study for organic chemistry tests.

Boyd stared aghast at the green and yellow streamers, the balloons, the soda cans in buckets of ice, the meeting table covered with snack foods and a white cake with "Congratulations, Boyd!" piped across its sweet, slick top in green icing.

"Oh, man, I told you," Seamus moaned, shrinking back.

"Come in here, young man!" Ooljee moved to the front of the crowd— her regal bearing lightened by a pointy, yellow party hat projecting from the left side of her head—and pulled him in with both hands. "Your grandpa got you good! He knew you'd never suspect a party here. You should've seen your face."

"But...what about poor, dear Clive?" Clare fretted.

Sam cracked, "Probably hasn't stopped running yet. Maybe he'll rejoin us after he goes home and changes his underwear."

Everyone laughed except Clare and the two remaining victims.

"I'll check on him," Seamus said, finding an excuse to leave the scene he'd warned against. If Boyd told more lies, it was going to be ugly, and if he came clean, it would be even uglier. Either way, Seamus didn't want to be a witness.

Lloyd stepped up, holding out his arms to greet his grandson. "I'm proud as can be of you, boy, and I look forward to doing this again when you get your bachelor's."

"Maybe not this exactly. I don't think you can fool Boyd twice with the same prank," Ooljee remarked.

"I barely figured out how to fool him once," Lloyd admitted, showing his full range of teeth in an explosive smile.

As they stood face to face Lloyd thought he knew the reason for Boyd's quizzical, almost despairing, expression. He figured his grandson was still coming to grips with not only the surprise party but also his grandfather arranging for him to visit the Prosperity Community Center after dark.

"Cat got your tongue, boy?" Lloyd teased.

"I'm in shock."

Lloyd had expected joy, at least enthusiasm. "Sorry I tricked you. It seemed like the only way to make this a surprise." Lloyd whispered his apology and then frowned, thinking of the risk he'd taken in allowing Boyd and the PIP gang to wander down the darkened corridor on their way to discover the partygoers. The only reason he'd given his grandson the gift of an evening in the Prosperity Community Center was because he didn't think anything would happen as long as Boyd was in a large group of merrymakers and confined to one room without an active history.

"It's okay," Boyd whispered back. He tried to loosen up and look appreciative. Plastering an affected smile on his face, he received a frosty can of Dr. Pepper—his favorite—from Ooljee.

Boyd popped the tab and took a drink. "Where's your mom? She okay?"

"She's fine, just didn't feel up to getting out tonight. She wanted me to give you this." Ooljee hugged Boyd, and then she pointed with her thumb to a table piled high with gifts. Her salmon-pink nail aligned with a big white box topped with a blue bow. "And that. It's from both of us."

"Uh, thanks. I didn't expect anybody to get me anything." Boyd was now beet red with shame.

"Why not, kiddo? This is a happy moment. Celebrate this thing! Celebrate your...oh...no..." Ooljee had stopped smiling by the time the last of her words left her mouth. She lowered her head at Boyd, finally interpreting the conflict steaming from his soul. She gave him a grievous stare. "Oh, Boyd, how could you quit and not tell your grandfather? This'll kill him."

Boyd seized on the psychic's final sentence. "You don't mean that literally, do you?"

Ooljee pursed her lips and stepped back, heartily disappointed. As she withdrew, the celebratory crowd swallowed her in a blur of smiles, goofy little party hats, plates of snack foods, and cans of soda.

A dimpled brunette in a ponytail and a white sundress emerged from the cheerful group. "Congratulations, Boyd," she said, approaching hesitantly, unsure if she'd be welcomed.

"Amy," Boyd muttered, completely caught off guard. "Uh…it's good to see you. It's been…"

"Five months since Mom and I were here on Christmas break," Amy said sheepishly, framing their last meeting in a more positive way than as the time when their relationship officially came to an end. "How've you been?"

"Okay, thanks, and you? I'm really surprised to see you. Did you drive up here just for this?"

"It's not that far. I got here in, like, an hour and a half. Lloyd was so cute when he called and told me about the party. He really is proud of you, you know."

Boyd didn't want to be reminded of that yet again. "So, how are you liking Phoenix?"

"It's a big change from Prosperity. My mom's having a hard time getting to know people."

"Sorry to hear that."

"It's hard going from a place where everybody knows everybody to a city where neighbors don't even talk to each other. I have friends at ASU, but Mom doesn't have anybody. After I graduate, I'm pretty sure she's going to move back here."

"What about you?" Boyd asked before he realized what he was saying.

Looking on the spot, Amy replied, "We'll have to see." She smiled tensely and backed away with another "Congratulations."

Lloyd moved in, and Harry and Jim approached, each one nursing a can of pop.

Jim slapped Boyd on the arm and lifted his cola in salute. "Hey, congratulations, man! I didn't know you were graduating 'til your granddad called and told me about the party."

"Yeah, didn't see you at the ceremony," Harry piped up.

"Ceremony? I didn't see you the last half of the semester. After you dropped the anthro class, I thought maybe you left. Rumor had it you dropped out of college altogether."

Boyd's eyes shifted to his grandfather, who watched the exchange with increasing confusion.

"You dropped anthropology?" Lloyd asked.

Boyd nodded, focusing on the aluminum can in his hand.

"But I talked to you on the phone right before you..." Lloyd choked down a breath as he processed the information. After a weighty pause, he asked, "Did you take that final?"

Boyd wanted to speak, to tell it all, but he couldn't form a single word. He kept looking at the can and shook his head.

Lloyd asked another question, one he hoped against hope would get a positive response. "Did you take any final?"

Chewing on his lower lip, Boyd shook his head again.

The room became clouded with awkwardness.

"Oh, sorry, man. I didn't mean to...you know," Jim repented.

Lloyd held back tears brought on by embarrassment and betrayal. "When were you going to tell me?"

By now, the room was quiet, and every face was toward the grandfather and grandson. Harry and Jim had fallen away, giving the men room for their moment of reckoning.

"I wanted to tell you. So many times, I tried to, but I...I couldn't. It never seemed right."

"And this seems right? Here, in front of all these people? At a party I arranged for your graduation?" Lloyd's lips danced. The tears he'd fought back were unleashed, and his whole face shriveled into an aggrieved mask. "I feel like a stupid old man."

Lloyd pushed himself away from Boyd, away from the crowd. His hands were shaking so much that he battled to pull open the door and free himself from the room. Slamming the door behind him, he sped away, seeking privacy while he came undone. As he stalked down the dim hall— staggering and stumbling—he became enraged. Tight fists pummeled the air. He looked up at the rafters, into the darkened recesses of the center, and shouted to the phantoms of the past that had lured his grandson away from him, away from his true love, away from his schooling, away from every other interest as far as Lloyd could tell.

"You did this! It's your fault!" he shouted into the ether, across the ages.

As his rage built, so did a pain in his chest. The man leaned on a marble pillar, finding support for his weakening body. He went dizzy as the sharp, debilitating sensation sliced into his chest and down his left arm. Lloyd grunted, fighting the unbearable agony. Without the use of his arm, he lost his hold on the column and slid down, knocking his head against the cold stone on his descent. His body lay crumpled and still until Seamus, who was wandering the halls, happened upon him.

"Mr. Chang?" The giant of a man threw himself down and urgently felt for a pulse. "Oh, Boyd, you've really done it now."

CHAPTER 18

Peter appeared unbridled, shirt collar unbuttoned, sleeves rolled up, a sweat stain marking a 'V' on his back. He didn't bother with pleasantries.

"You knew about me from the beginning, didn't you? I saw you watching me when I arrived at the Canary Cage."

"Come inside," Mae instructed, opening the screen door.

Peter slowly crossed the threshold and parlor and folded onto the sofa. Mae shuffled over to join him, lowering with the effort of one whose joints strain with every degree of bend and extension.

"I began dreaming about you around a month ago. My mind was drawn to you because you remind me of someone dear to me. Because we have the same abilities. Because I knew you'd be coming here, to Prosperity, to me.

Peter pressed on. "Why did I come here?"

"It's where you belong. You came to help and be helped."

Befuddled, Peter frowned at the woman, waiting for more.

"Tragedies and injustices fade in time, but they never really go away. They change their corner of the world forever..." Mae centered herself, breathing meditatively. "Something happened here long ago that's still affecting our town. Some people know parts of it. Some's written in a journal. But no one knows it all."

"And I can help with this?"

"You've already started gathering some of the missing pieces. You're going to help make sense of it...and what happened to Martin Schrader." Mae strummed the fringe of her shawl. "God's hand is on you, Peter. You're a special creation."

"Because I have second sight?"

"That's part of it."

"Am I a medium?" Peter guessed.

"No. Not me or Ooljee either. Someone may come to us in a dream, but…no, we're…well, our minds work different than most. We can feel what others do…or have felt…sometimes through their memories, sometimes visions. We can see pieces of the past, future, and present, pieces of other people's lives. And more." She held back for a second. "Don't you ever catch yourself knowing what other people are thinking, or influencing someone to say or do a certain thing?"

"I can't even remember my own past." Peter deflated in a hopeless sigh.

"You will. That blankness is your own doing. You put it there for a reason." Mae tilted her head, looking far into Peter. "Let me stir some memories." Fixating on the wounded boy inside, she immediately envisioned scenes from years gone by. They fluttered through her brain like a swarm of vibrant, short-lived creatures. "I see a house like a Greek temple…with a fountain in front."

"That's where I grew up," Peter said uneasily.

"There's a boy in bed. It's nighttime, but he's not asleep. He's afraid of what he sees. A soldier in a raggedy gray uniform stands in the corner, holding a rifle…he's a ghost."

Peter's mouth gaped, his eyes deepening with remembrance. "I'd forgotten about…that. He'd look past me, like he was watching something I couldn't see, and then he'd run away. Always the same."

"Like that little girl in pantaloons who'd skip down the driveway and vanish in front of you? Or the see-through man who sat on a stump by the stream sharpening an ax blade?"

Peter twisted toward Mae with fearful eyes. "How do you know all this?"

"The same way you've seen images from the past. We're alike, Peter, three of a kind counting Ooljee."

Peter listed against Mae, who hugged him.

"I know it's a lot to take in, child. But you'll understand…eventually. I can only tell you so much. Frankly, I don't know it all."

"Tell me what you can."

"Your talent's been buried a long time. You taught yourself to suppress it, kept it hidden. After a while, you forgot you had it and forgot all the things it had shown you. But deep down, it was still functioning enough to draw you here. And once you came here, where the energy of the past is thick, Prosperity jump-started your talent. It's trying to resurface."

"Why am I remembering other people's memories but not my own?"

Mae pushed Peter back so she could look him in the eyes. "Because your own experiences are what caused you to wall up your gift in the first place. You worked hard to lock it away. Why do you think you get those headaches? It's your brain rebelling against what you're doing to it. You're fighting the visions and the past with all your strength. But it's time for you to remember. The ball's rolling; you're allowing yourself to see things in dreams, when your body's dormant and your mind's open. It's only a matter of time before it starts to happen during waking hours."

Peter noticed Mae's shallow breaths. "Are you alright?"

"Mmmhmm, just not used to all this talk." She pulled in a few loads of air before saying, "I want to tell you a story. I think it may help you understand."

Mae braced herself for the tale. Her black eyes moved to the opposite wall, where a framed photo of a young, pig-tailed Ooljee smiled back at her. She wouldn't look at Peter while sharing this most private and precious story.

"There was this woman, name of Tansy Avendon, who sold herself into Mad Molly's service, along with her five-year-old son. Oh, Charles was lovely...deep brown eyes and waves of golden hair. Molly made a lot of money renting him out because girls, well, they were easy to come by, but little boys weren't.

"Plenty of bad men—and a few women—came for Charles, all ages and kinds, some seemingly respectable; you couldn't tell by looking. They did things to him..." Mae faltered, revolted by the memories. "Anything was allowed so long as it didn't mar his face...Molly charged extra if there was bruising or bloodshed."

Mae shuddered with grief, sopping up her tears with the yarns of her shawl. She never turned to face Peter, who watched her profile go from determined to defeated in an instant.

"Charles was a triumph of the human spirit. How he stayed so kind and good after everything...no one but me ever knew just how special he was..."

Peter put an arm around Mae, who reached down, grasped her necklace, and held out the pendant for Peter to see. "Charles gave me this rose. I pressed it under my mattress. Then, I kept it in my Bible, until it started to fall apart. Ooljee gathered up the pieces and took it to a jeweler and had this made for me. It's been around my neck since Mother's Day 1970."

"It's very pretty," Peter said, looking closer at the necklace he'd noticed before. "Charles must have meant a great deal to you."

"He was my kindred spirit. We were the same age, but he died at 15, and I kept going. That wonderful boy spent most of his life being hurt and degraded in the filthy rooms of the Crib District—then in Molly's private apartment—before dying to save me and this town on June 28, 1923."

Mae disintegrated into sobs, and Peter held her close until she gathered herself.

"You were 15 in 1923?"

"Yes, that was the year Molly died. Charles killed her...to set me free. He wasn't a murderer in my mind; he was a liberator. But he couldn't live with the notion of taking a life, not even one as evil as Molly's. He set fire to Sin Alley and died in the blaze, on purpose. It was his penance."

Peter thought Mae must have confused her own memories with her mother's, surely an easy thing for an empath to do. "Wasn't your mother, Rosemae, the one held captive by Mad Molly?" he gently reminded.

Mae shifted under the weight of Peter's comforting arm and answered with such authority that he couldn't doubt her. "I'm Rosemae. We're one and the same. Only Ooljee, Lloyd Chang, and now you know that. I kept the secret because I knew people would pester me about the old days, asking about Mad Molly and Wei Chang and Sadie Rue, and I didn't care to discuss any of that."

Peter gulped down his shock. "Understandable," he said.

"But the one person left out of Prosperity's lore is Charles. That boy was mistreated even in death. When people went through the ashes of the Crib District, they found two sets of remains in what had been Molly's apartment. They knew one was Molly and assumed the other was one of her henchmen—because they all disappeared after Molly's death. The sheriff and his deputy threw the bones into a mineshaft somewhere in the Sandspurs and took an oath not to tell where. Do you know how many shafts are in these mountains? To this day, both sets of bones are together, and I can't find them." Mae looked grief-stricken. "People think I'm all-seeing, but I'm just a human." She glanced aside, brows pushed firmly together, imparting hard-earned knowledge. "Someday, you'll learn that no matter how good you are, even at the height of your power, you won't be able to know everything you want to know. You'll fail. You'll be frustrated by the limits of your gift."

"I'm sorry about Charles, Miss Bennally."

Finally, Mae faced Peter. "May I?" She slipped her hands around his head, her thumbs at his temples, her fingers splayed across his scalp. "Don't be afraid, Peter."

Peter fully surrendered himself. He shut his eyelids and let the old woman latch harder onto his head, her fingers almost boring into his skull. He felt light, like air itself, and disconnected from his body, as if he was floating away. Then, his mind went blank—he saw only blackness and an explosion in the center of the darkness, and he was suddenly in another time and place. He was experiencing things as another person, seeing things through those eyes, feeling as that person had. He had no awareness of the present or his existence as Peter Jacoby.

"Were you stolen from your family?" The words were those of a girl.

He looked down at small, graceful, brown hands folded on a red skirt and black hair to either side of his face. Two bare feet kicked nervously from the edge of a sofa upholstered in opulent white brocade. He was witnessing the past from Rosemae's perspective.

The girl's shy glance rose, and the surroundings came into view, as did the person to whom she spoke. A boy in his early teens, dark blond, angelically handsome, in brown knee pants and a white shirt, sat on a padded ottoman not three feet away. He kept peeking at a closed door at the back of the room; occasional laughter and music came from the other side.

"No," the boy answered. He looked as uncomfortable with his answer as he did being so close to a girl his age.

"Why are you here?"

"My ma was one a Molly's girls afore TB done her in. She brung me with her when she come here from Tennessee." The boy peered down, then to the left, then to the right, finally aiming his wounded eyes at his companion's feet. "Is that what happened to you—you got stoled from your family?"

Rosemae emphatically jiggled her head. "I was watching my grandmother's sheep. A man grabbed me. He brought me to Prosperity on horseback and sold me to Molly for $100."

The boy looked pained by the information.

"Molly keeps me chained in an underground room. It's dirty and smells bad, and there are vermin. This is my first time outside there. This room's pretty."

"Yeah, Molly's apartment is posh. This here's the parlor. Everything in it cost a whole lot." The boy sneered at the gilded bric-a-brac and sumptuous furnishings, almost all of them pristine white. To his side was a white grand piano and, against a wall, a long table draped in white linen and set with unlit candles and silver ladles and serving spoons. He glared at the table a good long while, but when he dared to look back at the girl across from him, he smiled ever so slightly. "I'm Charles," he said. "Your name's Rosemae, right? I've heard Molly talk about you. You still got family?"

"My father is dead, but I used to live with my mother and grandmother and my brother and sisters. They don't know where I am."

"I'm sorry, Rosemae. Maybe someday you can beat it outta here and go back to your family."

"I will never go back," Rosemae answered. "I was told in a dream that this is where I must stay...always. I don't like Prosperity, but it is my home now."

"You have dreams that come true? No bull, you know things afore they happen?"

"I have visions."

"Visions. Yeah, visions. Sometimes, I have those, too. Honest, Rosemae."

The girl smiled.

"You and me, we're alike, ain't we?" Charles asked, grinning back. His lips slowly slid together, then dipped into a frown. "Those visions a mine ain't hardly ever good." The boy gave the floor a cold stare, like he was watching a tragic scene being enacted under his chin. "You never been to one a Molly's bashes, have you?"

"No."

Charles turned his distressed gaze to Rosemae. "Listen here, there'll be a bunch a gussied up people in there. Some'll act nice to you. Some'll act like you're nothing. They're all crumbs, every one, so don't trust 'em. Just do what they say and don't talk back, and it'll be over soon. I've a trick I use when they start to…do things. I think on a real pretty place. I think a everything: the color a the sky, the shapes a the clouds, the leaves on the trees, and lots a noise, maybe the rush a water or birds singing. I make up a world inside my head. Sometimes, I think I'm really there." The boy shrugged self-consciously. "It's foolish, but it helps."

"I do that, too. I imagine I'm back in my grandmother's hogan."

"We are alike." Charles gave a smile, so genuine and pure, and then let it disappear. "'Cept you're strong Rosemae. You been in the basement for…" he paused to count on his fingers, "'bout nine months. Ain't no girl never done that. Not even close. Molly only keeps girls chained up down there till they break, and then she knows they won't run away or put up a fight when she moves 'em to a crib. That don't never take longer than a month, but you been there all this time, getting yelled at and hurt bad by Molly's men, and you ain't given up. That means they can't break you. You ain't like me, ain't like the others. You got hope."

The click of an unlatching door sounded. Rosemae and Charles jerked in their seats, startled.

"'Member, do whatever they want, and go somewhere in here," Charles hurriedly whispered, knocking on his head with a soft fist.

A middle-aged snowy blond—pretty but hard edged—entered the room in a sleeveless white velveteen gown with layers of long fringe below the dropped waist. Pearls dripped from her earlobes and sat atop her wavy bob in a bejeweled headband. A long, brown cigarette burned in a holder that she held between silk-gloved fingers. Lifting the cigarette to her oxblood-red painted lips, she took a long drag and stared at the two teens.

"Okay, come on, my guests are ready for you," she said in a husky tone, swaggering back toward the door.

The scene faded and everything went black as Mae removed her fingertips from Peter's scalp and leaned away, weary, having imparted the powerful scene from her far-away past. For a brief flicker, Peter had no sense of consciousness. When he came to, he was breathless. But he retained the memory Mae had shared and held it as if it were his own.

He whispered, "That boy…Charles…I've seen him in dreams."

"I thought so."

"He reminds me of...me. I looked like that when I was a boy. What does that mean?"

"You're somehow related. Charles was from Tennessee, too. Mae narrowed her eyes at Peter. "You're even more alike. You understand?"

"Second sight?"

"Yes," Mae affirmed, though that wasn't the likeness she'd hoped Peter would recognize. "Did anything else trigger a memory?"

Peter didn't make the connection Mae wanted. "No, ma'am."

"I suppose I'm not the one to bring that out in you," Mae mused disappointedly. "At least you're one step closer."

Ever the empath, Peter was focused on Mae, not himself. "Did your family ever learn what happened to you?"

"After I was freed, Yee Chang took me in and sent word to my family. My brother and mother visited me, but my grandmother and sisters wouldn't leave Dinetah; they felt they couldn't set foot outside the People's land, just as I knew I wasn't to leave Prosperity. Now, this place is a haunted hill—no relation comes to visit. You must understand, Peter, that the dead are taboo in Diné culture. That is one reason I cannot return to my people—I keep too many ghosts' secrets."

"I see." Peter sat still for many minutes, head floating with new knowledge. Overwhelmed, he fought tears. "Miss Bennally, I don't know what to do now," he confessed.

"You're to stay here, and I'm to teach you. This is another reason you've come. It's a gift to us both."

Peter was dumfounded. Mae's proposition was at once strange and sensible.

"Many years ago, Ooljee came to me hurting and alone and unable to make sense of what her mind was capable of. I taught her to develop her abilities and understand herself. I'm going to do the same with you."

"What will Ooljee say?"

Mae placed a soft palm against Peter's unshaven cheek and smiled. "She's going to help me teach you what an amazing man Peter Jacoby is."

He sniffed, rubbing a fist at his nose. "Thank you," he whispered as he broke down, crying. He couldn't comprehend what was happening, but it finally felt right. It felt good. He believed in the tiny woman in the lavender shawl.

Mae's small fingers gripped Peter's arms and slid down to encompass his hands. "Ya'at'eeh shíye'. You're home, Peter. Things will be different. Now, you are my son."

Boyd awoke with a yawn and stretch and recoiled as he felt a crick seize his neck. He gingerly looked around and saw Seamus and Clive standing at a vending machine discussing how best to spend their collective $1.75: a two-pack of peanut butter cookies or a Texas-sized cinnamon roll. They'd narrowed down the options based on which products had the most mass.

"Our lad's awake," Clive crowed, noticing Boyd's stirrings.

Seamus hollered across the waiting room, "What sounds better: a cinnamon roll or cookies—the soft, chewy kind?"

"I don't care," Boyd apathetically answered.

"It's only until the cafeteria opens. Then I can use my debit card to get us some real food," Seamus explained.

Boyd curled up as if to sleep again, mindful of his neck. "I'm not hungry."

"Come on, man, you gotta eat. You've been here all night, and you've had nada. Didn't touch the corn chips or cupcakes we got you. You gotta keep up your strength."

"I have a better chance of keeping up my strength by not eating that crap."

Seamus strolled over to the horseshoe-shaped arrangement of furniture where Boyd rested, stopping along the way to review a map of the hospital's emergency escape routes. It had been almost six hours since he'd dashed to McBrideville Memorial Hospital on his motorcycle, stopping to collect Clive, and following the ambulance that ferried Lloyd and his frantic grandson to the emergency room. In the ensuing hours, he and Clive had mostly stayed silent except for offering occasional words of support to Boyd or talking about mindless subjects. It was enough for Boyd that his friends were there. That spoke volumes.

Clive put his money into the machine and selected the double-pack of cookies. He hungrily retrieved the treats and scanned the packaging as he joined Seamus and Boyd in the seating area. "I say, these have 10% of the RDA of iron and 6 grams of protein. They're practically health food." Tearing open the pouch, he slid out the cookies and gave one to Seamus.

"Sure you don't want one?" Seamus offered Boyd, who pulled himself upright and began gently turning his rusty neck in a therapeutic side-to-side motion.

Boyd made a sickened expression and shook his head, as if refusing a cow patty.

The widescreen television mounted high up in the corner of the room played CNN. The volume was below an audible level. Talking heads and remote reporters flashed on and off the screen, moving their mouths without actually imparting any news.

"I wish we could change the channel and turn that thing up," Seamus groused, consuming three-quarters of his gigantic cookie with one bite and quickly crumbling the rest into his mouth.

Clive nibbled genteelly on his snack. "You're tall enough, ol' chap. Give it a try."

Seamus peeped all around. There was no one in sight, but every so often someone in a medical uniform would walk hastily down an adjoining hall, either emerging from or disappearing into a set of automated swinging doors.

"I don't know. Maybe they want it left like that. I don't want to piss anybody off."

Clive chuckled. "Seamus, my boy, you look like a Viking warlord. Who's going to harass you?"

No sooner did Seamus stand than the double doors opened amid a mechanical hum, and a goateed man in a blue surgical cap and scrubs moved straight toward them.

"I knew I shouldn't try anything," Seamus whispered, as he guiltily retook his seat.

The man came so close that he hovered over the trio. "Are you with Mr. Chang?" he asked.

Boyd shot up, cringing at an acute reminder of his stiff neck. "I'm his grandson."

"Dr. Riordan." The doctor shook Boyd's hand and shifted to shake Clive's and Seamus', as well. "Mr. Chang is stable and sleeping at the moment, but he was alert before the procedure and able to speak with me at length. We're holding him in telemetry so we can keep a close eye…"

Boyd interrupted. "What procedure? A couple hours ago, the nurse said he was still undergoing tests."

"I'll take it from the top. Your grandfather experienced a severe episode of angina and struck his head, briefly knocking him unconscious. The fall left him with a concussion. Mr. Chang is also dehydrated, but that isn't a major problem; we have him on fluids. However…"

"Yes?" Boyd begged for the whole story.

"An underlying problem came to light during our evaluation. Your grandfather was not getting enough oxygen to his heart, so I proceeded with an angiogram and discovered he had one artery 85% blocked and another at 75%. I opened the arteries with stents."

Boyd screeched, "He had heart surgery?!"

"Not like you're thinking," Dr. Riordan explained. "The stents were inserted through a port in his groin and guided into position in the arteries. This is a relatively common procedure, and definitely a lifesaver. The only outward sign is the port, which is blocked with a dissolvable collagen plug. He needs to lie flat for a few hours and take it easy for a while, but he should bounce back quickly."

"Excellent!" Clive interjected.

Dr. Riordan agreed. "This probably doesn't seem like a positive experience, but your grandfather is a very lucky man. If he hadn't lost consciousness and been brought in here, it's likely he would have gone on, status quo, until he suffered a major heart attack. It's a miracle he hasn't had one yet...and functioned almost as normal. But I won't kid you. You need to stay on top of his health. He should have been making regular visits to his cardiologist and had this monitored."

The doctor gave an encouraging smile. "You'll see him soon. Any questions?"

Boyd's brain felt like a pincushion pricked by too many thorny thoughts. His mouth was cottony, inoperable. He swung his head "no."

Dr. Riordan patted Boyd on his shoulder and trotted off. Boyd watched the doctor until he disappeared behind the swinging doors. His eyes never blinked. The information he'd heard was still seeping into his brain. When it was fully absorbed, Boyd put his head in his hands and cried.

CHAPTER 19

Afton drove into the Sandspurs with a bundle of white hollyhocks shorn from her yard. She passed a roadside memorial and parked in the shadow of a rocky overhang, in a cloistered pullout used by road crews and horny teens. Dusk was descending.

Before she left her car, she texted a note of encouragement to Seamus, who was juggling dinner guests and the first of the nighttime partiers. "Give 'em hell, Bro," she wrote, wincing at the thought of their hard-drinking regulars discovering the Ghostly Grill was going dry. She felt guilty leaving Seamus and the staff to deliver the news, but she wasn't yet ready to return to work or the scene of her solitary encounter with Martin Schrader.

Afton glanced back at the memorial. The Prosperity Bible Church youth group had pounded a white wooden cross into the earth where Martin had swerved off the asphalt and soared into eternity. A string of blue silk flowers wreathed the cross. It was a kind tribute begun by a congregation unacquainted with Martin. Built upon by others—some who'd known the boy, some who hadn't—the site had become a messy pile of assorted offerings.

Afton considered laying the hollyhocks near the cross, but instead carried them with her to the crash site. Clutching the flowers between jaw and chest, she cautiously scooted down the bank on her butt, pausing where canyon sand mixed with crushed taillight glass and a broken life.

The fierceness of Martin's death was evident in the mangled metal before her. The bashed-in sides and flattened form of what had emerged from an assembly line as a Chevy Blazer indicated that the vehicle had made impact somewhere on the canyon wall and rolled into the sandy bed. Somehow that idea was far worse to Afton—more violent—than the thought of Martin's life ending with a single impact so jarring that it had immediately dislodged soul from body.

Pensively, Afton surveyed the steep incline she'd just navigated. About 20 feet up was the proof: a great gouge in the tan earth and below that, a broken trail of scraped ground, where the Blazer had come tumbling down. She averted her eyes with a shudder and moved toward the wreckage, looking over the Blazer's roof, peeled back like a lid on an opened tuna can. Her fingers reached for the blackened edges, where a welder's torch had seared through metal, allowing Martin's extraction.

She dangled the billowy stems over the driver's seat—a scrunched, stained wad—and let go. It felt more appropriate to leave her gift at the place where Martin's spirit had departed his body than the place where his vehicle's wheels had gone astray. Here, not the flat roadside above, was the scene of Martin's transcendence.

The fading sun painted the world with mysterious halftones. The temperature cooled, but Afton remained uncomfortably warm after her shimmy down the high bluff. She wove her hair into a braid and pulled out the neck of her T-shirt, blowing down onto her dewy, nearly flat chest. With her hair pulled back and her elfin body hidden inside baggy clothes, Afton looked like a young boy, not a woman of 30.

She walked to the far side of the Blazer and stared in, thinking of those few moments she'd spent with its driver. She was completely immersed in the setting and, she thought, alone in the wilderness, when a man appeared high above, peering down from the roadside.

He waved his arms over his head, like an island castaway trying to flag down a plane, then cupped his hands around his mouth and shouted, "I can see you, Martin! I'm coming!"

The man ran down the canyon bank, tripped over his own feet, and righted himself before taking another fall and sliding—bumpily—a great distance. He staggered upright and went into a jog, heading for Afton. She was caught off-guard. There was no place to run. No one to call for help. Doing all she could to prepare, she grabbed a fist-size stone and pulled herself into a runner's crouch, ready to dodge an assault.

The man swerved around the wreckage and came within a few feet of her before realizing his mistake. He stepped back, humiliated, putting proper distance between himself and Afton.

"I...I apologize, ma'am. I mistook you for...someone else." He wheezed a series of labored breaths.

Afton sidled further away, her fingers still wrapped around the rock. She didn't know how to size up the stranger. At a glimpse, he was a natural disaster—healing sunburned skin peeling off his nose and cheeks, clothes stained by his bumbling, bizarre plunge into the canyon—but little details spoke of gentility. His choice of words indicated an educated manner. His shoes were expensive leather creations. Though disheveled, his clothing was high quality, well matched, and suited to white-collar environs.

The man raised his hands to show that he was unarmed. "I mean no harm. My name is Peter Jacoby." He pushed his eyes toward the wreckage and explained, "I'm the one who found Martin Schrader. That's why I was yelling. I thought you were him." Peter cringed at his answer. "That sounds insane, doesn't it? Please accept my apologies. I've been an unstrung idiot ever since I found that kid's body."

Peter backed away, ready to make the strenuous climb back up the canyon wall.

"Peter Jacoby, huh? You know my brother."

Peter stopped, questioning Afton with his eyes.

"Seamus Burnside." Afton dropped the stone. She stood on tiptoe and reached as high as she could. "Six-foot-seven, red hair, beard. Can't miss him." She smiled.

Peter relaxed and walked back to the woman.

"Yes, I met Seamus this past week. Great guy." He was still panting from his downhill race.

"Sorry about the rock," Afton offered.

"I didn't exactly make a good first impression." Peter extended his hand. "Let me try this again. Peter Jacoby. Nice to meet you."

"I'm Afton."

"That's Scottish, isn't it? As in 'Afton Water.' Flow gently, sweet Afton…"

Afton was astonished. Peter was the only person she'd ever met who knew the origin of her name. "Yes! My mother was a huge Robert Burns fan."

The twosome stood awkwardly still, their eyes looking everywhere but at one another.

"Did you leave those?" Peter asked, noticing the blanket of hollyhocks inside the wreckage.

"Yes."

"I'm sorry for your loss. Did you know Martin well?"

"Not really, but I feel connected in a way."

Peter didn't want to press, and Afton wasn't up to airing her dirty laundry in front of a stranger. She hoped he would view her as only a benevolent member of the community, one who was moved to pay tribute to a dead boy with a bundle of flowers from her garden.

"I feel the same way…connected," Peter said. "Since the day I found him, I haven't thought of much else but who he was and why I was the one to recover his body."

As the sun's last light vacated the canyon, Afton started getting twitchy. "We should leave. It's not good to be out here after dark."

"Afraid of the canyon's spirits?" Peter asked, assuming Afton was, like most Prosperityites, a believer in the supernatural.

"Not exactly. The scorpions and snakes start crawling after sunset, and we're on their turf."

"Oh," Peter said, feeling very small.

He plucked a set of keys from his pocket. A miniature flashlight dangled from a Grand Canyon Hospital fob. "If it gets too dark, this should see us up the cliff." He flicked on the instrument, which had a powerful beam for its size.

The light reflected off something behind Afton. Something thin, long, and coiled. "What's that?" Peter shone the light directly on the object, directing Afton toward the discovery.

Edging up to it, Afton saw a spiral notebook laying facedown, its tan cardboard back camouflaged amidst the sand and dry grass. "Wonder why I didn't see that before?" she asked, picking up the object and dusting off its cover. "I was standing right on it."

She ran her fingers over the red cover, feeling the embossment of myriad doodles. Crudely rendered geometric objects were scribbled across the cover in black ink, along with creatures that, due to the artist's lack of skill, could have been either dragons or dogs. Flipping open the pad, Afton's eyes roved over a page of calculus problems and snapped up to the information scrawled on the inside of the cover: Marty Schrader; Calculus; Mrs. Kuticka, Room 105.

Afton went cold, as if winter had settled in her bones. "You won't believe this," she said, holding out the book for Peter to examine.

He didn't need to look. "It's Martin's, isn't it?"

Afton plucked the coil binding. "His mother should have this, don't you think?"

"Of course," Peter agreed, desperately hoping this was the reason Martin had dogged him for days. And yet knowing that was only partially true.

"Mr. Jacoby! I had no idea you were here!" Clare looked shell-shocked when Peter answered the door at 533 Hangman's Lane.

Peter was no less flabbergasted. Clare's was a face he'd hoped to never again see. His disapproval of her libidinous actions during his last night at the Canary Cage was on par with his embarrassment over them. The ghostly intervention she'd participated in the next morning did little to improve Peter's opinion of her. Nevertheless, being a well-mannered man, he held open the screen door and politely asked her to enter.

"Mae has already retired, but Ooljee will be home soon," he informed.

Clare balked, avoiding an army of winged insects that circled the porch light. "I shouldn't stay. I'll just drop off these homemade honey muffins," she said, transferring a red-gingham-covered basket into Peter's arms and chirping, "Mae has a fondness for them."

"I'm sure she'll appreciate your thoughtfulness. Thank you for stopping by." Peter began to shut the screen door, but Clare moved forward, sliding a foot over the threshold.

"Mr. Jacoby, would you spare me a minute? Out here on the porch?"

Uncomfortable with the request but too courteous to decline, Peter left the gift basket inside and walked out, softly shutting the wooden and screen doors behind him so as not to wake Mae. Clare was already seated on the porch swing. Peter leaned against the railing opposite her, elbows bowed behind him. His features were smoothed to perfection by the porch's soft amber light, and his beauty added to Clare's discomfort. She couldn't look into his sharp brown eyes, which were steadfastly set on hers.

"I've been thinking of what you said. I owe you an apology. My advances must have been insulting to a true gentleman such as you." Clare pushed her feet against the porch, propelling the swing slightly forward and back, rocking the contraption like a cradle. "I suppose I don't know anything about real gentlemen, so I didn't realize how my visit would make you feel. I've never been rebuffed before—not that I do that very often, mind you. I really was trying to help, but I was basically forcing myself on you...under false pretenses...while you were vulnerable. I see that now, and I can't express how sorry I am." Clare dared to look up at Peter. Her black cat-eye makeup was dripping down at the corners, where tears puddled.

"Don't think anything more about it," Peter said, pushing away from the railing to offer Clare a pat on the shoulder.

"What a terrible hostess I was! To make you uncomfortable and..."

"Please, Miss Bowers," Peter hushed, patting her again. "Let's forget it happened."

Clare sniffed and wiped the tears away with two long, red-nailed index fingers. "I think I only know one way to relate to men. My stepfather was forcing himself on me as soon as he moved in—I was 11. Then I had all those years on the strip—men with their eyes and hands all over me. I've gone through life offering my body to men because I thought it would make them like me. I'm smarter than that, but I can't get out of the habit. I put you in a compromising position because of my insecurity."

Peter imagined how unhappy a life Clare must have lived and how hard it must have been for her to transition from nubile sex goddess to geriatric innkeeper, especially when she'd been taught to value only her physical qualities. Clare seemed so lonely, and Peter knew how aloneness can erode sensibilities and make one think and do foolish things. He released all resentment.

"I accept the apology, Miss Bowers. Now, please, let's think no more of that night. And let's dispense with the formality. Please call me Peter."

The lights from Ooljee's red Prius shone up Hangman's Lane, leaching through the trees and hedges. Peter and Clare watched quietly as the car turned in and parked in the side yard.

Ooljee emerged, juggling her woven-grass purse and a paper sack, and slammed the car door closed with her rear. She stopped at the foot of the front porch stairs, sucking in air. "Yummm, someone uphill is barbecuing something fantastic! But I've got something even better." She writhed up the steps, dancing to her own humming, and dropped a cold, lidded Styrofoam container into Clare's lap.

"What's this?" she wondered.

"A pint of rum raisin from the Sugar Hut."

Clare's eyes swelled. "My favorite! Thanks, Ooljee! You always know when I need a little pick-me-up!"

"You're welcome. I had a feeling you'd be over after your evening social hour to check on Mom. Peter, I got you peanut butter and chocolate."

"Perfect," he confirmed.

"Thought so. You have a serious sweet tooth, my man. I can dig that."

Peter cracked a grin as Ooljee bustled by, unloading his pint along the way. "I'm going to put Mom's in the freezer for when she wakes up."

The screen door squeaked shut behind Ooljee, and soon flew open again as she emerged with three spoons and napkins. She scooted next to Clare on the swing, sending it from a gentle sway into hard rocking. The group took the lids off their respective pints and dug in, eyes rolling at the taste of the rich, creamy delights.

"Damn, that's good!" Ooljee sang.

"Very good," Peter and Clare uttered in unison.

"So, Clare, have you heard that Peter's going to be staying with us for a while? Mom's going to mentor him." Ooljee licked the rocky road film off her spoon.

"I'm so glad! Oh, I knew Mae and Ooljee were the ones who could help you. Why, I remember when I found out they were psychic. I was in the midst of restoring the Canary Cage. They came over to introduce themselves and invite me to dinner. I still remember it like it was yesterday. Ooljee was a teenager, loved to cook. She made chili rellenos and peach shortcake for dessert. She said she changed that at the last minute because she had a feeling I was allergic to strawberries. I am!"

Ooljee laughed at the memories of their first days as neighbors. "And remember when you invited us over the next day? Peter, you should've seen it. The Canary Cage was a musty old ruin, and Mom and I walk in, and there's Clare in one clean little patch in the parlor, dressed to the nines, with a silver tea service. We sat there and had tea and cookies while workmen carried lumber past us and electric saws went off in other rooms and sawdust came drifting down the staircase. I swear, when I went home, I blew my nose and sawdust came out."

"What was I thinking?" Clare asked through her laughter. "I should have served tea on the porch."

"Ah, it made for a good memory," Ooljee said. She slurped another bite of ice cream off the spoon and aimed the utensil at Peter. "Your turn. Tell us one of your favorite memories."

Peter stopped mid-bite. He breathed in the scents of grilling meat and blooming roses and enjoyed the taste of peanut butter and chocolate that lingered on his tongue. For the first time he could recall, he felt totally relaxed and accepted for who he was. He knew he was among friends.

"I remember being at my Granny Weston's house. It was a dilapidated old shack, but she kept it clean inside and had a jungle of flowers in the front yard. The house was roofed with tin panels, and when it rained, the drops on the metal sounded like music. I remember this one time sitting on her lap on the front porch. She rocked and held me and hummed songs while the rain fell on the roof. She told me fairies were up there dancing for me."

Clare's eyes misted up. "That's beautiful, Mr. Jacoby...Peter."

"That's better," he approved, shoveling up scoop after scoop until a thin chocolate ring appeared around his mouth; he gleefully licked it away.

"They say you can tell a lot about a person by the way he eats," Clare said.

"What can you tell about me?" Peter asked, looking into his empty container, "That I'm not lactose-intolerant?"

The trio guffawed, and Clare quickly made her appraisal of the situation. "No, silly. I can tell you're comfortable here at Mae and Ooljee's. When you ate at the Canary Cage, you were peckish. That uneasiness is gone."

"I like it here," Peter admitted, admiring the greenery and tiers of flowers. "This yard is like my granny's. Especially the roses. That scent reminds me of her." Peter eyed the huge yellow blossoms. "I don't think I've ever seen such large roses."

An impish grin crossed Ooljee's face. "That's where the outhouse used to be. When Mama had it torn down, she filled up the holes and planted rose bushes on top. You think those roses are something now...you should have seen them back when I was a kid. Yowza! Big as your head!"

Inside, Mae woke to the sound of laughter—Ooljee's, Peter's, and Clare's. She picked her head up from the pillow and strained to hear the cheery conversation taking place outside. Quite unexpectedly to Mae, Peter was bringing joy to the old house.

CHAPTER 20

The Schraders' living room was a scene of domestic apocalypse. Games, dolls, magazines, and empty pop cans cluttered nearly every square foot of space. Martin's funeral bouquets—floral scabs on rusty stalks—moldered throughout the space. Looking down on the debris were photographs of Martin that stood sentinel at every level of the room, holding his future at bay.

"I've been having real bad thoughts. They won't let me be." Emma held an opened can of Sure-Save Diet Cola in her hand, bringing it up to her mouth a few times but never making contact with her lips. The addictive elixir of aspartame, water, and caramel coloring was about all she consumed lately.

"My ma has the girls, and Martin Sr. is off who knows where. He's been staying at the restaurant late hours and leaving before I get up. I think this house reminds him too much of Marty. I remind him too much of Marty...too much for him to come close to me again." Emma drizzled some cola into her mouth. "I need my husband. Tricia and Sara need their daddy. I guess he don't need us, though."

Afton assumed her most sympathetic pose, hands folded on her knees, face contorted in commiseration. "Maybe he's hiding because he's overwhelmed by pain and doesn't want you or the kids to see him weak."

"Weak? Martin? Never thought of that." Emma looked over at the family portrait, which showed her husband at the top center, a lumberjack of a man with long brown sideburns and shoulders twice as wide as his wife's. "I seen Martin in terrible pain. Once, our pickup fell and pinned him when he had it jacked up, working on it. The earth cushioned him, but he had a broken collarbone, crushed ribs, and a punctured lung. I held his hand while we waited for help. I was bawling like a baby, but Martin never cried, never did nothing but grit his teeth and sweat. And while he was in the hospital healing, he didn't complain about nothing…except the food." The farmwife brushed a smile off her lips.

"But there's no medicine for the hurt in here," Afton said, laying a hand over her heart, looking like a woman well versed on the subject of inner turmoil.

Emma dragged on the cola like a suckling drunkard. "You're right. I know it. I don't want to think of my husband being weak, though. Not Martin. I could understand him flying into a rage or crying his eyes out, but running away from his family…that's a weakness I didn't think he had."

"Give him time. He's dealing with it the way he knows—keeping the hurt inside, refusing to deal with it, keeping so busy he can't think about it. Soon, he'll have to face it, and he'll need you when he does."

"You married?" Emma asked.

"Was. It didn't work out."

"What happened?"

Afton was never comfortable talking about her life, but she wasn't injured by the question. She'd been allowed so deeply into Emma's personal space that she felt she owed some confidentialities in return. "I must've been a lousy wife. Jason cheated on me inside of two years of marriage. Caught him red-handed, so to speak."

"It wasn't about you, honey. Sooner or later, that type screws around. Be grateful it was sooner rather than later." Emma tapped the side of her nose. "I understand these things. My sister was married to a man who couldn't keep it zipped. I'm glad Martin can. That ain't one of his faults."

Afton sighed, loosening up. "Well, I can't entirely blame the marriage failure on Jason's infidelity. Nothing excuses what he did, but I wasn't the easiest person to live with either. You see, my parents died almost a year to the day after I got married, and I guess I went a little crazy. I acted like your husband—ran away from my marriage, threw myself into work and tried to keep my mind on something other than my pain. Between caring for my brother and managing a bookstore, I never had time for a husband. I was gone so much that I didn't notice when Jason started fooling around with our neighbor. Didn't notice much of anything until I walked in on them. I left the creep, and then 10 days later, my brother swallowed a bottle of pills. Boy, that was a great month!" Afton paused for a derisive laugh. "But it put it all into perspective. Made me see that the ones we love are what matters. Losing or nearly losing them will rearrange priorities like nothing else can. You and I have learned that the hard way."

"We surely have," Emma sullenly agreed. "A few weeks ago, I was worried sick about how we were going to afford a new barn roof. Today? I couldn't care less if the whole thing rots." She held the cola out, indicating her house. "This place used to be spotless. You could've eaten off the floor. Now look at it. I haven't lifted a finger for housework since the day Marty went missing. I can't even find the energy to cook. Marty's all I think about." Staring at the aluminum can inside her bent fingers, she seemed like a seer gazing at a crystal ball that reflected scenes from the past, not the future. "I wish I'd spent more time with my boy instead of working around the house. I could've put the mop down and left the laundry to go on a walk with him, could've shot hoops with him more often. We were always close. We did things together, but it could've been more, you know? It should've been. Now, all those chances are gone."

The mourning woman provided the perfect transition. Reaching into her canvas tote, Afton pulled out the notebook she and Peter had stumbled upon. She had dusted it clean with a rag. "I have something for you."

As the item was directed into Emma's lap, her eyes clicked open with recognition. "That's Marty's!" She dropped the cola can onto the coffee table and clutched the notebook with both hands, every finger trembling at the touch.

"The man who found Martin's...body," Afton hesitated, "found that last night. I was with him."

Emma was dumbfounded. "Peter Jacoby?"

"Yes. He's gone back to the canyon a couple times. Your son's passing has deeply affected him."

"God bless him," Emma said, folding her arms, holding the notebook to her heart as tears skated along her cheeks. "And God bless you for bringing me this."

Afton felt renewed. "I want you to know that a lot of people have been touched by your son's life and his passing. Peter Jacoby, me, my brother, Coach Jensen. I went to see him the day I visited you. I needed the release of talking to him...not sure why, but I'm glad I went. He told me about your son, and I feel closer to Martin Jr. now."

"Coach Jensen is a great man. He was so good to Marty, keeping him on the team even after he started to get sick." Emma lovingly ran her hand over the front of the notebook, admiring each doodle as if it was the work of a master artist. "He took care of my boy."

"And trusted him. I don't know many teachers who'd turn over their car keys to a student."

Emma's hand stopped stroking the notebook. The woman looked at Afton with a curious expression. "What do you mean?"

Afton wondered which of her words harbored offense. "You know, how Coach Jensen sometimes let Marty use his Blazer, like that Friday, when he asked him to pick up supplies for the trip? I think that shows a lot of trust and respect, don't you?"

"Coach Jensen said he let Marty take his Blazer to get supplies?"

"Yeah."

Emma's lower lip danced. "When I called him that afternoon, looking for Marty, he said my boy had lifted his keys and stolen the Blazer from the school parking lot, but he didn't want to tell the police and get him in trouble. He was sure Marty would come back when he was ready." The woman's questioning eyes skimmed the room, the notebook, Afton. "Why would he lie?"

"Peter, it's Afton Burnside." Mae grinned mischievously as she waved the phone in the air.

With blushing cheeks and a "thank you," Peter took the receiver. "Hello Afton. How are you?"

"Okay, and yourself?"

"Fine, thanks," Peter lied for the sake of courtesy and brevity.

"Martin Schrader's mom just called me. She asked to meet with the two of us, didn't say why. Are you game?"

"Of course. Anytime."

"Great, I'll be right over. See ya."

"Goodbye." Peter hung up and, perplexed, turned to Mae. "Martin Schrader's mom wants to meet me."

Mae's playful grin flat-lined. "I expect she wants some closure. After all, you recovered her son's body." She smoothed down Peter's shirtsleeves and straightened his collar, fussing like a mother preparing her teenager for the prom. "I'm sure you'll be a comfort to her."

Mere minutes later, Afton and Peter were on their way to Santa Rita, Afton's Honda fighting against the current of tourist vehicles weaving up Salome Hill.

"Maybe Emma wants to thank us for the notebook," Afton speculated.

Peter didn't feel he'd earned gratitude for the discovery of Martin's body or his personal artifact. "I hope she doesn't feel that's necessary."

"Sure, but I don't know what else she'd want with us." Afton thoughtfully paused. "By the way, I think it's very nice of you to do this."

"Glad to," Peter said after a self-conscious "ahem."

The remainder of the ride east was filled with alternating bouts of awkward then easy conversation. Afton and Peter took relieved breaths when they turned into the Schraders' driveway.

Emma was waiting outside on a folding chair with the family's Queensland heeler at her feet. Her legs and arms were crossed, her body closed off. The woman looked more than weary and grieving. She looked empty.

"Emma, this is Peter Jacoby," Afton introduced.

"I'm glad to know you, ma'am," he said, reaching out. "Please accept my condolences."

"Thank you for everything. Thank you for coming," Emma answered, taking his hand for the slightest of shakes.

Martin's mother was exactly how Peter had imagined her—hardy and sweetly plain, with a fresh-scrubbed face and meaty limbs—except this was the eroded version. Normally, Peter was sure, she was the perfect picture of rural motherhood, the kind of mom to rise early; cook a big breakfast for her family; clean a house top-to-bottom; tend to livestock and pets; irrigate the crops; and still make the time to have homemade cookies waiting on the stove when the kids got home from school. But the woman Peter saw was not that mother. This was the Emma Schrader with no purpose, no energy, blue pouches under her eyes and no color at all where a healthy rosy gold usually warmed smiling cheeks. This was less than half the woman Peter knew she truly was.

"I don't know what to do," Emma whispered. She seemed in a trance.

Peter and Afton had not yet decided where they were to sit when Emma started talking. Without wasting time, they took the closest options: Peter going cross-legged on the grass and Afton sliding onto a mulberry stump, the two of them giving full attention to the woman.

"I never would've believed it. I don't know what to do."

Ever the businesswoman, Afton had prepared some materials for Emma—the name and phone number of a well-regarded grief counselor in Sedona and some printouts from the Web about coping with the loss of family members. She took the folded papers from her purse and tried to hand them over, but Emma didn't notice. Her eyes were spherical blue blanks, staring across the yard at an unmoving point that rested between planes.

"I read Marty's notebook. His suicide note is in there." Emma kept speaking without inflection or facial expression. "Half those pages are about what he was going to do and why. He meant for that notebook to be found. That's why he took it with him. It's my baby's last will and testament, his last words to me."

Afton instinctively crawled over to the woman, kneeling beside the heeler, who was already offering comfort by licking her mistress' ankles. Afton put a hand on Emma's knee. "I'm so sorry," she said.

"See? I was right. He meant to do it. He went to his favorite spot, a little shady grove over by the Verde River, the other side of Tuzigoot, where our family used to picnic. He sat under a tree and figured out how he'd do it, and then he wrote page after page in that notebook to explain his decision."

Peter's thoughts returned to the afternoon when he'd met Afton's brother, that lost day when he'd been drawn to Tuzigoot, then westward, along the banks of the river, summoned unknowingly to the place that Marty had loved so well, and then further on, to a desert ridge, to save a man's life.

"Said he didn't want any of us family or anyone he knew to find his body, so he was going to drive up to Prosperity, take a bunch of pills, have him a couple of drinks, and then wait it out and let it all end. He planned to order rum and colas. He didn't want the alcohol, but he thought it would make a faster-acting poison, and the sweetness of the cola would coat the taste of the pills." Emma beamed at the remembrance of a precious child. "Such a good boy…how many his age don't want liquor?"

Afton's fingers were clamped over her mouth, locking up the cries she would have made if she'd had the strength. She recalled how she'd run off Martin, sent him away to die alone. He had planned to die—or at least go into a fatal coma—there, in the grill, surrounded by people. He might have lived if he'd stayed, might have vomited up enough of the medicine to have been saved. But they would never know because Afton had sent him into the dark night all alone in a state that scarcely allowed him to maneuver a vehicle down a road. All the inhabitants of Prosperity and the Verde Valley knew how far he'd gotten: Dead Horse Canyon.

Emma droned on, head cocked, eyes fixed. "You'll never guess why he did it. I never would've. Not in a million years."

Afton and Peter knew the woman didn't need a response, probably wouldn't even hear one if it was given; so they sat there quietly, cocooned in empathy, listening.

"Coach Jensen." Emma's face changed. Her neck, then face flushed red, the color rising as her heart pumped blood and rage to her brain. Her eyes, still staring out at an invisible object, disappeared behind tears. She shook as if in an epileptic attack. "That bastard drugged my baby and raped him! Damn, low, son-of-a-bitch coach!"

A wail like nothing Afton had ever heard ripped itself from the woman's throat and flushed a pair of mourning doves from the overhead branches of an Arizona sycamore. Emma's jaws nearly unhinged as her head tipped back, eyes shut tight, the scream of a mortally wounded creature pouring out, louder and louder, a clarion cry of suffering that ended in kittenish whimpers.

Afton gathered the woman to her, needing to feel an embrace as much as she wanted to give her own.

"How could he?!" Emma shrieked.

Afton squeezed harder as the woman's voice lowered, and through the gasping, shuddering sobs, Emma outlined the accusation Marty had left behind scrawled in ink.

"My boy hadn't seen it coming. Marty thought the coach was just being friendly when he kept getting closer and closer, finding ways to be alone with him and touch him." Emma stopped. "That bastard!" she cursed, pressing a fist into the hollow of Afton's back, baring down like a woman in labor. After a moment locked in Afton's embrace, Emma pulled away and wiped her eyes, determined to tell the tale as clearly as possible.

"It happened in Flagstaff last year, at the retreat. The coach gave him a beer. He didn't want to drink it, but Coach Jensen said he deserved it because of the way he'd performed in the playoffs and that he was a man now and needed to taste alcohol. So, Marty drank it, and next thing he knew, it was morning and he was in his bunk. Said he didn't feel right and was real sore..." Emma paused, stifling the anger. "But he didn't know what had happened until that fall, when he started as the coach's assistant. When Coach Jensen wasn't around, Marty tried to look up something on his computer and found pictures of himself and the coach that were real bad, that the coach had taken—he could see his arm holding the camera in some. Marty said he didn't have no clothes on and looked dead, must have been passed out, and in some of the pictures the coach was doing...things to him..."

Emma couldn't go on. Her sobbing picked up to such a pace that Afton thought for certain the woman was having some kind of seizure. She grabbed Emma and held her close again, trying to steady her.

"Seeing those pictures must've jogged Marty's memory cause he said then he kind of remembered waking up during the attack, but it was hazy, like a nightmare. Then he started remembering the details and seeing those pictures in his mind...but my baby was too ashamed to tell anyone!" Emma lowered her face into Afton's hair, the words muffled by the red spirals. "He was too ashamed to come to me. Didn't he know it wasn't his fault? Didn't he know I'd love him just the same?"

"He knew," Afton uttered, rubbing Emma's arms.

It was nearly five minutes before the woman could speak again. "My boy thought about others to the end—always a team player. He noticed the coach starting to pay extra attention to Tyler. Marty was afraid he was planning to use the retreat to do the same thing to Tyler that he'd done to him. Marty couldn't let that happen. That's why he stole the Blazer and ran off. He thought that would make the coach cancel the weekend, and when his suicide note was found, the coach would get arrested."

Emma yielded to the last phase of a brutal cry, the salty drops from her eyes splashing into Afton's ringlets and dripping down to her scalp. Her mouth was slack, curled down on the ends like a loosened rubber band.

"What kind of mother am I that I couldn't tell something like that was happening? God forgive us! Martin Sr. and me, we made Marty stay on that baseball team! I ain't ever gonna forgive myself. Not ever! How could I not have known?"

CHAPTER 21

The details of Martin's confession would have troubled anyone, but they visibly agitated Peter, who rocked on his haunches and wiped his eyes, mouth, and neck like a man sweating out a withdrawal. Glints of memory were lighting his mind—Martin's memories and his own. A face here, a word there, the imagery patterned in a disorganized duel that reconstructed two boys' similar, life-altering experiences.

The melee inside finally got the best of him. Peter pulled himself up and walked away without Emma or Afton noticing. Besieged by dizzying revelations, he staggered between the trees of a peach orchard, using the rough trunks as crutches to move him onward. He reeled, disoriented and nearly blind, to the edge of a pond, where the soggy slickness of duck-trampled grass felled him. Slipping down onto the damp bank, Peter succumbed to a breakdown or break-through, whichever it was. He bent his legs and dipped forward, resting his head on his muddy knees. It was noisy in his mind, almost as cacophonous as the mallards that excitedly scolded him for treading too close to their watery home.

There was a scream. Peter wasn't aware of its source. It could have been him, crying out for mercy, or it could have been one of the boys in his head, the ones who burned with indignity and righteous anger. Perhaps one of them screamed at the moment it happened—the only time for Marty, or one of the many times it happened to Peter. In a split second, he remembered. Amid the confusion, he remembered.

"Deke, Deke, Deke," Peter monotonously accused, the repeated word blending with the calls of the ducks that took flight around him. It was Nanny Lotta's husband, Deke, the groundskeeper, who came stomping into Peter's churning consciousness. That egg-shaped man in overalls, who was always shuffling around the property with tools in hand, looking for some wayward natural formation to force into place. Deke's hound-dog face was as impassive as the stone wall around the Jacoby property, showing no anger, no pleasure, no remorse.

It all came back, steadily leaking through the pinprick puncture in Peter's barricaded mind.

The first time had been in the tool shed, with the scent of grease and pesticide in Peter's nose and the sharp steel blades of landscaping implements all around. Peter had been 10, still a boy in every sense of the word. It had happened so quickly, unexpectedly, and was so foreign a feeling—like being ripped apart by fire, down there, where only ugly things happen—that it had been pure shock. "That'll teach you for trespassing. This's my property," Deke had said after pulling up Peter's pants and booting him outside. Disbelief had held Peter until he went into the house to shower and discovered blood smeared against the backs of his thighs. The shame came later.

At dinner that evening, the cook ladled out the pre-entrée soup, and Peter tried his best to spoon it up, but he felt too sick to eat. He was all nerves and thumbs. And while he sat there, clumsily stirring the golden broth in his china bowl, he thought: did Lotta know she was married to a monster, and could his parents tell by looking at him that he was no longer whole? He was too afraid to lift his eyes to theirs and find out.

It had taken Peter more than a month to tell Lotta what had happened. By then, it had happened again, when Deke came upon Peter in the basement, pouring the old shavings from his whittling kit into the incinerator.

"Nanny Lotta, I have to tell you something," Peter had whispered, mustering every ounce of courage he had. "Deke pulled down my pants and…" Peter had gotten no further than that before Lotta slapped him hard across the mouth and told him to "quit fibbing." She wouldn't hear such things. They were improper, she said, and warned him not to repeat his experiences, lest people think he was a liar or a little pervert. "A child with your upbringing should know better. No one will believe you. You'll only bring shame on your family."

Peter knew Lotta must have said something because the next morning, when he walked down the drive to wait for the school bus, Deke was waiting for him at the main road junction, lurking behind a pine. The gardener wore a furious expression as he stepped into the sunlight and took Peter by the shoulders. He shook him hard and punched him in the belly before telling him he'd do even worse to his mother if Peter ever spoke another word.

The trickling recollections became a stream, then a wave that crashed over and through the barrier in Peter's mind. Everything came flooding into the present, so many images that he couldn't sort them. He saw Martin's face, lax and oblivious, cradled by Coach Jensen's vein-plumped hand. And then, as discomfort filled the teen, his eyelids snapped opened for a brief lucid moment that lasted long enough for his eyes to focus on his attacker and become blue eddies of humiliation, disbelief, rage, betrayal—all the named emotions Peter had felt himself so long ago, along with some emotions too raw and deep to be labeled.

Next, Peter saw his own attacker in a darkened room, fastening his overalls as he wheezed and grunted like a pig wallowing in muck. Martin's body. Peter's body. Both so young and lean and unblemished but for the injuries inflicted by those they trusted. Coach Jensen. Deke. Martin. Peter. The contesting images flickered back and forth in rapid-fire succession, from a lofty Southern estate to a seedy cabin in the Arizona woods. Martin's life and his own had become intertwined. The confusion created a pain so intense that Peter felt he was losing himself. He braced his forehead with cramping hands, squeezing, squeezing hard. Blinded to the external and petrified by the overpowering stimuli swirling through his brain, he went limp. There was a burst of internal light, and then it was over. Peter felt nothing as he slumped back against the muddy bank.

Boyd whizzed through the hospital cafeteria's hot food buffet and took a table. The ham and cheese omelet tasted better than it looked, and the hash browns were downright tasty. He was contemplating why hospital food gets such a bad rap when a familiar voice echoed through the nearly deserted dining area.

"Hey, stranger."

Boyd looked up, fork in hand, ogling his surprise guest.

Amy walked tentatively toward him, sandaled toes pointing inward, hands clutching a pink purse. In three days, Boyd's ex-girlfriend—completely out of his life for five months—had surprised him with two unexpected appearances.

"Amy?!" Boyd bellowed, spewing egg across the table. The girl nervously watched his Adam's apple bounce up and down as he coughed. She prepared to perform the Heimlich maneuver.

When he caught his breath, Boyd took a fast drink of orange juice and stood up, asking, "What are you doing here?"

"Why wouldn't I be here?"

"Uh...I don't know."

"We're still friends, aren't we?"

"We are?"

Boyd was a mess, all confidence gone from his face and posture. His body slouched inside wrinkled cargo shorts and a rumpled Hawaiian-print shirt that showed he hadn't slept for days. The bleached stripe in his hair was standing upright, but not from the support of gel; the whole front-left side of Boyd's hair was on end, while the right and back were tamped down from his sleeping sideways in the padded armchair in his grandfather's hospital room.

"Of course we're friends," Amy assured, emphasizing the word "friends." She smiled comfortingly as she reached out and lightly stroked Boyd's crushed sleeve, trying to smooth it. "And your grandpa's my friend, too. Mr. Chang is, like, the sweetest guy ever."

"Grandpa thinks the world of you." Boyd confessed, "He's still giving me grief for breaking up with you."

"You breaking up with me? That's not how I remember it."

"You know what I mean. Us breaking up, I should have said."

Amy shifted uncomfortably and changed the subject. "I would've come earlier, but I didn't know. I left the community center after you and your grandpa…after you guys…you know. Anyway, I'm staying with the Gabbards here in McBrideville. Last night, we had dinner at the Ghostly Grill, and Seamus told me what happened."

"I'm glad you're here."

A dimple punctuated each side of Amy's smiling mouth. "I am, too. They were taking your grandpa's blood, so I left his card and flowers at the nurses' station. One of the nurses said you were probably here and that you haven't left the hospital at all. I think that's commendable."

Boyd almost blushed. "Yeah? Thanks." He had to look away from Amy for a minute to compose himself. It was like they were on a blind date, verbally dancing around each other with polite phrases.

"Can I buy you breakfast?"

"That'd be great."

Boyd pulled out a chair and pushed it in before Amy was prepared to sit, knocking her from her feet.

"Oof," she grunted, landing hard and fast on the seat.

"Sorry! I didn't mean to do that." Boyd self-consciously assumed his own seat as Amy laughed.

"The ham and cheese omelet is really good."

"I'm a vegetarian now."

"Really? When did that happen?" Boyd asked as if he'd just learned some sordid detail of her life.

"A few months ago. We saw a film in my Environmental Ethics class that was so gross and sad. I had no idea what animals go through at factory farms, and I didn't know how those places pollute the land and water. Oh, Boyd, it was disgusting! I gave up meat right then and there. Although, okay, I admit I sometimes crave a cheeseburger with onions and pickles. I mean, it gets bad. Like, one time, I didn't stop myself until I was actually in the drive-thru at Whataburger. I felt like such a loser!"

Boyd's brown eyes glistened. Amy was so lively and pretty, so good-hearted and forgiving that here she was when he most needed her, acting as if they were still the closest of friends, playing his personal cheerleader.

He couldn't help but blurt out, "I'm sorry for that time I stood you up so I could go on an investigation, and the time I yelled at you for losing my EMF meter and then found it in my backpack later. I was a jerk to you."

"Um, it's okay," Amy replied.

"No, it isn't. I shouldn't have treated you the way I did. You've been my friend since we were kids, and you were always there for me. We had a lot of good times." Boyd sighed regretfully. "I always cared for you, Amy, but I know I didn't act like it sometimes. I took you for granted."

"You were really intense for a while. It kind of worried me. Everything was EVP this and EMF that and full-bodied apparitions here and residual hauntings there. It's like you didn't want to talk or hear about anything else."

Boyd reflected on the past few years. He could see how driven he'd been. "Yeah, I've always loved ghost stuff, but I got too caught up in it...Hey, remember, when we were in 7th grade and you and me and Ralph Garcia used to do ghost stakeouts in Prosperity's old buildings?"

Amy shivered, remembering. "I hated crawling through those dark places. They were scary. I just did it because you enjoyed it so much...and because I knew you joined the Junior Craft Guild because of me. Do you think I didn't realize you hated making mosaic trivets as much as I hated the ghost stakeouts?"

"Yeah, we had a good give and take, but when we got older, you stayed nice, and I got self-absorbed. I never took you salsa dancing, no matter how many times you begged me."

"So what?" Amy asked, shrugging. "I only went on two PIP investigations."

"At least you went. You tried my stuff and were supportive. I didn't do any of your things, and I didn't support you."

Amy's shoulders rocked with withheld laughter. "I don't know how supportive I was. I accidentally erased your EVP tape from the Skeleton's Closet investigation."

"Oh yeah. So, I guess we're even, right?"

Amy grinned and gave a nod, but Boyd grew serious. "My work's still important to me, but things are different."

"How so?"

"I've changed since Friday night. When I saw my grandpa being rushed out of the community center on a gurney..." Boyd gasped, holding in emotions, "it made me see what's really important. I still want to investigate the paranormal, but not at the expense of everything else in my life. I need to make time for the people I care about and things that matter to them. That doesn't mean give up my own pursuits, just stop being selfish. You know? I mean, would it kill me to go to my grandpa's Prosperity Historical Society meetings once in a while? Or learn how to salsa dance?"

As Boyd teetered on the verge of tears, Amy reached out and took his hand, giving it a soft squeeze. "You have changed. You finally grew up," she said.

CHAPTER 22

When Peter's eyes opened, they were a different color. The deep umber had paled to hazel, as if a light now shone behind the irises. Everyone in the hospital room noticed. The change was too dramatic to ignore and so strange a phenomenon that the excitement that should have been generated by Peter's emergence from unconsciousness was dampened by worry.

"At last, here you are," Ooljee cooed, sidling up to Peter, mindful of the IV tube that ran between a metal stand and his pierced arm. Peter didn't say a word as his eyes roved from one visitor to another—Ooljee, Afton, Seamus—reading the tender, tired, concerned faces.

"Mama can't be here, Peter. She wanted to, more than anything. But she can't leave Prosperity, you understand? Truthfully, even after all these years, I'm not sure I understand. It's just the way it's always been. She wanted me to tell you that you're not going to have any more headaches."

Peter didn't acknowledge the words. He was captivated by the silver bangles that wrapped around Ooljee's left wrist.

"Can you speak, Peter?" Ooljee asked. She tried to keep the panic from her face, but it became all the more evident when, after waiting a reasonable amount of time for an answer and receiving none, she patted his hands, told him to lie still, and politely excused herself. She jogged down the hall, thin bracelets jangling, looking for someone who seemed authoritative. "We need help in Room 23," she told a woman wearing raspberry-colored scrubs and a stethoscope twined around her neck like an exotic dancer's boa.

The nurse—mid-thirties, blond French braid, spherical saline breasts, fake tan—slowly looked up from a chart, obviously lost in thought and accustomed to having patients' loved ones turn hysterical over everything from a late meal delivery to the need for extra pillows.

"The patient in Room 23 is awake, but something's wrong. He can't speak, and his eyes are…weird."

The nurse glanced at the monitors positioned around the work station. "No alarms, but let's have a look," she patronized, setting out in an unhurried gait.

Ooljee took long steps ahead of her, looking back with perturbation at the lagging woman. She noticed the nurse's badge: Diane Phelps, RN.

"Can you please move a little faster, Nurse Phelps? A man's life may depend on this."

To satisfy Ooljee, the nurse stepped a bit livelier, but she didn't truly see the need. "Ma'am, it's a positive sign that your…" the nurse angled for the right term. "Husband?" she ventured, questioningly.

"Brother," Ooljee quickly corrected.

"Okay, it's a good sign that your brother is waking up, but you need to understand that his recovery could be slow. His eyes are probably readjusting to the need to focus. Remember, he's been out a long time, and we still don't know what's wrong with him…nothing from what we can tell, except he passed out. All his signs are fine, the EEGs have been fine. In fact, his brain has been quite active. No damage there that we can see."

The nurse stopped cold for a second, recognition enlivening her face. "Hey, you're that psychic who used to host *American Fugitives*. Ooljee Davis! I knew you lived in the area, but I've never seen you in person before. I loved that show!"

"Thank you. I enjoyed doing it." Ooljee smiled graciously and then pushed the nurse on with her own bounding steps. She knew that Diane Phelps was the expert on medical conditions, but it didn't take any special training to see that Peter had emerged from his coma far differently than he'd entered it.

"Here, you see?" she said, leading the nurse into the room.

Peter was seated on the bed, his sandy blond hair standing up like a rooster's comb atop his head.

"Well, well, nice to see you up, Sleeping Beauty," the nurse remarked without any expectation of a reply. She cuffed his arm and took his blood pressure. "One-ten over 70. Everything looks normal. He's fine," she announced.

"Fine?" Ooljee exclaimed. "Nurse Phelps, you don't understand. Peter hasn't spoken a word, and he normally has dark brown eyes."

"They look greenish to me," the nurse answered. "The problem is you're not used to seeing him like this. Visitors always comment about how different their family members look when they're laid up in a hospital bed."

Afton jumped in. "The problem is that those aren't his eyes. How can they just change color all of a sudden?"

The nurse made an exasperated frown and acquiesced by leaning over Peter and lifting his lids for a closer look. She took a small light from the pocket on her scrubs and shone it into his pupils. "His reactions are good. There's no discoloration, no yellowing or inflammation," she declared.

"It's his irises that have changed, not the whites of his eyes," Ooljee said with diminishing gentility.

"I wouldn't be concerned. Just see to it that he takes it easy."

Afton erupted with the irritation that Ooljee was keeping at a simmer. "Aren't you going to do something now that he's out of his coma and not talking? Shouldn't his doctor know?"

"One moment."

As Nurse Phelps prissily sauntered from the room, Seamus turned to Peter and gave a grin. "I'm jealous, man. I used to be the only one my sister would fuss over. Now you've got her and Ooljee watching over you like she-bears! Can't pry them away with a crowbar." Seamus didn't know if Peter heard or understood his words, but he had to say them, if for no other reason than to break the tension in the room. "There's only supposed to be two of us in here at a time, but Affie chewed off everyone's butts until they left us alone."

Peter slowly leaned back into the hospital bed, scrutinizing the acoustical tiles of the ceiling, seemingly unaware of the comments. Discomfort mounted as silence pervaded the room. For everyone there was a single haunting thought: was Peter's mind irreparably damaged? Only Mae, sleeping in her rocking chair at home and watching the hospital scene in her dreams, realized that Peter's metamorphosis into the being he was meant to become was, at last, well underway.

Nurse Phelps returned to the worry-filled room looking sourer than ever. "I've left a message for the hospital's internist, but he's very busy," she grumped with a look of pained self-sacrifice. She was backing out of the room when Afton's words caught her and reeled her back in.

"Hold on! What if Peter's had a stroke or something? I'm telling you, something isn't right. It would be nice if you acted like you cared."

The nurse tightened into a haughty pose. "Look, I can't spare a doctor right now," she reiterated, sounding like she was the personal dispensary for medical professionals. "But I can give him a thorough examination if that will make you feel better."

"At least it's something," Afton gibed.

"Fine. Some privacy please," the nurse requested.

Ooljee and Seamus stepped into the hall, but Afton stayed put, supervising the nurse with critical eyes.

Nurse Phelps decided not to force the issue. She shook her head and tried to calm herself as she walked to Peter's bedside. Bending down to take another look at his eyes, the source of unease and speculation, she softly protested, "Some days, this job just isn't worth it."

Peter tilted his pupils toward hers. His lips parted, and a soft, reassuring voice whispered, "It's alright Diane. I know about Bob. He'll come back to you, and he'll bring the kids with him."

The nurse flew back, stunned, her face drawn up in surprise. "What? How do you know...?" Quiet and blanched as a statue, Diane remained unmoving, flabbergasted, unable to look away from Peter.

"He knows you gave up the pills. He knows you've changed this time."

Nurse Phelps' fight or flight response finally kicked in, and her decision was to swiftly put distance between her and the unnerving patient. Thrashing backwards, arms and legs making exaggerated circles, she caught the IV tube in one careless rotation, pulling the needle and tube from Peter's arm and spraying the floor with saline and so many drops and slashes of blood that the spillage seemed to be a message in Morse Code.

Peter didn't feel any pain. Those mossy green eyes looked right into Diane, reading her thoughts, memories, every impression on her soul. She couldn't have known that all the times she'd put her hands on Peter since his admittance—altering his sleeping position, administering medication, taking readings, catheterizing him—he'd been connecting with her pain and delving into her mind, which was constantly occupied by regret and angst over a long-standing pain-killer addiction and her separation from her husband.

The nurse continued her clumsy retreat, tripping on her feet and crashing down as she tried to remove herself from Peter's gaze. Afton bolted forward to render assistance, but Diane righted herself before Afton could reach her.

"What's happening here?" Afton asked, trying to sort out Peter's words and the nurse's berserk reaction.

Peter started to get up and help the floundering woman from the ground, but she held up a hand, warding him off. "Stay away from me!"

Clambering across the floor, she screamed, "Stay back!"

Clawing at everything around her, she pulled herself up and shakily opened the door, passing Ooljee's and Seamus' curious faces. Diane Phelps, RN, was still screaming when she ran full-force down the hall, past the nurse's station, through the swinging doors into the maternity ward, and out an emergency exit, triggering a hospital-wide alarm. As the ear-piercing wail scraped through every room and corridor, Peter calmly rose from his bed, liberating himself from wire monitors and a catheter without even flinching.

"I don't know what that was about, but I think you better stay put," Afton said, feeling every logical explanation she reached for elude her mental grasp.

"There's no time. I have to see someone," Peter replied.

He scrounged through the supplies in his bedside table and found a packaged sterile gauze square. Pulling open its paper sleeve and unloosing the pad, he pressed it onto the bubbling wound on his forearm where Nurse Phelps had, quite by accident, removed his IV needle.

With the bandage in place, Peter shakily walked to the door and stepped out.

"Ah, man, you're not showing the world your best side," Seamus alerted Peter as he wandered into the hall with his unfastened hospital gown gaping, exposing his backside from neck to thigh. Peter didn't seem to notice, or at least to care.

"I have to find someone." In his hospital-issued blue terrycloth booties with white treads, Peter staggered ahead, prompting Seamus to run to take him by the arm before he toppled.

"You need a wheelchair, man."

"No time."

With a hard tug on the back of his gown, Seamus forced Peter to stop. He pulled the flailing sides together; they barely covered Peter's butt cheeks. "You let me get this, or they're gonna haul you off to a nudist colony," Seamus said, double-tying the laces. "There, now you've got a little privacy. So, where to?"

Peter stumbled forward at a quick but uneven pace.

Afton started to follow the men, but Ooljee held her back. "Let your brother do this," she said, and Afton silently agreed, watching Peter rush— quite inelegantly—from the ward, using Seamus as a rudder.

The medical staff hurried about trying to calm patients and allay fears after the brief false alarm. They paid no mind to Peter and the gargantuan redhead in the black and white uniform, who appeared to be a funky version of the Grim Reaper come to collect an expired soul.

Peter stopped at the junction of two long halls and looked right and left.

"Where are we going?" Seamus wondered.

"I have to see a man before he leaves here." Peter narrowed his eyes and lurched toward the right. "He's this way."

"Tell me his name, and I'll have someone look up his room number."

"Down there. The room in the corner," Peter said, leading the way with a pointed finger.

"You're shitting me! That's Lloyd Chang's room. They're gonna discharge him this morning."

"That's why I'm hurrying," Peter explained.

Seamus helped Peter into the room and looked around, surprised to not see Boyd at his post: the vinyl chair by the bed. "Hey, Mr. Chang. Where's Boyd?"

"He's having breakfast in the cafeteria." The older man looked antsy. "He's taking a long time; they're supposed to kick me out of here soon."

Lloyd watched Peter, waiting for an introduction.

"This is Peter Jacoby. Peter, this is Lloyd Chang."

Without sparing a word of greeting, Peter hobbled over to the bed and peered hard into the man's face.

Lloyd wondered at his out-of-sorts visitor, pegging him as either a paranormal buff or a fan of Arizona history. Either way, he assumed he was like so many he'd encountered over the years: someone who was excited to make his acquaintance because his bloodline offered a connection to Prosperity's storied past.

But Peter hadn't come to Lloyd's room to hear stories about old Prosperity or ask if he'd ever encountered any of his ancestors' spirits in the buildings of the haunted town. Instead, Peter would be the conduit to forgotten days and hidden knowledge.

"You dreamed about your father last night." That was a statement, not a question. "You were walking down a street, and Yee was behind you, trying to talk to you, but you couldn't hear him."

Lloyd made a move to speak but couldn't. The numbers on his heart monitor began to rise.

"I don't wish to upset you, Mr. Chang, but last night I saw your father's death and…felt his emotions. There are things you need to know."

"What is this?" Lloyd croaked.

Peter spoke quickly, trying to say everything he needed to before Lloyd threw him out or tuned him out. "I saw Yee on a couch, with a small red book in his hands and liquor bottles around him. He propped open the book before he died, hoping it would be read by whoever found him."

Lloyd's chin muscles spasmed and something akin to fear appeared in his eyes. He wanted to roll onto his side and shun Peter, but he couldn't.

Peter gently touched the man's shoulder. "Don't be afraid. I'm new to this, too." He drew a long breath and treaded further into sensitive territory. "What's been happening in the park is your father's doing, not Mad Molly's. He's tried to reach you for many years, but you haven't listened."

Overwhelmed by the shock and shame, Lloyd angrily asked, "Why?! What does he want?"

"Forgiveness. And for the truth to be known. What's in the book is important."

Lloyd explored Peter's eyes, feeling the powerful truth of the stranger's words, as he silently reviewed every unsettling occurrence in the park, the community center, his own home, until his lower lids cupped thick crescents of tears. How could he not have seen what was happening? How could he not have known it was his father trying to reach him and touch his mind and heart? He turned his face to the wall. "All this time…"

He thought of their last, dismal exchange when he'd cursed his father and fled with his mother, yet this time, remembering didn't hurt. The guilt lifted. So did the anger. His skin tingled, and a beautiful unnamed emotion filled him, like a balm to every injury his father had ever inflicted on his soul. He felt loved, warm, as if his daddy held him on his lap, the way he'd always wanted him to. Somehow, somewhere between this world and the next, Yee Chang had become more of a human being. Father and son had finally made peace.

All men should strive to learn before they die
what they are running from, and to, and why.

— James Thurber, "The Shore and the Sea"

PART IV: RESURRECTIONS

Journal of Yee Chang
May 27, 1953

I have not heard from my wife or son in three days. This evening, I walked
up Salome Hill to the Graham Boarding House. Twice I went by. On the
second pass, Rosemae came out, stood on the porch, and crossed her arms.
She asked if I wanted something, and I shook my head and said what a cool
evening it was. She nodded and went back inside. If ever she forgave me,
she has taken it back now. I have committed too many new sins.

There is no food left in the house except dried beans and rice. The
staples are enough to last me. I have beer and whiskey. I have toilet paper.
The radio works. And I have this journal to keep my mind occupied.

My back aches. Is this punishment? My own body must be on Xu's side.
Maybe it misses her. I miss her, and my son. I am surprised to find that I
long for them, as I long for the bottle and for peace. I cannot get right with
my family. I cannot square the past. Nothing can bring absolution, but
perhaps writing my confession will lift some of the misery of silence and
secrecy. I will try.

I came to Prosperity in 1899. I was a young 13 and glad to leave San
Francisco and the old ways, and my parents who wielded them, to seek my

fortune with my older brothers, Wu and Wei, and Wei's wife, Ting. We leased a building from Molly Petrova and opened Chang Brothers Restaurant on the bottom floor and lived in the apartment above. We worked hard and did good business. But Prosperity was not what we had hoped it would be.

It was wicked. After six months, we decided to sell and return to San Francisco, but Molly would not have it. We brought in much money for her. So she sent her muscle to intimidate us. A Cornish miner with knuckles that almost dragged the ground beat Wu to a pulp and delivered Molly's message: the Changs would stay in Prosperity until she had no use for them. He reminded us that people who ran afoul of Molly often ended up dead or worse; I learned very early that dead is not the worst thing a person can be.

We were trapped in an unholy existence. Every day, we feared for one another's welfare and wondered when Molly would demand a bigger cut or more concessions from us. Few people would have anything to do with us outside our restaurant. It was the easiest for me because I was the youngest. My siblings treated me tenderly and gave me time off for studies with Mr. Garibaldi, the school teacher. He was a good man who looked on me with pity when the townspeople would not allow their children to attend school with a Chinese student. Mr. Garibaldi ate dinner with us most nights, and then he and I studied in the kitchen. Year after year, he worked with me until I could read and write as well as any Englishman, perform complex equations, understand the laws of physics, identify any country on a map, recognize and speak about the masterpieces of Michelangelo and Renoir. Mr. Garibaldi called me his protégé and promised to begin teaching me Italian when I turned 17. He loaned me stacks of books and journals, some of which I still have because I had not yet returned them when he was robbed and knifed on Mine Cart Way. All he ever carried on him was $1 and the pocket watch his aunt gave him when he came to this country. Giorgio Garibaldi was 33 when he died, with no wife or child left behind. But I mourned him as I would have a father, and I began to fill with bitterness.

Life continued to be difficult, especially for Ting, who for many years was deprived of female company. Then in 1910, Sadie Rue came to work at the Canary Cage. Sadie was a looker and the top-paid girl in town, which put her at odds with the other prostitutes. As outsiders, Ting and Sadie fell into fast friendship and regularly confided in each other.

One evening, Sadie arrived with a black eye and cheek. Ting made her a poultice for the bruises and brewed strong tea for them both. They sat at the kitchen table as Sadie cursed herself for accepting a patron Gorley had warned her about. Gorley was the Canary Cage's muscle, a big Yavapai fellow, who had his own room on the ground floor, near the entrance, so he could screen the patrons.

This night, Gorley had opened the door to a stranger who introduced himself as Latreaux. The man was well groomed and held a big roll of cash while he explained that he was a man who accepted only the best and had heard the Canary Cage had the finest offerings in the region. Sadie said, to her regret, she stood up from the chaise she was resting on and haughtily announced that she was the best. Gorley tried to dissuade her. "He looks like a dandy to me. I can handle him," Sadie had said, and she took Latreaux upstairs.

Sadie said he was limp as an overcooked string bean no matter what she did. He explained that he required extra incentive and produced a set of brass knuckles with a claw on each hoop and put the device on his right hand. He pushed her face-down onto the bed and tried to slice her back, but she fought him off. He offered her extra money, but when she told him to put his clothes on and leave, he only got rougher and angrier. Sadie said he talked about how Molly let him use the claws on her ladies and even her pretty little blond boy as long as he did not damage his face. Sadie called loudly for Gorley. The big man was there in a heartbeat, pulled Latreaux from her, beat him senseless, and deposited him atop a pile of horseshit in the middle of the road outside the bordello.

When Sadie finished her story, she was shaking and bug-eyed. I thought that was because she had been attacked, and some of it was that. But she kept asking about the boy. Had Ting ever heard of him? What pretty little boy was Molly allowing evil men to carve up? She could not stop talking about the child Latreaux had mentioned. I would not think of this conversation again for years.

In 1918, the Spanish influenza claimed a fourth of Prosperity's population. It took three of my family. My brother Wu died in the first days of that plague. Later, Ting became ill. I had counseled her against volunteering to nurse the sick, but Ting was the kind to tend the needs of others. She died for that selflessness, as did her daughter, Yin. They departed on the same day, five hours apart. Yin was only seven.

After his wife and child died, Wei crumbled. I never knew a man to grieve so hard. My ever-solid brother was undone by the loss.

So was Sadie. She spent many hours in our apartment trying to care for us, as Ting had, but she was a terrible cook and knew nothing about running a home. Some of her efforts were comical. Even now, I smile when I remember Sadie frying a skillet of bacon at such high heat that the grease exploded. She threw her arms in the air, screamed, "Run for your lives!" and fled out the door while Wei calmly placed a lid over the pan and turned off the stovetop flame. It is a good memory.

Months passed, and we began to feel happiness again. Sadie knew good jokes and stories. She liked games. Gradually, she brought Wei back from the dark place he had gone. Friendship was strong among us. We considered Sadie our sister because Ting had called her that.

We continued to run the restaurant, but with Ting, Wu, and Yin gone, there was no meaning. We never made the fortune of which we dreamed. Molly extorted more and more over time. And often when we delivered food to Molly's establishments, we left without receiving payment or after being robbed. How we dreaded delivering food to those places! We were spat upon, taunted, shoved, and shot at. But more than any of this, when we entered those gambling halls and saloons, we were reminded of the innocent ones who suffered for Molly's profit. Sometimes we could hear their pleas and screams through the floorboards.

We had never seen the notorious basement rooms, but we knew where they were. A locked door behind the bar of the Red Garter Saloon led to a stairwell and cells, where the unwilling new girls were shackled and violated until they lost their resistance and could be transferred to the grimy cribs along Sin Alley.

Everyone knew this was happening, including the law, but nothing was done because Molly's syndicate was the most powerful and profitable in the state. The authorities who could not be bought would back down when their families were threatened. It was the same reason Molly, in the midst of Prohibition, openly operated four saloons. No one dared cross her.

The joke was that Molly made the lion's share of her fortune on the backs of women on their backs. But there was nothing comical about Sin Alley or the women who worked there. The youngest, prettiest prostitutes signed on with the Canary Cage or the Cajun Queen. This left the older, infirm, and unattractive workers for Molly, except for foreign slaves and those traded for coverage of debts, some of whom were young and comely. Molly kept business brisk by offering her ladies at low prices to anyone, though she lost a lot of "stock," as she called the women, to disease and violence and sometimes suicide. That meant she had to frequently replenish her holdings.

In 1921, word got out that Molly would pay a high bounty for girls and did not care how they were acquired. I heard that a man drove all the way from Tucson to offer his daughters. More than one youthful wife was turned over for the money, too. Sadie learned of a particularly unfortunate soul: a young girl stolen from the reservation. Molly did terrible things to break her. But it had been many months, and the girl was still in leg irons in one of the basement rooms. Her spirit, though not her body, was still intact. Sadie had cried when she talked about that child.

The following January, Molly placed a large order for a party at her apartment, which was the second and third floors over the Red Garter Saloon. Wei and I cooked all day and packaged the food into pails for transport. When we made the delivery, we were allowed inside Molly's apartment.

We were directed to prepare a buffet in the parlor, on a table set up along a piano. So, we transferred the food into silver bowls laid out on the white linen tablecloth. We arranged the servingware and lit the long white tapers and put a match to the smaller candles that warmed the chaffing dishes. We were almost through when a door at the back of the parlor opened and people began filing through it. Many were flushed, as though they had been dancing. They were all wealthy, by the looks of them. When they had emptied into the parlor and stood milling about, waiting for us to finish, I saw Wei freeze while scraping out a pail of dumplings. His eyes shone horror, and I followed their direction with my own, looking for what bothered him so.

In the backroom, one of Molly's hired muscle stood watch while two naked children dressed: a blond boy and an Indian girl. When the girl had put on a red dress and the boy was in knee pants, the guard pushed them out of the room. I will never forget the wounded looks of shame on those children's faces. The boy never raised his eyes, but the girl looked directly at Wei. Then one of Molly's crowd yelled, "Get to work, Chinamen! We're hungry!" and the guard shoved the children through the parlor and out the door.

I never saw Wei so angry. He could not calm down. I believe he saw Yin when he looked at that innocent girl. We stayed awake all night talking about what to do. Wei said he could not go on living in Prosperity knowing that children were being hurt like that. The next night, when Sadie came for dinner, we told her what we had seen. She was as angry as Wei had been, and when she cursed Molly, she cried because she knew what those children were going through. Again, we stayed up all night, and this time, with Sadie's help, we came up with a plan.

CHAPTER 23

Mayor Alvarez poked his head into the maintenance office and felt a stab of melancholy at the sight of Lloyd's empty desk. The light from the overhead fixture spotlighted Boyd, who was alone in the room, shifting some files and tidying up. He was a good kid, but a kid was how Sam still viewed him, not an able replacement for the elder Chang, who'd put heart and soul into caring for the Prosperity Community Center and all town property for 14 years.

Boyd heard the click of Sam's boots on the marble floor and gave a wave without turning around.

"He will be back, won't he?" the mayor asked.

Laying the files on the desk, Boyd turned and gave Sam his full attention. "The doctor said Grandpa will be fine."

"But he will be back?"

"Are you kidding? If he couldn't do this job, he'd go bananas."

Sam smiled, but worry came through as his gray mustache undulated over shaky lips. "Should you leave him alone so soon?"

"Ooljee's staying with him this week, while I'm here, and as he gets stronger, she'll look in on him during the daytime. He'll be spoiled rotten before you know it. The doctor said he can resume full-time work at the end of summer, as long as he doesn't do the heavy stuff. I'll handle that."

"You're a good grandson, you know that, Boyd? I wish my own grandkids took half the interest in me that you do with Lloyd. He's lucky to have you." Sam noticed the pile of papers and folders in front of Boyd and the overwhelmed look in the teen's eyes. "It doesn't all have to be done at once, you know."

"Okay, thanks."

"Is there anything I can do for you?"

Boyd thought for a moment. "Yeah, would you please explain things to

Roy, so I don't get shot or attacked by Captain if I have to work late?"

Sam chuckled. "Will do." He pulled the door shut, allowing Boyd to sort through his projects in quiet.

Boyd had been coming to the office since he was a kid, when he proudly and in awe watched his grandpa push papers at the big desk or rode through town with him on maintenance rounds and stopped by to pick up new orders or supplies; yet, for all his years of visiting the center or working in it, this was Boyd's first time alone in the room. It looked different without Lloyd at the helm, seated in the antique, swivel captain's chair behind the main desk.

There was a calmness in the office that Boyd hadn't expected. No presence, no oddness, nothing out of sorts. Overhead, a ceiling fan turned slowly, circulating cool, somewhat fusty air.

"I love the smell of old buildings," Boyd whispered, tasting the stale scent as he breathed it in.

What he didn't love was the thought of full-time maintenance work. He'd planned to stick to the part-time position until his grandfather retired, and he'd hoped with all his heart that wouldn't be long. Boyd thought a concussion, dehydration, and two stent placements would put the idea of retirement into Lloyd's head. But after only a handful of days away from his close-up look at mortality, his grandfather was anxious to get back to his old job. Boyd didn't see an end to his role as Lloyd's coverall-clad sidekick anytime soon.

"I always feel hoity here," Sam told Clare, who took up tiny silver tongs and deposited two sugar cubes into his cup before handing it over on a saucer with two petit fours and fresh raspberries.

Balancing his pale gray Stetson on his left knee, Sam watched her graceful actions with delight, receiving confirmation that his long-ago-bestowed gift of the hand-painted antique tea set had been the right choice.

Clare poured a cup for herself and leaned back. "I enjoy our visits."

Sam was a friend and, for a time, had been more. After his divorce, he and Clare had dated for a month, until they acknowledged they had the romantic chemistry of siblings and settled into a platonic relationship.

Slicking down his thick gray mustache with a thumb and forefinger, Sam began, "I'll come right to the point. I was going to call an emergency meeting of the historical society but then decided it would be better to speak to you about matters."

"What matters do you mean?"

"Mainly the Prosperity Days Festival. I don't want to entertain this idea, but maybe we should postpone or cancel, what with Lloyd's health and all. And now our guest speaker, that Doris what's-her-name from the mining board, has to back out of the lecture. I called and told Lloyd—since he's the one who made the arrangements. He was disappointed, of course, but then he called me back later saying he was going to give the lecture himself."

"Oh, he can't do that. He's practically bed-ridden," Clare retorted.

"I agree. I don't know what's going on in that brain of his. Is he maybe feeling guilty about leaving us in the lurch, so he thought he had to volunteer?"

"Goodness, I hope not. What does he want to talk about?"

"He wouldn't say except that it's about old Prosperity and should interest the entire crowd."

Both Clare and Sam were intrigued...and also somewhat edgy about what had spurred the recuperating town caretaker to volunteer for the speech and whether or not, in his fragile shape, he'd be able to pull it off.

Sam's shoulders fell. He moaned. "Should we cancel the weekend—or the lecture?"

Clare was speechless. The weekend had never been put off. It was the historical society's major fundraiser and brought in more money for Prosperity businesses than any event except the Halloween Costume Ball and Ghost Walk. She nervously rubbed a lipstick stain from the rim of her teacup. "Realistically, we can't forbid Lloyd from giving the lecture, and we can't cancel. If he doesn't already feel guilty, he will if we let this disrupt the festival."

"I hadn't thought of that." Sam balked at his lack of foresight. "Well, then, Lloyd is officially this year's guest lecturer." He inspected the tiny pink-icing flowers piped onto his petit fours before devouring both treats.

Clare watched Sam's brows rise and fall and bounce together. "Is there something else?"

"It isn't just the lecture. I'm so...stressed. Lloyd being out from work is causing some problems. I had a couple last-minute projects in the queue to prepare for the festival...and if the visitors' park gets torn apart anytime soon, there's no way Boyd can handle it alone."

"That is a predicament."

Clare doled out more petit fours, and they snacked in a reflective stillness that lasted but a minute. Throughout that time, Clare was turning over Sam's problem in her mind, and Sam was thinking of how elegant he felt in Clare's parlor, taking tea and dainties. He also thought of what a magnificent politician's wife Clare would make, genteel but with the right touch of scandal in her showgirl background. Then he remembered their clunky attempt at coupling, which ended practically before it began. On second thought, his two big mutts, Beau and Buck, were about the only permanent houseguests he could imagine devoting himself to at this stage of his life.

"You need someone young and strong to help until Lloyd gets back on his feet, which—good Lord willing—will be soon," Clare thought aloud. She drilled her sad eyes through the parlor's large window, in the direction of the Chang residence. Planting her teacup on the table, she sang out, "Oh, I know just the man!"

CHAPTER 24

"Please stop pacing, Peter."

Ooljee slid her half-frame reading glasses down her nose and looked up from the notes she was preparing for an upcoming women's expo appearance. It would be her 81st lecture on the use of psychics by law enforcement, and she was trying to think of a new angle.

Peter stopped mid-stride in front of the picture window. "I apologize. My mind is going wild. Right now, I'm seeing Jamie Clancy clip his toenails in his room in the Canary Cage. Why that? I don't want to see that. I don't want to see most of the things I've seen."

"Your mind's been unplugged after all these years and is being flooded with stimuli. Mama thinks things will level out once your brain settles into its groove."

"Good. This is aggravating. Not just the visions…I have so many new memories that I don't know what to do with them."

"Do you want to share some?"

"These aren't the kind one wants to share."

"Those can be the ones you most need to share. I'm your sister now. What's family for if not helping each other?"

"Right, yes. Family." Peter was still trying to figure out what that word really meant. "I'll tell you…someday."

Ooljee coolly raised an eyebrow. "That's a cop out."

Hands clasped behind his back, Peter walked to the middle of the parlor and peered down the central hall, which stretched toward a cabinet stocked with mementos from Ooljee's school days: a ceramic donkey so poorly crafted that it looked like a camel, knick-knacks made of shell, yarn drawings, a few small, framed photos.

"Has it always been just the two of you here?"

Ooljee pulled off her glasses and laid them on her stack of notes. "Yes.

We've had 48 years together here." Ooljee looked toward Mae's bedroom, where the old woman napped. "I wish you could've known Mama when she was at her peak. We'd talk all day and never use our mouths. She'd show me visions from half a world away. She was something else, and still is, but her mind isn't as strong as it used to be…though she's much better since you arrived. You've given her a new reason to be alive and engaged."

"But I've intruded in your lives and your home…"

"You haven't, and it's OUR home," Ooljee corrected. "You belong here. Frankly, not many people can handle it. Once, we tried to adopt three girls, sisters. Those poor kids didn't last a week before they were begging to go back to the group home. We explained what was happening and that they weren't in any danger, how nothing they saw or heard could hurt them, but every night, they slept with Mama and cried until dawn. So, Mama and I swore we wouldn't inflict our haunted house on other children…or pets. We had two cats and two dogs live out their days with us. We loved those guys, but animals are so sensitive, you know. They'd sense everything and were nervous wrecks most of the time. When the last one died, we decided it was unfair to bring others into our freaky house. Now we just feed the birds and the feral cats that live on the hill." Pushing a tumble of black curls behind her right ear, Ooljee cued, "I'm blabbing, and you're avoiding the subject—memories."

Peter trudged back to the window. "I saw everything," he replied in a graveled voice. "It's hard to believe something like that was gone from my memory for so long."

"I didn't see it all, but enough. It's stayed with me here and here." Ooljee touched her head and the area over her heart. "You're very brave."

"No. You saw what happened. I did nothing."

"What could you have done?" Ooljee asked. "You were a kid. A victim. You grew into a good man, and yes, believe me, that's a brave thing in itself. Do you know how many victims end up self-destructing or go on to victimize others? Some people suffer and do what they can to spare others that pain. Some suffer and don't care if others do, too; the worst of them want others to suffer with them, even at their own hands. Your attacker fit into the last category. You fit into the first. Be proud of that."

Peter leaned against the cool windowpane, trying to relieve his inner fever. Ooljee stayed seated, keeping her distance, not wanting to make him feel trapped and pressured into a confession. She watched from behind as he started to speak.

"I always felt I was a burden to my parents, maybe a mistake. Only my grandmother showed me love and support, and I loved her more than anything. Granny Weston tried so hard to be a part of my life, but my father did everything he could to keep her from me. Once, I heard him refer to her as 'that fat hillbilly' and say that he didn't want me around her because I'd pick up her ways."

Ooljee clicked her tongue, saddened and appalled by the callousness.

"She was the one person I should have told. But I was too ashamed. When it first started, I told my nanny. She called me a liar. Then Deke threatened to hurt my mother if I said anything. I thought he'd kill us both."

Peter sniffed back emotion. "I knew Granny Weston would believe me and protect us. She would have done anything for me and loved me no matter what. But the shame was…paralyzing. Even when I had the chance, I didn't tell her. Yet there was hope because I believed the bad things would stop if I ever did speak up." Peter paused until he could continue without crying. "Granny died when I was 12. I lost the one person who loved me. I lost hope. Then, I knew Deke's assaults would go on and on, and no one would care."

"Oh, Peter…" Ooljee lamented.

Peter stared out the unobstructed pane of glass, onto the green lawn and yellow roses the size of salad plates.

"Granny Weston worked three jobs to provide my mother a good education and opportunities. She was so proud of how she turned out. Mother was a local news anchor, and after she married my father—who was richer than King Midas—she became a major socialite. She was a big deal around Nashville. My father loved how the wealthy set fawned over her and wanted her at their parties, and how people would stop her on the street to tell her how much they adored her. What people thought about him and his family mattered more than anything to my father. That rubbed off on my mother. As I got older, the more like him she became, and the less I saw Granny Weston."

Raising one hand to touch his reflection in the glass, Peter asked, "Did you see my mother die?"

"Yes, and I saw some of what came before," Ooljee admitted. "But I don't know the whole story. That's safe with you."

"I don't want it to stay with me. I think you're right. I should tell you."

Ooljee scooted closer to Peter. "Well, then, I'm honored."

"Where to begin?" Peter mumbled. After a steadying breath, he launched his narrative. "I was 14 when it ended. Our groundsman had been abusing me for years. I hated it, and I hated him, but I was resigned. I was a scrawny kid, too small to fight Deke, and I accepted that no one would believe me if I told…or that worse would happen. So, I tried to cut myself off from the experiences while they were occurring. I'd learned to suppress the ghost images and visions and the thoughts that flew at me from other people's minds, but I couldn't always ignore Deke's physical assaults. How could I disregard his hands all over me and his fish odor and his breathing that sounded like a rasp on wood? I can still hear that grating sound; it was so heavy that I sometimes thought he'd die...wished he'd die.

"I never knew when it was coming, but I knew it would happen sooner or later, and it always hurt, and it was always a monstrous humiliation that I felt guilty about. Can you imagine that? I felt guilty for what that man did to me! I'd showered and cried the first few times, but after that, I stopped crying, and I stopped trying to wash Deke off of me, out of me. I didn't even comb my hair anymore. I didn't care, and I wouldn't have done anything but stay in bed if Lotta hadn't forced me to get up and go about life." Peter's hand tensed, his fingertips curled against the window, as if he were trying to free himself. "I thought that September day was going to be like all the other times—that Deke would do his thing, and I'd take it like an automaton—but it was so much worse. You can't imagine the disgrace I felt when my mother walked in." He clamped his teeth and bent forward, trying to hide his face. "I wanted to die." His throat tightened, turning his words guttural. "You know I killed her, don't you?"

"You didn't kill her."

"I let her be killed. If I'd told someone what Deke had been doing...if I'd moved to help her when Deke attacked her..."

"Don't do this to yourself, Peter. I know you feel responsible. I've sensed that since I touched you in the Canary Cage, but it isn't true. You were a scared, hurt boy. You tried to tell, and even if you hadn't, you have to remember that you're the victim. What happened to your mother—and you—is Deke's fault, not yours."

Peter nodded, trying to believe what she said. He opened his mouth to speak but shut it again, cowering at the remembrance.

"You don't need to say anything. I know how that day ended," Ooljee hushed.

"May I try something?" Peter timidly asked.

"Go on," Ooljee allowed, and Peter put his hands on her head, his thumbs plugged into her temples, fingers bracing the sides in the same manner Mae used when transmitting or collecting mental images.

Ooljee began to pull away, remembering the emotional scourging she'd endured on Raymond Aguilar's behalf, an ordeal that continued to disturb her slumber and her soul. But then, she leaned back in, deciding to take a chance for Peter's sake.

The connection occurred almost immediately. Peter's energy pierced Ooljee's mind and held her to the spot. There was no option but for her to remain motionless. Her eyelids spasmed, eyes drifting back and forth, looking at the objects and framework of a long-gone scene, seeing things as Peter had seen them that fall day of his 14th year. Instantly, Ooljee felt as he had, suffered as he had.

The setting was the bedroom she'd seen before when she'd grabbed Peter in the Canary Cage and was submerged in a visionary tidal wave from his past. It was a spacious L-shaped room lit by hanging brass lamps. Three redbud trees grew straight and slim outside a tall, double-hung window, which was opened wide. A brass bed swathed in a suede-patchwork comforter; an armoire; bookcases; and a cedar trunk topped by a chess set, situated between leather chairs, furnished the space. It was far too serious and sophisticated a room for a boy, and a strange setting for the distasteful figure of the family's groundskeeper.

Deke loomed like a thunderhead, his face clouding lustful crimson. His denim straps were unbuttoned, his overalls puddled around his legs. Between his puffy bullfrog throat and his thighs were rolls of hairless, bare flesh that resembled crowded pink hills. A stench like stagnant pond water came off him. It was the beginning of an encounter, not the end. Naked, Peter stood awkwardly still and gripped his headboard, wishing for it all to be over. There was no cognizance of Ooljee Davis and no thoughts or feelings of her own. She was living this moment exactly as Peter had when the memory was created.

Bent in submission, Peter felt the chilled air tease a million tiny prickles from the smooth skin of his chest and concave stomach. The boy's mind was kicking into self-preservation mode by drifting away to another place. Peter—Ooljee—concentrated on the chess set on the trunk, the pieces placed where he and Lotta had left them during an unfinished game. The mind escape was deepening. The focus shifted entirely away from Deke and held to a white rook. Every thought was about chess; total concentration; nothing to spare on what was about to happen in the room; no, Deke wasn't there; the whole world now revolved around chess. *White rook moves to open file. That's it. Yes. Check mate in two moves.*

In a split second, the illusion was shattered. The doorknob clicked and the bedroom door opened. The world was no longer a black-and-white chess set. Peter was back in the room with Deke, mortified beyond conception as his mother walked in, a martini in one hand, making a rare and unanticipated appearance in her son's room.

"Your father and I are driving to Memphis tonight to…"

The woman searched the vast room as she spoke, and when she laid eyes on Peter, her words clipped off. She wavered in her navy pumps, staring aghast at her son and the obese gardener paired together, unclothed, Deke's hands about to make contact with Peter. Silence ensued for only a short time as the woman comprehended what she was witnessing.

"Get away from him!" she fumed. Fury painted her face, which looked even redder set against her pale French twist. Samantha Weston-Jacoby seemed the consummate socialite in a tailored dark blue pantsuit and pearls, but her psyche was fraying as she realized the extent to which she'd been ignorant of her child's situation. If there was one emotion that competed with the wrath in her it was remorse for not having known what was happening and stopping it.

"Put on some clothes, Pete, and go downstairs. Don't be afraid. Go on," she instructed, conjuring her best, but obviously artificial, smile to comfort her son.

Ooljee's gaze remained stationary, indicating that Peter hadn't followed his mother's instructions. The reasons: incapacitating fear and, to a lesser degree, his reluctance to leave his mother in the same room as his foe.

Deke bent over to grab his overalls, but Samantha offered him no chance at dignity. Hurling her martini at him, she yelled, "Stay where you are, you son of a bitch!"

She sidestepped over to the wireless phone on a bookcase. Deke's eyes moved quickly to each side, looking for an escape route. He was a trapped animal, desperate to be free, a creature that would have gnawed off its own entangled foot. He was certain to bite and claw and go down fighting. Mrs. Weston-Jacoby lifted the phone, keeping an unbroken stare on her son's assailant. She began to dial, but Deke wasn't about to let her make the call.

Grunting like a charging rhino, the man lunged toward her, his gait slowed by his overalls-hobbled feet. Samantha made one loud, long scream for help as Deke cumbersomely barreled at her.

"Hush up, hush up," he chanted, seething.

The weight of his body knocked the wind from Samantha's lungs as he slammed her against the wall, ending her shriek. Where her head struck, the plaster cracked into a web of thick lines. The woman looked like a floppy chew toy flung from a puppy's mouth as Deke grabbed her and threw her sideways, her limp body crashing into the bookcase and sending a collection of texts onto the ground, around where she fell.

Samantha had been knocked from her pumps, and all Peter could see of her were pantyhose-enshrouded feet protruding from under Deke's squatting, naked body as his thick arms flailed away, his fists pounding out of her what life was left.

Desperate to help his mother, Peter took a step toward Deke, but his body locked in terror; he struggled to move on from the shock of being discovered in mid-violation and witnessing the desecration being visited upon his mother.

As Peter forced another step, his father appeared in the doorway, holding his hunting rifle at eye level. The balding man in a black Armani jacket and alligator shoes sidled in and quickly wheeled around, taking aim at Deke. Franklin Jacoby had often stared down that .22's barrel at innocent game flushed into the open by hunting tour guides, but he'd never faced dangerous prey worthy of his bullet and his ire.

Deke froze for a scant moment before gracelessly rising and stepping from his felled victim, backing away from the rifle, making no explanation. Corpulently nude, blood spattered across his torso and head, he was an image from the most perverse of nightmares.

Franklin looked left, mouth agape at the sight of his dead wife, her face an unrecognizable red mush beneath a swirl of blood-dyed hair. He then looked right, at his naked son, who only now was able to see what had become of his mother. Peter screamed, his broken adolescent voice pitched high like a hawk's cry.

Triggered by the sound, Deke kicked off his overalls and stumbled toward the opened window, exploring his only chance of a getaway. He crawled onto the sill, balancing between the white curtain panels, and looked down three stories. Whether or not he'd decided to risk the jump made no difference. His fate was sealed.

Peter flinched as a shot rang out, momentarily deafening his left ear. He saw a puff of smoke and a red circle with a dark bulls-eye appear on Deke's chest as he was blasted from the window. His last expression was a quizzical one—eyelids peeled back, eyebrows raised, mouth a perfect "o"—as if he couldn't believe what was happening. He flew straight back off the sill, and dropped, exiting like a cartoon character that briefly hangs in midair and then is gone.

Peter's numb hand reached out for Franklin, who leaned over his wife's body, horrified, his spent rifle flung on the ground. But the man rebuffed his son's touch as he looked up and asked, "What did you do?"

That was all Peter needed to share. It was the one complete, life-changing scene that had closed his mind for years and sweltered in his soul, poisoning his being, until Martin Schrader's blood-encrusted, faceless corpse began to dislodge it. He didn't need to go on with other memories, like watching his father being led away in handcuffs or watching him come home two years later with a distrustful stare that demonstrated how he'd never stopped blaming Peter for his wife's death. He didn't need to recount the ugly trial or his unhappy placement with his guardian—the vice president of his father's chemical company—or at the age of 19 walking into what had once been his parents' bedroom and finding his father dangling from a rope tied to the ceiling fan. Franklin had died without acknowledging—or inquiring about—Peter's victimization. During the trial, he maintained that Peter had been nowhere around when he found Deke over his wife's lifeless body; the police assumed the groundskeeper had attempted to rape Samantha Weston-Jacoby and beat her into unconsciousness when she resisted. The truth of Peter's long-term abuse never came out. It was one more thing the boy, and then the man, had learned to suppress.

Yes, Peter had shared enough. As he removed his hands, Ooljee crashed forward onto the parlor's floorboards. She wheezed, her fingers stretching into the air, reaching for aid. "He...help me," implored.

"Oh no..." Peter panicked, stooping down to lift Ooljee's head. Her eyes were crossed beneath half-closed lids.

"Please forgive me! I didn't know…"

Peter was spent from his experiment and had little strength to deal with the fallout. He tucked his arms under Ooljee's back and knees and strained to stand. "Miss Bennally!" he shouted.

By the time he was upright, holding Ooljee, Mae was in the room, worriedly inspecting the scene. She tottered toward her disoriented daughter and slid her hands against each side of her face. "Awee'," she called, patting her cheeks. "What happened?" she asked Peter.

"I think I killed her!"

Ooljee's head rolled. She cursed in Navajo and opened her eyes, hazily training them on Peter's face. "That was t'óó diigis! Don't ever do that again!"

"Thank God you're alive. Please forgive me! I didn't mean to hurt you."

Ooljee's facial muscles twitched as sensation returned. "Your energy was running through me like an electrical current. It's too damn powerful!" She wriggled about until Peter put her down and then woozily leaned on his shoulder. She held a finger between her eyebrows, putting pressure where the pain was the worst. "I'll be okay…but you have to learn how to temper what and how you share. Otherwise, your next human fuse box might get fatally overloaded."

CHAPTER 25

"SANTA RITA COACH RELEASED ON BAIL," screamed the *Verde Valley Trumpet* headline.

That was a shock. The Schraders didn't think Mark Jensen would be able to supply the $50,000 to buy his temporary freedom, but they underestimated both his wife's savings account and the community support from people who couldn't believe the coach who guided their hometown teams to victory season after season was capable of the most deplorable violation of trust. They didn't want to believe, refused to believe, that the man who stood inside the locker room as their naked sons toweled off had more than state tournaments on his mind. As testament to their faith in Jensen's character, several of his followers opened their pocketbooks for his bail money and defense fund, a development that sickened everyone who knew Martin hadn't lied when he took pen and paper and set down an accusation too scandalous for him to live with.

Ooljee answered the telephone and roused Peter from his chair at the kitchen table, where the breakfast dishes were scattered among cards. The trio had been playing poker, one of the more enjoyable tools they used to increase Peter's telepathy and remote sensing abilities.

"Let's take a break. I'm a tad worn down," Mae admitted, rubbing her eyes.

"It's Afton, and she sounds excitable," Ooljee notified.

Peter put the phone to his ear and greeted her, triggering a breathless outpouring. "You won't believe it! Mark Jensen is walking around a free man. Maybe not for long, but he's not locked up, and he has a team of idiots on his side rallying for charges to be dropped. Emma Schrader told me she and her husband received a couple of threatening calls from his rah-rah squad. Can you imagine?"

Peter's face was set in a grid of concern and repugnance.

"Unbelievable," he whispered.

"I feel so bad for the Schraders. How much pain do they have to endure? They've lost Martin because of that pervert, yet they're the ones being vilified. What's wrong with people? Oh, and guess what. The police can't locate any damaging photos on the coach's computer. Apparently, he got a new model this spring, and no one knows what happened to the old one. Convenient, huh?! That creep is cleverer than he looks. The guy's gonna walk. We both know it."

Peter was bleeding inside for a boy who'd been cruelly used and whose memory was now being sullied.

"Peter, are you still there?"

"I was thinking about the situation."

"Sure, hey, I'm the one who's sorry. I shouldn't have brought it up. You're still recovering. You've been through a lot yourself. Are you feeling better?"

"I'm getting stronger by the hour, thanks."

Afton had no idea that Peter's mind as well as his body was strengthening, and in terms that modern science couldn't explain.

"That's good to hear." Afton grew quiet, somewhat embarrassed by her impassioned call. "Well, I'll let you go. I just wanted to share the news. I figured you'd want to know."

"You were right to call, Afton. Thanks." As Peter hung up the phone, he was already planning how to help Martin Schrader once more.

"Mark Jensen?" Peter asked, confronting the muscular man crouched in front of a lawnmower set on bricks, changing the oil. The coach's hands were smeared with grease, his jogging shorts and orange Padsley's Gym T-shirt soiled with organic green stripes from a morning of heavy landscaping.

"Who wants to know?"

"Peter Jacoby."

The man recognized the name. It was apparent by the way his blue eyes shifted quickly down to the mower and back up at Peter, who did not put forth his hand for a handshake.

"My lawyer says to make no comments, so you might as well leave." The man hooked a crescent wrench around a bolt and gave a tug, channeling his embarrassed rage into the forceful twist of his wrist.

"I'm not interested in your comments," Peter answered.

"Oh yeah? Well, leave anyway."

"Not yet."

Mark pointed the wrench at Peter. "This is private property. You're trespassing."

"That's a small crime compared to yours, Coach Jensen."

"That does it. I want you out of here." The man pushed himself up, his arm muscles rippling with tension. Mark was no taller than Peter but more filled-out. He used his beefy stature to try to intimidate his visitor. Sticking out his chest and positioning his mouth close to Peter's ear, he angrily demanded, "Beat it. My wife'll be back from the store anytime, and I don't want her hearing whatever garbage you're about to unload."

"You mean you don't want her to hear the truth," Peter clarified. He compared the coach to his own assailant. Mark was a beautiful physical specimen, fit, tanned, young, whereas Deke had been old enough to be Peter's grandfather, a slovenly ovoid mass of ruddy, dimpled flesh. But appearances meant nothing. Martin's assault had been no less traumatic because his offender was attractive. Coach Jensen was a monster, just as Deke had been.

"I know how Martin felt," Peter said.

Mark snickered, "I don't know what you're talking about."

Peter pushed on, aware that his opponent was losing temper and nerve. "You see, I know what it's like for someone you trust to hurt you in so terrible a way that you think your life is over. I know how it feels to blame yourself for what that person did to you and carry such shame that you can't ask for help, even from the people closest to you. I've been where Martin was, but fortunately I came back from that dark place."

"Yeah, whatever. I still don't know what you're talking about." Mark shoved Peter aside so that he could disappear indoors and avoid further discomfort, but he didn't get far.

"You're going to know exactly what I mean. You're going to know what Martin went through, and you're never going to hurt another child. Never, you understand?"

Peter grabbed the man's head, fitting his palms atop his ears, remembering the grip Mae had used on him when she'd shared her own memories, the same grip he'd used on Ooljee when he'd almost, accidentally, sent her into a state of permanent disrepair. There was a brief, violent struggle as the coach reacted to the strange touch, but once Peter's fingers burrowed in, finding the indentations of Mark's temples, the scuffle ended.

With all his energy, Peter transmitted the memories stored inside his brain—his own and Martin's. He clamped his eyes so tightly together that pink tears bled out. His teeth were bared as he poured all his power into the transference, plunging Mark into scenes that were somewhat familiar yet also new and injurious in their updated context. Into the coach's mind, in vivid detail, came the cabin in Flagstaff. It was a recognizable backdrop, the events all too fresh, but Mark was not experiencing the moment as he had before, when pitiless urges moved him to find gratification in the unthinkable. No, now he was Martin, feeling, seeing, understanding as

Martin had. There was nothing pleasurable, only pain, fear, degradation, disbelief, and a sense of loss too great to fully comprehend. He saw his own face through Martin's blurred, drugged eyes, and it was not a handsome one. It was warped with selfish perversion, unidentifiable as the visage that greeted him in the mirror every day. Through Martin's lost vision, Coach Jensen saw himself as he truly was: an abomination.

Mark began to mumble; his eyes were opened to the daylight yet saw nothing but those images Peter willed him to view. And still, Peter held his focus, moving the coach back through time to his own first sordid moments with Deke, when he'd learned how frightening a place the world can be. That initial encounter, in the tool shed, brought tears from the coach and caused him to cry out in pain. "No more...pleash," he slurred between scenes, in a fleeting few seconds of coherence. But Peter had more to share.

He continued imposing memories on Coach Jensen: him sitting mortified in his 5th-grade classroom as he soiled his pants, unable to control himself after multiple violations; Martin driving to a Verde River refuge where, feeling damaged beyond salvation, he chronicled his abuse and plans for suicide. And still Peter went on. Offenses were imparted in rapid-fire succession, condensed in time but not magnitude, each tragedy building on the last, piling into an insurmountable emotional burden. By the time the last, gruesome scene of Martin sailing over the bank and into the bed of Dead Horse Canyon was recounted, Mark was bent, then prone, sobbing, breath rattling, feeling the indignity and horror of his victim and another like him. He'd taken into his being the physical, emotional, and spiritual wounds of two boys who'd been dishonored on every level.

Coach Jensen had felt the ruin of young lives, the sudden and violent loss of innocence, and for the first time ever, had been forced to understand the full weight of his actions. He was a broken man, both mind and body bent to Peter's will. Beyond the memories and emotions, the residue of Peter's raw power ripped through the coach's being, resonating in every aching, overtaxed corner of psyche and form. Mark was damaged, just as Ooljee had warned. Nineteen minutes under Peter's grip, and he was beyond hope. Despite his hard-earned muscles, he couldn't withstand the assault Peter had inflicted on behalf of a high-school baseball player and a soft-spoken boy from Tennessee.

"Now you know what it felt like to be on the other side," Peter crowed, leaving the coach twitching like a newly birthed creature, gagging on his spittle in his freshly manicured yard.

"There's no comparison, my good man! 1963's *the Haunting* is horror at its purest," Clive passionately bellowed. "It relies on psychological subtleties to tweak the viewer's deepest fears. The part with the unseen force holding Nell's hand…sheer perfection! It's terrifying because of what you don't see but can imagine."

Seamus smirked. "Subtleties shmutleties. Come on, man, what's a ghost gonna do to you? But the devil—man, there's nothing scarier. *The Exorcist* has frightened the snot out of more people than any movie! Ever! Afton—the Iron Maiden herself—slept with the lights on for a week after she saw it."

"Keep it down, guys. My grandpa's asleep upstairs," Boyd reminded, putting a finger to his lips. "If you're through, maybe we can get back to business, unless you want to fight about something else stupid. Most complex villain? Worst screen adaptation of a good book?"

"That would be the 1999 version of *the Haunting*, based on Shirley Jackson's novella, *the Haunting of Hill House*," Clive answered without pause. "Have you seen it? Abysmal! The blithering twit responsible for that travesty should be flogged."

"Here we go again," Seamus groaned.

Boyd yanked his hair and opened his mouth in a frustrated silent scream. "Okay, dudes, conversation about Shirley Jackson is off limits for the rest of the day."

The ghost hunters sat cross-legged on the Changs' living room floor, eating cheeseburgers and onion rings and reading submissions for PIP membership. They drew applications for review, like playing cards, from a three-inch-high stack at their center.

Boyd had created three piles for filing the submissions, which had been rolling into PIP's e-mail account since they posted the application form months before. Several papers were in the "Hell, no" pile, a few in the "Maybe," and only two in the "Definitely interview" group.

A cough came from upstairs, a manufactured one that said "I can hear you."

Boyd cringed. "Okay, seriously, dudes, let's keep the noise down and get focused. Ooljee will be back from Sedona soon, and I'll have to go to work."

"Hey, how's your granddad getting along?" Seamus quietly asked.

"It's hard for him to stay off his feet, but he knows he has to build his strength, especially now that he's giving the lecture for the Prosperity Days Festival."

"What's he gonna talk about?"

"No idea. He won't tell me."

"I'd like to hear him, and I wanna see the go-kart derby, but I don't know if I'm gonna be able to get away for any events this year. Afton's still being kinda flaky. Who knows when she'll come back to the grill? How about you guys? You going to any of the events?"

"I have to stick with my grandpa, so probably just the lecture. What about you, Clive?"

Clive was bent over a set of applications, sucking mustard off his fingers like a nursing child. "This chap must be soft in the head. He submitted separate forms for his spirit familiars since he says they'll accompany him on investigations. We have one for a dog, one for a Native American shaman named Brown Bear, and one for Belinda, a pioneer woman. The man writes, 'my familiars are frequently with me during the day and watch me while I sleep, telling me their thoughts.'"

"Dude, that's a serial killer in the making!" Boyd joked. He lowered his voice to a creepy whisper. "The dog told me to strangle the members of PIP and cook them on my patio grill. I made necklaces out of their vertebrae and teeth. Aren't they pretty?"

Clive slipped the applications into the "Hell, no" stack, and nonchalantly addressed Seamus' question. "I'm taking Clare to the dance and the lecture. Ergo, no SpecTours by Night outings this Saturday. I'm losing a fortune for love."

Clive picked up another application and began reading, while his cohorts ogled each other bewilderedly.

Boyd did some fishing. "Sam can't take her this year?"

"He and Clare are merely friends." Clive lowered the paper and, with a look of dawning realization, explained. "Sorry, old boys, did I fail to inform you that Clare and I are seeing each other?" Facing the blank looks of his colleagues, he added, "Romantically."

"Get out!" Boyd said, throwing an onion ring at the ghoulish entrepreneur.

The gravity of Clive's expression convinced Boyd that the unusual pairing was for real.

"Dude, she's, like, great-granny age!"

"Clare is a handsome woman. Besides, the soul is more important than the shell."

"Yeah, but that's a really old shell."

Ignoring the insult, Clive placed the application in "Maybe" and fetched another.

"You mean, you'd do someone that wrinkled?"

"I say, that's uncalled for! Don't speak of Clare in such crude terms!"

"I wouldn't worry about deflowering Clare. A few dozen, maybe hundreds, got there first." Boyd wrapped his arms around his stomach and rolled over, crying with laughter. When he picked himself up, his three remaining onion rings were squished flat and stuck to the side of his gray Billabong T-shirt. Boyd pulled them off and frowned at the fist-sized grease stain near his right breast. "I'm lactating oil."

"Serves you right," Seamus said.

"I'm just saying what you're thinking."

Seamus had witnessed enough. "Leave him alone, man."

"I can't. This is too good…"

"Jealous cause Clive snagged an ex-showgirl?"

Boyd was incredulous. "That's sick! She's, like, 150! Clive's only 28!"

"You wanna be quiet, man? Your granddad can hear everything with you yelling like that," Seamus cautioned, pointing upstairs.

Boyd whispered loudly, "Come on, Shay! Clive and Clare? That's wrong! It's gross!"

The air was thickening with bruised feelings and ugly words. Seamus wouldn't play any part in wounding Clive or maligning Clare, two lonely people with harmless eccentricities. "I never thought you were so close-minded, man. If they're happy and not hurting anyone, what's it to you?"

Clive sat up straighter. Every pretense fell away as he showed his vulnerability to the friend who had his back. In a perfectly plain American accent, Clive softly confessed, "Clare gets me…she's the only one who ever has."

"Go for it," Seamus encouraged, attempting to fist bump Clive, who made an uncoordinated jerk to the side and instead punched his own shoulder. As Boyd sniggered at the failed macho ritual, Seamus smoothly turned his motion into a congratulatory slap on the back. "I'm happy for you, man."

CHAPTER 26

Peter was practically hyperventilating when he coasted into the driveway. After driving around the Verde Valley for more than an hour, trying to calm down and let the Buick's a/c blow the sweaty patches off his shirt, he was still a revved-up mess. But he needed to get back to Mae. Ooljee was running errands in Sedona and then would be playing nursemaid to Lloyd Chang. It was up to Peter to keep an eye on the psychic centenarian.

He stepped out, raking his hair with his fingers, trying to look pulled together.

Mae was waiting for him on the porch, arms crossed over her chest, shawl wrapped around her though it was a sunny 90 degrees out.

"Want to tell me where you've been?" she asked before he'd made it to the steps. Her countenance was unusually hostile.

"I had business in Santa Rita."

"Business...hmph," Mae looked down her nose at Peter, shaking her head. "I know what business you've been up to. You almost killed a man this morning! He's never going to be right again because of you."

Peter was offended by the scolding. He'd expected Mae's questioning, but not outright derision, not for attacking a tormentor like Coach Jensen. He roared back, "He wasn't right to start with! He destroyed a boy...more than one boy. Martin Schrader wasn't the first, but he'll be the last. I saw to that!"

He stepped back, wondering if this was the end of his relationship with Mae and his stay in Prosperity. Finally, he thought, he may have crossed the line.

"Child, you don't have any idea what you've done."

"I'd call it justice," Peter said through stiff lips.

"I would, too," Mae answered.

Peter squinted at the woman. "You would? Then...why..."

Mae shuffled over to the porch swing and took a seat, patting the empty space beside her. She held her words until Peter was uncomfortably seated to her left.

"Oh, Peter, there are so many things to consider…"

"I just wanted to keep Mark Jensen from going free and hurting other boys."

"You didn't know if he'd go free. This case is only starting. He hasn't been tried yet." She restlessly wrapped a clump of lavender fringe around her fingers. "Be honest. Did you want to stop Coach Jensen or make him pay? Didn't you want revenge for Martin…and yourself?"

Peter glanced away from Mae, too ashamed to face her. "Maybe a little, but mostly I wanted to stop him."

"Mmmhmm," Mae hummed. "You can't risk this gift on vengeance. You have to be smart about using it, figure out the right ways of bringing folks to justice. These are the things you'll think on as you get older. You're a good man, and as you age, the pain you've inflicted—for any reason—will come to haunt you. You'll wrestle with the damage you've done because, unlike Mark Jensen, you have a conscience."

"I can live with it," Peter curtly replied.

It was like talking to a child, and Mae had to remind herself that, in a sense, that's what Peter was—still very young in terms of knowing himself and quite inexperienced in the understanding and use of his power.

"Won't be long before you start thinking about that man's wife and child and how they're going to spend years to come taking care of an invalid—how they'll lose almost all they have to afford it and how his little daughter will give up her carefree years to tend to her disabled daddy. You can tell yourself you meted out justice to Mark Jensen, but did you consider how it would affect those two innocent people?"

Peter flashed an unmoved scowl. "Criminals' families pay for their loved ones' crimes in many ways. Would it have been easier on them to lose their savings on legal fees and the child to grow up visiting her father in prison?"

"Then, think of this, Peter. You could've hurt yourself as much as that man. Putting out that kind of wrathful energy—my, that's dangerous! It's by the grace of God you aren't back in the hospital. And what if someone had seen you with your hands on his skull? What do you think would become of you? You'd be the one going to jail. Remember, him to whom much is given, much will be required."

Mae pulled air in through flared nostrils. "I don't want you to have made this journey in your heart and mind just to end up in jail or incapacitated. You have much to contribute yet."

Peter stood, shaking with indignity. "If everything I have and everything I am goes away today, I'd be satisfied. I stopped a child molester, Miss Bennally. I stopped him for good. I think that's an important contribution."

Peter stepped around her as she sat like a harmless little wren on the porch swing, lavender shawl wings folded around her.

"Excuse me, ma'am, I'll make us some lunch," he said, sending the screen door swinging behind him.

Mae threw her head back and sighed. "You still have much to learn, child," she whispered. "I pray I have the strength…and the time…to teach you."

"Well, well, the working man comes home to wait on me. It's an unfair world," Lloyd ribbed, turning off the television and sitting up in bed.

Boyd unloaded a dinner tray with two full plates and glasses of water onto the bedside stand. "Not too unfair. Ooljee made us tamale casserole."

Lloyd clucked pleasure at his pile of chili-sauce-soaked masa and cheese. "That there is a hell of a woman…and a hell of a cook. Don't know what we'd do without her."

"For sure. So, how are you feeling?" Boyd sat at the foot of the bed, ready for a visit.

"I'm tired of lying on my backside, and there's nothing good on TV. What happened to decent shows?" Lloyd sneered at the small, powered-off set on the dresser. "It's all trash. People suing each other or telling their filthy secrets to the world, like they're proud of them. Some nut was bragging about fathering kids by three different women—two sisters and their stepmother! And, can you believe the women started fighting over him?! I don't know who's the biggest horse's patootie in that lot. Couldn't watch anymore. Trash!" Clearly staggered by the debacle, Lloyd returned to the solace of his tamale pie, which was now cool enough to eat. "I did crossword puzzles until the news came on." After sliding a slim slice of avocado down his throat, Lloyd broke in a new subject. "Talked to Ooljee today about a possible replacement at work."

"What needs replacing?" Boyd asked, swirling cheese on his fork.

"Not what. Who. It's you, boy."

"Me? No way! What are…"

Lloyd cut him off. "I know you've been working that job to help me, and I'm grateful. Couldn't have done it without you these last two years. But it's time you start living your life the way you want to."

"This is the way I want to live," Boyd insisted.

"Clare, Mae, and Ooljee know a fellow who might make a good assistant for me. I've met him. I agree. He doesn't have any experience in maintenance, but then, neither did I when I started, and that turned out fine."

"Am I really that bad? I've only been fulltime two days. What has Sam been saying?"

"He says you're doing great. I'm proud of you, Boyd. I know you'd stick with that job until the cows came home if you thought that's what I wanted or needed. But that's not what I want or need. I'm holding you back, and it has to stop. Lying in bed so long has made me think about what I've done to you."

Boyd had just realigned his priorities to emphasize other people, and now the main person he wanted to focus on was pulling away. "Grandpa, I like working with you. I don't want to do maintenance fulltime forever, but it's good for now."

Lloyd wouldn't be moved. The decision wasn't purely about Boyd, anyway. When Ooljee approached him with the suggestion, she'd said, "This guy could use the influence of an older, wise male. The father he had was worse than no father at all." Those words had spun Lloyd's brain like a washing machine tub—churning up the foulest memories of a boy raised by a self-loathing drunkard—and had softened him toward the person in question. When Ooljee spoke the name "Peter Jacoby," the deal was sealed.

Lloyd already felt spiritually connected to the man. He recalled how determined and yet sensitive Peter had been at the hospital, how insightful. Lloyd hadn't shared that event with Boyd, and he'd asked Seamus not to either.

"Ooljee says this fellow is in roughly the same boat I was in when I began working for the town. Get my drift?"

Even if his grandson understood what he was saying, Lloyd recognized that a well-loved, sheltered young man like Boyd couldn't get below the surface of such understanding. He couldn't know what it's like to need to work that hard—straining muscles, employing every nerve and ounce of energy and concentration, until your head and soul clear and you drop from exhaustion into bed, finding relief in the deathlike sleep that keeps all thoughts at a distance.

"I'll teach him about Prosperity, to know its buildings, its history, and how to be a hard worker...maybe how to be a man. I need to help this fellow..." Lloyd timidly looked aside, "and I need to be needed. You understand?"

Slowly, Boyd gave his blessing, "Sure, Grandpa."

"It's time you do your own thing, and I'll support you. If that's ghost work, go on and do it. You want to go back to college, do it. Whatever it is, I'm here for you. Got it?"

"Yeah, got it," Boyd said, choking back emotion.

"So, what do you want to do?"

Boyd went blank. He'd never been asked that.

"Anything in the whole world."

"I guess be a paranormal scientist. Write books on the subject. Produce and host a show on the paranormal. Give lectures. Teach people." Boyd spoke tentatively at first and then, feeling the courage his grandfather's words inspired, he announced, "Maybe a degree would help my credentials...and give me something to fall back on."

"Okay, then, what next?"

Boyd raised his eyebrows, mouth gaping, unsure of the next step. "Look into relevant undergrad programs at ASU?"

"Seems a good plan."

Boyd began eating. Everything tasted bright, like the colors on the plate: orange, green, yellow, red. A bite of spicy casserole burned down his throat and roasted in his belly, but the feeling enlivened him. He felt on fire from the inside, like the furnace that fueled his life had just kicked on after lying dormant for many seasons.

"I'd like you to train this fellow over the summer, starting tomorrow," Lloyd outlined. "That'll give me a chance to rest up while you show him the ropes, introduce him around the community center and around town. Give him an idea of my ways. How I operate. What a pain in the patootie I can be." Lloyd winked mischievously. "Then, you go off to ASU, and I'll return to work with my new assistant. How's that?"

Boyd nodded.

"Your trainee will meet you at the center at 8:00."

"Don't you want me to take him on the morning sweep of the park? If we aren't there by sunrise, and Mad Molly's up to her old tricks..."

"We don't have to worry about the park anymore."

"No?" Boyd asked skeptically.

"Molly has a long list of things to answer for, but wrecking the park isn't on it. Trust me, boy. It'll make sense soon," Lloyd promised, mopping up the last of his casserole. "By the way, Peter Jacoby is the name of your trainee. Nice...and unusual...fellow."

"You're kidding!" Boyd's shoulders rocked with laughter. "That's so cool! He's going to be a blast to work with!"

CHAPTER 27

Peter looked like a sulking child sitting on the front steps, arms wrapped around folded legs, chin resting on knees. Only his eyes moved, watching a dragonfly flit between the green blades of iris leaves in the yard.

Ooljee moved onto the porch, into the waning daylight, clicking her heels to the Psychedelic Furs tune playing in her head. The melody had been running through her brain from the moment she'd opened her eyes that morning, through her time at the farmer's market in Sedona and while tending Lloyd, but she couldn't for the life of her remember the words or the title; she hated when that happened.

She drew closer to Peter, sensing the troubled energy coming off him like lightning bolts. "I have a feeling you got one of Mama's scoldings today," she said.

"And how," Peter answered, still as before.

The dragonfly sped off, wings humming as it went.

Ooljee took a seat on the step below Peter. Her positioning was intentional. She knew it would make Peter more comfortable if he didn't have to look her in the eyes.

"Those don't happen often, but when they do….hmm, they cut you to the quick, don't they?"

She didn't see him nodding, but she knew he agreed.

"I heard my first when I was 10. According to Mama, I'd gotten too big for my britches. There was this girl at school named Tammy Myers. Her daddy was an alfalfa farmer. He spoiled Tammy rotten—dang, she was a snotty little thing! Always picking on me for being different. There weren't a lot of African American-Diné kids at McBrideville Elementary back in the 60s." Ooljee laughed and quickly looked back at Peter. "I'm not sure there are many there today either. Anyway, I had a dream that Tammy's dad died in a tractor accident. The next day, Tammy was teasing me at morning recess, telling me how ugly and stupid I was, calling me a cocoa puff…the usual. It really got to me. Out of pure anger, I blurted out that her daddy was going to die choking on his own blood underneath a tractor. That quieted her down." Ooljee lowered her head. "What do you suppose happened that afternoon?"

"Tammy's father died," Peter guessed.

He watched as Ooljee's head bounced up and down, her loose, dark curls shaking, almost trembling.

"We were reading silently when the school secretary came in and whispered into Mrs. Cox's ear. She looked sick and whispered something back to the secretary. Both women went to Tammy's desk, and Mrs. Cox went down on her knees and said, 'Tammy, I want you to get your books and supplies together and go to the office.'" Ooljee rubbed her hands together and shifted her knees back and forth in an agitated fashion. "I can still see it so clearly. Tammy immediately twisted around in her seat and stared at me with these big, fearful eyes. I was so ashamed of myself. I couldn't believe I could be so vindictive. I knew I'd done wrong, and for a while, I thought maybe I'd lose my gift because of what I'd done with it. I think in a way I hoped I'd lose it except then I worried that Mama would send me away from her." Ooljee scooted around to face Peter. "Of course, Mama would never do such a thing. I know that now, but as a child, still wondering why she loved me and why she'd taken me in, I questioned that. You get what I'm saying, Peter?"

"I think so. You're saying that even though she doesn't approve of what I did, Mae still cares what happens to me."

"I'm saying she cares about YOU, and nothing is ever going to change that." Ooljee pressed a thumb into Peter's chest. "This kind of relationship probably doesn't make sense to you—I know you didn't feel this type of love from your parents—but just trust me on this, it happens. There are people who love unconditionally and will give their all for you. Mama is one of those people. There is absolutely nothing you could do that would ever make her stop caring about you. If she gave you a genuine Mae Bennally scolding, it's because she was worried about you and trying to teach you something."

Peter had to ask. "Did Mae tell you what I did?"

"No, but I think I know. I heard on the radio that Mark Jensen's in the hospital."

"Is he bad off?"

"Critical condition."

Peter waited a while, thinking, before following up with, "Do you think what I did was wrong?"

Ooljee gave a thin smile, as if compromised. "I'm not going to judge you, Peter. I'll level with you…I've done worse than the Tammy Myers cockup. Working with police and sheriff departments and hosting *American Fugitives*, I've had some pretty frustrating moments. In my mind, I've seen unfathomable crimes against the totally innocent and then watched justice slip right on by. And being able to feel—even relive—the victims' fear and torment and the perpetrators' rage, or worse yet, their pleasure…believe me, I understand what you did and why you did it. We want justice for the Martin Schraders of the world and can be hell-bent on getting it for them." Ooljee massaged the back of her neck, fatigued by the weight of memories. "I guess my advice is this: be smart about how you take action. If you ever need help, if you just need to sort things out, whatever, I'm here for you." Ooljee pulled herself up a step, beside Peter. "Come here, my brother," she said, protectively sheltering him under one arm, nudging his head onto her shoulder.

After a few minutes with their heads close together, Peter began to hum a tune. Softly, nearly undefined at first, it grew stronger until he sang the words, "love my way…" He leaned back and quizzically looked at Ooljee.

She replied with a playful chuck to his chin. "That's it! I couldn't get that tune out of my head, but I couldn't remember the words. It's *Love My Way*. Yeah, that's it, alright. Oooh, you're getting good, kiddo!"

Peter sat on the back porch, mentally preparing himself for his first day on the job with Prosperity Public Works. Distracted by the sweet-pungent scent of tobacco smoke, he tuned in to a conversation between two miners from the home's boarding house days. The smoke wasn't really there. Neither were the miners. But Peter knew they had once been as real as anything in the here and now.

He wasn't intimidated by the olfactory and auditory sensations—those experiences were becoming familiar, and the ones that surrounded him now were quite benign.

"Them girls at the Cajun Queen is a damn sight better than the Canary Cage's pickings. Canary Cage tomatoes is too high and haughty and no better looking."

"Bull! You take a gander at that Sadie Rue? I'd give my right nut for that biscuit."

"That's about what she costs, too!"

The miners' laughter was short-lived and blaring, like a shotgun blast.

Peter blanched, feeling like an eavesdropper, and then smiled at the lewd words that ran to his ears from somewhere far in the past. He noted women's voices in the present, and the opening and closing of the front door, but he sat still, right ankle on left knee, fingers clasped behind his head, elbows spread like wings as he closed his eyes and pictured the grubby gravel-throated men whose voices echoed around him.

"Pretty night, isn't it?"

Peter's eyes flipped open to see Afton. He jumped up. "Have a seat, won't you?" He gestured to a wrought iron chair across the patio table.

"Thanks." Afton took the chair and unhanded a cellophane-swaddled bundle topped with a red bow.

"What's this? Cookies?" Peter asked as she pushed the package toward him.

Afton shrugged self-consciously. "I never thanked you for what you did. How do you thank someone for saving your brother's life? I know it takes a lot more than cookies, but it's a start. I brought some for Ooljee and Mae, too. They helped me a lot that day Seamus went missing. I owe you all so much."

"You don't owe me anything, but thank you." Peter removed the bow and pulled back the cellophane film from the plate of cookies, taking one of the golden-brown discs and biting into it. It was rock hard, but the taste was good. He held the plate up, offering Afton one of her own creations.

She politely begged off. "I ate all the kinda burnt ones, so I'm full."

Peter could hardly hear Afton's words over the sound of his molars grinding the ossified dough. "They're very good."

Afton watched silently as Peter ate two more cookies. Each time he took one, he offered the plate to her, only to face her quiet refusal. When he'd finished, he dusted a fine sawdust-like blanket from his lap and again thanked Afton, whose face was much softer and happier than he'd ever seen it. Peter knew what was inside her mind. It didn't take any supernatural ability for that. She was mooning at him, her little pixie face a perfect pale circle inside a wiry red halo.

"You should know that I'm damaged goods," he regretfully declared.

"Aren't we all?" she answered.

"You deserve to know..." Peter wiped a hand over his mouth and with an anguished scowl admitted, "This is hard."

"Please don't be afraid to tell me."

"I'm not a regular man."

"How so?"

"I...uh...I've never had a lady friend."

Afton reared back a tad, feeling foolish. "Oh, sorry, I was way off track. I didn't know you're gay."

"I'm not. I'm...damaged." Peter cleared his throat over and over until he spit out, "I was badly hurt as a child..."

Afton's eyes tightened like she was trying to read his mind so that he wouldn't have to say the difficult words.

"...in a very private way," Peter finished, and Afton nodded, letting him know she understood what he was saying.

"The idea of intimacy has scared me for so long...I...I've never been on a date, never even held a woman's hand. Whenever someone showed interest, I pushed her away." He hesitated, lowering his voice. "I don't know what kind of relationship I can offer you."

Afton's heart palpitated as she felt herself drawn closer to Peter, admiring him all the more for his honesty. "Do you like me?" she asked, her teeth chattering ever so subtly, blue eyes deep with hope.

"Yes, I do."

"That's good, because I like you a lot. I haven't known you very long, but I know what you did for my brother, and I've seen how thoughtful you are with people. I know you're a kind and moral man. I can't think of a better foundation for an attraction to someone."

Peter's face went crimson. "You're being very nice to me."

"I'm being frank. And as long as we're confessing, I'll tell you about my baggage. I was married. I don't know if you knew that. It didn't last long. He slept around, and when I found out, it just about killed me. I hated men after that. Didn't trust them. Didn't want anything to do with them...except my brother, of course, but I consider him a whole different species. He's not like most men I've known. Neither are you. No kidding, I haven't even had a romantic thought in my head since I walked in on Jason and his bimbo eight years ago. I haven't wanted to try a relationship with anyone...until now."

Peter smiled. "We're quite a pair, aren't we?"

Afton smiled back. "I don't want to pressure you. I don't want you to feel like you'll hurt me by saying 'no.' I'm a big girl."

Peter's pupils widened, then constricted, as he trained himself on Afton. He'd sized up her character when they'd first met, but now he was able to make a deeper exploration of her being. What he sensed encouraged him to envision a future he couldn't have imagined even days earlier. There was a good heart in Afton, and unswerving devotion to those she loved, total honesty, too. She was a strong woman with a fractured heart. Sometimes the pain had been unleashed in frustrated rage, but the self-reflection forced by recent events had mellowed Afton and heightened the compassion she'd always possessed. Peter was taken by the empathy. He'd seen it displayed in Emma Schrader's presence, for both the grieving mother and her wronged boy, and he felt it now, like a life force, inside her. This was a woman he could trust.

"Please don't agonize over this. If you want to give it a shot, I'd like that. If you don't, I'll understand." Afton started to leave. "I'll let you think about it. You take care of yourself."

Peter reached out and grabbed her hand, almost toppling his plate of cookies. "Don't go," he said. "I want to try."

CHAPTER 28

Peter's uniform—which was on order—was the only part of his new job that he wasn't looking forward to. The high-waisted khaki coveralls reminded him of prison garb, though they seemed comfortable. He stifled a laugh imagining what his appearance-conscious parents would have thought of their son in such a getup...and doing physical labor.

"This afternoon, we'll go on a couple calls." Boyd unfurled a forefinger, then a thumb, as he listed the chores. "Gladys Mahoney put in a request for us to check out a sidewalk crack near the old jail. You'll find that Gladys is über vigilant and puts in at least one work ticket a week for things that no one else notices. Second, we'll get started planting a bunch of Arizona Cyprus near Prosperity's welcome sign—the town council wants a windbreak there. But, right now, I'll show you the building."

Boyd slid open the grated door on the antique Otis elevator and pulled it shut with a grinding clang once he and Peter were inside. "Hang on, Jacoby. We call this little baby 'the Rocket,'" he said as he pressed the fourth-floor button. Slowly, the metal cage ascended, groaning until it jerked to a stop at the top floor.

"Thanks for the warning. That was quite a ride," Peter joked.

"Yeah, so as you can see, it's usually faster to take the stairs, unless you're lugging heavy equipment. One good thing, though, the Rocket may look rickety, but it almost never breaks down. We still have a lot of original stuff around here—this old shit was built to last."

When they stepped from the elevator, Peter watched a woman in an old-fashioned nursing uniform rush by. It was the second ghostly figure he'd seen that day, the first being a legless man in a wheelchair, propelling himself down the first-floor hall, hands on wheels. Neither figure noticed Peter. They were shadows of the past, the kind he'd seen during his childhood and was now used to seeing in and around Mae's house. The figures didn't scare him at all, only startled him.

As he moved through the building, Peter glimpsed a few all-encompassing, panoramic bygone moments. They popped up in his brain, unbidden, at random intervals. They were short scenes or even snapshots of times gone by. The mental intrusions were jarring to Peter, who was still learning to gracefully incorporate them into his everyday life without giving any outward signs of what was happening to him.

Boyd unlocked a room and pushed the door aside, standing in the doorway. "This is Storage Room 405, our problem child. Almost every time it rains, the ceiling leaks."

When Peter first looked into the large room, he saw children lying in beds as nurses in white uniforms and surgical masks tended them. It wasn't until he'd blinked a few times that he saw steel-case shelves holding cleaning supplies.

"Only nonporous things for cleaning go in here. Buckets, jugs of cleaning solution, whatever. We don't put anything in here that might be damaged by rain. And this is all surplus, you know, the big stashes. We keep a good supply on-hand downstairs in the closet next to the maintenance office." Boyd started to close the door but noticed Peter still staring intently inside, his eyes moving as if following something.

"You okay?"

"Fine, thanks. I'm curious, do you know what this room used to be?" Peter casually asked.

"The fourth floor was the children's ward when this was a TB hospital. I don't know what it was when this was a regular hospital or an insane asylum. My grandfather would know." Boyd read more than curiosity on Peter's face as he pulled the door shut and locked it. "You saw something in there, didn't you?"

"Shelves of cleaning supplies."

"Give me a break, dude. You're forgetting that I know about you. What else did you see?"

After a small pause, Peter admitted having seen the sickly children and attendant nurses. "Sorry, I didn't want you to think I was crazy."

"Me? I'm the dude who chases ghosts through Prosperity, remember?" Boyd grinned, making Peter immediately drop what was left of his defenses. "There isn't a better town you could've come to for learning about this side of you...and learning about the paranormal. You're going to find maybe, like, two or three nonbelievers in the whole town. And, dude, nobody's better at psychic stuff than Mae Bennally. Ooljee's really good, too. You're lucky they took you on for training. Mae is your Yoda, and Ooljee's your Obi-Wan."

"My oh gee what?"

"Obi-Wan Kenobi. Dude, don't tell me you never saw any of the *Star*

Wars movies."

Peter shook his head.

"Have you been living under a rock? I'm making it my mission to educate you on all things sci-fi." Boyd considered Peter. "Hmm, are you more Spock or Data?" He held up his left hand, fingers splayed to form a "V," and pronounced, "Live long and prosper." Chuckling, he forced Peter to copy him. "Come on, do it with me, dude." When Boyd was satisfied with Peter's Vulcan salute, the tour continued.

"The rest of this floor is storage for the town's holiday decorations. There's a ton. See? Each room is labeled: Halloween, Christmas, 4th of July, yadda, yadda."

They walked the length of the hall and entered every room without incident, but when they returned to the elevator, Peter saw a man in a red and black uniform sitting on a stool by the controls. Boyd walked right through him, talking the whole time about how the floors have to be buffed once a month and what a pain it is.

"Dude, it's like wrestling an alligator. That freakin' buffer's heavy, and it gets hot and kind of takes off on its own."

The elevator operator disappeared as they dropped down to the third floor, and Peter felt more comfortable when only he and Boyd remained in the cage, though he didn't know why. It wasn't like an actual person had been in there with them. It was just a memory. The building's memory.

Summer children's classes occupied the next floor, which was so alive with laughter, shouting, playful chatter, and the music of Tom T. Hall's "Sneaky Snake"—which was the subject of a boisterous sing-along by preschoolers—that Boyd decided to save that part of the tour until later. On the second floor, the Verde Valley Golden Oldies were playing bingo in 210, and next door, in 212, volunteers were preparing a sloppy joe lunch for the group. Peter was amused by the comments of the bingo players, who were subjected to the children's noises filtering down from above. Half cheerfully mentioned the sounds of youth, while the other half complained to volunteers that they wouldn't be back for other Golden Oldies programs if something wasn't done about the hullabaloo. One crotchety coot in Bermuda shorts went into the next-door kitchen, shakily stood on a chair, and beat the bristle-end of a long-handled broom against the ceiling, yelling, "Stop that damn racket, you brats! I can't hear myself think down here!" A volunteer helped him off the chair and told him not to crawl up on anything while she went upstairs to ask the kids' wranglers to control them.

"That's Nate Desmond, from McBrideville," Boyd whispered. "And over there is his wife, Genna." He pointed to a silver-haired woman with droopy hot pink-glossed lips intently working four bingo cards. "She lives in Prosperity. Like most people, she can't stand to be around Nate for long, so they live apart. PIP investigated her apartment as one of our first outings. She lives over the old barber shop, and, dude, her place is really active. All residual stuff. I saw my first full-bodied apparition there—a woman in a white blouse and black skirt. She walked out of the wall and sank into the floor, like she was going down stairs. That's because where I saw her, there used to be stairs. Freakin' cool, huh?"

Back into the Otis elevator they went. This time, Peter didn't see the man in the uniform. It was just him and Boyd, talking shop in the suspended metal cage.

Stepping into the ground-floor lobby, Peter studied the fantastical bric-a-brac at the top of two marble pillars. Carved, gilded palm fronds splayed out, encircling the stately columns. Mirrored ovals, approximating date fruits, punctuated the tips of the fronds. Peter knew that, through the loving and attentive work of people like the Changs, those columns looked much as they had when first erected a century earlier.

"It's refreshing to find a building like this…a town like this. No chain stores, no modern artifices." Peter looked around at the generations of architecture in the community center, from the neoclassical pillars to the art deco flourishes on etched glass panels. "Once a building is gone, so is a link to the past. You've preserved more than buildings here in Prosperity. You've also saved ties to the people who once lived and worked here. You've protected history itself."

Boyd stretched his mouth back in a Cheshire Cat grin. "Dude, my grandpa's going to love working with you. You are so freakin' right for this job."

"Where are we?" Mae asked, confused. She looked out the car window at the rustic wooden structure with a framed menu by its double doors and shrank down in the passenger seat, as if trying to hide from the building.

Peter had never seen his mentor disoriented, and it unnerved as much as saddened him.

"This is the Ghostly Grill. We're going out for dinner."

The old woman looked down and up the road, at the parking lot, at her companion, and then her bewildered squint loosened.

"Oh, yes."

It was Mae's first meal out in a long time. It had been hard for her to get around for more than 20 years, but the last few had been especially bad. No food tasted good enough anymore to make the painful, slow journey out of the house, into and out of a car, and into a restaurant worth the effort. But Mae would make an exception for Peter. She wanted to buy him a meal recognizing his first day with the Prosperity Public Works Department. No one had ever celebrated his achievements—as a boy or a man. She had a lot to make up for with him.

"Are you sure you're up to this?" Peter asked, noticing the packed parking lot and thinking a crowded restaurant might produce another spell of puzzlement.

"Definitely, and that's that."

Peter practically had to lift the little woman out of the car. She was so light that it was no problem except for the awkwardness of where to put his hands. If it hadn't seemed an embarrassment to Mae, he would have offered to carry her everywhere.

Leaning against Peter, Mae took the front steps slowly.

"Whew, I'm already tuckered out. Maybe I can take a nap in one of the booths," she said with a wheezy chuckle.

The Ghostly Grill's double doors opened before them, Seamus' wide arms spreading them apart. "Miss Mae Bennally, we're honored," he said and then nodded at Peter. "Jacoby, how's it going?"

With great fanfare Seamus led them to the nearest open booth, making the walk as short as possible. He handed over menus, first using his apron to wipe the ubiquitous greasy fingerprints from the laminated pages.

"What can I get you two? Everything's on the house." He squelched Mae's budding protest with, "You know the saying: your money's no good here."

"Well, bless your heart. Did you know Peter finished his first day on the job with the Prosperity Public Works Department? He's now an official Prosperityite," she said, deflecting the attention.

"Congratulations, Jacoby!" Seamus praised. "Glad you're sticking around. I think you're gonna fit right in. Let's start this party with some drinks."

Mae became excited by the thought of an old favorite. "Can you make a Shirley Temple?"

"The best you ever had," Seamus confidently replied. "The tourists' kids love those. Only they don't know who Shirley Temple is, so we call it Boo Juice."

Mae beamed at Seamus. "Boo Juice sounds lovely."

"Make it two, please," Peter ordered.

"You got it," Seamus confirmed with a slap to the edge of the black Formica table. "I'll give you time to decide on meals."

Mae was dwarfed by the tri-fold menu. When she held it up in front of her, she completely disappeared. She pulled the menu up close and then far away, but her reading vision had evaporated decades ago.

"I went off and forgot my glasses. Peter, can you read me my supper options? All those tiny letters look like a bunch of ants crawling across the page."

Beginning with the house specialties, Peter read the outlandish names— Terrified Tacos and Rattlin' Bones Ribs being so silly as to make Mae laugh—and the descriptions of the items.

Seamus returned with the drinks and took the dinner order, leaving Mae and Peter with the time and privacy to get into a meaningful conversation.

"How do you like the job?"

"Very much," Peter said.

"Good. Thought you'd be happy there. Boyd's a good boy, and his grandfather's a good man. They'll treat you well, and Lloyd can teach you much." Mae twittered. "You can teach him a thing or two, also."

Peter pulled the conversation away from pleasantries. "I'm grateful for the job and all your help. Truly. But I don't know if I'm cut out for the…gift." He used the last word reluctantly. "I think I may go mad if I have to see sad, terrible visions and not be able to do anything about them."

"Who says you can't do anything about them? Or that they're all sad and terrible? Like anything in life, your attitude has much to do with it."

"I can control what I see?"

"Sometimes," Mae pulled the maraschino cherry from her drink and devoured it, eyes closed, savoring the intense sweetness. Opening her lids, she sighed. "My, that's good!"

After a happy breath, she explained, "Most visions just happen and are tied to powerful feelings like fear or anger or joy. But sometimes I see scenes that are…boring. Someone watching television. A dog playing in a yard. There isn't always a direction to my vision. You may or may not be the same."

"So far, all I've seen are horrible…or ridiculous things." Peter recalled the scene of Jamie Clancy clipping his toenails and the parade of other inane or profane images that had marched through his psyche.

"Child, since you came here, you've been marinating in negativity. Makes sense most of what you saw was negative. Course, you also saw images that fit together like a jigsaw puzzle. You didn't know it, but you were looking for those pieces. Once you saw Charles, you wanted to know what that vision was about and kept seeing things that related to him. You drew that information to you. When all these new feelings and memories settle down, you'll start to gain some control over your gift."

"Good," Peter said, relieved.

"I said SOME control. Visions will still come unexpectedly; some will make sense, and some won't. Some things that you'll want to see, you'll be able to, and others you won't, no matter how hard you try. It's not easy, but you have to learn to accept that."

The entrees arrived, and the couple stilled their voices. Their unusual discussion was to be a discreet one.

"One Gobble Goblin Turkey and one Ghostly Grilled Cheese," Seamus confirmed, placing the platters on the table. He noticed the half-drained glass at Mae's setting and started to grab it. "Let me get you a Boo Juice refill."

Mae halted him. "It's pure heaven, but I'll stop at the one. Doesn't this look delicious?!" she praised, immediately gnawing on the end of her dill pickle spear. She rolled her eyes. "Lovely. It's your mama's recipe, isn't it?"

"Why…yes, ma'am," Seamus said, amazed at her quick insight.

Mae winked his way. "She's mighty proud of you. Take my word for it."

After inquiring if he could bring anything else and asking them to save room for dessert—also on the house—Seamus left to check on other customers, and Mae had the chance to put Peter through his paces.

"What do you feel in this place?" she asked between bites of her sandwich.

Peter looked around. Families and couples were grouped throughout the dining room, eating and talking.

"It seems pleasant."

Shaking her head, Mae instructed, "Close your eyes and listen with your mind. What do you pick up? What's here? What memories? What energy?"

Peter closed his eyes and lowered his head. Quietly, he looked inward, as if through a telescope that extended deep into his soul and out into the vastness of time and space.

"I see kids in this booth…and at tables pulled up close. They're singing to a boy; it's his birthday. There are red balloons and a cake."

"Good, good," Mae encouraged.

"It's gone," Peter said. He began describing a new scene. "Now, there are two men fighting. They're bloody and wild. I think they're on drugs. One has a knife. He cut the other man's arm…here." Without opening his eyes, Peter raised a hand and touched his left bicep. He stayed quiet for another minute before surrendering. "That's all." He looked at Mae with disgrace, as if what he'd seen wasn't enough.

Mae nodded in her supportive way, happy with his progress.

"That's good, Peter. You're doing very well. And you see, we have the good as well as the bad all around us. Some of what you see is positive, and some isn't. When you start to feel overwhelmed by the bad, remember to concentrate on the good. Sometimes you have to look hard for it, but it's there."

Peter blinked quickly, processing the statement. "The good, as well as the bad…all around us," he murmured.

In an instant, he knew what to do, as if someone had whispered in his ear the meaning to his life. Now he knew this unnatural talent that had plagued him since its resurgence could be more than a tool of vengeance. He had an idea of how to use it for good. Mae had inspired him to see more than the obvious.

If his plan worked, Peter would, finally, view this onerous ability as the gift Mae described.

CHAPTER 29

"Assistant director? You're not jesting? I'm astonished and humbled, my good men!" Clive brayed, throwing up his arms and laughing maniacally.

The Ghostly Grill was populated by plenty of tourists, who reacted to Clive's outburst with delight or disdain. One uptight couple, looking frightened, packed up their twin toddlers and hurried out the door before ordering.

Seamus and Boyd took a measuring look at each other and quietly hoped their decision was for the best. They couldn't take back the offer now. Besides, Boyd had made it clear that he couldn't co-lead PIP in the near future. Other things would be eating into his time: looking out for his grandfather, Amy, taking over Prosperity's full-time maintenance position in the short term, and online college courses before transferring to Arizona State in the fall.

"Promise me that you're up to this," Boyd demanded, pushing an accusing finger toward Clive. "If you even think you're going to freak out on an investigation, it's your obligation to let Seamus know and not proceed. When I come back here after college, I'm going to resume co-leadership of PIP, so I don't want you making a joke out of this organization."

"You have my word, squire. I'll not let you down," Clive swore.

Seamus smiled weakly at Clive and, with a handshake, welcomed him to the upper echelon of PIP. It was a momentous occasion, the changing of the guard, as it were. Yet Seamus was uncomfortable with the possibilities introduced by Clive taking over a higher post. It was like putting Moe Howard in charge of a chemistry lab or appointing Yogi Berra debate team captain.

He and Boyd hoped to dilute Clive's influence with the introduction of two new investigators.

"You know we've been toying with the idea of injecting some fresh blood into PIP for a while. Training new investigators. Growing the organization. Well, now seems like the right time," Boyd explained to Clive, who was quickly losing enthusiasm. "You helped us narrow the pool to some good candidates, and Seamus and I extended offers to two this morning. They accepted."

"You did? They did? What?" Clive clucked, sounding like a hen that just squeezed out the biggest egg of its life.

Seamus turned over the paperwork on the recruits, letting Clive reacquaint himself with the chosen two. "They came by the grill for interviews and blew us away. I think they genuinely want to learn the ropes, and we all know we could use the help." He flicked the application Clive was reading and began a verbal summary of the first new investigator. "Josh Cameron: 23, McBrideville native, carpenter by trade, owns a cabinetry shop with his dad. He did two training investigations with the Yavapai County Ghost Brigade before they disbanded; they gave him high marks. This guy knows the equipment and technical side. His passion for investigating the paranormal really comes through when you meet him."

"Yeah, his zeal is admirable...but it could turn problematic, so keep him on task," Boyd chimed in, picking up with the next one. "Then we have Stella Garcon: 41, mother of two, lives on an organic farm outside Prescott, extensive research and documentation experience. She was the archivist at the Sharlot Hall Museum for five years and has a Ph.D. in U.S. Southwest History. Her thesis was 'Prescott Hauntings: A History of Reported Apparitions in Arizona's First Capital.'"

"Impressive credentials," Clive intoned as he used a thumb and forefinger to discard the applications—like used diapers—far from him. "But a female will change the group's dynamics. Are you comfortable with that?"

Boyd sniped, "Our dynamics have already changed. You're moving up. I'm taking a sabbatical. We have two new members. Besides, dude, it's the freakin' 21st century. Time to integrate the sexes, wouldn't you say?"

Clive flinched at the word "sexes" and nibbled at the crust of his Booberry Pie. "Here, here for Josh and Stella. Huzzah," he apathetically consented.

The group picked at their pie slices, pushing chunks of pastry and gelatinous filling around their plates with their forks. Boyd took a wistful look at the men seated with him. "So, this is it, huh?"

Clive wiped his mouth with his napkin, placed the piece of crumpled, purple-stained paper on his lap, and reverently folded his hands over it.

Seamus smiled, trying to brighten the heavy moment. "Guess so. But it's not like it's over, man. You're still gonna investigate with us when you have the time, right?"

"Sure, yeah. I'll be around Prosperity on breaks and weekends whenever I can. And you know if you run into something complicated, need some extra help or something, I'll be there for you guys."

"We know," Seamus answered.

"Well, uh, thanks for meeting me for lunch. I should get back to work. Peter might have the community center in ruins by now. I don't think that guy ever even changed a light bulb by himself. But he's learning fast. He's doing a lot better than I did my second day on the job. Remember that? I was digging a trench, and I put a pickaxe through one of the center's PVC irrigation system pipes. Looked like freakin' Old Faithful up there."

Seamus and Clive smiled wanly, nodding.

"Anyway, this place is going to be crawling with tourists soon. The big weekend and all."

"You know it, man." Seamus squirmed in his seat, wanting to do more, say more, until he finally stood and almost knocked both the table and Clive over as he reached out and bundled Boyd into a bear hug, unintentionally squeezing him so hard that the teen gasped and gurgled. "It's been a good run, buddy. A real good run."

"Remember me? Peter Jacoby?" He leaned around the opened screen door so Emma could get a better look at his face.

"Sure I remember." She ran her eyes over him, amazed at how quickly the tan, smiling man with perfectly styled hair had rebounded. "Won't you come in?"

Peter hesitated. "Could we go out by the pond?"

Emma left the house with a hangdog gait, her tennis shoes sliding rather than stepping across the ground. She was even more haggard than when Peter had last seen her—a mournful wraith who neither ate nor slept. Peter wondered how much more of her soul she could afford to lose before slipping away completely. Through the peach orchard and up, onto the pond bank, Peter tried to cheer her with pleasant chit-chat, but the woman only listened and answered out of courtesy. Her one genuine contribution was asking Peter how he was feeling of late.

The pond was a 60-foot-wide depression filled with dark water and partially rimmed by grass and reeds. Flotillas of green moss rode the surface, where the miniscule movements of tiny bugs and snails caused bubbles and rings to appear. A ragged, charred cottonwood stump jutted up from the bank with a rain gauge and an antique Coca-Cola thermometer nailed to its dead bark.

"This is a special place," Peter stated. He didn't tell Emma that he'd spent the last hour walking around it, trying to catch some of Martin's happy memories—or that he'd succeeded.

Emma agreed with a flicker of a smile. "Real sorry about what happened to you here," she said.

"I'm doing alright now. How are you holding up?" Peter knew the answer, but he wanted to give Emma the chance to verbalize her pain.

Her lips tightened, holding back words and feelings. Then, they started to tremble, and she cracked. "Martin Sr. isn't at the restaurant so much. He cried for the first time a couple nights ago, let it all out. The girls are still hurting, you know, but they're managing. I heard them laughing this morning; it's been a long time since I heard that sound. I need to be there for my family and help them recover...and start being a mom and wife again. But I'm not making progress like they are. I just can't move on from this. I've been asking myself what I could've done differently to let Marty know how much he was loved and keep him from doing what he did." She bowed her head, wiped a drop of snot from her nose and sucked in the remainder, then quickly looked up, letting the tears absorb back into her eyes. "God help me, I don't think I can go on," she divulged.

That gave Peter the opportunity he wanted. He moved in close, pulling Emma into his arms. He hoped he could get a good grip on her before she became uncomfortable and started to panic or pull away. But she didn't react. It was easy for him to position his fingers on her head, fingertips framing her sweaty blond hairline.

He closed his eyes and summoned the memories he wanted. Two beautiful moments that endured in space and time as evidence of Martin's 17 years of life as part of a loving, supportive family. With compassion and tenderness, he pushed those memories outward, mindfully directing them where he wanted them to go. Like electricity traveling a circuit, the mental energy flowed through and out him, into Emma, sinking into her psyche.

Emma saw and felt as Marty had during a brilliant summer day in his eleventh year. The family was picnicking by the pond, as they often did during the warm months. Marty was riding a tire swing that dangled from the shady cottonwood that stood guard over the pond before being felled by a blast of withering lightning. He was crouched on the tire, fists hardened around the rope, legs threaded through the center, laughing, yelling "higher," as he soared out over the water and then swung back to shore, where his dad tapped the tire with another push.

"Higher, higher!" Marty happily commanded.

"Higher than that?" Martin Sr. asked with mock incredulity.

"Yeah, higher!"

"Okay then. This one is going to be really, really high. Hold on tight."

This time, when the tire returned to the shore, Martin Sr. grabbed the rubber ring and pulled it back, back, stepping back, raising up on his toes, huffing as he lifted it above his head.

Marty let out an exuberant "oooooh," and looked to the opposite bank, where Emma sat with a picnic lunch and his little sisters—two shirtless, towheaded tots dipping their feet in the pond water and jabbering in high-pitched voices.

Martin saw fear in his mother's eyes. Emma jumped up. "Martin, that's too high!"

Marty giggled and yelled, "Don't worry, Mom!"

He threw his head back and screamed with exhilaration as Martin Sr. let go, and he whizzed out over the pond. When the rope reached its full extension, about 15 feet above the surface, Marty unwound his legs and released the rope, plummeting backwards in freefall. His back and thighs stung as he plunged in. The last thing he saw before going under was his mother, screaming on the bank, and his sisters watching him with faces like blank slates. The impact knocked the air from his lungs. Murky drafts shot up his nose, into his mouth; he choked on thick, fetid water. Under for several seconds, he reoriented himself, fighting through moss, head and chest aching. When he emerged with a gasp, his mother was almost to him, rapidly dogpaddling—the only swim she knew.

"Marty?! Are you okay, Marty?" she wheezed, awkwardly fishing him into her arms.

Marty spewed out a stream of water, aiming it at his mother's face, before erupting in laughter.

"Why...you...little booger! You almost...gave me...a heart attack," Emma gurgled, dragging him back to shore as she dogpaddled with one arm, working against the weight of her wet clothing.

She crawled onto the bank, pulling Marty up beside her. Hilarity from Martin Sr. and the girls echoed around them. Marty braced for a swat on his behind or at least a scolding, but his mother tugged him onto her lap, held him to her, and kissed him hard, keeping her lips against his cheek until her heart's beat steadied. Marty relaxed, feeling the explosive pain from lungs and muscles fade beneath his mother's all-encompassing love.

Peter replaced that scene with a new one, another family event from the same setting but a much later date. It was months earlier, on Valentine's Day, close to sunset. The weather was brisk. A campfire roared on the pond bank, where Sara and Tricia were counting out marshmallows and graham crackers and breaking Hershey bars into squares for s'mores. Martin Sr. was using his pocketknife to whittle down the end of a thin mesquite branch. He'd already whittled two, which Emma used to skewer hotdogs.

"Come on, Marty," Emma called. "It ain't a weenie roast if you don't roast a weenie!"

"No, thanks," Marty answered. He didn't move from the fold-out chair he'd positioned on the bank opposite the campfire. Keeping his distance, he watched his family maneuver near the flames, his sisters delighting in their task, his parents trying their best to lure him in.

"We need another roasting stick, Marty! Get out your knife and help me out over here. Bet I can whittle faster than you. I got two fresh mesquite twigs left. We'll see who's grand champion weenie stick whittler," Martin Sr. challenged.

"No, thanks," Marty repeated.

He observed his parents looking sadly at one another and halfheartedly returning to their chores.

Marty wanted to go over there, just to make them feel better, but he couldn't move. Every limb seemed made of iron. He was pinned to the spot by not just lethargy and depression but some physical force that was getting harder to fight every day. Marty thought back to a lecture in Mr. Hershbaum's astronomy class regarding exoplanets. He recalled the popeyed man speaking of a particular star, HD 114762, in the constellation Coma Berenices, around which a possible planet had been discovered. Mr. Hershbaum said it was most likely a brown dwarf, but whatever it was, it was huge—at least 11 times the mass of Jupiter, maybe 145 times that giant planet's mass. The teacher had pointed at Martin and said, "Your little sister Tricia would weigh more than a ton there," going on to note that, of course, such an environment couldn't sustain human life. These days, Marty felt like he was on that dense, mysterious planet, where it was impossible for a mere human to walk or breathe...or live.

Stuck in the fold-out canvas chair, Marty watched his family moving on without him; that was what he wanted. His mother dumped a can of Beanee Weenees into a cast iron pot and set it next to the fire to warm. She pulled deviled eggs from an ice chest and paused, looking his way with a sweet, worried smile. Martin Sr. whittled away at half the previous speed and without joy.

Princess padded over to Marty. He couldn't even lift a hand to pat her on the head, the way she expected, the way he always did to let the old dog know he cared. She curled up beside the chair and sighed deeply, resting her gray muzzle on her tail nub.

"You get the first s'more, Marty!" Sara shouted.

"We're gonna write your name on top with chocolate icing. Yummy!" Tricia hooted.

"And XX and OO because that means kisses and hugs!" Sara added.

Neither girl looked hurt by his lack of response. They danced over to their father, singing songs created on the spot, and began piercing marshmallows with the two other sticks he'd honed in the interim, taking time for a mock swordfight with the skewers before returning to the fire.

Rising through the inner emptiness that grew each day, in league with the strange, immobilizing weight, was the sense of love, the one feeling that—though it ebbed and surged—never left him. The smallest of smiles crossed Marty's face as he remembered the day when he'd taken the wildest tire-swing ride of his life. He thought of his father, straining to lift him higher and higher on that rubber disk, trying to fulfill his son's wish to fly, and his mother, so forgiving of his foolish act. The memory was overwhelming and precious. His throat tightened as he remembered those innocent days when, for better or worse, he existed in the moment, living life to the hilt. Everything had changed so much since then. Except the love. That never went away. He wanted to assure his parents that it never would, yet he was still paralyzed by the malicious personal gravity at his core. As he watched his parents labor to build a special moment for them all, he felt the love inside him build, feeding on gratitude, until he sensed a glimmer of joy. "XX and OO," he whispered.

Peter removed his fingers from Emma's scalp, letting her mind go blank, the first step in her returning to present and personal consciousness. He held her, steadying her so that she wouldn't fall when she became alert to her surroundings.

"Are you alright?" he asked, feeling her begin to stir in his arms. He waited for her to pull away, possibly curse him for the startling experience. Instead, she buried her head against his chest, wanting to hold on and go back for more. She'd lived two of her son's dearest moments, witnessing them from his paradigm, and those episodes had given her insight into his life—thoughts, feelings, the very heart of who he was—in a way she could never have comprehended. They'd confirmed that, despite all that had happened, Marty hadn't felt abandoned and unloved. He had, as his suicide note explained, loved his family fully up to the last moment and had known they'd done all they could to help him. "Don't blame yourselves," Marty had written. "You're the best parents. I love you guys."

Those words, scrawled in the chicken-scratch writing she'd teased her son about, flashed through Emma's brain, as they had often during the last few weeks. Finally she believed them.

"That's what Martin wants you to remember," Peter said, squeezing Emma against him.

She nodded her head, her greasy, sun-damaged hair scratching against his shirt.

"I don't know how you did that, but thank you with all my heart," she whispered.

CHAPTER 30

Boyd pushed his grandfather toward the podium. The big, rubber-padded wheels of the wheelchair made a soft "bump, bump" as they rolled over the wooden planks of the stage. Lloyd canvassed the crowd inside the community center auditorium and felt his freshly mended heart squeeze tight. Three-hundred-fifty-six Prosperity Days Festival attendees sat in stackable chairs, drinking from bottles of water or soda, ready to be enlightened—or at least entertained.

"How's that?" Boyd whispered, rolling Lloyd just past the podium and facing the crowd.

"That's good, boy."

The teen moved the gooseneck microphone to the side of the lectern and bent it toward his grandfather, who blew into it, then tapped on its bulbous end, listening to the amplified thumps resound throughout the enormous room.

Lloyd covered the microphone with one hand and cued Boyd, "I'll take it from here."

Boyd retreated offstage, into the auditorium, where Ooljee saved him a seat. Bumbling over Peter's and Mae's feet, he plopped down in the third row, between Ooljee and Clive and Clare, both dressed in Edwardian garb, Clare's sun-spotted fingers welded to Clive's pale, wrinkle-free hand.

Leaning forward in his seat, Peter glimpsed the contrasting, laced digits and considered how his and Clare's similar violations had resulted in very different outcomes. For Clare, the aftermath had been a life of flaunted sexuality and extroversion and an insatiable yen for physical intimacy, while Peter responded inversely by becoming a shadow of a man, who pushed away anyone who came near. Peter smiled, realizing that, though Clive was an oddball, he'd be nothing less than gallant toward Clare, the abused little girl who'd finally found someone to treat her like a cherished lady.

214

"He's looking good," Ooljee commented, and Peter's attention returned to Lloyd.

The rustling and murmurs of a fidgeting crowd ceased.

"Good evening, ladies and gentlemen. My name is Lloyd Chang. I'm the treasurer of the Prosperity Historical Society and a native of this town. Doris Whitaker will not be lecturing on the history of the Copper Prince Mine, as stated in your programs. My apologies for any inconvenience. In lieu of Ms. Whitaker's presentation, I'll be sharing a special story from Prosperity's past. It's one that few people know, and I think you'll find it interesting, especially those of you who are long-time residents—or historians—of the area.

"I've been under the weather, so please bear with me if I have difficulties…"

Lloyd pulled his reading glasses from his chest pocket, clumsily unfolding the arms and sliding them over his ears. His hands next went to the battered leather journal on his lap. His wide thumbs caressed the binding, stroking it, as Lloyd stared at the crimson cover, knowing his duty yet nervous about fulfilling it.

With a long, sobering glance over the top of his glass frames, Lloyd set the stage for the revelation.

"I've been ashamed of my father for a long time. Yee Chang died of alcohol poisoning when I was a boy. He was physically and emotionally abusive to my mother and a dreadful father. When I was 12, he told me something that made me even more ashamed of him. But he was my father. I hope you can understand when I say that although I was ashamed of him and despised the things he did, I loved him."

Lloyd lifted the small volume in one hand, showing the crowd. "After he died, I was given his journal. I read it, and I understood my father a little bit better. I was still ashamed. I still had anger. But I realized why he'd turned out as he had." Stopping to fill his lungs with air in a single grating gasp, Lloyd felt the enormity of what he was doing. A dizzy buzz spun his head, and he closed his eyes to regain his equilibrium. Upon opening his eyes, he saw Boyd leaving his seat to come to his aid. Lloyd shook his head, stopping him. "My father was a weak man who did some very bad things. I tried to protect his memory and honor my family by hiding his sins. But I came to see how much he regretted them and how much they affected other people, even people in this room."

At that, Lloyd looked across the mesmerized crowd. Bottles of water were suspended in mid-air, inches from opened lips. No one so much as blinked. Thinking they were going to hear a lecture on copper mining, they had instead become witnesses to a soapy family drama of historical proportions. Lloyd locked eyes with Mae, whose dark orbs shimmered with emotion. She tightened her jaw and lifted her chin, urging him on.

The man's fingers shook as he opened the journal to the page he'd marked with a stripe of red cotton yarn.

"I'd like to read my father's last entry. I look at it as his confession. It's the truth of what happened here many years ago. I hope it brings some peace to those who were wronged."

"Affie!" Seamus squealed. He hadn't expected to see his sister in the grill any time soon. Perhaps never again.

The restaurant was packed, with a queue of expectant diners holding down the planks of the front porch. The whole town was teeming with tourists for the Prosperity Days Festival, some at Lloyd Chang's lecture; some scouring the quaint shops; some haggling with the street vendors selling jewelry, blown glass, pottery, homemade soaps, and other goods along Spirit Street; others taking time out to refuel their bodies and quench their thirst.

"Thought I better come down out of my ivory tower and help out." Afton laced up her spidery apron. "I should've been here last night, too, Bro. Sorry I let you down. I'll try not to do that again."

Coming back was easier than Afton had expected, and she knew that was due, in no small part, to the tender relationship she was starting with Peter. Like a giddy teen in love, she felt all shades of positive.

Seamus grinned proudly. "It looks different, huh?"

Afton swept her eyes across the length of the balcony. "Yeah, where's the band's stuff?"

"They're gonna start playing here one weekend a month and the others at the Bloody Bucket Saloon. Some of our regulars were pissed about not having a place to drink and dance. You okay with that?"

"As long as the band is."

"Yeah, they are. But, when I said things look different, I meant the bar. It was Monette's idea to turn it into a buffet station. We've been doing an all-you-can eat family happy hour, with wings, taco fixings, salads, the whole shebang, and half-price fountain drinks." He gestured toward the smorgasbord, which was swarming with takers. "People are loving it!"

ZuZu jostled away from the kitchen, juggling a tray with three dinners and a pitcher of lemonade. "Welcome back, Boss Lady!" she hollered.

"Thanks. It's good to be back."

Things seemed to be going well despite the full-capacity crowd. Seamus and the crew had everything in order, much to Afton's surprise. And the surrender of the Ghostly Grill's liquor license hadn't hurt business. Of course, it was difficult to judge how an average Saturday night would be without the Prosperity Days Festival skewing the numbers.

Far behind Seamus, Afton saw Ordway's head bobbing in the kitchen pass-through window; he was listening to his iPod and cooking burgers, his gray goatee a seeming extension of the smoke rising from the grill. Up on the balcony, his wife, Monette, flitted among tables with pitchers of cola and water. The place felt more like home to Afton than she'd ever dreamed.

The front doors opened and 12 people entered. Seamus ducked down to look out the front window and saw an idling white passenger van with a blue dove and "Santa Rita Community Church" painted on the side.

In the past, when Afton was hostess, such a sight at a busy time would have left her frazzled. But Seamus was unruffled.

"Excuse me, Affie," he said.

Moving to the front, he warmly welcomed the church folk and cited a wait time of at least 30 minutes. The people discussed it briefly, nodded in agreement, and provided the name of their pastor for the wait list. Seamus thoughtfully explained a couple of options for passing the time: enjoying the views of the Verde Valley from the front porch or a quick visit two doors up the hill to the Skeleton's Closet Antique Shop, which—he was sure to mention—was having a sale.

Afton watched her brother swing into action with confidence. Hidden in the kitchen during days and behind the bar at nights, he'd never before had a chance to shine unless he was playing against his nature by intimidating clientele as the house bouncer. Now, Afton saw her brother's true strengths. The week of working the grill without her dominating influence, being forced to take the lead and make all decisions, had pushed Seamus to unfurl his talents and given her the opportunity to see them.

A putty-bellied man in golf shorts wiggled two fingers at Afton, beckoning her. "Pardon me, miss? Can we get some extra napkins? We had a spill."

"No worries, sir," Afton said, taking up a pair of dishrags and a handful of napkins. The mess didn't raise her blood pressure a single point. Quite the contrary. When she handed over the napkins to the man and his embarrassed wife and knelt down with the rags to clean the pool of ginger ale from between their chairs, Afton was softly humming.

CHAPTER 31

It was almost 15 minutes before Lloyd got through the opening pages of his father's final journal entry and reached the details of the mystery he had concealed so long. By then he was breathless and struggling for energy, but he couldn't stop.

"Sadie contacted one of her regulars, a Prescott rancher, who agreed to take in the boy and return the girl to her family. As thanks, Sadie planned to send along two cases of bootlegged liquor, good hooch, not that swill the local farmers made. We would transport the liquor and children in Deputy Warrington's mule wagon, which he lent us to haul supplies, as needed, in exchange for free dinners."

Lloyd's voice was growing rawer by the sentence. If not for the microphone that leaned in under his nose, no one beyond the stage would have heard him. His shoulders were rounding away from the wheelchair's back, and his eyes were straining, though he didn't really need to see the words on the journal pages. Lloyd had read them so often he could recite them almost verbatim.

"Sadie seduced Molly's chief bodyguard, Tarney. It took three months for her to get the goods without making him suspicious. From him, she learned that the blond boy was Charles Avendon, 14, the son of a dead prostitute. The girl, Rosemae, had been kidnapped from the reservation and was secured in the basement of the Red Garter. The keys to her leg iron, her cell, and the stairwell door were on a brass ring in the bar's cashbox. Molly kept another set with her.

"Sadie also learned that Charles had been sold regularly when he was younger, but when he got older, he became Molly's plaything and was moved to her apartment, where Tarney kept close track of him.

"Tarney divulged Molly's usual schedule and habits, including that she had begun sampling her own drugs and sometimes passed out for hours after inhaling heroin. Sadie joked to the bodyguard that the next time Molly took the white stuff, it would be comical if they had a rendezvous under her nose. Tarney arranged for his boss to have a good dose that Thursday, which was Sadie's night off work.

"Our plan was foolhardy, but we had to try. Being younger and faster than Wei, I would free Rosemae, while Sadie freed Charles. Wei would drive to the edge of town and wait for us.

"Sadie got her hands on a bottle of green liquid that rendered people unconscious. She said Madam Rooney sometimes added it to a glass of wine when one of her girls had an appointment with a disagreeable fellow. Sadie had used it herself and thought it worked like a charm.

"That Thursday night, she would go to the Red Garter and get friendly with the barkeep, who guarded the door to the basement. She would have a drink with him and slip some of the liquid into his whiskey. Then, she would go upstairs to Molly's and try the same trick on Tarney.

"Thursday night came. I rigged up the mule team and loaded the liquor. I did not want Wei sullied because he was dressed in his finest tweed suit and the tam Ting had made him. I knew he wanted to make a good impression when he arrived in Prescott, not for his sake but for the children's. No one could have dissuaded him from the plan. 'This must work,' he told me as he climbed onto the buckboard.

"It was 1:55 when he drove down Sin Alley. I watched him turn and wave good luck to me as he hawed the mules onto Spirit Street. That was the last time I saw my brother alive.

"I knew Sadie and Wei would not fail. But I was a panicked fool. I could hardly walk a straight path to the Red Garter. When I entered, I saw two men passed out on a card table. I moved behind the bar and almost stumbled over the barkeep, who was sleeping like a baby on the floor. I have never moved so fast or less gracefully as when I took the key ring from the cashbox and fumbled my way through unlocking the door to the stairwell.

"I found a pull-chain and yanked it, turning on a single bare bulb. I closed the door behind me and hurried down the stairwell. I fingered a big brass key and stabbed at the lock many times before making contact.

"As I pushed open the cell door, light spilled into the room, and I saw a girl shackled by one leg and wearing a soiled red dress sitting on a bare mattress. Her uncombed hair hid half of her face. There was a bucket in the corner, where she relieved herself, and the room reeked of the foulness.

"'I will help you,' I whispered to the child, whom I recognized from Molly's abominable party.

"The girl's hopeless expression did not change. I think she knew I would not succeed.

"I knelt by her. My hands were shaking so strongly that I dropped the key ring.

"'We must move quickly,' I told her as I fished up the keys and reached for the leg iron's padlock.

"Then I heard noises coming from above, and I froze. A door slammed and Molly yelled, 'What the hell happened? Where's Charles?'

"I looked at that helpless child, and then I looked at the light-filled corridor. As quickly as I could, I left the cell, sprang up the stairs on my toes, and pulled the light chain. I stood close against the wall, listening and breathing so hard I thought I would faint. I heard the click of Molly's high heels as she came down the steps from her apartment and moved near the door. I closed my mouth to quiet the sound of my breathing, and I swear I felt my hot breath come out my ears. Molly mumbled something about drunkards and kicked something. Then I heard her footsteps go outside, where she shouted profanities about her workers.

"That was my chance, and I knew it. I opened the door. The light from the bar shone into the stairwell, and I glanced back at the opened cell where Rosemae sat chained to the wall. I made my choice almost without thinking. Before I knew it, I was running through the bar and out the back exit, the one I used for food deliveries. I did not look right or left as I fled through the alley. I ran into our kitchen, into the storage room, and huddled amidst stacks of bagged rice and beans. I heard the ticking of my watch, pulled it from my pocket, and held it close. It was 2:41.

"I hoped that Wei and Charles would leave without me. I knew I should go to them and tell them what had happened so they could be on their way. But I was afraid. I was still cowering when I heard a woman shrieking and a commotion like Hell being unleashed on Salome Hill. I would find out later it was Sadie fighting a band of inebriates fresh from the Cajun Queen. Led by that perverted peckerwood Latreaux, they beat Wei and dragged him to Pearline Graham's Boarding House. There, they hanged him, after accusing him of possessing liquor, stealing the wagon and mules, and kidnapping a white woman. Sadie fought tooth and nail for Wei. Pearline and one of her boarders, a miner named Fred Waller, also tried to stop the hanging; they were clubbed unconscious for their efforts.

"Almost every Prosperityite had been served by Wei in our restaurant or on their doorsteps, when he delivered orders and inquired about their health and happiness. They knew how fine a man he was. Yet only three tried to stop his murderers. When I consider this, I think very low of the human race. I think even lower of myself when I consider that I was not among those three.

"They had waited for me. When Sadie saw Latreaux coming, she knew there would be trouble and told Charles to flee. He hid in the Sandspur Mountains for three days. I learned that from Rosemae years later. She said he came back for her but was captured by Molly's men, who found him in her cell, trying to pry off her padlock with a horseshoe nail. Charles had brought her a yellow rose, which she stowed under her mattress throughout her imprisonment. As far as I know, she still has that faded bloom pressed between the pages of her Bible.

"What I did, or failed to do, started a cascade of tragedy that went on for over a year. In July, dear Sadie was found hanged in her room. The official report read suicide, but that was untrue. Word spread that Sadie had spurned Tarney and run off with Molly's beau. Most thought the whole scandal, including Wei's lynching, was the fallout from a failed elopement. No one knew of our plan to save two children, and very few outside Molly's circle knew Charles' identity or history.

"Tarney was more than happy to take out the woman who played him for a fool. I saw Sadie's body in the casket; blue finger marks ringed her neck. People were afraid to attend her funeral. Only Pearline Graham, Gorley, and I stood at her graveside.

"The following summer, Charles Avendon did what I could not. The night of June 28, 1923, he saved Prosperity's unfortunates. Seizing a private moment with Molly, he stabbed her in the heart with a letter opener. He unshackled Rosemae and another innocent soul recently added to Molly's collection and told them to bang on doors and raise an alarm, so people could flee the flames that would soon engulf the block. He returned to Molly's apartment, torched it, and died in the fire.

"I was awakened by the commotion and went outside. Flames were shooting from Molly's. Burning pieces floated onto the roofs of other buildings, and soon, the whole block was blazing. I considered packing items to save but decided nothing mattered. Then I saw Rosemae emerge from the crowd, barefoot and dirty, with a pink band of flesh around her lower left leg, which was smaller than the right. She was in the same tattered red dress I had seen her in the night I should have saved her, but now it was much too small for her. The arms, neck, and waistband had been ripped to accommodate her growth. Older and taller but still a child, she limped toward me holding her only possession: a flat, dried rose. I was so ashamed that I could not look her in the face. Before I could back away, she took my hand and said, 'I know you tried.'

"We walked up the hill and sat in the mouth of a mine tunnel watching her prison burn. Watching the Crib District die. She shuddered and shed tears when the two floors above the Red Garter collapsed, sending what remained of Molly's apartment down to ground level. She stared long at the dried flower in her hand, and I could only guess what she was thinking.

"Hours later, rain started to pour. The abating inferno was drowned. We walked back to town. I was surprised to see Chang Brothers Restaurant still standing. A storage building at the far end of the block also remained, but the rest of Sin Alley was blackened rubble.

"I took in Rosemae. We ran the restaurant together. But every time I looked at her, I was reminded of my failings. I thought of Wei and Sadie and believed they would still be alive if only I had acted my part. I felt bitter and guilty when I served townsfolk, when I saw the Graham Boarding House, when I drove Deputy Warrington's wagon to McBrideville for supplies. I could not escape my sins, and I was craven. So I told people that Rosemae had killed Molly. I did not want anyone to know about Charles, lest they learn of his ill-fated escape and the events surrounding it. I let people believe that Sadie had tried to steal Molly's beau and that my brother was her accomplice and a bootlegger. Sadie and Wei carried the truth of my cowardice to their graves.

"Rosemae became a hero, but things were never the same between us. She remained kind, and neither refuted nor confirmed my claim when people asked about that fiery night, but I erased whatever residue of respect she had for me.

"Before I left to find a bride in San Francisco, I bought the boarding house for Rosemae. I thought it was right that she have her own home and that it be the place where my brother died for her. Rosemae graciously accepted the house and her role as caretaker of the Chang legacy. She is still there, growing flowers in soil nourished by Wei's blood, keeping our secrets, living with ghosts.

"There. I have written my confession. My father was right. Regrets are an old man's poison. There is no anecdote. We live, we make our choices, we age remembering what we did or did not do, and we die content with our choices or consumed by remorse. I have poisoned myself with thoughts, feelings, actions, lack of actions, and with drink. I need my bottle now. I want to feel nothing, and forget. I want this to end. Please let it end. Someone forgive me."

Lloyd closed the journal and held it to his chest. He was hoarse and exhausted, as much from emotion as from traveling to the center and relaying his father's final thoughts. He watched as, from out of the awe-struck audience, his grandson broke rank and dashed toward the east wing of the stage. He saw Mae's tear-streaked but approving face cradled against Ooljee's broad shoulder. Everything else was a hazy smudge.

"My father died after writing this. His body was found by Rosemae." One shaking hand pointed the cracked spine of the journal at the woman. "Many of you know her as Mae Bennally. She isn't Rosemae's daughter. She is Rosemae, and she lived through everything I just read." Lloyd lowered the book and removed his glasses, folding them back into his shirt pocket as he looked out to the third row. "Mae, I'm so sorry for everything that happened to you and everything my father caused…I'm…sorry…"

Lloyd's voice was silenced by a rush of emotion he hadn't expected. He pushed the microphone away and hunched forward, trying to hide his face

222

as it shattered into a thousand anguished lines that channeled tears in zigzags down to his shirt collar. Humiliated, he tried to flee, but he was trapped. His hands slapped at the wheels of his wheelchair, feeling for the brakes, which were too far behind him to grab.

With the hum of the crowd dizzying him, Lloyd was afraid to stand. He imagined pushing himself up from his seat, then losing balance and tumbling off the stage. Pawing at the sides in desperation, Lloyd weakly fought the wheelchair until he heard two clicks and felt the breaks release and inertia rock him. He was pulled back quickly, and turned about, rolled offstage, coming to a fast stop behind a heavy, royal blue curtain. Before he knew who had him or what was happening, he felt Boyd hugging him, his gelled hair stabbing the side of his face.

"I'm so proud of you, Grandpa," he said.

"What a lovely morning," Lloyd chirped, as Boyd nudged his wheelchair down the brick walkway of the Prosperity Visitors' Center Park.

Lloyd held a mug of decaf out to each side of his chair so the coffee sloshed over the ceramic rims and onto the ground, not his lap.

Situating himself on a park bench, Boyd took one of the mugs from his grandfather and admired the circles of marigolds they had planted—before Lloyd's surgery—in the raw earth where the fountain had stood.

The men sat quietly as they watched the earliest rising tourists step out to sightsee or rush to one of Prosperity's breakfast spots. Both drank every drop of coffee before any words were exchanged.

"Do you feel that?" Lloyd asked.

"Feel what?"

"Exactly. It's gone. That sense of dread that used to be here."

Boyd perceived the calmness. "We really won't have to worry about this place anymore, huh?"

Lloyd confidently shook his head. "Nope. Your great-grandpa finally got my attention."

"I can't believe all that time we thought it was Molly." Boyd silently tallied the money, time, and effort spent on the park's continual "recovery." It had all amounted to many early mornings of back-breaking work, but it had also created some cherished memories between him and his grandfather, pushing them together as a team, forcing them to learn from and depend on one another. Boyd suspected that had been part of the cosmic plan.

"I'm going to miss our pre-dawn cleanups out here," he admitted. He peeked sideways, watching Lloyd's eye rims grow red.

His grandfather cleared his throat and tried to look unaffected. "Not me. I'm too old for hard labor…and I'm tired of smelling like Ben-Gay."

CHAPTER 32

Fluorescent orange cones blocked the road where an officer stood watch, shooing back tourists who ignored the "Road Closed" sign. Led by Prosperity Chief of Police Tim Vulic, combined units from Prosperity and Santa Rita swarmed Dead Horse Canyon, determined to find evidence to help frame a case against Mark Jensen. Eight uniformed officers stood on the bank and peered down, watching a father-and-son team in hardhats and reflective vests securing utility chains around the wrecked Blazer that had carried Martin Schrader into death; the men formed a sling with the chains and attached the winch cable from a boom truck parked on the slight pullout high above.

Peter and Boyd were on the scene with the Prosperity Public Works pickup, which had hauled the equipment for the road block. Also on hand were a tow truck and a team of paramedics from McBrideville—just in case.

"Wouldn't it be cool to power that truck? Reeurrrr," Boyd screeched, pumping his hand like he was operating the crane.

The recovery of Martin's smashed metal coffin wasn't a light matter to Peter. To his left, within his frame of view, was the boy's roadside memorial, which had grown in the days following his death, and then leveled off as the tragedy faded in the public's mind. That didn't take long. Martin's shrine had become an untended collection of stuffed animals, candles, cards, and clumps of silk flowers and piles of dead real ones that crumbled and blew down the highway a few petals or leaves at a time. Soon, like Martin, the monument would be gone. If it hadn't become the focal point of the investigation, the wrecked Blazer would have shared a similar fate and stayed in the canyon forever, transmuting into a rusted husk.

Chief Vulic worked the crowd while waiting for the wrecking crew to finish their job. When he came to Peter, he lost his glibness. "Ooljee told me about your…ability," he said, removing his sunglasses. He confronted his reflection in the lenses as he divulged a case point. "The kid's note mentioned a flash drive with photos, but we haven't found it. I'm hoping it's not smashed flat or lost for good. Gonna be like finding a needle in a haystack." He waited for Peter to provide guidance. "Wanna hazard a guess where it's at?"

Peter could tell hopes weren't high, but he felt something there. Inside that twisted, weld-burned Blazer far below was something important. Whether it was a flash drive, Peter wasn't sure. Nor could he tell if whatever it was had survived the ballistic impact of the crash. He only knew it was there...somewhere inside the vehicle. "It's still in the Blazer."

"Bring it up!" shouted the father-son duo in the canyon.

The muffled talk among police officers and emergency workers ceased as the boom truck groaned, its outriggers digging in. As if the machines were conversing, the Blazer's metal frame answered with a nerve-grating, high-pitched squeal of stress. The winch began to slowly reel up, dislodging the vehicle from the canyon floor. Suggestive of a metallic yo-yo dangled by a giant robot's arm, the Blazer rose into the air. Sand, dirt, and chunks of shrubbery and grass dripped from the downward-pointing front fender, which had been punched back, almost flush with the mosaic windshield. The rapt audience watched as the SUV levitated higher and higher until even with the road. Their eyes moved quickly down, in unison, following the descent of a piece of internal gadgetry and five dried hollyhock stems that plummeted from the driver's side where, weeks earlier, welders had pried back enough metal to free Martin's corpse.

The Blazer had almost cleared the canyon, when, with a "chung," one of the chains slipped over a bolt on the vehicle's undercarriage and tightened quickly. Such a small thing, yet enough to send the SUV rocking. The winch operator panicked and hit the crane's swing function control, creating more inertia for the heavy, pendulous object. Resembling a wrecking ball, it struck the bank with enough force to push aside a large section of earth.

"Holy monkey!" Boyd said, watching a cloud of dust rise up from where the Blazer slammed the canyon wall.

The paramedic team rushed to the bank, hoping horrific work hadn't been created for them.

"Everyone okay?" a bug-eyed EMT called to the wrecking crew in the canyon.

"Yeah, but what the hell's going on up there?" the older man asked.

"Lester, you dick!" his son blindly roared at the truck's operator.

Father and son anxiously watched the crane lift up, scraping the SUV against the bank until it floated over the guardrail. The operator then deposited it onto the flat back of the tow truck and bent over in his seat, exhaling, hands shaking like an addict in withdrawal.

Police filed into the canyon, launching the search for onsite evidence.

Santa Rita Police Sergeant Dixie Reynolds strayed from the others and moved toward the bank, where the car had made landfall. Her poodle-curl bangs ruffled as she rushed a few paces, and then stopped herself quickly, teetering on the edge of an abyss.

"That crane opened an old mineshaft!"

The dislodged wooden cap rested in a pile of dirt against the guardrail. After decades in darkness, the 10-foot diameter pit shored up by split-timber braces was penetrated by sunshine.

Officer Reynolds motioned for Boyd and Peter to approach. "Let's recap this sucker! We'll need one of those 'Stay out, stay alive' signs from the mine inspector's office!"

Before they could move, Peter grabbed Boyd's shoulder and folded in two. "Unng," he grunted through clenched teeth.

"Whoa, dude!" Boyd reached for him as he stumbled onto his knees.

Peter couldn't see Boyd or his surroundings, couldn't make a sound. He was consumed by a vision so strong that every part of him—including vocal chords—was paralyzed.

A piece of the past was inside him, unfurling itself. It moved quickly across mind and soul, leaving its traces behind for him to remember. Peter saw Charles Avendon smashing bottles of brandy and vodka in what he recognized as Mad Molly's apartment. The woman's lifeless body lay on the floor, a letter opener protruding from her chest, a bloody abstraction on her white dress, her feather and pearl headband flapping back like a bad toupee. Charles, dripping tears, took a box of matches from a lamp stand, pulled out a stick, struck it, and flung it toward an alcohol-soaked sofa. He struck another match, and another, and another, tossing each tiny torch onto an area sodden with liquor. "I'm sorry it took so long, Rosemae," he whimpered, wiping his eyes so he could see. As flames erupted around him, he sat next to Molly's body and pulled his knees up to his chest, holding his shins. He sucked in the swelling, darkening smoke, and coughed a little, then more, until he began to gag and buckle with dry heaves. Charles lay back, writhing, struggling for breath, as black clouds of smoke ended the scene.

In an instant, before he returned to the present, Peter knew what had become of the boy. He felt it in his body, as if the knowledge had been implanted into every cell.

"Charles Avendon's...remains...are in that shaft with...Molly Petrova's. He's in a blue-flowered sack. She's in a red-striped sack."

Peter was still speaking when he opened his eyes and saw two paramedics bent over him, their faces more curious than worried. Chief Vulic was also there, further off, standing with Boyd.

Peter became panicked when he put his hands out and felt that he was on a gurney and his left arm was bound in a blood-pressure cuff.

"You passed out, sir," said a burly EMT, preparing to shove him in the ambulance.

"This is normal for me. I'm fine."

The bulky man doubtfully raised his eyebrows at Peter.

"Yeah, that *is* normal for him. It's part of his charm," Boyd wryly attested.

Peter sat up and gently pulled apart the Velcro tabs on the cuff. "Thank you, but this isn't necessary."

He was sliding from the gurney, steadied by Boyd, when Sergeant Reynolds stepped up to Chief Vulic and gave her report.

"Sir, that shaft is about 40–50 feet deep. The sides are in good shape. There's some fallout at the bottom but not much. I can see something down there."

"Two sacks?" Chief Vulic knew town lore as well as any Prosperityite and realized Mad Molly's bones had finally been unearthed. He wanted to test Mae Bennally's protégé. "Is one blue and one striped red?" he asked the officer, all the while eyeing Peter.

"Yes, sir, from what I can tell. How did you…?"

Chief Vulic cut her off with a nod. He shouted over his shoulder, "Don't go anywhere with that boom truck! We're going to need it again!" He looked back at Peter, giving a droll smirk. "Unless you can levitate those bodies out, Mr. Wizard."

"Hey, Affie, you left your cell phone on the counter, and it's vibrating!" Seamus palmed the phone and read the name off the screen. "It's Emma."

"Emma Schrader?" Afton asked, looking quizzically across the booth at Peter, who was downing an iced tea. "I better see what she wants. Excuse me, okay?"

Afton shot from the booth, took the phone from Seamus, and went through the swinging door into the kitchen for some quiet. Seamus snuck into Afton's vacated seat and twitched his head to the left, slyly indicating Clive and Clare, who cuddled and cooed over a plate of extra-spicy batwings at a secluded corner table.

"Check out Harold and Maude," Seamus cracked. "Maybe the third time will be the charm for Clare. After divorce and widowhood, she deserves to hit the jackpot. It's kinda hard to think of Clive as the jackpot, though, isn't it?"

Peter and Seamus inconspicuously spied on the pair over the back of their booth. As if on cue, the lovebirds heightened the action. Tipping their heads forward, they engaged in a long, wet kiss that entailed many twists of their necks. Clare's knobby, ring-laden hand held Clive's face against hers like she was sucking the life out of him.

Seamus quickly turned around. "I wish I hadn't seen that." He queasily stood up. "That's a sign. Time to get back to work."

As he retreated, Peter was left vulnerable. From his position facing the corner, it was difficult to keep his eyes from the canoodling couple. He pushed himself back, then to the side, his twill coveralls sliding easily over the vinyl. He couldn't escape the view.

"Are you ready for some good news?" Afton asked, returning to the booth with her cell phone—still lit up from use—glowing in the pocket of her black-widow apron.

"Please," Peter begged, relieved to have Afton back, distracting him from the curious make-out session in the corner.

Afton leaned over the table to quietly impart the details, the frizzy ends of her hair mopping across the black Formica.

"The police found the flash drive under the back seat. It had photos of Martin and Coach Jensen on it...proof of, you know...what happened."

Peter felt relieved yet heartsick. What a bizarre reality when the discovery of child pornography amounted to "good news." But it was a miracle to have the evidence unearthed and usable; he knew that, though he flinched thinking of Martin's final injury from the coach as complete strangers—cops, lawyers, jury members, and others—viewed his violation in intimate detail via the electronic images.

"And, drum roll, please," Afton said. "Another one of Coach Jensen's victims has come forward. He's an NAU freshman whose parents still live in Santa Rita. That's all Emma knew about him. Brave kid, huh?"

"Very. Good for him." Peter's mind drifted, as he contemplated the suffering of yet another casualty. His outer vision dimmed. Inwardly he saw boys, one after another, burn to ashes in a fiery pit—first Charles, then Martin—but another, new boy stood unscathed in the flames. This boy— straight, black hair chopped in a bowl haircut, thin brown arms outspread— rose like a Phoenix bird from the flames and soared into the sky. He was the survivor. Like Charles and Martin, he'd had the courage to say *enough.* Like Rosemae, his spirit had carried him out of the darkness, into a new life. This one could not be broken.

Peter smiled wistfully. "Good for him," he repeated.

CHAPTER 33

Mayor Alvarez pulled every string he could to make sure that Charles Avendon's bones didn't linger in a lab or get labeled for interment with the indigent. They belonged in Mae's care. And there was no doubt in Sam, after Lloyd's public disclosure and a conversation with Peter, that the bones were, indeed, those of the boy who'd suffered long at Mad Molly's hands and died ridding Prosperity of her evil influence.

Yet Sam couldn't simply drop a sack of bones at Mae's front door. The bundle was all that was left of a human being who'd loved, dreamed, smiled, cried, and grew in days and wisdom until being cut down just this side of adulthood. Reverence was required.

So, he bought an infant-sized casket from Lawning Brothers' Mortuary in McBrideville. The Heaven's Flower was their best model, dark walnut with a white crepe interior. At 33" long, it was just the right size to accommodate the pile of bones and shards. A lovely final resting place, as far as caskets go.

After a soul-wasting day of town business and personal finagling, Sam finally laid hands on the remains. He took the package—a jangly bag with its two top corners tied tightly closed—from Chief Vulic and gave a slow blink of his eyes in thanks.

"Where's Mad Molly going?" Sam asked.

"It'll be a long process before she gets sown. We've called in a forensic anthropologist to determine the age, gender, so forth…procedure, you know. I'll be in contact with the Prosperity Historical Society. This could be a big marketing moment for your group…hell, for the whole town."

"You can throw her back in the shaft for all I care," Sam spat.

Chief Vulic seconded that motion. "I was there when Lloyd Chang read his granddaddy's diary. I'm inclined to agree with you." He waited a beat and added, "That's why I'm not putting that boy through the same red-tape procedure Molly's getting. One sack of bones is a morbid curiosity; that other sack, well, that's somebody's loved one. It's the least this town owes Mae Bennally. You let me know if I can be of further assistance to her, will you?"

"Much obliged, Tim."

Sam stepped outside the chief's office feeling the heft of the sack and marveling at how a strapping teen boy had been reduced to 20 pounds of hardened minerals.

"Night, Sarah," he told the receptionist, who was locking desk drawers with her purse on her shoulder and a set of car keys dangling from pursed lips.

"Buh-buh," she squeezed out.

Sam tamped his cowboy hat on his head and left for home, walking as he did every work night to his mint green Victorian near the top of Salome Hill.

He entered the front door to the slobbery greetings and gyrating rears of his two lab mixes, who acted like they hadn't seen him in days. After telling them what good boys they were, Sam stood in the foyer and stared at the little, opened coffin on his kitchen table.

He listened to the swing of the doggie door as his pets went outside to bark at the scent of something wild that passed by. Sam moved to the box and laid the flowered blue sack inside. Shutting the lid, he left his hands on it and prayed.

After feeding the dogs and making dinner of a cup of coffee, five saltines, and a chunk of Colby cheese, Sam was ready to take Charles on the last leg of his journey.

At dusk, he carried the casket from his house, down a steep dirt road, down Hangman's Lane, to the Old Graham Boarding House, feeling quite ancient and feeble by the time he reached the chain-link fence, limbs quivering. When he bent over and set the box on the driveway, his back muscles seized.

"Hell's bells, what a pisser," he griped.

Sam didn't think he'd be able to stand again, but he braced his hands on his knees and breathed several restorative gulps, giving his lower back time to relax. Slowly, stiffly, he rose and, with fingers spasming with fatigue, opened the gate. Giving a muffled grunt, he cautiously squatted and took the hardwood box back into his arms.

Sam pressed his boots gently into the gray gravel and onto the front steps, trying to silently climb up. He made very little noise as he tiptoed across the porch and slid the box onto the front porch swing, quickly grabbing the chains that held the seat to two rafters, keeping them from squeaking.

With a sniff of his nose and a flick of his mustache, Sam took his hat off and spent a moment of silence in front of the mortal remains. Then, putting his hat back on his head, he rang the doorbell and trotted down the steps, pressing a fist against his back as he quickly limped across the driveway and disappeared up Hangman's Lane.

"Shit! Damn it! Shit!" he chanted as he hopped up the road, like Quasimodo making a getaway.

The form of his exit wasn't pretty, but it was effective. Sam was nowhere around when Mae opened the door.

"Hello?" she called.

She trundled outside and saw the coffin. Instantly, she knew what it was. And she was glad to be alone at this long-awaited moment. Mae lowered herself onto the end of the swing, her hands stroking the wooden lid, a tremor in her lips and eyelids. Her fingers curled around the edges. As she draped herself over the casket, she wept as she never had before.

The coffin sat on the dining room table for two days, while Mae talked to the bones and reminisced about the golden boy who'd loved her. Meanwhile, a grave was prepared.

At work, Boyd researched where the utility lines crisscrossed Mae's property, then spray-painted their routes—blue for water; green for sewer; orange for phone; red for electric—on the lawn and gravel to warn Peter away from those regions.

"This can't be legal, can it? Burying a body in a backyard?" Peter asked Boyd as he plunged his shovel into the hard ground and felt the reverberations shimmy up the handle and go right into his arm bones.

"Who cares, dude? It's the right thing to do. Nobody in this town is going to say anything. Shit, the mayor himself gave Mae the remains."

"If the whole town was against it, I wouldn't let that stop me. I just wondered."

Boyd was glad to help, but Peter insisted on doing all the digging. After a long day of hard work, he'd come home to more strenuous labor, and he loved it. It felt good to use his body and toil at something that provided physical evidence of his efforts. Mostly, he was glad to be giving Charles a fitting final harbor and peace to his surrogate mother. The process was spiritual.

It took Peter four attempts to find a suitable gravesite. The first three digs, all attempted in one night, were painful failures. Each time, he dug down a few feet, through petrified earth, only to hit solid rock and have to find a new spot to start all over again.

The next evening, on the fourth try, he shoveled down a foot, soaked the hole with the garden hose, let that sink in, dug down another foot, soaked the hole again, dug more, and eventually had a grave that measured

3' x 5' x 5'. After it was finished, Peter noticed the location: less than 15 feet from Mae's bedroom window.

Saturday morning, a select group gathered for the burial, the five people most affected—directly or indirectly—by the short life of Charles Avendon: Mae, Ooljee, Peter, Lloyd, and Boyd. The Changs arrived with a yellow rose bush in a 5-gallon container. Mae had asked for that. She couldn't think of a more appropriate marker.

"How are you holding up?" Lloyd asked.

"I'm betwixt joy and grief, but this is a good day," Mae said, accepting Lloyd's arm. "And you? How's that ticker of yours?"

Lloyd stuck out his chest and tapped his breastbone, carefully avoiding his yellow rose boutonniere. "Solid. Can't keep a Chang down."

The twosome unhurriedly walked to the open grave, which was sheltered by the lacy boughs of a plum tree. Ooljee stood beneath the leafy canopy with Mae's Bible in her hands. "Shall we begin?" she asked.

Boyd and Peter were stationed on either side of the grave, positioned to lower the casket, their dress shoes sinking into the piles of dirt Peter had somewhat untidily excavated. At the foot of the grave, Lloyd held Mae against his side and gestured for Ooljee to proceed.

"We are gathered here to remember Charles Avendon, who was born in Tennessee in 1908 and died here, in Prosperity, June 28, 1923. This formal farewell is long overdue, but we know this has all worked according to our Creator's plan." Ooljee spoke forcefully and beautifully, like a preacher and a poet. She looked toward the coffin and then at the sky, the trees, the house, the people. "We know you have been transformed, your spirit refined to know no pain or hatred, regrets or sorrow. You have traveled home, to your source—our source—and are fully in God's light. You are pure love. More beautiful than ever."

Mae watched her daughter with pride as Ooljee opened the Bible in her hands and went to the first section marked by a shiny crimson ribbon.

"I've chosen a few passages that seem significant to this occasion. First, a psalm." Ooljee used her polished nail as a prompt so she could forego her reading glasses; her eyes followed the line of text above her thumb. "Though you have made me see troubles, many and bitter, you will restore my life again; from the depths of the earth you will again bring me up. You will increase my honor and comfort me once again."

Sparing but a couple of seconds, Ooljee flipped the pages to the next marked section and began reading from Revelation, "He will wipe every tear from their eyes. There will be no more death or mourning or crying or pain, for the old order of things has passed away."

The last passage, Ooljee knew by heart. She shut the Bible and looked at her mother as she recited, "Greater love has no one than this, that he lay down his life for his friends."

As Mae felt the force of that line, she drew her hands up over her mouth and nose. She didn't look like she was crying, but Lloyd could feel the quake of her muscles. He gave her a supportive squeeze, and she brought down her hands, straightening her shoulders, setting her chin out.

"Let's pray," Ooljee said, and every head bowed.

"Almighty God, we thank you for this day and all you have put in our hearts. Thank you for Charles and for restoring his remains to us, so that we might have closure. We thank you for working through him to free my mama and help the people of this town that summer night in 1923. We know Charles is with you now and forever. Thank you for that, too. We also thank you for healing our friend, Lloyd, and bringing Peter into our lives, and guiding Boyd in making plans for his future. We ask your blessings and protection for us all. Please help us to do the work you put before us, and to do it willingly and well. Thank you, thank you. In Jesus' name, amen."

Ooljee stepped back and walked around the grave to her mother. She kissed the top of her head and, with Lloyd, held her as Peter and Boyd began their task.

Taking up the ropes slung under the small coffin, they positioned the casket over the grave and then began slackening the lines, lowering Charles' remains a few inches at a time. Like shipmates, working hand over fist, Peter and Boyd loosened the ropes until the coffin disappeared into the earth and rested on the damp soil five feet down.

Lloyd took the yellow rose from his lapel and handed it to Mae. He and Ooljee moved with her to the edge of the grave and watched her with tears of their own as she stared down at the wooden box for a long while, seemingly communing, perhaps just remembering.

Minutes later, Mae was still stoic, her eyes boring into the casket. Knowing her odd talents, Boyd half-expected the coffin to pop open and Charles' bones to dance up the side of the grave. But there was no spectacle awaiting them, only the quiet ending of a long-playing drama.

Mae broke from her trance and gently tossed the rose atop the casket. "My friend...my love," she whispered.

EPILOGUE

The inside of the Subaru held the unique fragrance of Kouros cologne and garlic; an assortment of objects Boyd had gathered throughout his 19 years of life; and a jug of water and snacks for the road. On the passenger side was a loose pile of his favorite CDs and his backpack filled with, not the usual paranormal investigation gear, but his laptop and a 3-ring binder.

It was going to be a big adjustment for Boyd, moving to a stucco condo in central Phoenix, where Amy and her mother would provide room and board for his beginning semester at Arizona State.

"Are you sure about this?" Boyd asked, standing eye-to-eye with his grandfather. The teen wasn't thinking of how daunting it would be to go from a town of under 500 people to one of the biggest cities and universities in the nation or how strange it might be to live in the same home with his girlfriend and her mother or how hard it would be to find a decent job that accommodated his class schedule. He was only thinking of his grandfather's needs. Would he be okay physically? Emotionally? What if his heart acted up and he was alone? What if he fell down the stairs? Boyd's refocused attention illustrated how much he'd grown in the last couple of months.

"I'll be fine. I'm going to have my second youth. Now that I have the house to myself, who knows what I'll do? Maybe join the Verde Valley Golden Oldies. Movies and popcorn on Tuesdays, Bingo on Thursdays. I'm going to live it up with that Widow Johnson, and I won't have to pay for a single date."

"Be serious, Grandpa. I want to know how you really feel."

"Well, I'd rather go after Genna Desmond, but I can't do that until her husband, Nate, croaks."

Boyd lowered his chin to his chest, a frustrated grin on his face. "Okay, I can see I'm not getting anywhere."

Opening the car door, Lloyd leaned on the doorframe and looked inside at all the untidily piled belongings, remembering when many of them were acquired—the We the Kings CD during a trip to Flagstaff; the backpack a Christmas gift from Ooljee; the fuzzy brown bear-paws bedroom slippers—which were sticking out of a box—a gag birthday gift from Seamus that first year the Burnsides arrived in town.

When he looked back at Boyd, his grandson was gazing at him like he was trying to read his mind.

Lloyd dropped his guard. "I'm going to miss the hell out of you, and I'm a little scared. But I'm excited, too, because I know this is all good. We're both going to learn and grow. You'll have Amy and her mom to help you out. I'll have Ooljee and Mae…and now Peter. I won't be neglected. Ooljee's already got my cardiologist appointments lined up, you know." Giving a rap on the roof of the car, Lloyd urged Boyd to be on his way. "I'll be here when you return. I got confirmation from Mae. This crazy little town and I will be waiting for you, boy."

His skunk-striped bangs flopped on Boyd's forehead as he nodded and hugged his grandfather goodbye and then dropped into the front seat of the car. Lloyd shut the door and stepped back, giving his grandson room.

Boyd felt his throat tighten as he started the ignition. He looked ahead of him, his eyes scouring the limestone bricks of his house. Memories— good, bad, and indifferent—caught him up for a moment. Peripherally, he saw his grandfather's form, smaller and more stooped at the shoulders than he recalled. When he turned his head and set his eyes directly on him, it was like seeing him for the first time in years: Lloyd Chang had become an old man, and Boyd couldn't recall witnessing that process. *Don't cry, don't cry,* he told himself. Rolling down the window, he leaned out and called, "I love you, Grandpa. Let me know if you need anything."

My, how things have changed, Lloyd thought, his heart breaking and warming at the same time. "I love you, too, boy!"

Peter walked the same route to work as he had for almost two months: up Hangman's Lane, waving at Mrs. Acevedo as she puttered in her front yard, taking a left onto Mine Cart Way and sauntering in the shade of Chinese sumac trees, until turning right onto the dirt road that ran directly to the Prosperity Community Center. Dangling from the black shoulder strap over his left arm was an insulated cooler carrying a lunch Mae had packed; she liked fussing over Peter, and he enjoyed the attention.

The day was beginning like any other, except in one major respect. It was Peter's first day on the job with Lloyd Chang. Before he entered the parking lot, Peter stopped and took a cleansing breath as he looked down Salome Hill, onto the terraced roofs of Prosperity and further, to the shimmering Verde Valley, where two semis traveled the interstate looking as small as Matchbox cars. He pulled his cell phone from his khaki coveralls and punched buttons until he'd selected the contact labeled "Afton."

"Good morning, Sweetums," she answered in a cheery tone.

"How are you today?"

"Great. I got a full eight hours of sleep last night. Can't remember the last time that happened. How about you? I hope you're rested for the big day. Nervous?"

"Not really. I'm looking forward to working with Lloyd. I think I'm going to learn a lot."

"No doubt. He knows everything about Prosperity," Afton said. "If you guys don't make other plans, come on by the grill after your shift. Dinner's on me. Lloyd may need the diversion, since it'll be his first day without Boyd."

"Very thoughtful, Afton. I'll do my best to get him over there tonight. Wish me luck today."

"You got it. Let me know how it goes. Hang in there."

"Thanks. See you tonight."

Peter put the cell phone away and straightened his collar, pulling the zipper on the unappealing coveralls to just below his clavicle, so that it hid all but a small triangle of his white undershirt.

"Hideous," he proclaimed with a laugh, looking down at the uniform. Lifting his eyes, he said, "But that isn't."

He stood still for a few seconds, studying the Spanish mission-style building at the end of the thin dirt road and pea-graveled lot. It was a beautiful old structure, and he felt privileged to be working there, where history survived in every stone and stripe of mortar. His gaze was pulled up, to the third floor, where he watched a nurse in a white cap and dress look out the window. He was used to her by now. She was there almost every morning, and Peter wondered why she'd been drawn to that window, and why her imprint remained there so strongly through the ages. Bit by bit, he was learning her story through visions and intuition: her name was Pearl, she'd worked there when it was an asylum…and more, he figured, would come later. He was in no hurry. There were others, too, at the center and throughout the town, whose images intrigued him. Mysteries were all around him. Mae had told him that would happen. He was still trying to narrow his focus so as not to become overwhelmed.

Nearing the entrance, Peter noticed a figure move into the opened doorway. At first, he thought it was an image from the past, but then he realized the figure was wearing the same khaki coveralls that he was. It was Lloyd.

Peter smiled as soon as he thought he was close enough for the man to recognize his expression. He sped up his gait and pranced up the five bulky front steps.

"Morning, Peter." Lloyd wasn't smiling, but his face looked friendly, and a sense of welcome and affinity flowed from him. "Are you ready?" he asked.

Peter crossed the threshold, accepting everything he knew that question entailed. "I am, sir."

"Good, then let's get started."

Peter followed Lloyd into the foyer, where they both greeted the front receptionist and, a few paces later, the postmistress and two program volunteers.

As the men walked down the long hall, shoulder to shoulder, discussing the day's duties, they didn't notice each hall sconce flicker, fade, and then brighten at their passing. It was a sign. The spirits of Prosperity were pleased.

www.ingramcontent.com/pod-product-compliance
Lightning Source LLC
Chambersburg PA
CBHW051454170626
46811CB00002B/477